WARRIORS IN THE DUST

MAJOR MARK DENTON: In California he has just demonstrated "the Package," his new, coordinated concept in Special Forces warfare using A-teams, light helicopters, and high-tech weaponry. Now he's loading the whole thing on a giant C5-B cargo plane, heading for war . . .

CAPTAIN ROCCO BIRELLI: He took language training for his men seriously. Among the Baluchi tribesmen in Iran it's paying off—as his team trains the primitive soldiers to fight against the Russians . . .

CHIEF WARRANT OFFICER RED STEPHENS: He came to war with a pair of lady's silk panties in his pocket and an unparalleled knowledge of army helicopters. In a nonstop air-mobile battle, the Green Berets will need everything he could give them . . .

SERGEANT CAT WHITAKER: She's one of the army's top chopper mechanics. But in the heat of battle she'll have to do more than keep the "killer eggs" flying—she'll become the first woman gunship pilot in combat . . .

SENIOR LIEUTENANT VALENTIN POPOVICH VALNIKOV: In Afghanistan he learned that you could find out more about the Red Army from the BBC than from your superiors. Now he knows that he's going up against the Green Berets—and it will be a fight like no other before . . .

DICK MEDLIN: The CIA's #1 operative in the Near East, serving in Afghanistan and Tehran. Through contacts with local tribesmen, he'll give the Green Berets all the intelligence they need to ambush the Red Army . . .

CLASH OF STEEL

L.H. BURRUSS

POCKET BOOKS

New York London Toronto Sydney Tokyo Singapore

An *Original* Publication of POCKET BOOKS

POCKET BOOKS, a division of Simon & Schuster Inc.
1230 Avenue of the Americas, New York, NY 10020

ISBN: 0-671-70017-0

First Pocket Books printing October 1990

10 9 8 7 6 5 4 3 2 1

POCKET and colophon are registered trademarks of
Simon & Schuster Inc.

Printed in the U.S.A.

This book is dedicated to my mother,

Frances Moore Burruss

Soldier's daughter—World War I
Soldier's wife—World War II, Korea
Soldiers' mother—Vietnam, Iran, Grenada

Author's Note

This is a fictional account of combat in Iran. It does not reflect actual contingency plans, events, persons, or command arrangements. The MH-60P Stealth Hawk helicopter does not exist. The dedicated and able pilots do, however; they call themselves the *Nightstalkers*.

Thanks to Paul for the quick response, to Mike and Jon for the Soviet order of battle, to Alan for the maps, and to Frosty and his gang for logistical support.

Anyone who wonders why military operations are conducted on Zulu, or Greenwich Mean Time, needs only to consider the effect of multiple time zones, daylight savings time, and odd time zones such as Iran's, which is three and a half hours before Greenwich Mean Time (not to be confused with British Summer Time).

PROLOGUE

2250 hours Greenwich Mean Time (1850 hours Eastern Daylight Time) 18 September
Headquarters, 1st Special Operations Command, Fort Bragg, North Carolina

Brigadier General William Porter punched in the code numbers of the cipher lock and entered the door of the 1st Special Operations Command briefing room. A master sergeant, clipboard in hand, looked around from the wall-mounted maps on which he was working and said, "Oh, hello, General."

"Hi, Pete," Porter replied. "Where's everybody else?"

"Gone to chow, sir," the NCO replied. "They weren't expecting you till 1930."

Porter, 1st SOCOM's deputy commanding general, was still in civilian clothes. He and his wife had spent the previous ten days on leave, renovating the secluded old farmhouse he had bought as a retirement home near Madison, Virginia. They had left their teenage children at their quarters on Fort Bragg and had isolated themselves from the outside world at the old house. They had rarely had any time together away from the professional and social duties and their family in recent years and had been enjoying themselves immensely. But then a Virginia state trooper had showed up at the farmhouse with a message for Porter to call his headquarters.

He had telephoned the headquarters from Madison to acknowledge the message, then driven straight to Fort Bragg, arriving at the headquarters only moments before.

"Well, the Virginia state cops gave me an escort to the Carolina line," Porter said. "I haven't driven that fast

1

since I was a bachelor lieutenant. . . . Now, what the hell's going on, Pete?"

Porter took a seat, and the NCO turned to a map of Southwest Asia and said, "Well, sir, since the Soviet invasions of Afghanistan and Iran—"

Porter bolted upright in his chair. *"What?* When the hell did *that* happen?"

"Sir?" the sergeant said. "You mean you didn't know about the invasion?"

"Christ, Pete," Porter muttered, "I'm afraid I haven't heard a bit of news in over a week. When I left there were reports of a lot of Soviet troop movements into Turkestan because of all the civil unrest down there. But there was no projection of another damned invasion of Afghanistan. Sounds as if Gorbie has lost it. And Iran, too? I guess you'd better take it from the top—just a broad-brush outline of what's been going on for the past week or so. I'll go over all the message traffic in detail later tonight. Why the hell didn't the old man send for me sooner, anyway?"

"Well, sir," the master sergeant said, "the chief of staff recommended it to him several times this week, but the old man said you hadn't had a leave in two years. Until this morning he said to leave you alone—that the way things are going, you might not get another leave until the end of World War III."

CHAPTER 1

2255 hours Greenwich Mean Time
18 September
Over the Indian Ocean south of Iran

Captain Rocco Birelli, commander of Special Forces Operational Detachment A-326, helped his comrade-in-arms, Captain Bill Davidson, put his parachute harness on over the load-bearing equipment Davidson was already wearing. Next he helped Davidson attach his M-16 rifle to the left side of the harness and tie it loosely to his leg. Davidson checked the snap fasteners and weapon tiedowns, then pulled his bulky rucksack in front of him. He made certain that the H harness around the rucksack was properly affixed, and that the pockets of the heavy, bulging rucksack were secured. Satisfied with his inspection, he attached the lowering line to his harness, then squatted and, with Birelli's assistance, hooked the snap fasteners into the equipment rings of his parachute harness. Holding onto Birelli to assist him, Davidson stood, put on his Kevlar helmet, and pulled the chinstrap down over his chin. Davidson was sweating profusely as he faced Birelli and held his hands above his head.

With his eyes following his hands, Birelli began at Davidson's helmet and checked to assure himself that the equipment—parachute, weapon, and rucksack—were properly rigged and fitted. Satisfied that everything on the front of the other Special Forces officer was correct, Birelli spun Davidson around, checked his back, then unhooked the static line snap hook from the back of the parachute and passed it over his right shoulder.

Davidson took the snap hook and instinctively moved

3

to hook it onto the top carrying handle of his chest-mounted reserve parachute, as he had done the last fifty-odd times that he had jumped—then remembered that he wasn't wearing a reserve. For an operational jump from an aircraft flying five hundred feet above the ground, there was no need to wear a reserve parachute. From five hundred feet, by the time a jumper ascertained that he had a malfunction and activated his reserve, and the reserve deployed, it would be too late to do him any good. And since the total weight of the equipment Davidson and his men had strapped on them already was well over a hundred pounds, the useless reserve would only be one more item to carry off and bury when they sterilized the drop zone.

Turning back to face Birelli, Davidson gave him a nervous grin, then stuck the static line snap hook between his teeth and sat uncomfortably down, the bulky rucksack between his legs, his left knee locked as a result of the weapon tied to that leg.

Rocco Birelli patted Bill Davidson on the shoulder and yelled above the noise of the MC-130 Combat Talon's four engines, "I'll help Sergeant Slater give the rest of your guys a jumpmaster check!"

Looking toward the rear of the aircraft, he saw Slater motioning one man at a time to the open space between the ramp and the rows of nylon seats that ran along the sides and down the middle of the sophisticated aircraft.

In the troop compartment, the Combat Talon aircraft didn't look like a product of high technology. It looked almost like any other C-130 transport—for decades, the workhorse of the Military Airlift Command—except for a curtained-off compartment in the front area of the cargo bay. But within that compartment, and in the cockpit above it, were the instruments of American technology that made it possible for the crew to take the aircraft deep within hostile territory undetected.

From the outside, too, the Combat Talon looked much like any other C-130 transport, except for its mottled black radar-absorbing paint, the shape of its radar dome, and the presence of several innocuous-appearing attachments hanging beneath the wings. It was the sensors and electronic countermeasures inside these attachments that enabled the Combat Talon aircraft to escape detection by the less sophisticated technology of the Soviet Union and her allies and surrogates.

The loadmaster at the back of the airplane grasped Master Sergeant Slater by the arm and said something to him. Slater finished his jumpmaster check of one of the men in his team, then stood in the middle of the aircraft, stamped his foot, and, holding up all ten fingers, yelled, "Ten minutes!"

Rocco Birelli helped Master Sergeant Slater check the last two men of Davidson's team, then moved to one of the empty troop seats—near the door, but out of the jumpmaster's way. Slater, helped by two other members of his twelve-man A detachment and the air force loadmaster, removed the tiedown straps from the door bundles his team would kick out of the aircraft before they followed.

By the dim glow of the red interior lights they wrestled each bundle near the troop doors on either side of the fuselage. Slater pulled the static line from the top of each bundle's parachute and hooked it to the steel anchor line cable that ran along each side of the cargo compartment. Again, the loadmaster heard over his earphones a report from the copilot and passed it on to the jumpmaster, Master Sergeant Slater.

Slater turned toward the other members of his team, held up all five fingers of one hand and one finger of the other, and yelled, "Six minutes!"

From the cockpit, the Combat Talon's crew chief, Chief Master Sergeant Duke Riley, made his way between the nylon seats on which the two A teams were seated, giving each man he recognized a brotherly slap on the shoulder and a smile. He moved past Slater to the sloping ramp at the rear of the plane, plugged in his intercom headset, then donned a safety harness and hooked it to the anchor line cable above him.

Before beginning the commands that would lead to his team's parachute descent to the dark earth five hundred

feet below, Slater hooked his own static line snap hook to
the steel cable, inserted the safety wire that would keep it
closed, then tugged on it several times to ensure that it
was firmly attached. Then he faced the other members of
his detachment and yelled, "Outboard personnel, stand
up!" His hands, palms upward, signaled them to stand.

As Slater shouted "Inboard personnel, stand up!" the
aircraft lurched, causing several of the Special Forces
men to grab for something to hold on to. Rocco Birelli
caught Davidson before he stumbled back onto the nylon
web seats and said to him, "Do good, Bill, ol' buddy."

Bill Davidson looked at him and smiled weakly. While
Slater commanded "Hook up!" Davidson said, "Yeah,
we'll try, Rock. Good luck to you and your guys, too."

Sergeant Slater was giving the command to "Check
static lines," and Davidson wasn't even hooked up yet, so
he reached up, snapped his static line snap hook onto the
cable above him, and inserted the safety wire. The
aircraft seemed to drop into a hole, then hit bottom.
Davidson fell back into Birelli's lap. Birelli looked at the
commander of his sister Special Forces A team, grinned,
pursed his lips as in a kiss, and said, "You sweet
motherfucker, don't you never die! See you later, Bill."

Davidson struggled to his feet again and checked to see
that the yellow static line that would deploy his MC-1C
main parachute was routed directly from the anchor line
cable above him to the parachute on his back. He took a
bight in the static line, then stepped forward and signaled
to Slater to turn around. Satisfied that his team sergeant's static line was not misrouted, he stepped back
behind the door bundle on his side.

"Check equipment!"

Davidson looked down, feeling the snap hooks of the
H harness by which his rucksack was attached to him,
the quick-release loops that would enable him to lower it
after his parachute opened, and the tiedown that held his
M-16 rifle against his left thigh. The man behind him
slapped him on the butt and shouted, "OK!" Davidson
pointed to Slater and yelled, "All OK!"

The aircraft cut power, causing Slater to have to reach

up and grab the anchor line cable to maintain his balance. The crew chief, Duke Riley, who had been serving on Combat Talons since they were invented during the Vietnam War, walked to the right-side paratroop door and pulled it in and up, locking it open. At five hundred feet, the air that swirled into the plane's troop compartment was warmer than the refrigerated air that had filled the area before the door was opened. Riley kicked the hinged jump step down so that it was outside the door of the aircraft, then stomped on it to make certain it was in place. Across from him his loadmaster was doing the same thing in the left troop door. Riley took Slater's static line, now whipping in the wind that swirled around the back of the aircraft, and leaned his head over the jumpmaster's shoulder.

"Two minutes, Jimmy!" he said.

Slater nodded, waved his arms, and held up two fingers of one hand. "Two minutes!" he yelled to his teammates, then he went to the door, stomped on the jump step to verify that it was seated, and thrust his head out of the door. While Riley held his static line, Slater checked the darkness outside, looking forward, down, up, and to the rear. All he could see were stars twinkling brightly above the dark earth.

He pulled his head back in and looked at his team. Captain Davidson gave him a nervous wink. The other ten men in their team looked ready to jump, each steadying himself with his outboard hand on the frame of the troop seats, his inboard hand above his shoulder, holding a loop of static line up near the anchor line cable to which it was attached.

Riley tapped Slater on the shoulder and thrust an index finger in front of his face. "One minute, Jimmy!" he called, then he added, "Good luck, bud!"

Slater nodded, then raised one finger to his team and shouted, "One minute!" He saw the first two men in the stick on each side of the aircraft move forward and grab the door bundles to move them nearer the doors. Satisfied that all was ready, he again thrust his head out into the slipstream of warm air. He made a quick check of the darkness surrounding the aircraft, then looked forward and down. There! Low and ahead, he could see a pattern of four lights on the ground, one of which was blinking on and off. He wasn't certain that the lights were arranged in the exact pattern they were supposed to be—but then, during scores of infiltration jumps he had jumpmastered during training, he'd seldom been able to distinguish the pattern anyway. The fact that there were lights down there—one of which was blinking—at the right time, somewhere in the wasteland of southeastern Iran, where the Combat Talon crew had brought them after two midair refuels and a seemingly endless flight, was all he could have hoped for. He looked back into the aircraft, gave a thumbs-up to indicate that he had located the reception party's lights, then commanded, "Stand in the door!" and moved out of the way to enable the first jumpers to push the team's bundles to the edge of the doors.

Peering over the top of the bundle in his door, Slater waited until the lights were almost directly below him, then looked at the warning lights on the frame of the paratroop door. When the light turned from red to green he shouted, "Go!" and helped the man on his side push the equipment bundle out into the dark night. He looked at the other door just in time to see the second bundle disappear, with the man who had pushed it following right behind, before he even ascertained that it had cleared the aircraft. On that side the air force loadmaster was taking the static lines to pull them out of the way so they wouldn't snag on the men's bulky equipment.

At the door on his side Slater grabbed the static line that each man in his stick slid along the cable to him, holding them out of the way. He suddenly realized that all his teammates were gone, and for a split second he was gripped by fear—the fear that he was being left behind. A quick glance at the other door confirmed his realization, and without checking to see that no one was hung up outside the aircraft, Slater leapt into the darkness.

Special Forces Operational Detachment A-325 was

committed to the operation—an infiltration to link up
with Baluchi tribesmen in the hilly wasteland of southeastern Iran, to organize, train, and equip them to do
battle with the Red Army of the Union of Soviet Socialist
Republics.

"I'll be damned. We're really going," Captain Rocco
Birelli said aloud. For the first time he was absolutely
certain that his team, SFOD A-326, was going to be
deployed on an actual operation.

When he had first been alerted and isolated with his
team at Camp MacKall, a small camp just west of Fort
Bragg that was normally used as a base for training
Special Forces recruits, he had thought at first that it was
just another EDRE—Emergency Deployment Readiness Exercise. The seriousness of the 3d Special Forces
Group staff, however, had soon convinced him that they
were there to make actual preparations for his team and
others to infiltrate Southwest Asia and organize the
region's Baluchi tribesmen into an armed guerrilla force.
The fact that he and his teammates were given full access
to intelligence from sensitive, compartmented sources—
including satellite photos of their unconventional warfare operations area—reinforced his belief that their
preparations were for a live mission. But he still didn't
think they would actually go. The possibility of American soldiers becoming directly involved in combat operations against Soviet forces was something he just
couldn't believe. The world was supposed to be turning
into a peaceful planet. But now the damned Russians
seemed to be casting Gorbachev aside, and reverting to
their old, failed ways. . . . Even when they were issued
live ammunition—not only small-arms ammo but also
Stinger and Dragon missiles for use against aircraft and
armored vehicles—he had thought that they would be
used only to train and equip the tribesmen, and that the
Special Forces teams would be withdrawn before the
Russians actually arrived, if they ever did.

Only when the commander-in-chief of the United
States Special Operations Command showed up at Camp
MacKall and announced that a Soviet airborne force had

landed on the southeastern coast of Iran, in the vicinity of the small port of Chah Bahar, did Rocco Birelli and his teammates realize that the Soviets had defied world opinion and their own alleged demilitarization policy and had invaded Iran.

Still, Birelli and his men had refused to believe that they would actually be committed into a combat situation.

Even during the long flight from the Special Forces Operations Base in England to the almost useless wastes of southeastern Iran, Birelli had expected their infiltration jump to be aborted. Now, though, the doubts had all dissipated—vanished, like Davidson, Slater, and their team, out the doors of the Combat Talon aircraft.

Once that realization struck Birelli, it was as if he underwent a transformation. There was no denying it now. They were going to war.

As the crew chief and his loadmaster recovered the static lines and the parachute deployment bags of Davidson and Slater's team, Birelli's years of training for this day took control of his thoughts and actions, and he was transformed from a naïve young peacetime soldier to a professional Special Forces officer on the verge of leading his team into combat.

The exit of his sister team meant that Birelli and his team were twenty-five minutes from their drop zone. He rid his mind of all other concerns, and, turning to his own team sergeant, Master Sergeant Jake Brady, he said, "All right, Jake, let's get 'em rigged."

By the time the MC-130 crew chief signaled "Ten minutes," the men of Special Forces Operational Detachment A-326 had donned their parachutes, had strapped on their cumbersome rucksacks and weapons, and were ready to jump.

Four minutes later Rocco Birelli acknowledged Duke Riley's six-minute warning and stood to assume his duties as jumpmaster. He hooked up, took his men through the jump commands, got their door bundles positioned near the paratroop doors, then, as the crew chief warned, "One minute," he leaned out the door of the airplane and searched the darkness ahead for the drop-zone markings.

Far ahead he saw several pinpoints of light on the ground. They were in the form of an inverted L, and the outermost light was flashing "dot dot dash . . . dot dot dash," Morse code for the letter "U." That was the prearranged signal verifying that it was A-326's drop zone, manned by a CIA agent and the Baluchi tribesmen they were to train and equip to do battle.

Captain Rocco Birelli stood back from the door, ordered the team's stick leaders—Master Sergeant Jake Brady and the team executive officer, Chief Warrant Officer Fred Kaminski—to "Stand in the door!"

When the jump lights again switched to green Captain Birelli commanded, "Go!" and the twelve men of Special Forces Operational Detachment A-326 were out of the airplane and drifting toward the dark earth below.

2320 hours GMT (1920 hours EDT), 18 September
Headquarters, 1st Special Operations Command
Fort Bragg, North Carolina

Brigadier General William Porter drew himself a cup of strong coffee from the urn at the rear of the briefing room, then returned to his seat and, in his mind, reviewed the information he had just received, trying to absorb it all.

He looked at the map of Southwest Asia as he considered the events of the previous week.

At the top of the map was Kazakhstan, the Soviet republic whose largely Muslim population had been creating civil disturbances for months, seeking greater independence from Moscow. Numerous red symbols covered Kazakhstan's southern border, indicating the locations of Soviet military units—units that had been reported, when Porter went on leave ten days earlier, as being there to quell the civil unrest.

South of Kazakhstan, on the east, was Afghanistan. It, too, contained a number of symbols for Soviet forces for the first time since early 1989, when Gorbachev had directed their withdrawal from the decade-long war against the anti-Communist Mujahadeen guerrillas.

Eight days earlier the Mujahadeen had been poised for a final push on the capital of Kabul to overthrow the puppet Communist government there. They were massed in a valley just outside the city, preparing to use the last of the dwindling munitions supplied to them by the U.S. government in a bid for their long-sought victory. But the Soviets, who were aware that the Mujahadeen had expended all of their American-made Stinger antiaircraft missiles, denied them that victory. On 10 September they launched a series of massive airstrikes against the concentrated guerrilla forces, killing hundreds of them and wounding many hundreds more. The following day, 11 September, they reentered Afghanistan in force, employing one motorized rifle division and one tank division. Most of the forces were being used to mop up the battered Mujahadeen, but one regiment from each division had moved southwest to Afghanistan's borders with Iran on the west and Pakistan on the south. The assessment of America's intelligence community was that these forces were poised to invade Iran.

Iran had been in turmoil since the assassination of the Ayatollah Khomeini's successor, Hashemi Rafsanjani, with none of the various political factions able to gain the upper hand in their efforts to take control of the country. Tudeh, the Iranian Communist party, applauded the Soviet reinvasion of Afghanistan, and—seeing it as an opportunity to gain control of Iran for their party—requested Soviet intervention to "restore order and stability to the Islamic Socialist Republic of Iran."

Early on the morning of 14 September the Soviet high command convinced the Politburo hard-liners—over General Secretary Gorbachev's protests—to use Tudeh's request as an excuse to realize one of their long-sought goals—the seizure of a warm-water port on the Indian Ocean. A Soviet parachute regiment was landed at the small port of Chah Bahar on Iran's coast, and at the airfield located twenty-five kilometers across a bay from the port town.

The response of the United States had been swift and—so far, at least—effective. An exclusion zone was declared in the Indian Ocean. From the coast of Iran at the Strait of Hormuz, east to the coast of Pakistan, for a distance of two hundred nautical miles offshore, the Indian Ocean was declared to be under the sole control of the United States Navy and her NATO allies. Any vessel other than civilian oil tankers and cargo ships entering those waters, or aircraft entering the airspace above it, would be attacked and destroyed. Two carrier battle groups, one of which had been en route to relieve the other of duty in the Indian Ocean, were present to back up those threats. The battleship *Missouri* and her escorts were dispatched to reinforce them.

The Iranian Navy was the first to challenge America's declaration. During the evening of 14 September one of Iran's two remaining frigates, accompanied by three small raiding craft, entered the exclusion zone from the Strait of Hormuz. An American guided-missile cruiser, the USS *Yorktown,* was guarding that sector of the exclusion zone. She blew the Iranian vessels out of the water with her deadly ship-to-ship missiles.

The second challenge to the exclusion zone declared by the United States came the following morning, 15 September. A Soviet Bear reconnaissance aircraft transited Iran from the north and entered the airspace of the exclusion zone. A pair of F/A-18 Hornets from the supercarrier *America* intercepted the Soviet aircraft and, when it ignored signals to turn back, downed it with automatic cannon fire. A search-and-rescue helicopter from the *America* rescued the surviving Russian crewmen, who had since been turned over to the Swiss for repatriation.

Porter swallowed the last of his coffee and walked to the urn to get another cupful. He wondered, as he did so, whether the desperate diplomatic efforts of his own government and those of much of the rest of the world would succeed in preventing the tense situation from exploding into a major war. The forces of NATO and the crumbling Warsaw Pact in Europe faced each other across Europe in disarray, many armies unsure of which side they would be on if the volatile situation exploded into war. But the forces of United States Central Command—CENTCOM—had no such uncertainties about their mission. They were being marshaled for deployment to Southwest Asia by aircraft and America's fleet of roll-on, roll-off ships, prepared to do battle with the Soviet forces there.

The command of which Porter was the deputy commanding general—1st Special Operations Command—had placed the 3rd Special Forces Group on alert the day the Soviets reentered Afghanistan. The 3rd Group detachments that were targeted against Southwest Asia had been placed in isolation at Camp MacKall that same evening, to review their area studies and the contingency plans for them to infiltrate the area to organize, train, and equip potential resistance movements.

On the 14th, after the Soviets seized Chah Bahar and the nearby airfield on the southern coast of Iran, the decision was made to activate a Special Forces Operations Base—SFOB—in England, to provide command and control for any Special Forces detachments that might be committed to operations in response to the aggressive actions of the Soviets. In addition, a forward operations base, along with CENTCOM's forward command post, was set up on the island of Masirah, in the Indian Ocean off the coast of Oman.

On 15 September, when it became apparent that the Soviets might attempt to reinforce their airborne regiment at Chah Bahar with armored units from Afghanistan, the decision was made to commit two twelve-man A detachments into southeastern Iran, with a backup A team to Masirah Island.

Porter took a gulp of the strong coffee, then walked to a map of the area. He studied the map from south to north.

At the bottom was the Indian Ocean, with Masirah Island tucked in close to the coast of Oman beneath the point at which the Arabian Peninsula juts into the ocean.

Some three hundred miles north was the southeastern coast of Iran, with the crescent-shaped bay around which the Soviet airborne regiment was deployed. There were two large blue ovals drawn on the map, like goose eggs stacked one above the other.

The bottom oval, which rested on the coast of Iran and extended east and west of Chah Bahar for about fifty miles, and north well into the rugged Makran mountain range, was labeled Unconventional Warfare Operations Area SHARK. Atop it was another blue oval, extending east-west for a similar distance, and north from the Makran mountains to the Iranian town of Khash. The top oval was labeled Unconventional Warfare Operations Area TIGER.

It was into each of these areas that a twelve-man A team was now infiltrating by parachute. Porter studied the map from the top of UWOA Tiger's goose egg to the points at which the red symbols of the Soviet armored forces had been drawn to indicate their latest known positions. They were less than 300 miles away from the northern boundary of Tiger. Unless there was some way to impede them, the Russians could easily cover that distance in three days. And the latest intelligence reports estimated that the Soviets would have their support units with them, be fully resupplied, and be ready to move into Iran in two or three days.

"Five days. September the twenty-third," Porter said.

"Sir?" the master sergeant with him said.

"I said 'five days,' Pete," Porter replied. "The goddam Russians could be into UWOA Tiger within five days. That's just two days after our guys get their automatic resupply dropped to them."

"Yes, sir. Not much time to get the Baluchi equipped, trained, and ready to fight, is it?"

"No, it sure as hell isn't," Porter agreed. "Look here, Pete," he continued, pointing to a hill mass just southwest of the Afghanistan-Pakistan-Iran tri-border area. "Has any consideration been given to putting some direct-action teams in here, well north of Tiger? If we could hit them along these two roads, at least it might slow the bastards down long enough to give the guys in Tiger and Shark a few more days to get ready to deal with them."

"Well, yes, sir. That was considered—briefly. But the chances of getting any teams in there and set up before the Russians got past didn't seem worth the risk of capture. And all they'd be able to carry would be Dragons. TOWs are just too damned heavy to lug around. And without any mobility . . ."

Porter studied the map a moment longer, then said, "Get the Corps G-3 on the secure phone for me, will you, Pete?"

As the NCO dialed the number of the XVIII Airborne Corps operations officer Brigadier General Porter picked up a blue grease pencil and, with a dashed line, drew a third big oval on the map of southeastern Iran. This one, sitting atop the oval labeled Unconventional Warfare Operations Area TIGER, lay just west of the Pakistan border from the town of Khash, at the top of UWOA Tiger, north for about a hundred miles to the Iranian town of Zahedan. Porter labeled the new oval UWOA SWORD.

CHAPTER 2

2325 hours Greenwich Mean Time (1625 hours Pacific Daylight Time), 18 September
Edwards Air Force Base, California

Timing is everything, Major Mark Denton thought as he watched the helicopters being loaded aboard the big airplane. He couldn't remember who was credited with making the statement famous, but it didn't matter. All that mattered was that it was sometimes true, and that this was one of those times.

The rest of "the Package," as Major Denton, the members of his team, and their equipment were collectively known, was already aboard the C-5B Galaxy. The nine members of the 3rd Special Forces Group who had been tasked to help Denton demonstrate the capabilities of the Package were up in the passenger compartment of the airplane and were probably asleep by now. They deserved the rest. For the past few days they had gotten little sleep as they hid in the barren terrain of the National Training Center at Fort Irwin, California. The Special Forces men and the six members of the 1st Special Operations Aviation Detachment (Provisional) —four warrant officer pilots and two ground crewmen— had performed well during the demonstration of the capabilities of the Package. In fact, they had proved more valuable than Denton had dared hope.

The National Training Center at Fort Irwin is a huge base in the mountainous high desert of southern California where the combat maneuver battalions of the United States Army go to practice war. There is a permanently based force there whose sole mission is to simulate the tactics and equipment of the Soviet Army, and, after years of practice, they do a credible job of it. The commanders of the U.S. Army infantry and armor battalions and armored cavalry squadrons who pass through Fort Irwin agree almost unanimously that it is the most realistic training, short of war, that they could possibly provide their soldiers. The few who disagree with that assessment usually do so because they fail miserably, as a result of bad tactics or poor leadership, to make a decent showing against the opposing force.

Thanks to Major Mark Denton and the Package, the commander of the 3d Battalion (Airborne), 73d Armor, 82d Airborne Division, was not one of those who failed. In fact, his battalion, reinforced by the Package, had performed better against the 32d Guards Motorized Rifle Regiment—as the simulated Soviet force was designated—with his aging, lightly armored Sheridans than most tank battalions equipped with the army's newest and best tank, the M-1A1 Abrams main battle tank.

The concept of the Package was fairly simple: get a Special Forces A team equipped with state-of-the-art electronic equipment, team them up with a pair of armed light helicopters, and infiltrate them into the enemy's rear area—or an area he is expected to occupy—along with a substantial cache of fuel and munitions. Then turn them loose and let them locate and attack key rear-area installations in quick night raids. In addition, they would be in position to report on enemy movements and to harass enemy columns moving toward the front. He was confident that they could operate in the enemy rear for an extended period of time, as long as three conditions were met: there was an adequate number of places to cache supplies and hide from the enemy; they didn't conduct their raids too frequently; and the right men were assigned to the mission. The last condition, Mark Denton felt, was the most important.

For Denton, the opportunity to demonstrate the Package in an environment simulating realistic combat had not come easily. As the Force Developments Officer of the 1st Special Operations Command at Fort Bragg, he had found it easy enough to come up with the concept of the Package, put it on paper, and forward it through channels. His superiors had found the concept interesting, but getting them to commit the resources necessary to gather the men and equipment to test the concept had, for months, proved futile. Then the Panama operation had occurred, and Denton's concept had been all but forgotten. He had nearly given up on trying to get the concept through the bureaucrats, who, even if they finally approved it, wouldn't get around to testing it until long after Denton had completed his stint as a staff officer and had returned to his favorite job—commanding troops.

But one day the deputy commanding general of the 1st Special Operations Command, Brigadier General William Porter, had been making the rounds of 1st SOCOM's Fort Bragg headquarters to ensure that everyone was gainfully employed, and he entered Denton's cramped little office. He had read Denton's concept, and he asked him what progress was being made with it. When Denton explained that it had apparently become hung up in one of the bureaucracy's many bottlenecks, Porter asked for a more detailed briefing on the concept. After Denton pulled out his butcher-paper charts and gave an enthusiastic briefing on it, the general said, "You know, the assistant division commander of the 82d and I were talking the other day about how we might help his Sheridan battalion survive their stint out at NTC. This package of yours might be just the ticket."

Porter telephoned his counterpart in the 82d Airborne Division and arranged for Denton to brief him on the concept. Soon after, Major Mark Denton found himself —along with two Hughes H-500MD helicopters and their crews, an understrength Special Forces A team, and much of the equipment listed in his concept paper— attached to the army's only airborne armor battalion, the 3d of the 73d Armor.

He spent a week briefing and training the helicopter

crews and the Special Forces team on the concept and the equipment. They were all pleased to have the opportunity to get away from the relatively dull routine of normal training and to be part of the test of a new tactical concept and of equipment about which they had, for the most part, only heard.

They also came up with new ideas to improve the concept and were happy to find that Major Denton not only agreed to implement many of their ideas but encouraged them to come up with more.

Then, after spending three days and nights training with the 3d of the 73d Armor and their battalion of M-551 Sheridan airborne armored reconnaissance vehicles and their crews, they had deployed with the battalion to Fort Irwin to do simulated battle with the simulated Soviet forces there.

It had proved to be no contest. The ADC of the 82d Airborne had arranged with the commander of the National Training Center to not brief the OPFOR—opposing forces—on the fact that the 3d of the 73d Armor was reinforced by Major Denton's "Package" of two modified H-500 helicopters and two four-man Special Forces teams, plus a Special Forces radio man to serve as Denton's radio operator. Denton had equipped the SF teams with remote electronic OPs—observation posts—laser target designators, and a small, unmanned remote-control vehicle which had been given to the army to test by the corporation that invented it.

The Weasel, as the men had nicknamed the remote-control vehicle, or RCV, was capable of being controlled by the user from four kilometers away. It was only a meter and a half long, less than a meter wide, and a meter high. Within its shapeless fiberglass body were storage batteries, an electric drive motor, and a remote-control steering system. Mounted atop the body on a telescoping mast was a low-to-high light level television camera with a four-power zoom lens, also remotely controlled for deflection, elevation, and zoom. Beside it was affixed a remotely activated laser target designator. The top plane of the fiberglass body was covered with solar power collectors. The Weasel's ancillary equipment included a remote-control transmitter, a two-foot-wide dish receiver for the TV camera's signals, and spare batteries and solar collectors. Because the Weasel was too heavy to be man-carried, the team that operated it had a three-wheeled all-terrain vehicle with a small trailer to move it over long distances. There was another version of the Weasel that was satellite-controlled, enabling it to be manipulated at unlimited ranges, but Denton had not been able to acquire it for the demonstration.

The two modified H-500MD scout helicopters from the 1st SOCOM aviation detachment were equipped with systems similar to those carried by the army's OH-58D Kiowa helicopter: a mast-mounted sight through which long-range TV and infrared target acquisition systems enabled the crew to observe the battlefield without exposing the helicopter; weapons system mounts that could carry either the army's standard heavy anti-tank missile system, the improved TOW 2—an acronym for *T*ube-launched, *O*ptically-tracked, *W*ire-guided missile—laser-beam-riding Hellfire missiles, Stinger fire-and-forget antiaircraft missiles, 70-millimeter rockets, or either a .50 caliber heavy machine gun or a 5.56 millimeter, rapid-firing minigun.

Because the H-500MD was smaller than the OH-58D, it couldn't carry as heavy a load of ordnance as the '58, but it was quieter, more agile, and easier to maintain and hide, and therefore better suited to the Package's mission than the '58 would have been. For the purposes of the demonstration, the two helicopters had carried TOW and Hellfire missile systems on their weapons mounts.

Denton's teams had been allowed to infiltrate the training area two days before the training exercise actually began. The second night, which was the night before the airborne armor battalion and the OPFOR deployed to the training area, helicopter fuel and dummy loads simulating other supplies were dropped off at the locations Denton had selected as drop zones. Under his concept, these supplies would be airdropped to and cached by the men, but for the purposes of the test they were dropped off by truck, then hidden at the sites the Special Forces men had selected as caches.

The armed scout helicopters, their pilots well trained at flying with night-vision goggles in almost total darkness, flew out to their hide sites the night before the simulated Soviet regiment began its pre-dawn attack on the airborne armor task force.

Well forward of the helicopters one of the four-man Special Forces teams had set up a series of remote observation posts across the avenues of approach the enemy was expected to use. From their position atop one of the rocky hills they settled in to manipulate the OP's remote TV cameras. To their rear the second team had split up, with two men working another series of remote electronic observation posts, while their teammates stood by with the Weasel-towing all-terrain vehicle, ready to move to the location where the forward teams deemed they could best intercept the enemy.

An hour before dawn the forward OP detected the enemy moving into position to attack. The OP team immediately informed the task force commander, who ordered a simulated artillery strike on the enemy forces, while the men manning the OPs' small monitors continued to update their exact locations. On hearing the accuracy with which the strike was delivered, the controllers "killed" several of the enemy vehicles.

Meanwhile, the H-500MD crews hopped into their little choppers and flew to positions behind a small hill in front of the enemy's advance elements, and they reported to the forward OP team that they were in position to simulate launching two Hellfire missiles each. Ignoring the lead vehicles of the attacking column, the OP team manipulated the camera of one of their electronic OPs onto the vehicle they suspected of being the enemy commander's. Then the operator depressed the "on" switch of the OP's laser target designator and radioed, "Target illuminated!"

The pilot of one of the choppers popped up, acquired the laser beam, and called, "Identified!"

"Fire!" the OP replied.

"On the way!" the pilot replied as he triggered the Hellfire missile simulator.

The OP operator kept the laser target designator on his target for several more seconds, then turned it off.

Meanwhile, the man beside him had been tracking the lead tank with the camera of another OP, and as soon as his teammate declared, "Target destroyed!" he hit the LTD On switch and called, "Target illuminated."

While his wingman buzzed away to another firing position, the pilot of the second chopper popped up, sighted the laser beam, and fired his Hellfire simulator. One of the enemy crewmen sighted the second laser beam, too, and had several tanks fire on the position with blank rounds. The controllers ordered that OP out of action, even though pinpoint accuracy would have been required to hit the little, well-camouflaged electronic OP. But the forward team still had two operational OPs, and they took out two more enemy vehicles before the helicopters buzzed back to the first hide site to rearm their aircraft. The enemy called for artillery on one of the sites from which a laser beam had emanated, and the controllers declared another OP "dead."

Now the second line of electronic OPs was brought into play, and the H-500s' Hellfires took out four more of the enemy tanks after another accurately called artillery strike had made the controllers declare two other enemy vehicles "dead." The first echelon of the attacking force had already been severely depleted, and all they had been able to do in return was "destroy" two unmanned electronic OPs. The Package was working almost flawlessly.

The two helicopters, which still had not been spotted by the enemy, dashed back to the second hide site, and the crews quickly changed the armament from Hellfires to TOWs, which didn't require lasers to mark their targets.

The enemy's movements, as reported by the OP teams, had made it plain which portion of the friendly sector they were intending to attack, and the Weasel team quickly moved to intercept them. Meanwhile, the second attack echelon had appeared near the forward OP, and the Special Forces team called another artillery strike on top of them, then adjusted it to keep it abreast of the attackers. By the time the second echelon caught up to the badly depleted first, and continued the attack through them, it was daylight.

The choppers were in action again by then and, with their mast-mounted sights, were hovering out of sight behind hills nearly three kilometers to the enemy's front, still well ahead of the Sheridans and TOW vehicles the "Soviets" were expecting to have to fight. One at a time the little choppers popped up momentarily, fired their TOW simulators, then disappeared behind the hill with only their mast-mounted sights exposed to direct fire. As soon as enough time had passed to simulate the flight of a TOW missile to its target, the chopper that had just fired would buzz away to another hidden firing position, hovering far enough behind the protecting hill to preclude the wash of its rotor blades from raising a dust cloud. In less than five minutes they had been credited with four "kills" and buzzed away to the second hide site to rearm and refuel.

The Weasel didn't get into play that first day. The all-terrain vehicle broke down, and the team had to camouflage it and hide as the remaining enemy vehicles rattled past. But the TOW systems on the H-500 helicopters accounted for three more kills by the time the enemy came within range of the friendly task force's Sheridans, with their 152-mm Shillelagh missiles and smooth-bore guns. With the vehicle-mounted TOWs of the airborne-capable task force, they made quick work of most of the remaining enemy force, and by the time the controllers called a halt to the mock battle, the 3d of the 73d had suffered the loss of only two Sheridans and two TOW vehicles. The simulated Soviet force had lost more than thirty armored vehicles—twenty-two of them at the hands of Major Denton's Package and the artillery strikes they directed.

That afternoon, as the task force prepared for an attack against the reconstituted enemy, Major Denton was allowed to administratively recover the OP teams and their equipment, and to debrief the men. The commander of the National Training Center and the assistant division commander for operations of the 82d Airborne Division attended the debriefing.

Several of the Special Forces men commented on the fact that, had they cached TOW missile launchers near their OPs, they could have accounted for even more kills, but Denton quickly pointed out the fact that they would then have certainly been discovered. It wasn't worth it, he said.

"I disagree," Sergeant First Class Harry O'Neill, the leader of the forward OP team, said. "I mean, from the position we were manning, yes, they would have gotten us. But we could just as easily have been way up on one of those mountains on the flanks. Up there, by the time they reacted, even with artillery fire, we could've taken the launcher, hauled ass to a hide site, and got away clean."

"Yeah," one of his teammates agreed. "Just like the Mujahadeen used to do against the Sovs in Afghanistan."

"'Used to do' is right," the general from the 82d Airborne said, interrupting the briefing. "Those air-strikes the Russians hit them with the other day all but wiped them out. And now they've sent two divisions back into Afghanistan to finish the job."

Standing and facing the rest of the men in the room, he said, "For a change, it looks like we're not going to just sit here and let them get away with it this time, gentlemen. I learned a few minutes ago that the division has been alerted for deployment."

There was a murmur of approval, then the general continued. "I'm heading back to Bragg right away. The 3d of the 73d is to follow as soon as possible." Turning to Mark Denton, he said, "From what I saw of this 'Package' of yours today, Major, I intend to recommend to the division commander that you all be attached to us for this deployment. Can you handle that?"

Denton smiled. "You're damned right I can, General," he replied.

The other members of the Package voiced their approval, and the general smiled and said, "Good. Now, get me the standard name lines of yourself and your men before you leave. Then I want you to put together a list of all the equipment you'd need to operate for, say, a week in this sort of terrain. And include weights and cubes, if you can, then get the people here to fax it to my G-3 at Bragg."

Now, a day later, Mark Denton was loading the Package aboard a giant C-5B cargo plane and heading for Pope Air Force Base, the busy Military Airlift Command base adjacent to Fort Bragg. The G-3 of the 82d Airborne had sent a message confirming that Denton and the fifteen men supporting him, along with all their equipment, were, until further notice, attached to Headquarters & Headquarters Company, 82d Airborne Division.

"Yeah," Denton said again as he headed for the airplane, "timing is everything."

CHAPTER 3

2346 hours GMT, 18 September
Unconventional Warfare Operations Area Tiger
Southeastern Iran

Twenty-five minutes after Captain Bill Davidson and his A team parachuted into Unconventional Warfare Operations Area Shark just north of the Soviet airborne regiment's positions around the port of Chah Bahar, Captain Rocco Birelli's team jumped into UWOA Tiger, well to the north of Davidson and his men.

Although both teams were to contact the Baluchi tribesmen in their respective areas and organize, train, and equip them to fight the Soviets, Davidson's efforts would be directed against the Soviet airborne forces already on the ground. Birelli and his men were to prepare to engage the Soviet units that were expected to try to reinforce their airborne comrades from the north.

When Birelli felt the tug as his parachute deployed he quickly looked up, saw that it was fully open, then looked down at the drop zone. The lights of the reception committee were already out, and he could make out nothing on the ground. As the sound of the Combat Talon faded he released his rucksack and felt the yank on his harness as it reached the end of the lowering line. He grasped the steering toggles above him to turn his parachute into the slight breeze he felt against the right side of his face, but before he could turn he heard his rucksack thump onto the hard ground below. He got his feet and knees together just before he hit the drop zone and, tucking his head, rolled to the left. His weapon

27

banged loudly against a rock as he did so, causing him to wonder if it was damaged. By the dim light of the stars he could make out another jumper standing and climbing out of his harness just a few feet from where Birelli had landed.

Before he got up to recover his parachute Birelli struggled out of his harness and untied his weapon from it. He slung the M-16 rifle over his shoulder, then followed the lowering line from his parachute to his rucksack. When he reached it he pulled open the top flap and removed a small night viewing scope he had stored there. With it he was able to observe the drop zone and the other members of his team. One man remained prone on the ground, and two other men were standing over him. Someone had apparently been injured on landing.

In the pale green light of the pocketscope Birelli saw his team sergeant, Master Sergeant Jake Brady, moving toward him.

"Looks like we have one injury, sir," Brady said when he reached Birelli. "Carter. Compound fracture of one leg. His other one might be broken, too."

"Damn!" Carter was the team's senior radio operator. "Did you find Hanson?" Birelli asked, hoping to learn that his team's other radio operator had landed safely.

"Yes, sir. I told him to set up the satellite radio and to punch in a request for an immediate STAR."

The team had a contingency for the evacuation of anyone injured during the infiltration, provided the injury was serious enough to warrant it, yet not so serious as to preclude recovery by the use of the exotic STAR system, the acronym for Surface-to-Air Recovery. The Combat Talon aircraft would, if directed to do so by radio, return to the drop zone and paradrop a bundle containing the ground-operated portion of the recovery system. The STAR system consists of a lift suit—into which the evacuee is placed—connected to a five-hundred-foot-long braided nylon lift line. A blimp-shaped balloon is attached to the other end of the lift line and, when inflated by a bottle of compressed helium included in the kit, used to raise the lift line to its full length. Twenty minutes after dropping the STAR bundle the Combat Talon aircraft would return to the recovery zone and snatch the evacuee from the ground.

"Do the medics think he's not too badly hurt to get skyhooked?" Birelli asked, using the slang term for the STAR system.

"Norton's putting pneumatic splints on both legs. He's going to give him a local anesthetic before the STAR, if he needs it. Sergeant Carter understands the necessity for getting him out of here. He's ready to go for it."

"All right then," Birelli said. "Has anybody made contact with the Baluchi?"

"Yes, sir," Brady replied. "Mr. Kaminski's moving to the rally point with Esquire to find their chief now."

"Good," Birelli said as he began to roll up his parachute. "Is Esquire who we thought he was?" Esquire was the code name of the CIA agent who had entered the region and made contact with the leaders of the men Birelli's team was to equip and train.

"He sure is," Brady replied. "None other than ol' Dick Medlin himself."

The Baluchi tribesmen—more than half a million men, women, and children spread across the wastelands of southwestern Afghanistan, western Pakistan, and southeastern Iran—are a seminomadic group of Sunni Muslims who pay little heed to international boundaries, referring to the lands they occupy as "Baluchistan." Only Pakistan had ever tried, in modern times, to bring them under government control. The cost in blood to both sides had been heavy, and, as their lands are largely unproductive anyway, the Pakistani government had eventually simply left them alone.

The Central Intelligence Agency had long recognized their potential as a force to resist possible Soviet intervention in the area and had maintained contacts with their tribal leaders since 1980.

Dick Medlin had been working with Baluchi tribesmen on and off since the mid-eighties, providing their northernmost faction in Afghanistan with equipment to fight the Soviets and their Afghan Communist puppets. Prior to that he had served as a covert agent in Tehran during the ill-fated attempt to rescue the American hostages from there in 1980. And before that the courageous former Special Forces officer had been a leader during the attempt to rescue American prisoners from the North Vietnamese at the Son Tay POW camp near Hanoi in 1970.

"Man, that's great," Birelli said. "No wonder we were getting such good premission intel." Rocco Birelli had met the legendary Dick Medlin during the Special Operations Staff Officer Course at Fort Bragg, where Medlin had been a guest speaker. Jake Brady had been on Medlin's team years earlier. When the intelligence reports the team had been given during their isolation at Camp MacKall proved to contain exactly the sort of information they needed, Brady had remarked that there was only one man he knew of who could produce work like that—Dick Medlin.

It was a relief to Birelli to learn that his team sergeant's hunch had been correct. Medlin's talented presence could make the team's job less difficult.

"You'd better get on up there, meet them, and give Hanson permission to release the STAR request, sir," Brady said. "I'll get the drop zone sterilized and set up the beacon for the Talon."

"Right," Rocco Birelli said, hefting his heavy rucksack onto his back. He put his pocketscope to his eye and saw a small group of men standing at the leading edge of the drop zone, and he moved off toward them.

He arrived to find that the group included his executive officer, Chief Warrant Officer Fred Kaminski; the team's uninjured radio operator, Sergeant Percy Hanson; and three men in Baluchi native dress. To the men in native garb he said, in Baluchi language, "God's greetings. I am Captain Rocco Birelli, United States Army Special Forces."

"Hello, Captain Birelli," one of the men said in English. It was Dick Medlin. Birelli shook his hand as

Medlin said, in Baluchi, "Let me introduce the chief of the Talwar Allah, Chakur Nothani."

"Talwar Allah," Birelli thought as he shook the Baluchi chieftain's hand. "The Sword of God." Good name for a guerrilla force.

"God's blessings, Captain Birelli," Chakur Nothani said, then he turned to the third robed figure and said, "This is my military commander—the point of the sword—Lakha Nawaz."

Nawaz shook Birelli's hand and said, "In the name of God, welcome to Baluchistan."

Kneeling over his radio on the ground beside them, Sergeant Hanson said, "Sir, I'm all set up to send the STAR request."

"Send it," Birelli directed, and Hanson pressed the Transmit button on the satellite radio's digital message device group. The DMDG transmitted, in a split second, the surface-to-air recovery mission request that Hanson had typed into its memory bank. It was received by a communications satellite in orbit twenty-two thousand miles above the Indian Ocean and retransmitted immediately—on a different frequency—back to earth.

There were three stations capable of receiving the data and decoding it: 3d Special Forces Group headquarters at Fort Bragg, the Special Forces Operations Base (SFOB) in England, and the one that mattered most at the moment—the MC-130 Combat Talon, which was now far to the northwest, going through a series of deceptive flight legs while the crew waited to learn if they would be required to return to one of the drop zones for a STAR or could head for the aerial tanker waiting for them over the Gulf of Oman.

While he waited for confirmation of the STAR request Rocco Birelli accepted the offer of the Baluchi guerrilla force's commander to take some of his men and go with Kaminski to help the team clear the drop zone of parachutes and equipment. When they were gone Birelli explained that he needed to see his injured man, and the chieftain, Chakur Nothani, replied, "Of course. Wish

31

him well, and say that I am sorry he has to go without drawing Russian blood."

While the Baluchi tribesmen helped other members of the Special Forces team clear the drop zone Birelli went to where the team's medics were preparing the injured Sergeant Carter for exfiltration back to England.

"How you doin', Sergeant Carter?" he asked.

"Been better, sir. Sorry about this, but I didn't get my rucksack released in time. Seemed like I'd just got out the door, and I hit the ground like a ton of shit."

"Yeah, there's not much time from five hundred feet, is there? You sure he's in good enough shape to get skyhooked, Sergeant Norton?"

The senior medic of A-326, Staff Sergeant Chuck Norton, looked up from his medical kit and replied, "I think so, boss. These pneumatic splints will keep the breaks immobilized, and I got a good dressing on the puncture wound, so he shouldn't lose any more blood. He'll be a lot better off once he gets in the airplane than he would if we tried to drag him around out here."

"How many Gs do you pull when you get skyhooked, sir?" the injured Carter asked.

"Not many, so they say," Birelli said. "In fact, it's supposed to be less of a shock than the opening shock of a parachute."

"That's right," the medic said. "The lift line is woven so that it acts like a big rubber band. It stretches when the plane snags it, lifts you off the ground a little way, then, when it contracts, you get a quick but smooth acceleration."

"Right," Birelli agreed. "Damn quick. Zero to one-sixty in a few seconds."

"Christ!" the broken-legged Carter moaned. "You sure my legs can take it, Doc?"

"No sweat, buddy," his teammate said. "These pneumatic splints will work fine. And that ol' crew chief, Riley, is the best in the STAR business. He'll have you winched in in no time. You just make sure you're well into the plane before they unhook you."

Hanson, the team's remaining radio operator, walked

over to report that he'd received confirmation of the STAR mission. "They'll drop the bundle at 0016 Zulu — that's about eleven minutes from now. The pickup run will be twenty-two minutes later—0038."

"Roger," Birelli replied. "What track will they be flying?"

"Two niner zero magnetic. Same track they dropped us on."

"OK," Birelli said. "Find Sergeant Brady and have him set up the beacon and IR strobe, center of mass of the drop zone. The Talon crew will use the onboard computers to figure in wind drift and forward throw. Move."

Within five minutes Jake Brady had an SST-23 transponder beacon set up in the center of the drop zone. At 0012 hours Zulu, or Greenwich Mean Time, he turned on the SST-23 and an infrared strobe light. He checked the IR strobe with his night-viewing pocketscope to ensure that it was flashing, since it was not visible to the naked eye.

A minute later he saw the dim interrogation light on the SST-23 transponder flicker, indicating that the Combat Talon radar was "interrogating" it, and that the transponder was "replying." The low-flying black airplane was homing in on the drop zone. It was less than a minute from them before the men on the ground heard it. In the moonless night they didn't see the aircraft until it passed low overhead.

At first Rocco Birelli thought it had failed to drop the STAR bundle, but then he saw the dark shape of the parachute drifting toward where he, the medic, and the injured Sergeant Carter were. The bundle landed with a thud less than twenty feet away, and the parachute settled onto the three men. As they struggled to disentangle themselves from the nylon canopy and suspension lines Carter muttered, "Damn, this just ain't my day, is it?"

Birelli laughed. "You just better hope that the old saying about 'bad things happen in threes' doesn't hold true tonight, Carter."

"Jeez, boss, you really know how to instill confidence, don't you?" Carter said.

Brady and two of his teammates ran to the bundle and derigged it, and a few minutes later they brought the lift suit to Birelli and the medic, Chuck Norton. They had to slit the legs of the suit to get it over the pneumatic splints on Carter's fractured legs. The sewn-in harness that would bear Carter's weight as he was snatched from the ground was unaffected by slitting the legs of the suit.

Meanwhile, Brady inflated the big balloon and made sure that the inch-and-a-half-thick lift line was properly secured to it. Birelli checked to ensure that the other end of the five-hundred-foot line was properly attached to the harness of the lift suit. That done, he checked his watch.

"Zero zero three two," he announced. "Six minutes to pickup."

The radio operator, Sergeant Hanson, checked his own watch and replied, "Roger. I show zero zero three two and ten seconds." One of his duties as the radioman was to make certain that the team always operated on the correct time, since many of the activities of Special Forces operations require precise timing.

"You want me to deaden your legs, Hank?" the medic asked Carter.

"Naw, I'll be all right," Carter answered. "I'm so goddamned scared right now, I don't feel a thing."

"OK, then," the medic said. "I'd rather not shoot you up anyway if the pain's not too bad. They can give you a hit of morphine on the airplane if you need it. And be sure to take a piss as soon as you can."

"Ha! I'll probably pee on the way up."

"Let's get him out there," Birelli said, and they carried Carter to the center of the pickup zone.

Master Sergeant Brady double-checked the lift line connections, then turned on the small lights near the balloon and slowly released the coiled line from its container. The big balloon climbed into the starlit sky.

"Two minutes, thirty seconds," Birelli announced. "You ready, Sergeant Carter?"

"I guess," Carter answered. "You guys give the bastards hell, sir."

Birelli, Brady, and Norton shook hands with their teammate, then Brady said, "You just get your ass healed up and back out here, boy. Meanwhile, get with the Group sergeant major and make sure they're sending us what we need."

"Will do, top. . . . How much longer?"

"Just over a minute," Captain Birelli answered.

"He's interrogatin'," Brady said, seeing the light on the SST-23 flicker.

A moment later they could hear the Combat Talon approaching the pickup zone, and Carter, sitting on the ground facing it, with the lift line above him, said, "Oh, shit! There he is!"

The others stepped back from him. "Hang on, buddy," Norton said as the big, dark aircraft arrived overhead.

The yoke on the Combat Talon's nose slammed against the lift line, and immediately the coupling in the center rotated, grasping the line securely as the balloon broke loose and drifted away. It would rise thousands of feet into the air and would eventually burst and drift to earth scores or even hundreds of miles away.

The line drew taut, stretched, and lifted Carter off the ground a few feet. He hung there momentarily until the line reached full stretch, then, as his teammates watched in amazement, he accelerated swiftly and zoomed off high into the darkness.

Standing on the open ramp of the airplane, Chief Master Sergeant Duke Riley heard over the earphones in his helmet, "Good pickup!"

He immediately dropped an iron bomblet off the ramp. It was attached to a line with a hook built into it, and as the contracting lift line caused Carter to swoop up to a point even higher than the ramp Riley snagged the lift line with the hook. Immediately his assistant began to winch the bomblet in, pulling the lift line in with it. Riley guided it onto the winch drum, and it began to rotate, catching the line and wrapping it around the drum. He let it make several turns, then locked it into place and announced on the intercom that it was secure. Riley's assistant recovery master announced confirmation, and the copilot released the nose coupling. Riley pulled in the portion that had been hooked into the nose, tied it off, then began to winch Carter, swooping behind at almost two hundred miles an hour, toward the aircraft. A minute later Carter was almost to the ramp, flying along on his back with his head toward the airplane. As the winch pulled the wounded man toward the frame attached to the top of the cargo compartment, Riley and his assistant grabbed him and set him down on the ramp. Hooking a safety line to the steel ring of the lift suit, the airmen disconnected Carter from the lift line and carried him to the floor forward of the ramp.

"Recovery complete!" Riley announced as he closed the ramp.

Carter, lying on the floor of the Combat Talon, was breathing rapidly, his eyes squeezed tightly closed.

Kneeling over him, Riley laughed and said, "OK, Sarge. You can open your eyes now."

Two minutes after being snatched from the ground the injured soldier was safely back aboard the airplane from which, less than an hour earlier, he had parachuted into the wasteland of Southwest Asia.

Far behind him Captain Rocco Birelli, his ten remaining troops of Special Forces Operational Detachment A-326, the CIA's Dick Medlin, and the Baluchi guerrillas who called themselves Talwar Allah—"the Sword of God"—moved off across the rocky hills of southeastern Iran. They had no time to waste. Within a few weeks they were expected to have the guerrilla force prepared to do battle with the invading army of the Union of Soviet Socialist Republics.

0040 hours GMT (0410 hours local time) 19 September
Unconventional Warfare Operations Area Shark
Makran Mountains, north of Chah Bahar, Iran

Captain Bill Davidson sat huddled around the small campfire with his A team and the leader of the Baluchi tribesmen who had been waiting for him on the drop zone in UWOA Shark. They were picking bits of flesh from the carcass of a goat the tribesmen had roasted as a welcoming meal for their American advisers. After a brief introduction of the members of his team Davidson had been invited by the chieftain to sit with him at the fire and dine on the roasting goat. He would have preferred to move out of the area as quickly as possible and establish their base camp well away from the drop zone, in case the drop was detected by hostile forces. But the establishment of rapport with the Baluchi leader and his men was key to the mission, and it would have been rude and untrusting of Davidson to insist that they leave the area without first partaking of the meal offered to them.

Davidson knew what was coming when the chieftain used the point of his dagger to pluck one of the goat's eyes from its socket. It was considered a delicacy and was traditionally offered, in this part of the world, to the guest of honor.

Davidson thanked the tribesman for the honor as he plucked the spongy eyeball from the dagger and popped it into his mouth. He pretended to chew it several times, then attempted to swallow it whole. It wouldn't go down.

"God," he thought to himself, "please help me get this down without embarrassing myself and the team."

The chieftain was watching him, waiting for a compliment on the delicacy, so Davidson steeled himself, bit into the spongy eyeball, chewed several times, and swallowed. The eyeball refused to stay down, though, and he swallowed several more times before he was finally able to keep it down. Fighting off nausea, he forced himself to smile.

"That was delicious," he lied. "But now I think we would be well advised to get moving and establish a training base, so we can begin training to fight the Soviet paratroopers around Chah Bahar."

The chieftain agreed, and as they prepared to move out, Davidson's team sergeant, Jimmy Slater, chuckled and said, "You really enjoyed that eyeball, eh, boss?"

"I'd rather fight the whole damned Russian army than do that again," Davidson replied. "Next time, *you're* going to be the damned guest of honor!"

CHAPTER 4

2020 hours GMT (1620 hours EDT), 19 September
Pope Air Force Base, North Carolina

Major Mark Denton was tired, angry, and in no mood to put up with bureaucratic ineptitude. Yet here was a full colonel in the same army as he, waving a sheaf of papers in Denton's face, and demanding to board the C-5 aircraft that had the quickly modified version of the Package aboard. He was demanding to be allowed to see the equipment Denton and his men had spent the whole day inspecting, rigging, and loading into the big airplane.

"Sir," Major Denton said to the colonel, "with all due respect, unless you get somebody here from 1st SOCOM—somebody who can verify your need to know—you're not going to board this aircraft. This is a classified activity, and you're not on the access list. Now, if you'll excuse me . . ."

The colonel was the president of the Airborne and Special Operations Test Board, and some of the equipment Denton and his men intended to use against the Soviets had been commandeered from that organization. The loss of the equipment would interfere with his test officers' long-drawn-out evaluations of it.

Fortunately, Brigadier General Porter, the deputy commanding general of 1st SOCOM, chose this moment to arrive and check that Denton and his men were getting ready to depart Pope Air Force Base for the forward operations base that was being established on Masirah Island. It was on Masirah that Denton and his men would make their final preparations before parachuting into Iran ahead of the Soviet advance.

The irate colonel was poking Denton in the chest with his finger and threatening to ruin his career when the general's sedan pulled up beside them. The colonel didn't notice the sedan, but Denton did, and, as General Porter got out and walked toward them, Denton called "Attention" and saluted.

Porter returned the salute and asked what all the fuss was about, and the colonel gave an obscenity-filled version of Denton's refusal to allow him to board and inspect the aircraft.

"I see," the general said. "Now, Colonel, let me explain the chain of command for this activity. There's the president, then the commander, U.S. Special Operations Command, then there's me. And working directly for me is Major Denton here. Now, did you hear your name in there anywhere, Colonel?"

"Uh, no, sir. But—"

"Correct," Porter said. "So I suggest you move out, Colonel, and let Major Denton and me get on with it."

The colonel saluted, gave Denton a look threatening eventual revenge, and departed.

"Thank you, General," Denton said, smiling. "But wasn't your chain of command a little off? I didn't hear the CG of the 82d Airborne mentioned."

"That's right, you didn't, Major Denton. It's been changed. We're not certain when—or even if, at this point—the 82d will be committed. Meanwhile, the decision's been made to get you and your Package in there as soon as possible. Let your people know that your scheduled takeoff time is at 2115 local—that's less than five hours from now. Then hop in my car, and let's get over to the cage so the staff can brief you on the new plan."

Five hours, Denton thought as he went aboard the aircraft to tell the members of his team of the new plan. *Jesus, I haven't seen Jean and the kids but a few hours in the last couple of weeks, and now I'm leaving in less than five hours to go to war against the Soviets.*

It was the first time he wondered if he would ever see his family again. It wouldn't be the last time that thought crossed his mind.

A few minutes later he found himself sitting with General Porter and the 1st SOCOM Operations Officer (G-3), an old Special Forces hand named Billy Boyatt.

"Mark," Colonel Boyatt said, "we don't have much time to knock this operations order together. Now, here's the mission from USSOCOM: 'Special Forces Operational Detachment B-30'—that's you—'infiltrates Unconventional Warfare Operations Area Sword by air no later than 232400Z September to conduct surveillance and harassment operations against Soviet forces within UWOA Sword. Be prepared to acquire and designate targets for air fires. On order, support other friendly forces' offensive operations.'"

Colonel Boyatt unfolded a map of Southwest Asia on which UWOA Sword was drawn, and he allowed Denton to study it for a while before continuing.

The operational area was huge for a force as small as Denton's. It consisted of a corridor in eastern Iran with an average width of one hundred fifty kilometers, bordered on the east by Pakistan, from its tri-border area with Iran and Afghanistan, south to the town of Khash—a distance of about 200 kilometers. The western boundary of the UWOA bordered on the uninhabited wastes of Dasht-e Lut, a salt-crusted desert, and south into the inhospitable sand and rock wasteland west of Khash, into the foothills of the Makran Mountains.

"As you can see," Boyatt said after Denton had examined the map, "you've got one hell of a big operational area—about thirty thousand square klicks. But the key to it all is these two roads that loop out in opposite directions from Zahedan south to Khash. They're the *only* two routes the Soviets can take, unless they decided to invade Pakistan, too, which is extremely unlikely."

"So," Denton said, "I should hit them along those roads and use the rest of the area to take resupply drops, establish caches, and hide in."

"Exactly," Boyatt said. "The problem is, you've got to get in there quickly, get yourself set up, and start hitting them before they get much past Zahedan."

The general said, *"Damn* quickly, Major Denton. If we can prove that your concept will work to slow them down significantly—and I'm convinced it will—then we may get permission to reinforce you farther south. But we've got to have time, and your little team is about the only thing we have, without escalating this thing into a real asskicker of a war."

"Now, for obvious reasons, I can't tell you exactly where, but we've already got some A teams in the area south of your AO," Colonel Boyatt said. "If you can delay the lead elements of the Soviet force long enough, one of the teams and their guerrillas will be ready to pick up the action when the Russians get past you. By then, the other team and their guerrillas will begin hitting the airborne regiment that's down on the coast.

"And XVIII Corps should have two brigades ready to go in by that time, and . . . well, I'd better not give you too much info, in case the Russkies pick you up," the general said.

All three officers realized the likelihood of that. If Denton's force was as effective as they hoped it would be, the Soviets were bound to make a major effort to destroy them, and it was quite possible that some of the members of the newly formed Special Forces Operational Detachment B-30 would be captured in the process.

"I understand, sir," Denton said, managing a weak smile. "But they're going to have hell to pay before they get to us, I'll guaran-damn-tee you that. . . . Now, how do we get the choppers from Masirah to UWOA Sword?"

"You'll jump in two nights from now with your first load of fuel and equipment," Boyatt said. "Meanwhile, the helicopters, with no weapons or ammo aboard, will hop out to one of the carriers. The night after your infil, they'll fly from the carrier to your first hide site, refuel, then ferry your team up to your second hide site, where they'll hide out with you. The following night they'll do the same thing, up to your third area. Following that, we'll drop their weapons and ordnance in, and you can start operating. . . . What do you think?"

Mark Denton thought about the proposed plan. If they did it that way, it would be nearly a week before they began operations against the Soviets, and they'd need even longer to begin delivering blows in the coming fight. He said, "That's an awful long time, sir. When do you expect the Russians to start moving from their staging area in Afghanistan?"

"At any time," the general said. "In two or three days, at the latest. We think all they're waiting for now is for their logistical tail to catch up."

"Then we need to get set up more quickly, sir. Can you give me half an hour to come up with a quicker option?"

The general smiled. "Anxious to get after them, are you, boy?" he said.

"I'm just afraid that, if we do it the way Colonel Boyatt said, they'll be past us before we start pecking at 'em. I think we can find a way to speed up B-30's timetable."

"Good," the general said. "Colonel Boyatt, you work up the concept with him. Just make sure he doesn't get unrealistic and come up with something unworkable. See you in half an hour, gents."

When the general returned Denton briefed him on the new timetable.

"Colonel Boyatt's gone to make sure the air force can fly the missions we need to get this done, sir. But he doesn't think there'll be any problem."

"I'll make certain there isn't, Mark," the general replied. "Now, what's the plan?"

"We'll go straight to Masirah, arriving there early the morning of the twenty-first, Masirah time. By then we'll have the bundles reconfigured to meet our needs."

The general interrupted to ask if he'd be able to do that in flight, and Denton said, "Yes, sir. There's plenty of space, and all we need is a couple of riggers to help. The colonel's getting them alerted right now.

"Once we get to Masirah," he continued, "we'll transload the first load to the Combat Talon that's taking us in, then rest up and have our final briefing. As soon as it's dark the helicopters will head for the carrier. We'll coordinate with the Talon crew and make our infil two nights from now—the twenty-first."

He laid the map he'd been using for planning in front of the general and said, "The first three men—two SF men and one of the ground crew—will jump here, with a bundle that's mostly fuel cans." He pointed to a small circle in the southern portion of UWOA Sword, and the general looked at it, then nodded.

"The second drop—four men, including the other ground crewman—will go in here," Denton said, indicating another proposed drop zone, this one near the center of the team's unconventional warfare operations area. "They'll have with them about half the remaining fuel, and about half the ordnance."

He paused to allow the general to digest that part of the plan, then pointed to a third drop zone, about thirty kilometers southwest of Zahedan, the town near the northern edge of the UWOA where the road divided and looped south in two arcs. "The remaining four of us will jump in here with the rest of the fuel and ordnance and the choppers' weapons pods. And a whole lot of water. We'll cache the gear, then rest up through the next day.

"Meanwhile, the choppers will refuel on the carrier and hop on up north to the ship nearest to the coast. They'll top off aboard her, then head for the hide site near the first drop zone. They'll need to rest up there during the day, refuel, and cache any fuel that's left over. As soon as it's dark they'll head for DZ number two, taking the three men who jumped in first. That'll put eleven men, including the pilots, at the second site. There they'll refuel again and take four men on a short flight up to here."

Again Denton pointed to a small circle on the map, this one between the center and the northernmost of the three drop zones.

"The pilots will then fly on up to us, and we'll arm and refuel them. Then they'll settle into the hide site. Got it so far, sir?"

"What'll that give you, as far as who's where on that second night in Iran?" General Porter inquired.

"We'll have three men near DZ Two, four men about halfway between there and the northern DZ, and the rest, including the chopper pilots and their birds, at the northern DZ."

"What happens next?" Porter asked Denton.

"OK, sir. That night, while we're arming the choppers, we'll get our second resupply drops. They'll consist of fuel, water, rations, and more ordnance. Half of it will be delivered to the three men at DZ Two. They'll establish another cache there. The other half of the drop will go to the four men at yet another drop zone south of us, where they'll set up the final cache."

"That's an awful lot of drops to coordinate and operate in two nights, Major Denton."

Denton smiled. "Yes, sir, it is. But with the GPS satellites finally in orbit, it's no sweat."

Since the space shuttle program was finally back in full swing, the Department of Defense at last had its Global Positioning System satellites in orbit, constantly broadcasting their positions to earth. The miniaturized GPS receivers that Denton's team was equipped with took these signals and immediately translated them into the receivers' exact coordinates. It was almost impossible for anyone with a map and a GPS receiver to be lost.

"Yeah, I guess that's right," Brigadier General Porter said. "But are you sure the choppers can make the distances you're planning, and the times you're counting on?"

"Pretty sure, sir. I've sent for the lead pilot to verify the ranges and times, but I think I'm right. Even if I'm not, it'll only delay their arrival by one night. That means they'd be getting there four nights from tonight, instead of three. That's still a hell of a lot better than six or seven nights from now, like the original plan called for."

Porter looked at the map again. "What about these drop zones you've selected? You sure they're in uninhabited areas, and suitable for jumping?"

"Colonel Boyatt has taken their locations to the image interpretation detachment. They'll check them against their satellite photos to be sure. They'll also give me DZ reports for alternate drop zones throughout Sword."

The lead pilot of the two Hughes 500MD helicopters arrived and, after checking Denton's figures, said, "I don't know, boss. The distances are OK, but I'm not sure we can make the times if the wind's blowing the wrong way."

"Any reason you couldn't fly the first leg during daylight?" the general asked. "After all, you'll be within the exclusion zone. Nobody'll see you except Uncle Sam's navy."

"Hey, sir, that's right," the pilot said. "We can do the first overwater leg, or maybe two, during daylight. It'll be easier for us than flying on goggles all night, anyway. And it'll sure as hell give us all the time we need to play with over land."

"Great," Denton said. "I'd better go check on all these drop zones. We're running out of time."

Major Mark Denton had less than an hour with his family that evening. He tucked his children into bed, then spent a few moments holding hands with his wife, Jean, in the backyard of their Fort Bragg quarters. When she moved into his arms, with her head against his chest, she said, "It's going to be a tough one, isn't it, Mark?"

She had heard him enthusiastically discussing his concept of the Package with his fellow officers during his brief periods at home over the previous month. She didn't understand much about it, except that it had to do with small teams fighting against much larger forces of the Soviet army, especially tanks and armored vehicles. She recalled one of his skeptical comrades saying, "Hell, Mark, those guys wouldn't stand a chance. They'd be wiped out within two days."

And now he was apparently going off to test his concept in combat—an environment he had never experienced before, except in training.

"It's going to be all right, Jeannie," he said, with little

confidence that it would. "I'll be home before you know it."

"I just don't understand how it could have come to this," she said. Like many Americans, and others around the world, she had thought that Gorbachev and Bush would be able to negate the chances of Americans and Russians facing off in an armed confrontation. But the failure of Perestroika to take hold quickly enough, and the rising demands of autonomy in the satellite states of the Soviet Union, had weakened Gorbachev's hand with the old, hard-line members of the Politburo. There had been little President Bush could do to help his Soviet counterpart. In fact, his efforts to do so had only fueled the hard-liners' mistrust of their president and general secretary. And the upheaval in Iran resulting from the assassination of Khomeini's successor, Hashemi Rafsanjani, coupled with the final push for victory of Afghanistan's Mujahadeen, left Gorbachev with little choice. He could yield to the hard-liners' demands and exploit the situation with the Red Army, or he could be forced out of his position of leadership, as the moderate members of China's Communist party had been, and see his country revert to its old, failed system of economics and oppression.

"You know, honey," Mark Denton said to his wife, "maybe it won't turn into a fight—not a direct one between us and the Russians, anyway. I mean, maybe this is just some saber rattling Gorbachev has to do to stay in power."

But neither of them believed it, and Jean Denton buried her face in her husband's chest and wept until he kissed her gently and said, "Good-bye, Jeannie, darling. I've got to go. I'll see you before too long."

An hour later Major Mark Denton, commander of the newly constituted Special Forces Operational Detachment B-30, was aboard the big C-5B Galaxy that his wife, still standing in the backyard of their army quarters, watched rise into the night sky from nearby Pope Air Force Base.

CHAPTER 5

At the base camp of the Baluchi guerrilla group led by
Chakur Nothani, Captain Rocco Birelli had called a
meeting of the members of SFOD A-326. He was gathering their assessments of the organization, state of training, and military potential of the tribesmen who called
themselves Talwar Allah—the Sword of God.

Master Sergeant Jake Brady, the senior sergeant on the
team, reported on their strength. "There are forty-eight
men here. There's a headquarters section, with the
military commander, Lakha Nawaz, in charge. His staff
consists of an operations man and a supply man. The
others are divided into three elements: a heavy weapons
platoon of nine men, and two infantry platoons of twenty
and sixteen men. Nawaz says, though, that he already has
runners out to collect the rest of Talwar Allah, and
he expects to have between a hundred and twenty
and a hundred and forty men by the day after tomorrow."

Turning to Dick Medlin, the CIA man who had
contacted the guerrillas and gained their permission—
and help—to bring the A team into their tribal area,
Birelli said, "You think he'll be able to raise that many,
Dick?"

"Certainly," Medlin replied. "Maybe more. He would
never have given you a figure if he wasn't sure he could
get at *least* that many men."

"All right. What about equipment, Fred?" Birelli

asked his executive officer, Chief Warrant Officer Fred Kaminski.

"Very little," Kaminski replied. "They've got a few AK-47 assault rifles, but most of their weapons are old bolt-action jobs. There're even a couple of muzzle loaders. The only crew-served weapons they have are the ones we brought in. As we thought, we'll have to outfit 'em from top to bottom."

"Communications?" Birelli asked Percy Hanson, the team's radio operator.

"Just the two short-range bricks that Mr. Medlin gave them," Hanson replied. "They rely on messengers to get word to the outside. The guys who are out rounding up the other guerrillas are on horseback."

"From what I've been able to ascertain, they've got one horse for about every four men," Dick Medlin interjected.

"Well, they could be damned useful, especially for moving supplies and crew-served weapons," Birelli said. "What's their medical capability like, Doc?"

"Almost nonexistent," the senior medic, Staff Sergeant Chuck Norton, said. "A lot of 'em have packets of *khor*—dirt from one of their shrines. They eat it to ward off sickness, but it's bound to do them more harm than good. The closest thing they actually have to medicine is *nass,* which is really nothing but narcotic snuff. It makes them feel better, but that's all it does. They've got a sour milk drink that they spike with herbs, but I'm not sure if it has any real medical properties. The biggest problem I anticipate is water. There just ain't much in this godforsaken area. Fortunately, they don't seem to need much. They can go several days on one goatskin bag. But at least they have a good handle on the location of what few water holes there are out here."

"You think we need to include water on our resupply drops, Chuck?" Mr. Kaminski, the XO, inquired.

"Definitely, sir. We need to put in some emergency caches all over the UWOA. Apparently the water holes are in pretty good shape right now, but that's only because they had one of their rare rainfalls a couple of weeks ago."

The A team members discussed all they had learned in the two days they'd been with the team. The morale of the Baluchi tribesmen was excellent. They were eager to get their hands on the equipment the Americans assured them was on the way, and more and more men were showing up hourly in response to the call of their chieftain, Chakur Nothani. The weapons men of A-326 reported that, at the insistence of Nothani's military commander, Lakha Nawaz, they had already begun training a cadre of guerrilla leaders on the use of the Stinger antiaircraft missile and the Dragon antitank missile training devices the team had packed in their door bundles. The Baluchi tribesmen seemed to have a natural ability for quickly adapting to the use of such sophisticated weapons.

"And they're damned attentive and eager to learn," the heavy weapons man, Sergeant First Class Alex Nichols, added. "I'm going to start some of them on the 60 millimeter mortar this afternoon."

"OK, good," Birelli said. "You got the recovery party all organized for the automatic resupply, Jake?" he asked the team sergeant, Jake Brady.

"Yes, sir," Brady said. "We've got Washington, Bohl, and two Baluchi maintaining surveillance on the drop zone now, and I'll leave with twenty men and four horses as soon as the sun sets. I need to get with you, though, Mr. Kaminski, and decide exactly what we want to cache near the DZ, and what to bring back here."

The team would receive their automatic resupply— the pallets of weapons, ammunition, combat rations, and other equipment—that night, seventy-two hours after their infiltration jump. They had packed and rigged the equipment while they were in isolation, and it had been flown to the forward operations base on Masirah Island. From there, it would be paradropped into their UWOA by one of the air force Combat Talon aircraft. There would be enough in the resupply to arm and equip 120 of the Baluchi guerrillas.

1115 hours Greenwich Mean Time, 21 September
Masirah Island, in the Indian Ocean off the coast of Oman

Mark Denton watched the little Hughes 500MD helicopters lift off beside the long runway on Masirah Island and head northeast toward one of the carrier groups that was enforcing the exclusion zone in the Gulf of Oman.

Far to the north, a controller aboard an E-3A Airborne Warning and Control System—AWACS—aircraft, in orbit high above the Strait of Hormuz, saw the helicopters on his radar screen and made a radio call to them to verify their identities.

"Aphid Flight, this is Roulette Three. If you copy me, turn to heading zero eight zero."

He had been ordered to vector two rotary-wing aircraft from Masirah to the USS *America,* and although the two blips had appeared departing the island at precisely the planned time, he wanted to be certain that the aircraft he saw on his screen were the right ones.

Without answering on his radio, Chief Warrant Officer Red Stephens, the leader of Aphid Flight, as the H-500s had been designated, turned right to the requested heading of eighty degrees. A half minute later Stephens heard the controller's voice again: "Roger, Aphid. Come left to heading zero two five. That will be your heading to the target—range, one one zero miles."

Stephen's wingman, Aphid Two, flew up alongside him, and the copilot gave him a thumbs up to indicate that they, too, had heard the transmission from the AWACS aircraft. They would maintain radio silence throughout their flight into UWOA Sword, except in an emergency.

Over the intercom Stephens's copilot, CW2 Bart

Evans, said, "Well, Red, ol' buddy, what have you got me into this time?"

They both laughed, then Stephens said, "A place in history, Bart, my man. Why, don't you realize that one day you'll be sitting with your grandson on your knee, and he'll say, 'What did you do in the great World War III, Grandpa?' And you'll be able to say, 'Little Red'—I'm sure you'll want to name him after me for makin' you a hero—you'll say, 'Little Red, I fired the first shot. . . . I *started* World War III!' "

"Stephens," the copilot said, "you've got a *weird* sense of humor."

The two small helicopters reached their second refuel ship just before dark. They were well ahead of the schedule they'd need to maintain in order to reach the first drop zone at the prescribed time. Three of the other members of SFOD B-30 would, with a load of fuel, parachute into the drop zone an hour before the helicopters were due to arrive.

Once they had their helicopters refueled, Stephens checked his watch and said to the other three army aviators, "Since we've got over an hour before departure, why don't we check and see what kind of chow this here boat has to offer?"

On Masirah, the MC-130 Combat Talon that would drop the ground force of Denton's SFOD B-30 into Iran taxied into position behind another Combat Talon—the one that would deliver the automatic resupply to the A teams of Captains Davidson and Birelli.

Denton's Talon sat there for nearly twenty minutes after the first one had taken off, then pulled onto the runway.

"All set, Major?" the crew chief asked.

Denton looked at the other ten members of the team and saw that all, like him, were strapped into their seats, sitting uncomfortably in the harnesses of their parachutes. Their rucksacks all were tied down in the center of the aircraft. They would strap them on when they were twenty minutes from their drop zones.

Denton gave the crew chief a thumbs up, and the aircraft began its takeoff roll. He sighed deeply and said a silent prayer. He was soon to be a leader of men in combat, and he prayed that he would not let them, nor his country, down.

The next thing Denton knew, he was being shaken awake by the senior NCO on his team, Sergeant First Class Harry O'Neill. Denton had been so exhausted that he had fallen asleep as soon as the Combat Talon left Masirah.

"We're over the coast, sir," O'Neill reported. "Twenty-two minutes to DZ One."

The three men who would jump on the first drop zone were struggling to hook their rucksacks to their parachute harnesses. It was terribly cramped in the airplane because of the two pallets of equipment that would be dropped—followed by four men each—at the second and third drop zones.

SFC O'Neill was going to act as jumpmaster for the first two drop zones, and Denton decided that the best thing he could do would be to climb up onto the flight deck, to make a little more room for the others to attach their rucksacks and be given a jumpmaster check by O'Neill. Anyway, he was sure he could get some coffee from the pilots.

When Denton got onto the flight deck the navigator handed him a headset. When he had put it on, Denton whined over the intercom, "How much farther, Daddy?"

The pilot laughed and looked around. "What say, Nav?"

"On my mark, two-zero minutes," the navigator said, then several seconds later he said, "Mark!"

From the back, the crew chief said over the intercom, "Twenty minutes. Jumpmaster acknowledges."

"Anything on the fuzzbuster?" the pilot inquired, and from the electronic countermeasures officer in the curtained-off booth in the forward portion of the cargo compartment came the reply, "Negative. No radar hits from anybody but the AWACS. Guess they're still mourning Rafsanjani down there."

The pilot looked around at Denton and smiled. "Care for a cup of coffee, sir?"

It suddenly dawned on Denton, when the pilot called him "sir," that he was the senior man on the airplane. Here they were, violating Iran's sovereignty, infiltrating men and equipment to engage one of the earth's two most powerful nations, and he was, in all probability, the senior American officer directly involved.

"Yeah. Coffee sounds good," Major Mark Denton answered. While the engineer poured him a paper cup of coffee, Denton considered his situation. From what the deputy commanding general of 1st Special Operations Command had said, there were apparently two twelve-man A teams in Iran. They were commanded by captains. His B team—the Package—though it numbered only sixteen men, brought the total number of American soldiers in Iran to forty. Of them, Denton was the highest-ranking. And he was about to do battle with hundreds of Soviet armored vehicles and aircraft manned by thousands of troops led by scores of officers of greater rank than his. And it was not just the numbers that worried him; it was their combat experience as well. Having battled the Mujahadeen in Afghanistan for almost a decade, they were bound to have learned many lessons about fighting the elusive guerrillas.

Denton's thoughts were interrupted by the pilot saying on the intercom to the copilot, "Take it for a minute, Jim. I gotta pee while I have the chance."

When he returned to the flight deck the pilot sat beside Denton on the bench seat at the rear of the cockpit.

Patting Denton on the shoulder, he said, "You look worried, sir."

Denton managed a smile and said, "Yeah. I was just thinking about how many of those bastards there are, and how much combat experience they have."

The air force officer didn't know Denton's exact mission, but it was obvious enough that he and his men were taking in equipment that was to be used to engage the Soviet forces that were expected to invade Iran at any time.

"Well, sir," the airman said, "remember this, though. They got their asses kicked the last time they tried this. And they weren't fighting Americans."

Denton smiled at him, and the pilot said, "I'd better get back to flying this thing." He held out his hand to the army major and added, "Good luck. And remember this: If you need anything—you call, we haul."

Denton shook his hand. "Thanks. I'll remember that."

2245 GMT, 21 September (0215 local time, 22 September)
Unconventional Warfare Operations Area Tiger

Well to the northeast of Denton's aircraft, the other Combat Talon had already dropped its automatic resupply bundles to Captain Bill Davidson and his A team in UWOA Shark. It was now on final approach to the drop zone manned by Master Sergeant Jake Brady, the team sergeant of Captain Rocco Birelli's team, A-326.

Brady saw the light on the SST-23 transponder beacon he was using to mark the drop zone blink as the Talon's radar interrogated it.

He checked his watch. It was two minutes to the scheduled drop time, so he called, "Two minutes. Light 'em up!" to the other members of the drop zone marking party.

He turned on his pocketscope and looked at the other members of the marking party to make certain their infrared-filtered flashlights were on, as the lights were not visible to the naked eye. Satisfied, he turned in the direction from which he knew the aircraft would come and began flashing the authentication signal that would confirm to the Combat Talon crew that the drop zone had not been compromised.

Aboard the dark airplane the navigator called, "One minute."

"One minute," the loadmaster acknowledged, and he

made final preparations to cut the tiedown that would release the A team's bundles over the drop zone.

The aircraft was thirty seconds from the drop zone when the electronic countermeasures officer called, "Radar contact! Bogey at eleven o'clock, uh, eight miles! Bearing three three zero."

"Aw, shit!" the pilot responded, just as he saw the drop zone lights through his night-vision goggles.

From the back the loadmaster asked, "You gonna drop, sir?"

"Christ!" the pilot said. He knew the men on the ground needed the supplies, and he was almost over them. The radar contact from an aircraft eight miles away didn't necessarily mean his aircraft had been "painted" by the enemy radar.

"Yeah, we'll drop!" he replied.

"Stand by!" the copilot said. Then, as the plane reached the drop zone lights, he said, "Execute, execute!" and turned on the green lights in the rear of the plane.

The loadmaster released the bundles as the aircraft nosed upward, causing the bundles to roll along the rails in the floor of the cargo compartment and off the ramp. The bundles disappeared into the night.

"Clean drop," he called, and he began closing the ramp and the door above it.

The ECM officer announced, *"Two* radars, five miles, bearing three five zero! Looks like choppers."

"Roger," the pilot replied. "Nav?"

The Combat Talon was almost on a collision course with the unidentified helicopters, so the navigator said, "Come left to three six zero."

Four miles to the front of the approaching aircraft the Combat Talon pilot increased power, made a hard left turn, and ordered, "Set TFR to two five zero!"

"TFR to two five zero," the copilot acknowledged, and he adjusted the terrain-following radar from five hundred feet to two hundred fifty. The TFR would sense the airplane's height relative to the terrain ahead and below and automatically keep it two hundred fifty feet above the ground.

It was shortly after the bundles hit the ground that Jake Brady heard the approaching helicopters.

The team's heavy-weapons man, Staff Sergeant Willie Washington, heard them, too, and yelled, "Helicopters! Approaching from the north!"

"Everybody to the rally point!" Brady ordered in Baluchi, and there was a mad dash to a small depression on the west side of the drop zone.

Brady arrived there to find the guerrilla military leader, Lakha Nawaz, telling his men, "Wait until they are nearly here. When I tell you to shoot, shoot until you run out of ammunition."

"Wait, Nawaz," Brady said. "We must not. We must move quickly and hide."

"You've come all this way to *hide* from the enemy, when God *delivers* him to us?" the Baluchi commander asked.

Just then Staff Sergeant Washington saw, through his pocketscope, the helicopters passing a quarter of a mile to the west. "There they are, Sergeant Brady!" he called. "Two Hinds and two Mi-6's. They're about five hundred meters to the west, heading south. I don't think they saw us."

Brady scrambled to the edge of the depression and looked southwest with his pocketscope to see two Mi-24 Hind helicopter gunships escorting two big Mi-6 Hook cargo helicopters at an altitude of about a thousand feet. He watched them until they disappeared from sight beyond a ridge a mile to the south, then listened anxiously for another minute until the sound of their rotor blades faded away.

"Christ," he muttered with relief. Then he said to Washington, "Probably just shuttling supplies or reinforcements to their airborne regiment down at Chah Bahar. Make sure you get the time, location, direction of flight, and all that, so we can burst a spot report back to SFOB."

He returned to where Nawaz was standing. "They've gone on south," Brady said. "They didn't see us. Now, come with me and let me show you what the airplane brought us."

As they derigged the bundles of equipment Brady showed the various items to the guerrilla leader, explaining the purpose of those with which Nawaz was unfamiliar. The small arms were all of Soviet or Chinese make: AK-47 and AKM assault rifles, SVD sniper rifles, PKM machine guns, and a few Markarov pistols for the leaders. There were also several Soviet-made 12.7-mm heavy machine guns and RPG-7 rocket-propelled grenade launchers. The rest of the weapons were American-made. Brady showed Nawaz the 60-mm company light-weight mortars, the Dragon antitank missiles. And then he hoisted the *pièce de résistance*—the shoulder-fired Stinger antiaircraft missile. It was the weapon that, more than any other, had nearly led to the Mujahadeen's defeat of the Soviets in the war in Afghanistan. If the Afghan rebels had not run out of Stingers after America's withdrawal of support when the Soviets withdrew in early 1989, the Russians would never have been able to bomb the massed Mujahadeen forces and reinvade.

"With these," Master Sergeant Brady declared, "the next time God delivers the Soviets within range, we will destroy them."

A hundred kilometers south of Brady and the drop zone in UWOA Tiger, Captain Bill Davidson, his men, and their Baluchi guerrillas were moving away from the resupply drop zone in UWOA Shark. For their operations against the Soviet airborne forces around Chah Bahar, Davidson and his men had selected a different mix of weapons. They would rely heavily on 60-mm mortars and on 40-mm M-203 grenade launchers, which were attached beneath a third of the M-16 rifles they had just issued to most of the tribesmen. In addition, there were six M-202 rocket launchers, each of which carried four 66-mm incendiary rockets. Davidson's force also had several 12.7-mm and two 14.5-mm Soviet-made heavy machine guns.

As they moved in a long file away from the drop zone Davidson turned to his team sergeant, Jimmy Slater, and remarked, "Well, Jimbo, I just hope Birelli and his boys up north can buy us enough time to train these guys and hit the Russkies before they get reinforced. This stuff won't be much good against tanks."

"I heard *that*," Slater replied. "But if they don't, and we get our asses kicked, at least we won't have to worry about eating goat eyes at a damned victory celebration!"

CHAPTER 6

2350 hours GMT, 21 September (0310 hours local time, 22 September)
Over southeastern Iran

The AWACS aircraft over the Strait of Hormuz picked up the Soviet helicopters soon after the Combat Talon narrowly avoided detection by them and sped for the forward operations base on Masirah Island. The Soviet flight path was well to the east of the second Combat Talon's route, but the controller aboard the AWACS informed him of the enemy helicopters' presence nevertheless.

The Combat Talon with Mark Denton's team aboard had slowed and lowered its ramp in preparation for the drop of the first three men and a load of fuel at drop zone one.

The jumpmaster, SFC Harry O'Neill, knelt on the ramp with his head outside the aircraft. He was wearing a flight crew helmet, and he heard over the earphones, "One minute." By the light of a half moon, just rising above the horizon, he saw that the aircraft was entering a narrow valley. O'Neill pulled his head inside long enough to signal "One minute" to the three jumpers standing behind the container in which the fuel they would take in with them was packed. Two of the men released the tiedown straps securing the A-21 container to the ramp and leaned against the container, ready to push it off the ramp and follow it out.

Because it was a blind jump—there was no one manning the drop zone—they would rely on the computed air release point of the air crew to determine when they jumped. But with the Global Positioning System readout available to them, the jumpers were confident that they would be on target.

O'Neill stood, pointed down at the ramp with both hands, and called, "Stand in the door!" The jumpers shoved the heavy container nearer the edge of the ramp, and when the jump lights changed from green to red, O'Neill yelled, "Go!" The men pushed the container over the edge of the ramp and, as they watched its parachute deploy, stepped off the ramp behind it.

O'Neill was able to see all three personnel chutes deploy, then he pulled the static lines back into the aircraft, and the crew chief closed the ramp.

Facing the next three jumpers, whom he would lead out at the second drop zone, SFC O'Neill stamped his foot, flashed the fingers of both hands twice, and yelled, "Twenty minutes!"

From the cockpit of his Hughes 500MD helicopter, Chief Warrant Officer Red Stephens saw the dark coast of Iran ahead of him. He looked at his GPS readout and verified that he was in the right location to cross the coast, then climbed from his wave-skimming altitude of twenty feet to a height of fifty feet. "How do the gauges look?" he asked his copilot.

Bart Evans scanned the dimly-lighted gauges on the instrument panel and reported, "AOK." Then he glanced off to his right rear and said, "Aphid Two's tucked in tight." With the doors having been removed from the helicopter, he could see the second chopper clearly in the light of the half moon. Unlike Stephens, he had not flipped his ANVIS-7 night-vision goggles down in front of his eyes. It was standard procedure for only the man flying the helicopter to use his goggles, except when they were in the attack.

"Well," Stephens said as he saw waves breaking on the beach just ahead, "here goes nothing. Welcome to Iran."

The AWACS controller who had been monitoring their

progress across the Gulf of Oman saw the blips of the
H-500s cross the coast and made a blind transmission to
them—one that he knew would not be answered.

"Aphid Flight, this is Roulette Three. You're on course
with negative bogeys in sight. Good luck, guys." He had
no idea what Aphid Flight's mission was, but he could
tell by their radar signature, their speed, and the fact that
they had landed on ships that Aphid Flight was two small
helicopters. And since he had not been tasked to vector
them across the gulf when they returned, he assumed
that they were going to Iran to stay for a while. He shook
his head, pleased that his job was in the relative comfort
and safety of the Airborne Warning and Control System
aircraft.

When Specialist Four Hardin Boone heard SFC
O'Neill announce "Ten minutes," he made a decision.
Boone, the H-500 ground crewman who was to jump
with O'Neill and two other men into drop zone two,
stood, released his rucksack, and began taking off his
parachute.

"What the hell are you doing, Boone?" Sergeant Tom
Vance, seated beside him, asked. Vance, too, was to jump
into DZ Two.

"What's it look like?" Boone said as he shrugged off
his parachute. "I'm not gonna do this stupid shit."

Harry O'Neill saw Boone also and, burdened by his
own parachute and rucksack, waddled to where Boone
had dropped his equipment and was now sitting on the
troop seat. O'Neill grabbed him by the collar of his
desert camouflage uniform and yanked him to his feet.
"Pick up that parachute *now*, soldier, and put it on!"

Boone shoved O'Neill hard, causing him to tumble
over backwards across the equipment strapped to the
floor in the center of the cargo compartment. Sergeant
Vance pulled off his heavy Kevlar helmet and smashed
Boone in the back of the head with it. Boone crumpled to
the floor across O'Neill's legs.

As O'Neill struggled to his feet he told Vance and one

of the other Special Forces men, "Get him back to the ramp."

The two men dragged the stunned soldier past the equipment bundles and back to the ramp of the aircraft. O'Neill picked up the discarded parachute and followed them.

While the other two men held the semiconscious Boone on his feet, O'Neill strapped the parachute on him.

The crew chief leaned over to O'Neill and said, "Six minutes to drop," then asked, "You want me to tell your major up in the cockpit what's going on?"

"Negative," SFC O'Neill replied. "This is just among us enlisted guys. Vance, get his rucksack and strap it to our bundle."

Boone, regaining his senses, began struggling and said, "No! No, goddammit! I'm not going!"

O'Neill pointed to the revolver in the Combat Talon crew chief's holster and said, "Loan me your heat, Chief."

The crew chief handed the pistol to O'Neill, who shoved it under Boone's chin and said, his face close to Boone's, "You're going, Boone. You're gonna jump, or I'm gonna leave your brains splattered on the ramp."

Boone began sobbing then, and O'Neill handed the crew chief his pistol, then slapped the sobbing soldier hard.

"God damn it, Boone," he said, shaking him, "I'm not gonna let you screw up this operation. Now hook up, you son of a bitch!"

As the dazed paratrooper hooked up, Vance returned and said, "I got his ruck strapped on the bundle. Here's his helmet."

O'Neill shoved the helmet on Boone's head and pulled the chinstrap over his chin.

"Two minutes!" the crew chief warned as the aircraft powered back and he began to lower the ramp.

Major Denton arrived from the flight deck as O'Neill was hurriedly going through the jump commands. The crew chief and loadmaster were rolling the team's big equipment container onto the ramp in preparation for the drop.

"Where the hell's Boone's rucksack?" Denton asked Sergeant Vance. "And why's he look so dazed?"

"It came loose, so we hooked it to our bundle," Vance lied. "I guess he's sick, or a little scared."

O'Neill signaled "One minute," and the jumpers moved closer to the rear of the aircraft. Denton climbed to a position from which he could watch the big equipment container leave the ramp. He wanted to be certain that he saw the cargo chute deploy. If it failed to open, and the bundle crashed to earth, the aircraft would circle and return to the drop zone, and Denton and the others, instead of going on to drop zone Three, would follow their bundle onto O'Neill's DZ. He heard O'Neill command, "Stand in the door!"

The loadmaster cut the tiedown strap loose, and when the jump lights turned to green the aircraft nosed up slightly, and the equipment container rolled off the ramp and into the darkness.

So intent was Denton on watching the cargo chute deploy through his pocketscope that he didn't see Boone, whom O'Neill had placed in front of him, attempt to refuse to jump. But O'Neill shoved Boone, and he fell off the ramp backwards. When he did, his static line whipped around his neck, and as Boone fell into the night it snapped his spinal cord. For a moment he was towed along behind the airplane, then his body twirled, the static line unwrapped from his neck, and he fell away. O'Neill and the other two Special Forces NCOs followed off the ramp.

"Good canopy!" Denton said, then he scanned the darkness with his pocketscope until he saw the four canopies of the jumpers' parachutes. It looked like the jump onto DZ Two was off to a good start, so he turned to the three men who would infiltrate the last drop zone with him and shouted, "OK, guys! Twenty minutes!"

No one told him what had happened while he was on the flight deck, nor that Boone's static line had wrapped around his neck.

Twenty minutes later Mark Denton and the three other men leapt into the darkness at drop zone Three.

As soon as all four men had gathered at the equipment bundle, Denton directed his radio operator to send a short message over his satellite radio's burst device indicating that his element had arrived intact on DZ Three. To the others he said, "All right, let's get this bundle broken down and cached and sterilize the drop zone."

Red Stephens and Miles Goodwin slowed their helicopters and popped up to one hundred feet when their GPS readouts indicated they were a kilometer from drop zone One. Stephens' copilot flipped his night-vision goggles down, scanned the darkness, and said, "Bingo! They're at two o'clock." He had seen an infrared strobe light blinking off to his right front.

Stephens flashed his infrared-filtered landing light twice, and the team on the ground responded with four flashes of a filtered flashlight. The helicopters eased their way to the refuel site and settled onto the ground beside the stack of fuel cans.

Within an hour they had topped off the fuel tanks of the helicopters, buried the empty cans, and hidden the few remaining cans of fuel in a cache. Then they flew to the nearby site the ground team had selected as their overnight hiding place. After folding up the blades of the choppers and draping them with the shredded canopies of two of the parachutes, five of the men lay down to sleep while the other two climbed atop the hill above them to stand guard.

By the time the helicopters were hidden, Denton and his element, well to the north, had completed recovering the equipment from their bundle and had stashed it, along with their air items, in three separate caches nearby. While two of the men finished camouflaging the caches, Denton and his radio operator climbed the small, rocky knoll they would use as a hide site.

When they were settled into an outcropping of rock the radioman set up his satellite radio, and Denton said, "All right, Sparky. Let's see how the other guys are making out."

The radio operator punched a short message into his digital message device group (DMDG) indicating that they were set up near DZ Three and prepared to receive message traffic. Then he transmitted it to the satellite in orbit above the Indian Ocean, and it was retransmitted back to earth.

A minute later the DMDG received and decoded a burst of radio waves, storing them in its electronic memory and illuminating a small light indicating it had done so. The radio operator presed the Read button, and across the small face of the DMDG scrolled the stored message:

SECRET: OOOO SWORD DE BASE: DROP ZONE ONE REPORTS MISSION COMPLETE, TWO HELOS, SEVEN PAX IN HIDING VIC DROP ZONE ONE. BT. DROP ZONE TWO REPORTS ONE CASUALTY; BOONE, SPC HARDIN L. KILLED DURING INFIL (NON-HOSTILE). DZ TWO ELEM WILL BURY BODY AND REPORT EIGHT-DIGIT COORD FOR EVENTUAL RECOVERY. WILL INFIL REPLACEMENT WITH AUTOMATIC RESUPPLY TO-MORROW NIGHT. CONFIRM DZ REPORTS NLT 230200Z. SECRET. AR.

"Damn," Mark Denton muttered as, leaning over the radioman's shoulder, he read the report of Boone's death. "We haven't even gotten started yet, and we already have one dead."

"Well, I'll tell you, sir," the Special Forces NCO said coldly, "if we had to lose anybody, I'm glad it was that sniveling son of a bitch."

Denton let the comment go. Boone *had* spent too much time complaining about the mission—even about the long hours of work required during the demonstration they had conducted at the National Training Center. If he'd had time to do so, Denton would have had Boone replaced. But he hadn't, and now the young soldier was dead—the first American killed in the battle to stem the Soviet invasion of Iran.

CHAPTER 7

0600 GMT (0930 local time), 22 September
Southeastern Iran

Early the next morning, the Special Forces detachments
on the ground in Iran—the A teams of Captains Birelli
and Davidson, and Major Mark Denton's B team—all
received the same intelligence report from the Special
Forces Operations Base:

> Lead elements of Soviet 68th Motorized Rifle
> Regiment and 121st Tank Regiment crossed Iranian
> border from Afghanistan vicinity of coordinates
> 41R LP 705680, escorted by a flight of four Mi-24E
> gunships. Immediate objective appears to be
> Birjand-Zahedan road. Mujahadeen conducting
> sporadic harassing ambushes and mine laying but
> have very limited resources remaining. They have
> been directed to concentrate efforts on follow-up
> support forces, especially fuel and ammunition ve-
> hicles. Lead elements are being refueled by Mi-26
> refuel helicopters. Advise SFOB of earliest date
> you can commence interdiction operations along
> Zahedan-Khash-Chah Bahar axis.

The report went on to give additional details about the
Soviet forces involved in the invasion and concluded
with, "Imperative that all elements conduct operations
to harass, delay, and disrupt enemy movement with all
available resources. Advise soonest."

Mark Denton considered the situation of his detachment. During the coming night he would receive a paradrop of additional fuel and munitions at two locations between Zahedan and Khash. One would be at drop zone Two. The other would go in on a DZ to Denton's south, where the helicopters would drop four of the men—no, three, now that Boone was dead. The helicopters would then continue to Denton's location, where they would be armed and refueled from the nearby cache sites. If necessary, they could be used to ferry Denton and his men to positions along the two roads that arched east and west out of Zahedan, then reconverged north of Khash.

If all went as planned, Denton's detachment would be prepared to hit the Russian force in twenty-four hours. He sent a message to the Special Forces Operations Base indicating that fact, but adding that their preparedness would be much better if they could have forty-eight hours to get ready. From the SFOB, the 3d Special Forces Group commander replied that in all likelihood it would be at least forty-eight hours before the Soviets reached Zahedan.

At the guerrilla base some two hundred kilometers south-southeast of Denton, Captain Rocco Birelli and his teammates, along with the Baluchi chieftain, Chakur Nothani, and his lieutenant, Lakha Nawaz, were considering the message.

"It should be at least four or five days before they get into our area of operations," Birelli said.

They were holding their discussion in Baluchi, and Birelli was pleased that everyone on the team except Hanson, the radio operator, was conversant in that language. Birelli, the detachment executive officer, and the senior weapons man were, in fact, rated as near-native in their language proficiency. It was a point of great pride with the team that they were so well-trained in the language of the area toward which their team was targeted, for so many Special Forces detachments gave language training mere lip service. But Rocco Birelli had gained permission to take his whole detachment to the

Defense Language Institute for six months, where they had undergone an intensive course in Baluchi. Since their return they had spoken only Baluchi whenever possible at work, and the commanding general of 1st Special Operations Command had been so favorably impressed with the results that he had ordered each battalion in his command to have one detachment at a time at the language school, training in the language of the region toward which they were targeted. The program was paying off.

Master Sergeant Brady, the team sergeant of A-326, asked the executive officer, "Did we get all of the new men their equipment, Mr. Kaminski?"

"All except the last four, who just arrived last night," Kaminski replied. "We only had equipment for a hundred and twenty. We won't be able to get them—and any others who show up—any gear until our next re-supply."

"When will that be?" Nothani asked.

"We haven't sent in a request yet," Birelli replied. "They usually need at least three days notice before they can deliver."

"Well, this ain't 'usually,' sir," Brady said in English, then he reverted to Baluchi. "If they expect us to start fighting the Soviets in a few days, they're going to have to get us the weapons and ammunition we need to do it, and get them to us fast."

"Yeah, you're right," Birelli agreed. "We'll burst them a request as soon as we figure out what we need and tell them to get it to us within the next couple of nights. Now, let's talk about where we are in training."

They discussed the status of training of the guerrilla cadre. Fortunately, the Baluchi were already skilled rifle marksmen—some of the best in the world, in this region where "one round, one kill" was a credo. And most of the modern weapons the team was training them on were, although of sophisticated technology, easy to use. The Dragon antitank missile was simple to put into operation and required only that the gunner keep the crosshairs of his sight on the target. The wire-guided missile system's built-in wizardry would take care of the rest. The same went for the larger, longer-range TOW 2 missile system. And the Stinger shoulder-fired antiaircraft missile was also relatively simple to operate. Once the target was acquired by the weapon's infrared sensor, all the gunner had to do was elevate it slightly and fire. The missile's IR sensor, already locked in on the heat signature of the aircraft's engines, took over and homed in on the target. It would have been somewhat more difficult if the team and their guerrillas had to be concerned with the IFF—identify friend or foe—electronics in the Stinger. But since there would be no friendly aircraft involved in their battles—at least for the time being—they could ignore the IFF aspect of the system.

The 60-mm lightweight mortars, whose employment involved fire-direction computing, were more complicated to operate properly. But the A team's weapons men could do the plotting, and the heavy-weapons leader, SFC Nichols, indicated that the guerrillas who had been chosen to be mortarmen were already becoming adept at setting deflection and elevation on the weapon's sights, and preparing the rounds for firing.

By the time Birelli's team meeting ended, several decisions had been reached. They would request the additional war materiel they needed and ask that it be dropped within the next forty-eight hours, on two separate drop zones near the Russians' expected route of advance. They would split up into two elements and, as soon as possible, begin moving toward the DZs in the area where they intended to do battle. They would conduct what training they could en route, concentrating on tactics while they were on the move, and on weapons when they were halted.

When the meeting ended, Dick Medlin, the CIA man, and Chakur Nothani, the Baluchi chieftain, took Captain Birelli aside.

"Nawaz will be in charge of the guerrillas now," Medlin informed him. "Nothani and I are taking off."

"Taking off? What do you mean?" Birelli asked.

71

"We'll be in Zaboli initially, then Sarbaz, and, if we have time, Khash."

All three towns were on the roads the Soviets were expected to use on their advance toward Chah Bahar, where their airborne forces awaited reinforcement.

"I see," Birelli replied, for he knew without asking what the chieftain and his courageous companion would be doing. They would organize underground intelligence and sabotage nets in those towns to assist the effort to blunt the Soviet assault. Birelli embraced the Baluchi leader, kissing him on both cheeks and saying, "Go with the blessings of God."

"May His sword, Talwar Allah, be sharp and swift," Nothani replied.

Birelli shook hands with Medlin and said in English, "Be careful, Dick. Will we see you again?"

"Hard to say," Medlin answered. "If things work out, we'll be operating in Sarbaz most of the time. Send one of Nawaz's men in there in a couple of weeks. If we can, we'll let him lead us to you. Meanwhile, give 'em hell. It's important."

"We will," Birelli promised, then he rejoined the members of his team and their band of guerrillas.

1850 hours GMT (2220 hours local time), 22 September
Unconventional Warfare Operations Area Sword
Southwest of Zahedan, Iran

The two Hughes 500MD helicopters arrived at Major Mark Denton's hide site two hours after darkness that night. After they shut down, Chief Warrant Officer Red Stephens climbed out of his helicopter, found Denton, and said, "Why, howdy, Major! Which way to the bar?"

Denton chuckled. He was glad to see the aviator in good spirits. "Right over there, Chief," he said. "Let's see, we've got Hellfire cocktails, TOWs on the rocks, and Stingers, straight up. Name your poison."

"What?" Stephens said, "No minigun margaritas?"

"Yeah, we've even got them. Welcome to Club Iran."

"Sorry about my boy Boone packin' it in on us, boss," Stephens said. "He was a pain in the ass, but he knew more about how to keep these 500's flying than anybody, except maybe that hard-working Cat Whitaker."

"Well, maybe that's who they'll send in to replace him," Denton said. "They promised us somebody on tonight's drop."

"I doubt that, boss man. 'Cat' is short for Catherine. They ain't gonna send no split-tail out here to get shot at."

"You never know, Red," his copilot, CW2 Bart Evans, said. "Don't forget those sailorettes we saw on that last boat we got gas from."

"Yeah," Stephens said. "Check this out, Major D." He reached into a pocket of his flight suit and pulled out a piece of fabric, then held it up in front of Denton's face.

"What the hell is it?" Denton asked.

"All-American, well-worn sailorette's silk panties," Stephens said. "We were in this ship's mess, and this gorgeous little thing was serving chow. She says, 'What would you like, sir?' and I say, 'How 'bout some drawers for we who are about to die?' Next thing I know, she comes to the table, hands me this little pot with a lid on it, and says, 'Here's the dessert you requested, sir.' I opened it up and found these. Thought the ship's exec was gonna choke to death on his iced tea."

"Stephens," Denton said when he stopped laughing, "you're one crazy son of a bitch."

"Yeah, I guess so. We all are, or we wouldn't be here at Club Iran. Now, what's the plan for dealing with these Russkies, Major D.?"

The men sat in a circle in the dark, and Denton said, "First I need to know if you can fly back down to DZ Two, where you dropped the four guys off, and help them cache the load they're gonna get, then bring your new ground crewman and a couple of my guys back with you."

"Sure," Stephens said. "In fact, if we only take one

pilot, and just enough fuel to get there and back, we can bring all four of your guys *and* Boone's replacement, as long as they sling their rucksacks underneath."

"Great," Denton said. "Then, if there's enough time left before daylight for me to give the guys a quick brief and send 'em on their way, I'd like for you to ferry them out to their OP sites."

"What time's the drop coming in?" Stephens asked.

Denton checked his watch. "About an hour and twenty. With your guys helping, they should be able to cache the gear within, say, two hours—maybe less."

"Let's see," Stephens said. "That would put them back here in about four and a half hours. What time's it start getting light?"

"Around 0250 Zulu. That means we'll have something like three and a half hours of darkness to work with after they get back. Give them about an hour here, and they'll be ready to go . . . No, on second thought, I'll have two of the guys here with me ready to go as soon as the choppers get back. While you're putting them in, I'll brief the others."

"Sounds good," Stephens said. "I'll let the copilots do the flying down to the DZ and back. Miles and I will stay here and go over where you want the teams to go in. We'll start shuttling them as soon as the birds get back and refuel."

The helicopters, flown by the copilots, departed for the drop zone a short time later. Denton, Stephens, his wingman, Miles Goodwin, and the two Special Forces NCOs who would be first to go out to establish their electronic OPs, went over the locations where the teams would be dropped off.

Each team would emplace two electronic observation posts. They would monitor them from hide sites on the high ridges above the roads. Each electronic OP would have a laser target designator mounted parallel to its remotely manipulated TV camera. In the hide sites each man would have a Stinger antiaircraft missile and a Dragon antitank missile.

"If the Russians don't show up before tomorrow night," Denton said, "we'll use the choppers to set up an alternate site south of here for each team as well, where we'll put chow, water, and more Stingers and Dragons."

"And AT-4 rockets," one of the Special Forces NCOs added. "We'll have time to go down and aim them in on the road, too, if they give us tomorrow night to work with."

The pilots napped while they waited for their copilots to return with the helicopters, and Denton helped the OP team rig the bundles of equipment that would be slung beneath the helicopters. By the time the helicopters returned, they had prepared bundles for all three of the teams that would be deployed that night.

When the helicopters had shut down and the pilots and their passengers climbed out, Bart Evans called to Stephens, "Hey, Red! Look who they sent us."

"Hi, Mr. Stephens," a feminine voice said.

"Oh, Christ," Stephens said, then to Major Denton, as the woman approached, "Sir, meet the newest member of your team—Sergeant Cat Whitaker."

"Sir," she said as she firmly shook Denton's hand, "I know you're surprised to find a woman out here, but there wasn't any choice. I was the only jump-qualified H-500 mechanic they had."

"Well," Denton said, "I hope you'll be all right out here, Sergeant Whitaker. There aren't any sanitary facil—"

"Major," she interrupted, "I just finished my period a couple of days ago. If you can get an extra can of water in here within the next month and let me have a few scraps of parachute cloth, I won't be any more trouble than the rest of the team. Now, if you'll excuse me, I have helicopters to maintain." With that, she turned and began walking toward the little aircraft.

As she did Denton said, "Sergeant Whitaker?"

"Sir!" she said, stopping and looking back.

"I hear you're a damn fine chopper mechanic."

"Yes, sir, I am. The best."

"Then welcome aboard, and carry on."

It was madness to send a woman out here, he thought. But it was done. And right now he had better things to do than worry about a decision made halfway around the world by somebody else. He had OP teams to brief and deploy.

CHAPTER 8

1650 hours GMT (1935 hours local) 25 September
Southeastern Iran

The Soviets didn't appear in UWOA Sword for almost three days, and then it was only in helicopters, flying through the valley above the westernmost of the two roads between Zahedan and Khash. They appeared at dusk, two Hind gunships and two big Mi-6 Hook cargo helicopters. Denton sent a flash message to the SFOB asking if his detachment should engage them. By the time Denton received a reply of "Negative," the aircraft had passed his position and were flying toward the UWOA of Rocco Birelli and A-326—UWOA Tiger.

Birelli's radio operator and that of Bill Davidson's A team to the south received a different message on their DMDGs shortly after Denton reported the enemy helicopters:

SECRET: ZZZZ TIGER AND SHARK DE BASE: FOUR SOVIET HELOS, TWO MIKE INDIA TWO FOUR AND TWO MIKE INDIA SIX ENTERING YOUR AREA FROM THE NORTH. BELIEVED EN ROUTE CHAH BAHAR XX CHAH BAHAR. PERMISSION GRANTED TO ENGAGE AT WILL. IMI, ENGAGE AT WILL. SECRET: AR

Birelli, Lakha Nawaz, and half of Nawaz's guerrillas were due north of the drop zone they had used to receive the team's automatic resupply several nights earlier. If the helicopters were following the same flight route they had used that night, when they had been on a near-

77

collision course with the Combat Talon, they might pass within range of the team's Stingers. Birelli ran to Nawaz and explained the contents of the message to him and the senior American NCO with his half of the split A team, SFC Don Parker.

"How much time we got?" Parker asked.

"Don't know," Birelli replied. Pointing to the top of a rocky hill several hundred meters to their north, he said, "Get every man with a Stinger up there now!"

They had received four of the missiles in their automatic resupply bundles, and Parker ran to find the men carrying them.

Birelli and Nawaz scurried to the top of the hill and searched the darkening sky to their north. Within a few minutes all four Baluchi Stinger gunners and the light weapons leader, SSG Willie Washington, joined them atop the hill.

"Sir," Washington said in English, "you think we ought to put Americans on the Stingers?"

"Negative," Birelli replied. "Let the guerrillas shoot— if the bastards show up. It'll give the Baluchis confidence in the weapons we're supplying them. You just make sure they've got the night sights attached and they go through the proper prefire checks."

SFC Parker arrived on the hilltop then, and Birelli said, "Don, get back down and organize an assault party. Move about two hundred meters south, and if we knock any choppers down, sweep through and finish 'em off. But make sure you're in covered positions. I'd hate for one of them to crash on top of anybody."

"Wilco," Parker said. "Prisoners?"

"Roger, if you can take any."

Parker trotted off down the hill, and Washington said, "Prefire checks completed, Captain."

"OK," Birelli said. "Now assign each man a specific target. It should be two Hinds leading, and two Mi-6s right behind. Wait till they're abreast of us or just past, then fire a salvo."

"Wilco," Washington said, then he went to the gunners and assigned one of them the leftmost Mi-24, one the rightmost, one the lead or leftmost Mi-6, and the other the trail or rightmost Mi-6.

In the deepening darkness he ran the gunners through several repetitions of a mock engagement, then told them to sit down and rest until they heard the helicopters. All four men faced to the southwest—toward Mecca—knelt, and prayed to their God to deliver the enemy helicopters within range of their missiles.

Just under an hour later, their prayers were answered.

Nawaz heard them first, then, almost immediately, the newly trained Baluchi antiaircraft gunners heard them. Unlike their American advisers, whose eardrums were damaged by extensive weapons training and the rock music of their youth, the tribesmen's ears could hear any sound that broke the silence of the desert night.

By the time Birelli heard the sound of rotor blades, the gunners were already on their feet, facing the distant sound with their missile launchers on their shoulders.

The formation of Soviet helicopters appeared a minute later, about a kilometer to the guerrillas' northwest.

Washington saw them first with his night-vision goggles and said, "There they are! Two gunships on the flanks, with the Hooks in trail between them."

The gunners began to pick them up in their night sights moments later, and Birelli could hear the increasing number of beeping sounds as the Stingers' infrared sensors acquired the heat signatures of the helicopters' turbine engines. As they had practiced earlier, the gunners announced, "One ready . . . Three ready . . . Two ready . . . Four ready!"

"All ready," Washington acknowledged. "Stand by!"

When the formation passed three hundred meters to their west, the Stinger gunners following their respective targets as the weapons' acquisition indicators beeped madly, Birelli grabbed Nawaz and pulled him off to the side so they would be out of the backblast area.

As soon as he could see through his goggles that the helicopters were not masking one another, Washington shouted, "Stand by! . . . Fire!"

There was a flash and roar as, almost simultaneously,

the Baluchi gunners launched their heat-seeking missiles. Four red fireballs sped at the helicopters and, within a split second of each other, struck home. One of the missiles, its IR sensor confused by the presence of more than one source of heat, veered slightly and struck the same engine as one of the other Stinger rounds. The Mi-6 they hit exploded instantly in a giant fireball, its airframe and cargo splashing toward the ground. Each of the Hind gunships took a round in one of their top-mounted engines. The Hind on the right of the formation rose higher into the air, hung there a moment, then nosed over and dived straight into the earth. As it did so the other gunship veered to the right, slammed into the undamaged Mi-6, then cartwheeled forward and landed on its top, rolling twice before it burst into flames. The cargo chopper it had hit during its death throes had its tail rotor knocked off. It spun around twice, crashing to the ground as it did so. By the time it hit the ground the weapons of the Baluchi guerrillas, seventy-five meters to its east, were ravaging the wreck with small-arms fire.

All four Soviet helicopters, three of them ablaze almost instantly, had been reduced to heaps of rubble within an area one hundred meters square.

"Holy Jesus Christ!" Mark Denton said, while beside him the Baluchi Stinger gunners and their commander, Lakha Nawaz, dropped to their knees and chanted, "God is great. Thanks be to God!"

Sergeant First Class Don Parker, leading the Baluchi assault force, swept through the carnage. Before he could get the tribesmen under control, the four crewmen of the most nearly intact Mi-6, who had survived the crash, were dead from small-arms fire.

Rocco Birelli surveyed the scene before him. The four Soviet helicopters, which only moments before had been flying in neat formation to resupply the airborne force near Chah Bahar, were lying in shapeless heaps on the rocky ground below.

The ammunition in the Hind gunships began cooking off then, some of it careening through the dark sky like fireworks at a Fourth of July celebration. With Nawaz at his side, Birelli scrambled down the hill toward the burning wrecks. At the foot of the hill his radio operator, Sergeant Percy Hanson, yelled, "Captain Birelli! Should I send a spot report to base?"

"Yeah," the A team leader responded. "Let's see . . . tell them, 'Sighted Soviet suckers, Stingers smashed same.' Then add, 'Detailed report will follow.'"

By dawn of the following morning Nawaz's guerrillas had stripped the crash site of everything of military value. They got little from what remained in the wreckage of the two gunships and the Mi-6 that had burned. But from the less damaged cargo helicopter, which didn't burn, they recovered a large quantity of equipment. There were SA-14 shoulder-fired antiaircraft missiles, RPG-16 rocket-propelled grenade launchers equipped with improved sights. There were more than two hundred rounds of RPG-16 ammunition and new, elongated warheads for them. Birelli deduced that the tandem warheads were designed to defeat reactive armor—that is, armor covered with an explosive surface so that, when struck by point-detonating, shaped-charge munitions, a portion of the explosive armor would detonate. The effect was that, instead of allowing the shaped charge to penetrate the armor with a concentrated jet of superheated gases, the detonation of the reactive armor would disperse the gas jet, greatly lessening the damage. Most American antiarmor weapons employed tandem warheads now, as well. By detonating the explosive surface milliseconds before the shaped charge hit, the first, small warhead negated the effect of the new type of armor, allowing the second warhead to destroy the target.

The guerrillas also recovered six new radios of a type none of the Americans had ever heard of before. They appeared to have speech security devices built into them, and Birelli knew they would be of great value to the U.S. government.

The biggest find of all, though, was a briefcase containing military documents. No one on the scene could read Russian, but Birelli and his men were convinced that the documents were of significant intelligence value. Each was stamped with what appeared to be classification markings and another stamp that appeared to indicate it was copy number two of only five copies. There was also a transparent overlay with a number of symbols on it, although the men didn't know what the symbols represented.

When the force was prepared to move out with their captured booty, Birelli shot holes in the undamaged fuel cells of the unburned helicopter, then tossed a thermite grenade into the wreckage. By the time he and his band of men crossed the crest of a ridge two kilometers to the northwest, the sun had risen. Looking back, they could see a column of black smoke rising from the still-burning wreckage.

Once they reached a suitable site in which to disperse and hide through the day, Birelli directed two of his men to begin making handprinted copies of each Soviet document and the overlay. He felt the papers were valuable enough that he should make an additional copy, in the event the originals were lost. Meanwhile, he prepared a message for Hanson to punch into his DMDG and burst to the Special Forces Operations Base. While he was preparing it, Hanson received a message from the base:

SECRET: OOOO TIGER DE BASE: WELL DONE. SIGINT HAS NEGATIVE EVIDENCE THAT HELOS SENT MAYDAY. ENEMY AT CHAH BAHAR ARE ADVISING THEIR HEADQUARTERS THAT EXPECTED HELOS NEVER SHOWED. BE PREP FOR ENEMY REACTION FORCE FROM NORTH OR SOUTH. ADVISE ASAP XX ASAP OF CRASH SITE COORDS AND ANY SIGNIFICANT INTEL. BT FM CDR THREE SIERRA FOXTROT GOLF QUOTE DO NOT BITE OFF MORE THAN YOU CAN CHEW. BUT KEEP BITING EXCLAM UNQUOTE. BT SECRET AR

Birelli composed a detailed message on the engagement, what they had recovered, and the fact that they had counted the bodies of twenty-two Soviet servicemen amid the wreckage of the four helicopters. Then he requested disposition of the captured documents, emphasizing his belief that they were of significant intelligence value.

A short time after Hanson sent his detachment commander's message, he received a reply from SFOB indicating that the Combat Talon that would deliver his next resupply two nights hence would be prepared to recover the documents, and two each of the new RPG-16 launchers, tandem warhead rounds, and SA-14 antiaircraft missiles, as well as all of the captured radios.

At mid-morning a Soviet reconnaissance aircraft arrived over the area, accompanied by a pair of fighters. The aircraft remained at high altitude, however, and the American Green Berets and their Baluchi guerrillas stayed in hiding until the enemy aircraft were gone.

While they hid, Sergeant Hanson tuned in the world service of the British Broadcasting Corporation, and he and Birelli listened to the news.

They learned that the world was now aware of the fact that a Soviet airborne regiment was entrenched in and around Chah Bahar, and that other Soviet forces were moving south in an apparent move to reinforce them. According to the news, they would, in spite of harassing attacks by Mujahadeen guerrillas all along their route of advance, reach Zahedan at any time.

The broadcast included excerpts from a news conference with the President of the United States. In response to a question about whether or not the United States was going to mount an assault against the Soviet forces in Iran, he said, "We hope and pray that such a thing will not become necessary. It's my belief that the Soviet people won't allow it to become necessary. The civil unrest in the Soviet Union is growing daily, and I think that in the end, Mr. Gorbachev and the more moderate elements in the Soviet government will prevail, and the Soviet forces will be withdrawn. Meanwhile, though, we obviously can't stand idly by and wait for that to happen. To ensure that the flow of oil continues unimpeded through the Persian Gulf, we'll do whatever's necessary to enforce our control of the exclusion zone. As long as the Soviets don't violate that zone, and unless they try to reinforce the airborne force they so foolishly dropped at Chah Bahar, I see no reason for us—for the moment, at least—to mount an effort to dislodge them. As I said, I think the cooler heads in the Kremlin will soon prevail, and they'll be withdrawn. But I must say our patience is limited, and they need to get those people out of there—and elsewhere in Southwest Asia—and they need to get them out soon."

When asked about the rumor that there were already American Special Forces teams in Iran equipping, training, and advising guerrilla forces, the president replied, "Look, I'm not going to deal in rumors. Military operations are, especially at a time like this, classified. But if we feel the people of Afghanistan and Iran need help in throwing invaders out of their sovereign territories, then we're going to assist them in that effort."

"Sir," the questioning continued, "you said that you saw no reason, at present, to commit U.S. forces to dislodge the Soviets from Chah Bahar unless they were reinforced."

"That's right," the president replied. "Or unless they demonstrate hostile action or intent. Right now they're apparently just sitting there in defensive positions."

"Well," the questioner asked, "isn't the thrust from Afghanistan toward Zahedan an obvious effort to reinforce Chah Bahar?"

"It does appear that maybe that's their ultimate goal, in spite of Soviet claims that they're only pursuing the Mujahadeen and responding to the request of Tudeh—that's the Iranian Communist party—to go in there temporarily and stabilize the area. That's the same argument they used when they invaded Afghanistan during Christmas of '79, remember. They got kicked out eventually then, and if they don't abandon this ill-advised adventurism now and withdraw to their own borders soon, they'll get kicked out again. But going back to your question of whether or not this is an attempt to reinforce Chah Bahar, let me just say it had better not be."

"And how far south do they have to get before you're convinced it's a reinforcement, Mr. President?"

"Not much farther south, I'll tell you that."

"But *how* much farther, sir?"

"Well," the president said, "we're not going to draw some line in the dirt and dare them to step across it. What we want to see, and see soon, is the Soviets moving in the other direction—back to their own country. You know, these decisions have to be based on much more than the momentary locations of military forces. But if they were to get beyond Khash, for example, I don't think there would be any doubt in anybody's mind that they're trying to reinforce Chah Bahar. And *that,* we and our allies have already clearly stated, is under no circumstances acceptable."

The interview ended there, and the BBC reporter went on to other, more mundane news.

Hanson switched off the radio to preserve battery power, and Rocco Birelli said, "What he's *really* saying, I think, is that CENTCOM won't have enough forces marshaled and forward deployed for a while longer. Sounds like he figures the Russians will be around Khash before we're ready to commit our forces. Then the shit *really* starts! And our job, obviously, is to give CENTCOM as much time as we can."

"You think there's anybody north of us, Captain?" Hanson asked.

"You mean more SF teams? I doubt it. They wouldn't have enough time to train and equip their guerrillas. Could be they've put some people in to help rebuild the Mujahadeen. Could be a couple of recon and surveillance teams—even direct action teams. I don't see how they could do much good fighting tanks on foot, though."

CHAPTER 9

0800 hours GMT (1130 hours local), 26 September
North of Zahedan, Iran, near the Iran-Pakistan-Afghanistan
tri-border area

More than two hundred kilometers to the north, as Birelli and Hanson were listening to the BBC news, so was Senior Lieutenant Valentin Popovich Valnikov of the Soviet Army. It was a habit he had picked up in Afghanistan several years earlier, although then it was strictly forbidden—a punishable offense that made it necessary for the listener to sneak away with his radio to learn the truth of what was going on around him. He had continued the habit when he returned to the Motherland after the withdrawal of Soviet forces from Afghanistan, and had done so openly. It was still forbidden, in the army, to listen to Western propaganda. But, as one of his soldiers had remarked when Valnikov caught him listening to the Voice of America just after they were alerted for their current operation, "What are they going to do, Comrade Lieutenant? Take away my blue jeans and send me to Afghanistan?"

The fact was, they learned more about where they were and where they were headed from free world broadcasts than they did from their own chain of command.

And here they were again, back in the same sort of harsh terrain in which Valnikov had first tasted the fear and exhilaration of battle—when his socialist idealism had been replaced by the reality of death and wounds and destruction. Now all he wanted to do was to keep his men alive until this expedition was over.

Valnikov found it incomprehensible that it had

happened—that the old hard-liners were, for the moment at least, being allowed to prevail. What was Gorbachev thinking? Didn't he know that virtually every one in Russia—and in the satellite republics as well—would back him if he demanded that the old men step down?

He laughed to himself, and his gunner, seated beside him and leaning against a roadwheel of their T-80 main battle tank, looked curiously at him.

"What's he saying that's funny, Comrade Lieutenant?" The BBC broadcast was in English, and the gunner, as anxious for news from an uncensored source as Valnikov, was waiting for his company commander to translate it for him.

"The American president says that he'd like us to go back to Mother Russia, Sergei Ivanovich," Valnikov replied, turning off the small transistor radio and placing it in the pocket of his coveralls.

"Is he going to fight us, Comrade Lieutenant?" the gunner asked. "Have the Americans put any forces ashore yet?"

Valnikov looked at the young gunner. "Perhaps a few *Spetznaz,* Sergei Ivanovich. But nothing for us to worry about."

But his gunner *was* worried. If a bunch of backward tribesmen like the *dushman*—the Mujahadeen—could not be beaten by the Soviets, what would the Americans be like, with their technology and numbers, both nearly the equal of those of the USSR? If the *dushman* could hold out against men like his company commander, how could he and his young comrades-in-arms expect to overwhelm sophisticated American troops?

Valnikov was worried, too. It just made no sense. Rumor had it that the operation was a compromise—an attempt to polarize the support of the Soviet people by giving them a common enemy. An attempt by the old men to show Gorbachev and his progressive moderates that America and her allies had no real resolve. After all, what had they done in the last real crises in this part of the world? When the Soviets had invaded Afghanistan in

1979, all they did for several years was boycott the Moscow Olympic Games. And when the Iranians held fifty diplomats hostage the following year, all they did was send a pitifully small force of *Spetznaz* in a half-hearted attempt to rescue them.

Yet what had *this* American president just said? That if we get beyond Khash, he'll fight? True, Iran was a long way from Panama, but look at what this president had done *there*.

Valnikov climbed into the commander's hatch and extracted his large-scale map from his map case. He located Khash and, seeing the short distance between his current location and there, mumbled, "Then it's going to be a fight, Mr. President. We'll be in Khash in a few hours."

0820 hours GMT (1150 hours local), 26 September
South of Zahedan, Iran

Not far to the south of Valnikov and his comrades, Major Mark Denton's SFOD B-30 was making eleventh-hour preparations to oppose the Soviet advance.

He had two two-man teams on the ridges above each of the pair of roads that ran south from the town of Zahedan.

Each two-man team had emplaced several remotely fired AT-4 antitank rockets covering the road below its positions. In addition, each had established two electronic observation posts well up on the rocky slopes above the road and had tested the small TV cameras and parallel-mounted laser target designators—LTDs—to ensure that they were operational. The pictures the men received on the little high-resolution monitors that were radio-linked to each camera were sharp, and the radio link to each, which enabled the operator to manipulate the direction, elevation, and zoom lens of each camera, also proved to be functioning.

In their well-camouflaged hide sites atop the ridges, each two-man team also had a Stinger antiaircraft missile, a Dragon antitank missile, a hand-held LTD, and two briefcase-sized electronic OP remote control and monitoring systems, which they referred to simply as "briefcases."

In nearby cache sites each team had hidden an additional Stinger and Dragon, spare food and water, and extra batteries. Many miles to the south the men had used the helicopters, during the second night they had waited for the Soviets to appear, to establish cache sites for later use. The first night the helicopters had been used to bring forward the three men and some of the equipment they had received from the resupply drop of the previous evening.

Now Denton's little force had weapons, fuel, food, water, and other equipment cached along the entire length of his operational area between Zahedan and Khash—a distance of nearly two hundred kilometers.

In addition to the eight Special Forces men in the observation posts, Denton had four warrant officer helicopter pilots, his radio operator, and two helicopter mechanics—one of whom was the woman, Cat Whitaker—in the main hide site beside a valley several kilometers to the southwest of the OPs.

The two little egg-shaped Hughes 500MD helicopters, their Plexiglas bubbles draped with parachute cloth, their outlines broken up by lightweight camouflage nets, sat nearby. On the sides of each were two weapons pods. For the initial engagement each was armed with a pod of two Hellfire laser-guided missiles, and, because of the report that the enemy's advance elements were escorted by helicopter gunships, each also carried two "fire and forget" Stinger missiles. On the valley floor nearby were cached spare missiles for each system, as well as TOW 2 antitank weapons pods and missiles, and two 5.56-mm miniguns and 10,000 rounds of ammunition. There was also enough fuel to allow the helicopters to operate for about twelve hours each.

For communications, each team and helicopter had small AN/PRC-117 frequency-hopping FM radios. Because they skipped from frequency to frequency many times per second they were nearly impossible to detect, except by the most sophisticated radio direction-finding equipment.

In addition, Denton's detachment had LST-4 satellite radios equipped with digital message device groups—DMDGs—for long-range communications and messages to and from 1st Special Operations Command headquarters.

Denton's primary plan for striking the Soviets was based on the assumption that they would employ standard Soviet tactics. Intelligence reports from 1st SOCOM headquarters indicated that they were, so far, doing so as they moved through Afghanistan, then south through Iran.

Where the two Soviet regiments were required to move in a single column, the motorized rifle regiment led the tank regiment. When they were able to advance on two axes, the tank regiment would move up and travel parallel to them. Denton expected, therefore, that as they moved south from Zahedan the rifle regiment would appear first and take one of the two roads south. The tank regiment, he assumed, would take the other road.

Leading the motorized rifle regiment would be a combat reconnaissance patrol consisting of four or five BTR-80 eight-wheeled armored personnel carriers carrying a rifle platoon and an engineer recon squad. Denton intended to allow them to pass untouched.

Following them by five to ten kilometers would be the forward security element of the regiment. Led by a combined arms team of two BTR platoons and one tank platoon would be engineers, a mortar battery, and an artillery battery. Denton planned for the forward security element to be the first unit he dealt with.

Behind them by another five to ten kilometers would be the main body of the regiment's advance guard battalion. It would have two motorized rifle companies, a tank company—minus the platoon of tanks in the forward security element—an antitank platoon, and an antiaircraft section.

The rest of the regiment would be well to the rear of

the advance guard battalion—as much as twenty kilometers.

The helicopter force supporting the Soviet column appeared to be one that had been task-organized especially for the operation. If intelligence reports were correct, it consisted of eight Mi-24E Hind gunships, six Mi-8 Hip assault transports, and several huge Mi-26 Halo cargo helicopters. Each Halo was capable of carrying more than a hundred troops, or up to twenty tons of cargo.

The Hind gunships were what Denton and his men feared the most. They were being employed in pairs and, since the Mujahadeen had been shown to be out of Stinger antiaircraft missiles, one or two pairs had been covering the flanks of the advance guard. Denton's men had been given the Hinds as their first-priority target. Thus, each manned OP had a Stinger at the ready, and the H-500MDs each carried a pod with two of the air-to-air version of the Stinger missile.

If SFOD B-30's sophisticated ambush went as planned, it would begin with the Stingers taking out any Hinds in the area. Next the electronic OPs would be used to mark targets for the H-500s' Hellfire missiles. While the helicopters rearmed, the OP teams would watch the points at which their AT-4 antitank rockets had been aimed. Any Soviet vehicle passing those points would be engaged by the observers remotely firing AT-4s with their M-122 remote firing devices.

When the H-500s returned to the battle area they would first look for additional Hind gunships arriving to support the Soviet ground troops and engage them with their Stingers. Once the air was cleared of enemy helicopters again, the OP men would manipulate their electronic OPs to mark targets for the next salvo of Hellfires. They would then fire the remaining AT-4s to preclude the enemy from capturing the rockets, and to add to his confusion.

Finally, the OPs would fire a Dragon missile and, while the H-500s searched the skies for enemy helicopters to engage with their Stingers, the OP men would scurry to their alternate positions, from which they would launch their other Dragon.

SFOD B-30 was ready, and through the morning the men—and the lone woman—of the untested and anxious detachment waited in the dry, oppressive heat of the Iranian September day.

Mark Denton tried to sleep, but he could not. In a few hours men would die terrible, violent deaths, and he would be responsible for it.

"War is an ugly thing," he thought, remembering the beginning of a quotation, "but not the ugliest of things . . ." He couldn't recall the rest of the quote, and the thought was replaced by the image of a training accident he had seen at Fort Bragg. A Huey helicopter had crashed, and four men were burned to death in the wreckage. He remembered the grotesque, charred bodies, the awful stink. He was aware that the weapons he commanded would create the same sort of instant hell, or worse, within the Soviet armored vehicles and aircraft they hit.

He thought, too, of the television pictures he had seen of Chinese students crushed to death by the tanks of their own army in their brief quest for freedom in Tiananmen Square. And now another totalitarian Communist government was returning to its old oppressive ways. There had been so much hope all across the world. And then came China, and now the Soviet Union, resorting once more to the use of force to maintain corrupt power. Still, Gorbachev might prevail if he could show that the price for these policies was too great. In the case of the invasion of Iran, Denton and his men were resolved to make that price as steep as their little force could—at least until U.S. Central Command could, in a few more days, land the forces that would make the price unbearable.

Denton's small detachment, poised to hit the vastly superior Soviet armored force, seemed for a moment as vulnerable as the lone demonstrator who had placed himself in front of a column of tanks during the Chinese demonstrations for democratic reform. The tanks had halted, and the young man had—for the moment, at least—been allowed to live. For Denton and his men, the American Special Forces officer knew, the Communists' tanks would not willingly pause. But this time the tanks would face a more formidable task than simply crushing human flesh beneath their treads. This time it would be a clash of steel.

Denton moved to where Sergeant Catherine Whitaker sat beneath the mottled shade of a camouflage net reading a technical manual. It was an operator's manual for the Stinger antiaircraft missile system.

He sat beside her and asked, "You ever trained with the Stinger, Sergeant Whitaker?"

"No, sir," she replied. "The pilots have, but only in the air-to-air mode. I was thinking maybe I should learn to use it, though. I mean, suppose we were sitting here refueling and rearming the killer eggs, and a Russian plane showed up?"

"Killer eggs?" Denton said. "Is that what you call the choppers?"

She smiled. "You haven't heard them called that? If they look like eggs, and they shoot like killers, then they must be killer eggs, right?"

"Yeah," he said, chuckling. "I guess you're right. . . . Killer eggs. I like it."

"You're qualified on the Stinger system, aren't you, Major?" she asked.

"Yeah. You know, you're right—you and the other mechanic *should* know how to fire it, too—just in case. Go get him. I'll get a Stinger, and we'll do the training right now."

An hour later he had them familiar with the operation of the antiaircraft missile launcher.

"Thanks, Major Denton," she said as she placed the launcher into her camouflaged hiding place on the rocky slope. "Never know when this thing might come in handy."

"Let me ask you something, Sergeant Whitaker,"

Denton said. "How'd you manage to get sent out here to what's about to become a war zone?"

"Just like I told you, sir. When Boone got killed they gave me two hours to get my stuff together and get to Pope airbase. From there they put me on the next C-141 headed for Masirah. From there on I just followed your resupply pallets. First onto the Combat Talon, then off the ramp behind them. I've never been so damned scared in my life as when I stepped off that ramp into the darkness."

They sat in silence for a time, then Sergeant Whitaker said, "Sir, I hope you realize that I think it's just as stupid as you do for me to be out here. I mean, it's not that I can't do the job as well as a man—in fact, as far as maintaining those killer eggs down there, nobody can do it better. But, well, I'm not sure the American public is ready to start seeing servicewomen coming home in body bags. . . . You know what I mean?"

"I know exactly what you mean," Denton said. *"I'm* sure as hell not ready to see it. Still, it's bound to happen, with women getting jobs closer and closer to the battle area—especially if this thing heats up. Damn near happened in Panama, I understand."

Whitaker thought a moment, then said, "You know what I see myself as, sir?"

"What's that?"

"I think of myself as being like the pioneer women a hundred and fifty years ago. You know, like the circled wagons are being attacked by Indians, and it's my job to keep reloading rifles and passing them up to the men."

"Yeah," Denton said. "Yeah, Sergeant Whitaker, I'd say that's a pretty good analogy. As long as—"

"Sir!" the radio operator called from the camouflaged command post. "They're coming! OP One reports some movement on the west road. Looks like armored personnel carriers, and he hears helicopters!"

"Stephens!" Denton called the chief helicopter pilot. "Enemy vehicles and choppers on the west road! Your killer eggs ready to fly?"

"Roger!" Red Stephens acknowledged. "Crank 'em up?"

"Not yet," Denton said. "Come up here, and let's see what the OPs have."

With his AN/PRC-117 radio he called observation post One: "Oscar One, this is Base. What you got, over?"

"Oscar One here. I've got four BTR-80s in column on the west road, about thirty meters separation, moving at about, oh, ten miles an hour. Also, I can hear rotor blades in the distance, over."

"Roger," Denton replied. "How far from the kill zone are they?"

"About a kilometer right now."

"Roger. Let them go on by, as planned. Give me a report on the helos as soon as you see them."

"This is Oscar One. Wilco, out."

"All Oscars, this is Base. Remember the plan. The forward security element should be five klicks or more behind. Those are the vehicles we want, but we have to take out the choppers first. Three, do you have anything on the east road?"

"This is Oscar Three. Negative," came the reply from the men in the northernmost OP covering the other road.

Good, Denton thought. *The rifle regiment's moving out of Zahedan ahead of the tank regiment. There shouldn't be anything on the east road for quite a while yet—not until after the initial battle on the west road.*

"Base, this is Oscar One. I've got the choppers now. It's a flight of two Hinds at about a thousand feet. They're . . . hang on . . . they're turning back. Once they caught up with the point element they turned back. Must be working between the recon and forward security units. Will advise, out."

The second observation post on the west road called a moment later to report that the BTR-80s were now within sight of his position, adding, "They're entering the kill zone now."

"Roger that," Denton replied. "Keep me informed." He wished now that he had set up his command post near the road, or between the two roads, so he could see the action, instead of placing it several kilometers to the west. But with his limited personnel resources he had decided to stay near the helicopters so he could brief the pilots face to face and, if need be, assist in helping the ground crewmen rapidly rearm and refuel the H-500s. Once this initial battle was over—if it worked out as he hoped—he would reconsider moving to a position from which he could directly observe the battle.

He turned to Stephens and his wingman, Chief Warrant Officer Miles Goodwin. Their copilots were already at the choppers, ready to strip away the camouflage and start them up.

"OK," Denton said, "we should have about half an hour before the forward security element shows. As soon as that happens, crank up, scoot up north behind the ridge, and try to get behind the Hinds. If you can take 'em out without the OPs having to use their Stingers, do that. It'll keep them from having to give away their positions."

"Will do," Stephens said. "If there's only two of them, it won't be a problem. But we'll need the OPs' help if there's more than two."

"OK, Red. You guys ready?"

"We're ready, Major D. I just wish we had a couple more choppers backing us up."

"Yeah, me too, Red. And look . . . if I start asking you guys to do something that'll hang your asses out too far, say so. Without you guys, we won't be much good."

"No sweat, sir," Goodwin said. "If it doesn't sound right, we'll let you know in a heartbeat."

"All right, then," Denton said. "Stand by the killer eggs. I'd better burst a flash message to headquarters and make sure they're ready to start World War III."

He dictated a message to the radio operator. It was short, employing the code words that meant "Soviet forces sighted" and "I am prepared to engage." It read:

SECRET: ZZZZ BASE DE SWORD. WATCH XX WATCH. SMITE XX SMITE. SECRET AR

It took less than two minutes for the reply to arrive:

SECRET: ZZZZ SWORD DE BASE. RGR UR WATCH AND SMITE.
CRUSH XX CRUSH XX CRUSH. BT GOOD HUNTING. SECRET
AR

"Crush." It was the code word that meant "engage at will." Now there was nothing to do but wait until the Hinds, tanks, and armored personnel carriers of the motorized rifle regiment's forward security element appeared.

CHAPTER 10

1054 hours GMT (1424 hours local time), 26 September
Unconventional Warfare Operations Area Sword
Southwest of Zahedan, Iran

Just over twenty minutes after SFOD B-30 was given permission to engage the Soviet forces entering UWOA Sword, O'Neill reported spotting the lead elements of the forward security element.

"There are three tanks—T-72s or T-80s—leading. About a forty-meter interval. Behind them is a whole line of BTRs. I see seven or eight already. And here come the Hinds, over."

"How many?" Denton asked.

"I see two," the steady voice of Harry O'Neill replied.

"Roger, roger," Denton said. "Aphid Flight, you ready to crank?"

"That's affirm," Stephens replied over the radio. "Comin' hot!"

As the lead tanks pulled onto the three-hundred-meter-long straight stretch of road that the team had chosen as its primary killing zone OP Two reported, "This is Oscar Two. Lead tank's in the kill zone."

A moment later Red Stephens said, "Coming out. Where's the Hinds, and what's their altitude and direction?"

"They're a klick north of me," O'Neill replied, "flying north. About five hundred feet—lower than the ridge line, anyway."

"Roger. Aphid One and Two on the way. Give us about three minutes."

Flying two hundred meters apart, in trail, the two little

U.S. Army helicopters buzzed north, well below the ridge line and hugging the hillside to avoid being spotted. When they were about two kilometers north of OP One, Stephens heard OP Two report, "The lead tank's halted in the south end of the kill zone!"

"Where's the Hinds?" Stephens asked.

"This is Oscar One. Can't see 'em right now. Sounds like they're pretty far north."

"Roger," Stephens said. "I'm gonna ease up and take a peek."

His wingman went into a hover well below the crest of the ridge, far enough from the ground to avoid kicking up dust with his rotor blades. Stephens, also staying far enough back from the ridge to avoid blowing dust, eased his little helicopter higher and higher until his mast-mounted periscope enabled him to peek over the top of the ridge. He moved the tail from side to side. He was unable to see the road directly beneath the ridge, but he could see it about a kilometer north of him, for a distance of about two kilometers. It was covered with Soviet vehicles, some maintaining an interval of thirty to forty meters, others bunched up.

"Holy shit!" he said. "Looks like the whole damned Russian army! I can see about fifty vehicles. And there's the Hinds. They're turning back this way—heading south again."

"This is Oscar Two. Be advised, the tanks have all pulled off the road and stopped. And the BTRs are pulling off the road about a hundred meters behind them."

"This is One," O'Neill reported. "Looks like the whole column's stopping."

"Hey, Base!" Stephens called. "The Hinds have their gear lowered. Stand by. . . ."

What the hell's going on? Denton wondered. "Do you think they've spotted you, Red?" he asked.

"Negative. The gunships are slowing and descending. Can you see 'em yet, One?"

"This is One. Negative. Wait . . . yeah, here they come. Looks like they're landing on the road."

OP Two said, "That's a roger! I see 'em now. They're gonna land right behind the tanks."

Stephens swung his chopper's tail around and looked to the north. Above the column he saw a large helicopter approaching from the north.

"OK, Base," he called. "I've got another chopper headed this way. Looks like a Hook, or maybe a '26."

Although Mark Denton couldn't see it, he surmised what was happening. "A refueler!" he called over the radio. "It's probably a refueler for the Hinds or the vehicles. The gunships are probably landing to let him refuel them."

"This is Two. You could be right, Base. The Hinds are setting down on the road now."

"OK, everybody," Denton said, "get ready. Aphid, can you take out the refueler?"

"Not yet. He should be passing me in about a minute, though, and I can take him then."

"OK, standby. One and Two, can you illuminate the Hinds?"

"This is Two. I've got one camera on each now."

"One here," O'Neill answered. "Can't see the Hinds, but I've got a BTR with lots of antennas and another BTR on TV."

"This is Base," Major Denton said. "Aphid, take the refuel chopper as soon as he passes. Oscar Two, as soon as he fires, illuminate the Hinds with your lasers. Aphid Two will hit them. Oscar One will illuminate the BTRs next for Aphid One's Hellfires."

"Aphid Two's coming up now," the second helicopter called.

"Oscar One, roger."

"Oscar Two, roger."

"Aphid One. OK, the big bird's passing me now. . . . Here we go!"

In the cockpit of Red Stephens's H-500 the copilot, Bart Evans, said, "Two Stingers armed."

Stephens lifted his helicopter above the top of the ridge and placed the crosshairs of the through-the-mast weapons sight on the engines of the big Mi-26 Soviet helicopter.

He heard the beeping of the Stingers, indicating that they had acquired the heat signature of the enemy helicopter's engines, just as his copilot said, "Both Stingers locked on!"

With his hand on the weapon selector switch Stephens triggered the first missile, switched to the second, and fired it a moment later, then dived behind the ridge.

His wingman, Miles Goodwin, hovering behind the ridge five hundred meters to his south, watched the Stingers speed to their target, trailing plumes of white smoke. The Mi-26 took a rocket in each engine exhaust, and Aphid Two saw the engines burst apart, the rotor blades flying off in all directions. The body of the refueler exploded in midair a split second later, showering the column of vehicles below it with thousands of gallons of burning fuel.

"Target destroyed!" Goodwin called, then he turned his attention to the Hinds, now sitting in the road, their rotor blades barely turning as they shut down.

"Illuminate target, Oscar Two," he called when, a second later, his copilot said, "Hellfires armed."

Miles Goodwin saw the laser beam from one of the electronic OPs on the rear Hind and acquired it with his sight.

When the copilot announced, "Target acquired," Miles fired the laser-guided Hellfire missile, then ducked back behind the ridge. The ground-mounted laser target designator would guide the first streaking missile without further assistance from the helicopter that had launched it. Miles didn't see the missile slam into the rocket pod on the side of the enemy gunship, where the LTD's beam was fixed. Most of the thirty-two 57-mm high-explosive rockets in the pod exploded, detonating many of those in the pod mounted beside it as well. But several blasted out of their launch tubes and slammed into the other Mi-24 just ahead.

Seeing that both Hinds were knocked out by the first

Hellfire, Oscar Two called, "Both Hinds hit! Change target!"

While he remotely manipulated the electronic OP's TV camera onto one of the tanks, he heard Harry O'Neill in OP One announce, "Aphid One, Oscar One. Target illuminated."

"One fired," Red Stephens called a moment later.

Aphid Two had moved to another firing position by the time OP Two's remote camera zoomed in on the turret ring of the lead T-80 tank. "Aphid Two ready," Miles Goodwin reported.

"This is Oscar Two. Target tank."

"Illuminate," Goodwin directed. By now dozens of weapons were raking the ridge line in the areas where the earlier missile attacks had taken place, but Goodwin had moved his helicopter to an alternate firing position a half kilometer from his last Hellfire launch. He popped up above the ridge, acquired the laser beam, and punched off the Hellfire round. As he dived behind the ridge again he announced, "Aphid Two is on the way to rearm."

En route to the rearm point, Goodwin heard Stephens say, "Aphid One's ready. Illuminate, Oscar One."

"Target illuminated," O'Neill reported as he turned his laser target designator on.

"Two fired!" Stephens said. "I'm dry. Be right back, Oscar One!"

"This is Oscar Two. Target destroyed."

"And Oscar One, ditto!"

As the little gunships sped back to their hide site to rearm with another pair of Hellfires each, Mark Denton called SFC O'Neill. "Oscar One, this is Base. Status report?"

"This is Oscar One. We have one Mi-26 helicopter destroyed. It crashed onto four or five BTRs, all of which are burning. The first Hellfire destroyed another BTR—I think it was a command vehicle, because of the antennas—and the second one took out one other BTR. They're shooting the shit out of the ridge up here, but they're firing at ghosts. Also, they're blasting away at one of my electronic OPs, but they haven't hit it yet. We're ready to illuminate again when the choppers get back."

"Roger, roger," Denton said. "Any more Hinds around?"

"This is Oscar One. Nothin' I can see or hear, over."

"Roger, break. Oscar Two, this is Base."

"This is Oscar Two. I've got two Hinds burning in the kill zone. Also one tango eight zero tank. Quite a few bodies . . . wait."

A moment later he said, "This is OP Two. Another tank moved in line with one of my AT-4s. We got him in the ass, and he's burning, too! They're all shooting where the AT-4 was launched. There's nothing but confusion down there now, over!"

"This is Base. What's the status of your electronic OPs?"

"This is Oscar Two, wait." Denton heard as he watched the first H-500MD land in the rearm site. Cat Whitaker and her fellow ground crewman were standing ready, each hefting a Hellfire missile. Before OP Two called back, both missiles had been loaded and Aphid Two was lifting off.

"Aphid Two is en route to the kill zone with two hot Hellfires," Goodwin reported.

"Base, this is Oscar Two. They've knocked out one of my TVs, but I've still got one working. Also, I've fired one AT-4—three left. Ready to illuminate the next tank when Aphid Two gets back, over."

"This is Base, roger. OK, be sure to shoot your AT-4s whenever you have a target, guys. Aphid One's landing to rearm now. As soon as we shoot these loads I'm gonna have the choppers shut down and hide until we see how the Sovs react, over."

"Oscar One, roger."

"Oscar Two, roger."

"Aphid Flight copies."

Denton checked his watch. It hadn't been ten minutes since the first round had been fired. His team had destroyed three enemy helicopters, two T-80 tanks, and three BTR-80 armored personnel carriers. Four or five other BTRs were burning from the Soviet refuel helicopter's fiery crash. God only knew how many Russian soldiers and airmen had been killed or wounded. And all his team had lost was one electronic observation post.

But Denton didn't intend to push his good luck too far. He would have everyone lay low after the H-500s fired two more Hellfire missiles each and wait to see how the Soviets reacted to the devastating high-tech ambush.

"Base, this is Oscar One," O'Neill reported. "There's all kinds of artillery hitting up here now, over."

"Roger, Oscar One. How effective?" Denton replied.

"Not very. They just seem to be pokin' and hopin', over."

"Aphid Two is rearmed and coming out," Red Stephens reported from the rearm position.

"Aphid Two, Oscar One is ready to illuminate two BTRs when you're ready to shoot," O'Neill called.

"Roger, Harry. Gimme a couple of minutes."

Before Aphid Two could get into position to fire, O'Neill reported, "A BRDM just moved in front of one of my AT-4s. We got him. There are troops assaulting the location it was fired from, over."

That meant that the Soviets would soon know that remotely fired antitank rockets were being used against them. Once they found the AT-4's disposable launcher and the remote firing device wired to it, they would realize that they were being hit by command-detonated munitions. But what their response would be Mark Denton could only guess.

His thoughts were interrupted by the radio transmissions between the H-500 pilots and the Special Forces men in their hidden observation posts.

In short order, all four Hellfire missiles were loosed at the enemy, accounting for the destruction of the last T-80 tank in the forward security element and two more BTRs. In addition, another BTR moved into the kill zone of one of Oscar Two's AT-4 antitank rockets and was immobilized.

A few minutes later the killer eggs returned to the hide

site and shut down. While the flight crews folded the rotor blades and camouflaged the helicopters, the ground crew rearmed and refueled them.

From two ridge lines to his east Mark Denton could hear sporadic artillery fire as the Soviets searched in vain for their hidden tormentors.

Half an hour later both Oscar One and Oscar Two reported that dismounted enemy troops were spreading out along the road and moving up the steep, rocky ridge line. SFC O'Neill, the leader of OP One, said, "Tell you what, boss. I think we'd be well advised to fire off the rest of the AT-4s and the Dragon we have up here, then hightail it for the next ridge line before they can get up here to us. What say, OP Two?"

"Roger, roger!" the senior NCO in OP Two said. "If we don't, they're gonna roll us up!"

"This is Base," Denton said. "Do it. Are you going to destroy your alternate caches?"

"This is Oscar One." O'Neill reported. "I'm gonna drop down there and pick up the Dragon now. We'll blow up the electronic OPs, then fire both Dragon rounds. Also one of the Stinger rounds, just to get rid of it. Then we'll haul ass out of here with the briefcases and the other round in the Stinger launcher, in case another Hind shows up. Can you handle that, Two?"

"Affirm. But hustle. I'm blowing my AT-4s now, before the Russians get to them, over."

"Roger, Two. Me, too. Report when you're ready to fire the Dragons."

"This is Two. Wilco."

It was several minutes before Oscar Two, breathing heavily, called O'Neill. "OK, One, this is Two. Gimme a minute, and I'll be all set up."

O'Neill replied, "This is Oscar One. Roger. Let me know when you're ready to blow the OPs. Once that's done, we'll get set with the Dragon and Stinger, over."

A minute later Oscar Two said, "One, this is Two. I just blew up one of the OPs in the Russians' faces. I'm blowing the other one now."

O'Neill picked up the M-122 remote firing device

transmitter and punched in the code for the receiver that was wired to one of his electronic OPs. It was the same transmitter the OPs had used to remotely launch their AT-4 antitank rockets. But the receiver with the code he had now selected was connected to a blasting cap, and the blasting cap was in a block of C-4 plastic explosive that O'Neill had molded around the top of the electronic observation post. He pressed the Fire button, and the pound and a quarter of C-4, with a detonating velocity of 26,000 feet per second, blew the miniature TV camera, laser target designator, and remote control device to bits. O'Neill then punched in the code to the receiver wired to his other remote OP, and the same thing happened.

All four electronic OPs the four Special Forces men had used were now blown to bits. Even though the TV camera of one of them had been hit by enemy fire, the remote firing device was still working, and it destroyed the damaged OP.

The detonations of the exploding devices caused the Russian infantrymen to drop to the ground and fire wildly in front of them. Their fire caused no damage, but it gave the men on top of the ridge above them time to prepare their Dragon and Stinger missiles for firing.

"Oscar One's ready to fire our Stinger and first Dragon," O'Neill announced.

"This is Oscar Two. We're ready."

"All right, Two. Stand by . . . fire!"

From both positions there was a blast, and two Dragon missiles sped down the slope past the prone Soviet infantrymen. Another BTR-80 exploded, and yet another was badly damaged. Seconds later two Stinger missiles streaked down from the ridge top, hit the ground, and exploded. One explosion caused only psychological damage, but the other occurred between two Soviet soldiers, wounding both.

The two Americans in each OP dashed from their hidden positions, each team taking their remaining Dragon, Stinger launcher, remote control "briefcases," radio, rucksacks, and rifles. In spite of their heavy, bulky loads, they were gone before the Soviets' fire began raking their former firing positions.

While his teammate reloaded the Stinger launcher from the cache behind the ridge, one man from each team moved well away from the points at which the enemy fire was concentrated. They attached the sight to their remaining Dragon round, crawled to the top of the hill, and fired another antitank missile. O'Neill was able to keep his sight's crosshairs on his target and destroy still another armored personnel carrier. The other Dragon gunner began receiving fire from an AGS-17 30-mm automatic grenade launcher while his missile was still in flight. He dived for cover. The rocket smashed into ground and exploded harmlessly.

Then, burdened with their heavy loads, the four Special Forces soldiers began a mad scramble down the back side of the ridge. By the time the Soviet infantry officers were able to get their troops up and moving, the Americans had reached the valley and scrambled across it. When the Russians finally reached the top of the ridge their adversaries had taken cover amid the rocks near the bottom of the next ridge line.

One American had twisted his ankle, and all were panting thirstily and nearly exhausted. But they were safe—for the time being, at least.

Sergeant First Class O'Neill called his commander on the radio and reported that all four men were safe.

"We got a few more vehicles before we hauled ass," O'Neill reported. "We'll stay here until after dark, then start making our way to your location."

"Roger, copy," Denton replied. "Can you observe the ridge line you just left?"

"Affirmative," O'Neill replied. "The Sovs are just milling around up there right now."

"OK, Oscar One. If they start coming after you again, give me a holler. The killer eggs have dropped their Hellfires and mounted miniguns, in case you need their help."

"Roger that," O'Neill said. "Right now all we need's a few cold beers, over."

Denton was pleased to hear that bit of humor from his subordinate. It had been a dangerous, stressful experiment, this first test of a handful of Americans versus vastly superior numbers of Soviet men and materiel. But the American men had performed with unhesitating courage and had inflicted heavy damage on the invading Soviet force. Even in the face of pursuit by scores of infantrymen supported by artillery and heavy machine guns, they had held to their positions as long as possible before withdrawing.

It was a magnificent performance, and Mark Denton's only regret was that he had not personally taken part in the fight. As he tallied up the results of B-30's first battle for his report to headquarters he resolved to get more directly involved.

1225 hours GMT (1555 hours local time), 26 September
On the road southeast of Zahedan, Iran

While the Americans of SFOD B-30 were wreaking havoc on the Soviet motorized rifle regiment on the western road between Zahedan and Khash, the tank regiment on the eastern road was momentarily halted. The regimental commander had called a hasty meeting of his subordinate commanders, and Valnikov and his fellow company commanders had joined their battalion commanders at the tank regiment commander's vehicle.

"All right," the aging colonel said, standing atop his armored personnel carrier. "Our sister regiment has been hit on the west road. It appears to be a well-armed force of *dushman*—perhaps Iranian- or even American-advised—with Stingers and antiarmor missiles. They're probably concentrated over there, judging from the amount of damage they've done, so it isn't likely that we'll be hit. We need to move quickly though, since our comrades have been temporarily held up. But the presence of the *dushman* and their weapons is not the most disturbing news from our sister regiment. More worrisome is the fact that some of the infantrymen have acted cowardly—questioning their officers, failing to react to their orders, shying away from battle. Their officers have had to shoot several of the bastards, including one gutless company commander."

He paused and looked each of his assembled subordinates in the eye. "That's what this pig shit *glasnost* has led to. Now, let me make something perfectly plain. Any—*any*—failure of a member of this regiment to react immediately to orders, or to hesitate to do his duty, or to complain about *any* single thing will be met immediately by a bullet from his officer's pistol. Further, if I hear of one instance of an officer tolerating a single breach of discipline, *this* will be his fate!"

The colonel drew his Markarov pistol, aimed it at the chest of a captain of artillery standing before him, and fired three rounds in rapid succession.

The other officers gasped, those nearest the groaning, mortally wounded artillery officer not daring to move a muscle.

"Comrade Captain Pig Prick there," the colonel said as he holstered his pistol, "decided to ignore the order against listening to imperialist propaganda broadcasts. What you have just witnessed is a demonstration of how I expect each of you to handle any such breach of discipline. Now return to your units and prepare to move."

As he trotted back to his tank Senior Lieutenant Valnikov, realizing that his colonel's pistol could just as easily have been used on him, slipped the little radio from his pocket and tossed it aside. The colonel was right, of course. An army exists to obey the will of its government, and without discipline an army cannot function. So be it. He would obey his orders, enforce discipline in his company, and let the politicians decide when and where the army fought. Still, this campaign seemed to make so little sense. . . .

CHAPTER 11

1814 hours GMT (2144 hours local), 26 September
Unconventional Warfare Operations Area Tiger
A drop zone south of Khash, Iran

Captain Rocco Birelli watched the approach of the Combat Talon aircraft through his night-vision monocular. The airplane was on approach to make a surface-to-air recovery of the Soviet equipment Birelli's team and the Baluchi guerrillas had taken from the crashed resupply helicopter two nights before. He saw the yoke on the nose of the black four-engined Combat Talon hit the lift line attached to the equipment bundle on the ground below. The bundle lifted off the rocky drop zone, hung there momentarily, and was gone.

By then, the other Special Forces men and the guerrillas had completed the job of recovering and dividing up the equipment the Talon had dropped to them by parachute twenty minutes earlier.

There were TOW 2 weapons systems, Stinger and Dragon missiles, 60-mm mortar and small-arms ammunition, and antitank mines, as well as combat rations, water, and some lightweight camouflage nets in desert patterns. There was also a sizable quantity of oats in fifty-pound bags—feed for the Baluchi tribesmen's horses.

Birelli moved to the edge of the drop zone where the men were loading up the horses and preparing to move out to their next base camp. His half of the A team and seventy of the Baluchi guerrillas would move north to hit the Soviets as they entered A-326's unconventional warfare operations area, UWOA Tiger, from the north.

Their efforts would be concentrated along the road between the towns of Khash and Zaboli. South of them, the rest of A-326, under the command of the detachment executive officer, Fred Kaminski, would be preparing to engage the Soviets from Khash south to Iranshar.

Intelligence reports from the Special Forces Operations Base in England indicated that the Soviets' progress had been considerably slower than expected. They had encountered heavy resistance around Zahedan, the report said, and Birelli assumed that the Mujahadeen guerrillas there had been resupplied by the U.S. and were slowing the Soviets. Whatever the reason, Birelli was glad that he'd have a few more days to prepare his guerrillas to take on the Soviet armed forces when they arrived.

1832 hours GMT (2202 hours local), 26 September
Unconventional Warfare Operations Area Sword

At the command post in the barren mountains southwest of Zahedan, Major Mark Denton was awakened by Sergeant Cat Whitaker, who was on radio watch.

"Sir. Major Denton," she said, shaking his shoulder. He bolted upright, at first unable to connect the woman's voice with his surroundings. Then he said, "Oh, Sergeant Whitaker. Yeah. What's up?"

"Oscar Three just called, sir. He's got a column of vehicles approaching his sector, about five kilometers north."

Denton pulled on his boots, stumbled to the AN/PRC-117 radio, and called OP Three. It was the northernmost of his two observation posts on the eastern road between Zahedan and Khash.

Staff Sergeant Darryl Tippy, the NCO in charge of the two OPs on the eastern road, said, "I've got four or five vehicles a few klicks north of me now, and a bunch more following them by a couple of klicks. Can't identify the type yet, though, over."

"Roger, Three. Any sign of aircraft, over?"

"Negative, Base," Tippy answered. "Haven't seen anything since those jets over your way this afternoon." Late in the afternoon two Soviet jets—probably reconnaissance aircraft—had appeared above the site of the earlier battle. After making several passes over the ridges to the west, dropping magnesium flares to fool any Stinger missiles that might be fired at them, the aircraft departed.

"OK, Three. It's probably the tank regiment's recon element, followed by the forward security force. I'm gonna get the killer eggs standing by. Keep me informed."

The pilots were sleeping near their camouflaged helicopters. When Denton woke them and explained what was happening, Red Stephens said, "Tanks, huh? Well, let's get these weapons systems changed, men. I want a TOW pod and a Hellfire pod on each bird." Immediately the ground crewmen and the copilots went to work to remove the minigun from each chopper, replacing it with a two-round TOW 2 antitank missile launcher.

Staff Sergeant Tippy called from OP Three while they were making the change. "I've got the lead vehicles in sight on my north TV," he reported. "Tracks. Looks like three BMPs and a ZSU-23, over. . . . Wait, make that three BMPs and *two* ZSUs."

"This is Base, roger. I'll pass that on to the pilots."

The tank regiment was leading with three BMP armored personnel carriers—each carrying an AT-5 Spandrel antitank missile, a 73-mm gun, and a coaxially mounted 7.62-mm machine gun in its turret—and two ZSU-23-4 self-propelled antiaircraft systems. The ZSU-23-4s each mounted four liquid-cooled 23-mm automatic cannons and a fire-control radar. Each vehicle could fire about sixty rounds of 23-mm high-explosive ammunition per second, to an effective range of 2,500 meters. It was a potent weapon for defending against armed helicopters and could be used with great effect against ground positions as well.

Birelli informed the pilots of the presence of the

ZSU-23 vehicles in the lead element of the enemy regiment.

"Oh, shit!" Miles Goodwin exclaimed. "I'd rather have a sister in a whorehouse than take on a ZSU-23."

"Now, Miles, my man," Red Stephens said, "don't talk like that. The major will think we don't want to fly for him, and we'll *never* get no Distinguished Flying Cross that way. We'll just sneak up and take those dudes out first. Now, let's get these killer eggs hummin' and go get us some more Commies."

Denton had intended to let the small lead element of the enemy force pass before hitting them, as he had done on the western road. There would be many more vehicles available as targets in the brief engagement that way—what was called, in Pentagonese, a "target-rich environment."

As if reading Denton's thoughts, Stephens said, "We'll let the point element get well past your boys before we hit 'em. We should be able to take out all five of them, then come back here and rearm before we start using the OPs to lase targets for us."

"Well, just be careful, Red," Denton said.

"No sweat," Stephens replied. "If the fuzzbusters go off, we'll duck." Turning to the other pilots, he added, "OK, let's get it done."

Three minutes later the helicopters lifted off. As they buzzed south, hugging the valley floor, Denton saw a glint of light as the waning moon reflected off the Plexiglas bubble of one of them.

They flew south for several miles, then turned left into a narrow valley leading toward the first of the two roads running south from Zahedan. As they approached the road Stephens directed his wingman to hover while he eased his aircraft forward to check the road. Looking at the FLIR—forward-looking infrared—screen as Stephens turned his aircraft to the left and right, the copilot said, "Nothing along the road down here that I can see."

"Me neither. OK, Aphid Two, let's cross."

The choppers continued east until they got to the second road, then repeated the road-crossing procedure.

They continued east, crossed another ridge line, then turned north, toward OPs Three and Four.

"Oscar Three, this is Aphid Flight. We're one ridge east of the road, headed north. What's the story there?"

"This is Oscar Three. The five vehicles in the point element passed here about five minutes ago. Should be a klick or so south of us by now. The other vehicles are still about two klicks from us."

"Roger, three. Aphid's gonna kill the five vehicles that just passed you—knock on wood. Then we'll go rearm and come back to your area."

"Uh, OK, Aphid. But don't take too long. They'll be passing here before long."

When, according to his global positioning system readout, he was three kilometers south of OP Three, Stephens eased his helicopter up beside the ridge between him and the road. When his mast-mounted sight was able to peer into the valley below, he saw the vehicles coming down the valley road. Lowering his helicopter behind the ridge, he said, "OK, Two, they're about five hundred meters to my north. Ease up here a couple of hundred meters north of me and find yourself a firing position. I'll take the lead ZSU, which is third in line. You take the second one—the last vehicle."

Goodwin buzzed past him, then brought his H-500 to a hover and lifted it until he could see above the ridge. "Got him in sight."

"Roger," Stephens said, easing his chopper higher until he acquired his target. "On my command. . . . Arm Hellfires."

"Hellfires armed."

"Identify and acquire target."

"Target ID'ed and acquired."

"Fire at will!"

Both helicopters rose above the ridge top momentarily, keeping the crosshairs of their mast-mounted sights on their targets. "Laser on," each pilot directed. The copilots activated the laser in the mast of each chopper. They were both on target, and the pilots fired their Hellfire missiles, lighting the top of the ridge. Before the crewmen of the Soviet vehicles could react, the missiles struck home. Stephens reported, "Target destroyed!" as he saw his target explode in a ball of flame.

"Shit!" his wingman exclaimed. "Dud round!"

Goodwin dropped behind the ridge and dashed two hundred meters north, then popped up above the ridge again. It was easy to spot his target. The undamaged ZSU-23-4 was already pouring bursts of 23-mm tracer ammunition at the location from which Goodwin had fired his last missile.

Goodwin activated his laser but couldn't keep it fixed on his target, which was still moving. The ZSU gunner saw the laser beam and shifted his fire toward its source. Aphid Two dropped behind the ridge before the fire reached him.

Looking south, Goodwin saw a laser beam from Stephens's helicopter, five hundred meters away. The ZSU shifted the fire of its four cannons toward Stephens, and, as Aphid One "ducked," Goodwin popped up again, acquired the target in his sight, and fired his laser. Before the ZSU could again shift its fire, Goodwin launched his second Hellfire at it.

The second round detonated, and the tracked vehicle exploded. In the other burning vehicle the 23-mm ammunition was cooking off and exploding.

"Two," Stephens said, "I'm gonna head south, cross the road, and hit 'em from the other side of the road. I'll call when I'm ready."

"Roger that," Goodwin replied, turning north. When he was five hundred meters north of the burning vehicles he peered over the ridge, acquired the rear BMP in his sight, and directed his copilot, "Arm TOW!"

"One armed!"

He lifted the little helicopter until the weapons pod was above the ridge, fired the missile, then eased down behind the ridge until only the rotor-top sight was exposed. He held the crosshairs of his sight on the rear of the BMP as the optically tracked missile zoomed toward its target, trailing an ultrathin guidance wire behind it.

The troop door in the rear of the BMP was open, and

the missile entered it and exploded. Goodwin watched in fascination as the vehicle's turret lifted thirty feet into the air atop a giant fireball.

"Rear 'bimp' destroyed!" he called on the radio. "Your turn next, Aphid One."

"Good job. Gimme a minute, Aphid Two," Stephens said.

"This is Oscar Three," Staff Sergeant Tippy reported from his observation post several kilometers to the helicopters' north. "Be advised the infantry in the forward security element is dismounting and moving off the sides of the road up here! We're gonna have to start firing our AT-4s before they find 'em!"

"Aphid One, roger. We'll finish up here, rearm, and get back to you quick as we can."

The men in OPs Three and Four scanned the points at which their 84-mm remotely fired rockets were aimed. A T-80 tank rumbled into the kill zone of one AT-4. The man observing it on his remote TV monitor fired the rocket, and it struck the reactive armor on the tank's turret. There was a bright flash, but the Soviet tank rumbled on. The reactive armor had done its job, and the AT-4's shaped-charge warhead was rendered ineffective against the tank, although fragments wounded several nearby infantrymen.

To the south, Red Stephens—now behind the ridge to the west of the enemy point element—popped up and engaged the lead BMP with a TOW 2 missile. While Red's missile was still in flight, Goodwin launched one from the ridge above the opposite side of the road. Both BMPs were destroyed.

Stephens changed position. With his second Hellfire he engaged the only vehicle in the element that wasn't burning. It, too, exploded in flames.

"Aphid Two's expended," Goodwin announced over the frequency-hopping radio. "I'm heading for base to rearm."

"Roger," Red Stephens answered. "I'll be there shortly." He raised his helicopter to an altitude that enabled him to see over the ridge. In the valley below him all five

Soviet vehicles in the tank regiment's point element were burning. On his FLIR monitor he could see the forms of a number of men huddled together off the side of the road. He fixed them in his sight, popped up, and fired, holding the crosshairs on the group of men. The TOW missile exploded in the midst of them.

"Poor bastards," Stephens said, then he keyed his radio and announced, "Aphid Two's en route to base to rearm."

Senior Lieutenant Valnikov heard the panicked calls of the regimental commander's radio operator trying to raise the reconnaissance element that was several kilometers to their south. He was about to call to inform the man that he was on the wrong net, when he saw a flash well forward of him in the long column of tanks. The commander of the company forward of him yelled, "This is Minsk! We just took a hit! No damage, though . . . the reactive armor took care of it."

Valnikov heard his battalion commander order the attached infantry company to dismount and sweep along the sides of the dusty road for security. The column halted, and Valnikov said aloud, "No! Keep going, you fools! Get past them!" But he saw another explosion in the column of tanks far to his front as, to his left, a BMP roared past. It was his battalion commander, rushing forward to direct the unit's reaction to the enemy ambush.

Miles Goodwin was lifting off when Stephens landed at the rearm point. While the ground crew reloaded two Hellfires and two TOW missiles into the weapons pods, Stephens hopped out of the chopper to urinate. Before he finished, Cat Whitaker slapped him on the back and said, "You're loaded, chief! Go get 'em!"

On the way back to support OPs Three and Four the helicopter pilots heard Oscar Four report, "I just got a tank with an AT-4. It blew his track off, but he's firing at the empty launcher."

Five minutes later the H-500s were operating from

behind the ridge line to the east of the tank regiment's forward security element. They had each engaged a T-80 with a Hellfire, destroying one of them and disabling the other, when Goodwin said, "Aphid One, this is Aphid Two. I'm gonna buzz up north a couple of klicks and see what's up there. Be right back."

Red Stephens, holding his sight at the point on a T-80 tank where the turret and hull joined, watched the TOW streak toward it and didn't answer until after he saw the tank explode. Then he said, "Roger, Two. See if you can find something with lots of antennas on it." Antennas meant radios, and any Soviet vehicle with more than one or two radios had occupants that included someone of considerable importance. Knocking out such vehicles would do much to add to the enemy's confusion.

During Goodwin's flight north Stephens, heeding his own advice, destroyed a BMP with three antennas.

Valnikov saw three explosions in succession as the unseen enemy's antitank missiles did their job. The radio nets of both the battalion and his own company were filled with panicked calls, and on his net he ordered, "Get off the net! Get off the net, you bastards, and direct your guns toward the flanks—odd numbers left, even numbers right!"

He lifted his field glasses to his eyes and attempted to scan the ridges to his left front in the dim moonlight. As he did so his peripheral vision caught a flash of light from his left rear, and he lowered his glasses and glanced in that direction. Suddenly, several vehicles ahead of him in the column, his battalion commander's BMP lifted noticeably into the air as it exploded. He grasped the commander's override and traversed the tank's turret toward the area from which the missile had been fired. He dropped into the turret and peered through the sight, triggering the coaxially mounted machine gun. He watched the green tracers rake the area where he suspected the *dushman* had fired their weapon, hoping that, if he didn't kill them, he would at least cause them to flee. It was a futile effort. By the time he fired, Stephens had dropped his killer egg behind the ridge and sped off in search of another target.

When Goodwin, in Aphid Two, was four kilometers north of Stephens, he lifted his chopper's mast-mounted sight above the ridge and searched the column of vehicles for one with several antennas.

He spotted an artillery command and reconnaissance vehicle and told his copilot, "There's an ACRV. Arm a TOW."

"One TOW armed!"

Goodwin eased his helicopter above the ridge, put the crosshairs of his sight on the side of the ACRV, and fired a TOW 2 missile. As Goodwin tracked the missile's flight to its target the gunner of a ZSU-23-4 antiaircraft system, who had seen the glint of the moon reflecting off the Plexiglas canopy of the helicopter even before it fired, brought his guns to bear on it. He loosed a burst of fire from his four 23-mm rapid-fire cannons.

Miles Goodwin saw two simultaneous flashes. One was from his TOW missile exploding on the Soviet ACRV; the other was from a 23-mm high-explosive round detonating on the canopy of the Hughes 500MD helicopter. The copilot took the brunt of the round's fragments. Several shards of hot metal tore into his face and chest while one piece ripped into Goodwin's right arm. He nearly lost control of the helicopter but regained his grip on the control stick and dived behind the ridge as the ZSU gunner's second burst of fire passed just overhead.

"You all right?" he asked his copilot. The man beside him in the tiny cockpit said nothing but slumped forward against his shoulder harness.

Goodwin keyed his radio, scanning his instruments as he did so. "Aphid One, this is Two. I've taken a hit. Still flyable, but George is hurt. I'm headed for base."

"Say your position," Stephens called.

"I'm, uh, about a mile north of where I last saw you."

"OK, Miles. Are you hurt?"

"Little bit. Something hit my right forearm, but I can't check on it right now."

"One copies. You need to set down and trade pilots?"

"Negative. I'm OK to get to base—so far, anyway. Kill all the bastards you can before you break off. I'll see you back there."

"Roger!" Stephens had another T-80 tank in his sights, and he launched his remaining TOW at it. The round hit the reactive armor on the tank's turret, but the tandem warheads negated the armor's effect, and a jet of super-heated gases from the shaped charge blasted into the tank's ammunition, triggering a massive explosion.

"Tank destroyed! Aphid One's dry and headed home. Where you at, Miles?"

"I'm right behind you. Just saw you shoot and scoot."

"OK, follow me home." Stephens didn't bother to check the east road before he crossed it. He knew that they had destroyed all five vehicles of the point element on that road. But when he reached the west road he told Goodwin, "Hang on here a minute, buddy. Let me check the road before we cross." They had allowed the point element of the Soviet column on that axis—four eight-wheeled BTRs—to pass untouched earlier in the day. The BTRs hadn't been seen since.

Stephens pulled up behind a low hill near the road and peered over the top, executing pedal turns to scan the road with his FLIR.

"There!" his copilot announced. "They're laagered on both sides of the road, about a klick and a half north."

"All right, Two," Stephens said, "we'll move south another klick before we cross."

Major Denton came on the radio as the helicopters made their way back to the hide site. "Aphid Flight, be advised that Oscar One and Two are here now. The medic's standing by to help your wounded man. Break. Oscar Three, what's your situation?"

From OP Three Staff Sergeant Tippy replied, "I've got one AT-4 left to fire. Still haven't used the laser in either OP, and they're sweeping too far down the ridge to find them. What about you, Oscar Four?"

"This is Four. I've expended two AT-4s and have two left. Another BMP's about to . . . wait, out."

Ten seconds later he said, "All right! Scratch one more 'bimp!' I now have one AT-4 left. We haven't used our lasers, either, but one of them's pretty close to the road. They might find it, but I'll blow it up if it looks like they're going to. They're as fucked up as a soup sandwich down there right now, though. There are tracked vehicles burning all over the place, and ammo cookin' off in most of them. People running around everywhere, over."

"This is Base, roger," Denton said. "Just sit tight and keep reporting. Are you taking any fire?"

"This is Three, negative. They shoot the shit out of the launcher every time we fire a rocket, but there's nothing coming up here."

"This is Four," the other observation post reported. "Same here. They fire away at the AT-4 blasts, but other than that, it just looks like they're cutting loose at shadows."

"This is Base. Roger that. Keep your heads down, keep reporting, and I'll get back to you when we get the killer eggs sorted out," Denton said.

CHAPTER 12

1944 hours GMT (2314 hours local time), 26 September
Detachment B-30 hide site in the mountains southwest of Zahedan
Unconventional Warfare Operations Area Sword

The helicopters landed one behind the other beside the rearm/refuel point. Stephens and his copilot hopped out and ran to the helicopter behind theirs, where the Special Forces medic from SFC O'Neill's team was already checking on the severely wounded copilot.

"Let's get him out," the medic said, and several people helped him do so.

As Miles Goodwin climbed out holding his injured forearm, Stephens asked, "What happened?"

"Fuckin' ZSU," Goodwin said. "I was hitting another track and didn't see him. One round in the bubble—at least, I think that's all."

They examined the windshield on the copilot's side. There was a jagged four-inch hole where the 23-mm round had detonated.

"You gonna fly again, Mr. Stephens?" the female helicopter mechanic, Cat Whitaker, asked.

"Maybe. Anyway, go ahead and rearm and refuel me, then check this one for any other damage. Let's have a look at that arm of yours, Miles."

Goodwin's right forearm had a deep, jagged gash in it, but it wasn't bleeding much, and he could rotate his wrist, though with some difficulty. "I'll be all right," he said. "What about George?"

Stephens moved to where the medic was working on the wounded copilot, Warrant Officer George Jones. The medic had cut away Jones's fire-retardant flight suit and was inserting a needle in the man's wrist to start an IV. Another Special Forces soldier was holding a bandage over a hole in the aviator's blood-covered chest. There was also blood spurting from a small wound in his neck, and the unconscious man's face was covered with blood.

Major Denton said, "Let's back off and give him room to work." While one of the Special Forces NCOs dressed Goodwin's arm, Denton and Stephens stood in the dark and discussed their situation.

"By my count," Denton said, "we've knocked out well over twenty vehicles today, and three choppers. I think it's time to pull back, see if we can get Jones evacuated—"

"From the looks of him, I don't think he'll make it, sir," Stephens interrupted.

"Yeah. I hope you're wrong, but it doesn't look good."

Cat Whitaker came to them and said, "One's topped off, armed, and ready to go, Mr. Stephens. We've only got two Hellfires and two TOWs left—three, counting the ones in Mr. Goodwin's tubes. I'm going to check his bird for damage now."

"OK, thanks, Cat," Stephens said. Then, to Denton, he said, "Sir, if we're going to pull out of here, let me expend what we have left. They're so confused down there that they're sitting ducks right now. I could be finished in half an hour."

Denton considered Stephens's request. Perhaps it would be good to expend the remaining ammunition from this cache while the situation allowed it. "I've got to get Oscar Three and Four headed this way, anyhow. If you could shoot from the east ridge while they're firing their Dragons from the west—"

"You got it," Red said. "I'm outta here. Let's go, Bart!" he called to his copilot.

Denton called observation posts Three and Four and told them to be prepared to expend the four Dragon missiles they had when Aphid One arrived, then start moving south.

"What's with Aphid Two?" Tippy asked from OP Three.

"He took a twenty-three-millimeter round," Denton answered. "Two's down, for now."

"Understand," Tippy said. "Advise One that I've got another ZSU on TV right now. Let me know before he pops up, and I'll use my first Dragon on the ZSU."

"Aphid One copies. That would be a giant help, Tip, ol' buddy."

As Stephens's H-500 buzzed away to wreak further destruction on the Soviets, O'Neill came over to Denton and said, "Sir, Mr. Jones is dead."

"Oh, Christ," Denton muttered. "OK, Harry. Get him ready to bury, then start breaking down here. As soon as Mr. Stephens shoots the last of his missiles we've got to start moving south."

"Wilco, sir. What about the miniguns and their ammo, the fuel, and all of that?"

"We'll have to see if the damaged chopper's gonna be flyable first. We may have to destroy it, along with the other stuff. I'll let you know."

2013 hours GMT (2343 hours local), 26 September
Unconventional Warfare Operations Area Sword

Red Stephens came to a hover behind a ridge well south of where the four BTR-80s of the recon element on the west road were laagered. He rose until he could see them, sighted in on one with its rear to him, armed a TOW, and fired. He held the crosshairs on the target until the missile detonated, then sped across the road and through a gap in the ridge ahead of him. He crossed the second road, climbed over the ridge above it, then turned north toward the glow of the burning Russian armor.

When he was behind the ridge abreast of the OPs he called to ask if they were ready.

"That's affirm, Aphid One," OP Three replied. "I'm sighted in on the only ZSU-23 I can see, ready to give him a Dragon."

Stephens's mast-mounted sight was above the ridge

top, and he zeroed in on a T-80 tank and said, "I'm ready when you are."

"Here goes!"

Stephens saw two flashes atop the opposite ridge as the OPs each fired a Dragon. He activated his laser, brought his helicopter up slightly, and launched a Hellfire. The three missiles hit almost simultaneously, though one of the Dragons struck a tank's reactive armor, doing little damage. The Hellfire ignited the tank, and Tippy's Dragon detonated into the ZSU's ammunition, creating a secondary explosion.

While the men in the OPs scooted off to their next Dragon firing positions, Stephens flew north a half mile in search of another ZSU-23-4 antiaircraft system. After several peeks over the ridge he still hadn't found one, but he saw a BMP mounting several antennas moving forward past the line of halted vehicles. He hovered behind the ridge until he heard OP Four announce that he was ready with his next Dragon.

"OK, Four. I'm firing now," Stephens said, then cut loose with a TOW. He dropped until only the mast was above the ridge while the missile sought the target in his sight. As the BMP erupted, a burst of 23-mm fire cracked past above the helicopter. A ZSU about a kilometer north of him had spotted the TOW's launch and was aiming for the source of fire. By the time it fired a second burst, Stephens was behind the ridge, headed south.

He heard Oscar Four announce that he was ready with his last Dragon. Stephens was about to peek over the ridge in search of a target when the helicopter's radar detection device began to buzz in his ear. He dropped lower behind the ridge, but the buzzing continued.

Denton's voice came over the radio. "I hear jets!" he said. "Jet aircraft to my east!"

Stephens quickly maneuvered his helicopter in for a landing at the foot of the ridge, telling his copilot, "Down-looking radar! They've got us painted."

It was probably an Su-27 counterair fighter, Stephens thought as he bounced to a landing and killed the

H-500's engine, the radar detector still buzzing in his ear. The Su-27, with the NATO code name "Flanker," was the only Soviet aircraft he knew of that had a look-down/shoot-down capability.

As he jumped from the helicopter Stephens pulled out the small carbon dioxide fire extinguisher from the cockpit. He pulled the pin and began spraying the engine cowling with it. He hoped the fire extinguisher's cooling effect would fool any heat-seeking missile locked on the engine. When it was empty he ran for cover with his copilot.

High above him the Soviet fighter pilot saw the radar blip of his target disappear as he launched an air-to-air missile. The missile lost the heat signature it was following and slammed harmlessly into the ground a mile or more from Stephens's helicopter.

The fighter pilot continued to search the skies around the burning heaps on the road below him but was unable to acquire another radar target amid the ground clutter. His quarry had apparently escaped. He and his wingman continued their search for more than half an hour, until they were low on fuel and had to retire.

They were replaced by two Su-24 Fencer ground attack fighters, which began to bomb and strafe the ridge lines on either side of the east road. But, although the OP teams were barely missed on the first run, the Fencers' bombs and cannons did the Americans no harm. When they made their second run, Staff Sergeant Tippy, halfway down the ridge to the west, acquired the trail aircraft's twin engines with his Stinger and fired. He dropped the launcher and dashed down the hillside in search of cover, not waiting to see that the Stinger caught its target and exploded in one of the tailpipes.

The Soviet Fencer pilot tried for several minutes to maintain control of his aircraft as it climbed toward the south. Finally, unable to make the aircraft respond, the two-man crew ejected from their smoke-filled cockpit fourteen thousand feet above Khash, Iran.

When he could no longer hear the sound of aircraft overhead in the still night air, Red Stephens returned to his helicopter and turned on the power to his radios. Staff Sergeant Tippy was talking to someone.

"OK, Base," Tippy was saying, "we'll keep heading south while the other chopper's looking for them. If we see anything, we'll give Aphid Two a call."

Stephens couldn't hear the response from Base. There were too many ridges between the two stations, and the FM radios couldn't reach each other.

"Oscar Three, this is Aphid One, over."

"Say again call sign?" Tippy responded.

"I say again, this is Aphid One. We're down behind a hill to your east. We had a continuous radar hit on our fuzzbuster and had to shut down. We're OK, though, over."

"Roger, roger, Aphid One. Base, you copy? . . . Affirm. He's behind a hill east of us. Says he's OK. . . . Wilco, break. Aphid One, this is Oscar Three. Will you be returning to base?"

"That's most affirm. We're cranking now."

2128 hours GMT, 26 September (0058 hours local time, 27 September)
Unconventional Warfare Operations Area Tiger, south of Khash, Iran

Far to the south, several of the Baluchi tribesmen with Master Sergeant Jake Brady were scanning the skies above them. They had heard a jet aircraft making unusual noises and then had seen a flash before the aircraft's engine noise stopped.

There was a flash on the ground well to their south, and Brady watched the glow from there momentarily, then searched the starlit sky with a pair of night-vision goggles. One of the guerrillas, looking through a pocketscope, shouted, "There! Parachute!"

Brady looked where the tribesman was pointing and saw a parachute drifting in the wind. It looked to be several thousand feet in the air.

"Get some horses!" he said. "It's the pilot. See if you can capture him."

Four men quickly put bridles on their horses, jumped onto their mounts' bare backs, and moved off toward the area where the parachute was descending.

It was more than an hour before they returned. They had with them two Soviet airmen, both trussed and slung across the backs of horses.

Roughly the tribesmen pulled their captives off the horses and threw them to the ground in front of Brady. One of the Soviets groaned loudly.

"Search him," Brady said to his intelligence sergeant, Sergeant First Class Don Parker. "I'll check the other one."

A moment later Parker said, "Hey, Jake, this one's got a compound fracture of the leg."

The medic with Brady's half of the split A team checked the Russian pilot's leg and said, "Yeah, it's a mess, Jake."

"Do what you can for him then, Doc," Brady said. "OK, Don, let's see what Ivan here knows."

They untied the Soviet officer's hands and gave him a canteen of water. After he took a long drink from it Brady sat down in front of him and said, "All right, Ivan Ivanovich, don't pretend like you can't speak English, because we know almost all Soviet officers can. Now, let's begin with your name, rank, and the type of aircraft you were flying."

0608 hours GMT (0238 hours local time), 27 September
Unconventional Warfare Operations Area Sword

At SFOD B-30's hide site southwest of Zahedan, ten American soldiers were gathered around the grave into which they had just lowered the body of their comrade-in-arms, Chief Warrant Officer George Jones.

Major Mark Denton said, "One day we'll return here to recover the remains of this courageous American. For now, we can only pray, each in his own way, for his soul. Let us pray. . . ."

They prayed silently for a minute, then Denton said, "Attention! Present . . . arms!"

They saluted the body of their fallen comrade, then Denton ordered, "Order . . . arms!"

Two of the men began to cover the body with their entrenching tools, and Denton said, "Red. Harry. Come on up to the CP, and let's talk about where we go from here."

They were discussing their coming move south when Staff Sergeant Tippy called on the radio.

"We've linked up with Oscar Four south of the lead BTRs. We're gonna cross the road here and try to make it over the next ridge before daylight. That'll put us about three klicks from your position, but I don't think we'll be able to make it in tonight. Too damned tired, over."

"Roger, Three," Denton said. "Just make sure you get into a good hide before you crash. And let us know the coordinates of it. Have you got enough water to get you through tomorrow?"

"We'll make do, Base. What's the plan for tomorrow?"

"We'll rest up during the day, then head south tomorrow night. I'll let you know where to link up with us after you send me your final location tonight."

"OK, sir. We're movin' out."

All fifteen of the surviving members of B-30 were dead tired. Tippy and his three men would have to keep moving for a while, but Denton ordered everyone in the base camp with him to go to sleep. He would take the first watch while he prepared and transmitted a report of the day's brutal action to 1st SOCOM headquarters.

It took him nearly half an hour to punch his message into the burst device. Including the BMPs that the last two Dragons from the OPs had damaged, the little team, battling the lead elements of two Soviet regiments, had demolished thirty-three enemy armored vehicles and damaged five or six others. They had also destroyed three enemy helicopters—two Hind gunships and a big refueler—and damaged a fighter.

Included among the enemy vehicles destroyed were

fifteen BTR-80 armored personnel carriers, with several more damaged; six tracked BMP carriers; eight T-80 main battle tanks, with an additional one immobilized; three self-propelled ZSU-23-4 antiaircraft systems; and an armored artillery command-and-reconnaissance vehicle.

Denton had no idea how many Soviet soldiers had been killed or wounded in or near the exploding vehicles. He estimated the casualties at between one hundred fifty and two hundred men.

When he transmitted the data to his headquarters, he was directed, a short time later, to check his figures and retransmit his message.

The staff officers at 1st SOCOM found it impossible to believe that the little detachment could have inflicted such heavy casualties on the enemy.

He retransmitted his message, adding, "Satellite coverage will confirm these figures."

Staff Sergeant Tippy called to say that he and the other men from observation posts Three and Four had crossed the west road and the ridge above it. They were spreading out to find hiding places on the back side of the ridge before they began falling from the exhaustion and stress of battling the Soviets and hauling their heavy equipment up and down the rock-strewn hills.

Denton studied his map with a red-filtered flashlight in an effort to come up with a plan for the following night's move south, where his detachment would again hit the Soviets. But he, too, was asleep almost immediately.

CHAPTER 13

At the morning intelligence briefing in Fort Bragg's 1st Special Operations Command headquarters the G-2 was briefing the commanding general on the previous day's action in Iran.

"As you can see from the satellite photographs annotated by our image interpreters, sir, our operations have been even more successful than we could have hoped—"

" '*Our*' operations, Colonel?" the deputy commanding general interrupted. "You mean Major Denton's operations, don't you?" The G-2 had argued against Denton's plan from the time it had been proposed, and the young brigadier general would be damned if he was going to let this military intelligence corps colonel forget it. "How long have you had Denton's report?"

The G-2 looked at the NCO who had the briefing copy of Denton's message listing the numbers of Soviet vehicles destroyed.

"His message was received at 0640 Zulu, sir."

It was after eight A.M. Fort Bragg time, which meant that 1st SOCOM had been in receipt of the message for nearly five and a half hours.

The commanding general looked at his deputy. The point had been made. "What's the precedence on his message, Sergeant?" he asked the man with the message file.

"Operational immediate, sir."

"Then why in *hell* am I just now being notified?" the CG asked.

The G-2 colonel reddened. "It, uh, it seemed somewhat inflated to me, sir. I wanted to get this morning's satellite coverage before I briefed you."

The general stared at the colonel for a long moment, then stood, faced his staff, and said, "Gentlemen, let me remind you of something."

He studied the faces of the men before him, then continued, "Halfway around the world there is a small group of men—and one young woman, thanks to a decision I still can't understand—who have, on the orders of the Joint Chiefs of Staff, attacked two—*two*—Soviet regiments. Now, we still don't know if they've fought the first battle of World War III, or the first battle to try to *avoid* World War III. But to them, it probably doesn't matter. By now they're realizing just how alone and vulnerable and tired—and damned lucky, losing only one man—they are. And we—we, here in the comfort of our air-conditioned headquarters, in our nicely pressed uniforms—instead of asking them what we can do from here to help them continue to succeed . . . and to stay *alive*—we have the unmitigated *balls* to be so skeptical of their courage and ability that we sit around waiting for a goddam satellite photo to prove their results before notifying their commanding general of what they've done."

He banged his hand on the table before him and said, *"That* is not only *wrong,* gentlemen, it is goddamned *stupid!* Criminal! Now, G-3," he said, looking at his operations officer, "I want an immediate message to Denton telling him that I'm damned proud of him and his men, and that I want him to do whatever's necessary, for the time being, to avoid losing any more of his people. I want to know what additional resources—men and equipment—he needs to continue his mission, and whatever it is," he continued, looking at the rest of his staff, "I want you people to get it headed for Masirah, and headed there *now!"*

He looked at his deputy and said, "Bill, you keep on top of it. I'm going to get a secure conference call with the chairman, CINCCENT, and USSOCOM to try to get permission to send Denton whatever it is he decides he wants. Is there anything else I need to know before I call?"

"Yes, sir," the master sergeant with the message file responded. "UWOA Tiger—A-326—reports the capture of two Soviet pilots. Apparently they're the crew of the plane that B-30 hit with a Stinger."

"Any hot intel from them yet?"

"No, sir. If there is anything in their next sitrep, we'll pass it straight up the line."

"All right," 1st SOCOM's commanding general said, "let's get cracking!"

1228 hours GMT (1558 hours local time), 27 September
Unconventional Warfare Operations Area Sword

It was midafternoon in the hilly wasteland of eastern Iran when Mark Denton received the message from 1st SOCOM asking what more he could use in the way of men and materiel.

By then the message, as encouraging as it was, was not his top priority. Staff Sergeant Tippy and one of his men were surrounded by Soviet infantrymen on a ridge just a few kilometers east of B-30's hide site.

It had occurred at midmorning, when the two men had moved back up on the ridge to determine if the Soviet motorized regiment on the east road was on the move again.

It was, but the Soviets had adopted a new tactic for defending against the elusive enemy who had mauled them the previous day and night. They were using heliborne forces to secure the ridges overlooking the road.

Tippy had just reported the fact that the enemy column was on the move again, headed south at eight or ten kilometers an hour, when he heard the sound of rotary-wing aircraft to his north. He had no Stinger with him, so he remained in hiding to observe the helicopters' activity.

Two Mi-8 Hip helicopters appeared above the ridges on either side of the road. Each landed a squad of troops, lifted off, and deposited another squad a kilometer farther south.

One of the squads was dropped just fifty meters from where Tippy and his mate lay hidden among the rocks. Half the Soviet squad moved down the ridge line a hundred meters, passing within ten meters of the Americans' hiding place.

When he dared raise his head to observe them, the Special Forces staff sergeant could see that their attention was focused primarily on the neighboring valley and ridge and the skies above them. And he noted that each of the Soviet elements was armed with both PKS 7.62-mm machine guns and SA-14 shoulder-fired antiaircraft missile launchers.

Tippy switched his PRC-117 radio to the "whisper" mode, fully appreciating for the first time the wisdom of that capability. In the whisper mode, the frequency-hopping FM radio automatically gave the sound entering its microphone a ten-decibel boost.

The men from the Oscar Four element, several hundred meters down the ridge from Tippy on the side away from the road, had reported the Mi-8 helicopters landing on the ridge. They had thought at first that Tippy and his teammate had been spotted and were about to be captured. They had readied their remaining Stinger to fire at one of the Soviet choppers but had then thought better of it when they saw that the squad of soldiers who got off didn't appear to be in pursuit of anyone. Instead, the Soviets set up one machine gun facing across the valley to the west, then split into two groups, one of which moved a hundred meters south along the ridge and set up the other PKS.

Now Staff Sergeant Tippy whispered his situation to Major Denton.

"Do you think you can hide from them until dark?" Denton asked.

"Affirmative, affirmative," came the whispered reply.

"All right. We'll see what the situation is then. I'll send Oscar One and Two up onto the ridge line to your immediate west, and if you get in trouble, they'll be able to support you with Dragons and their M-16s. Also, we'll arm Aphid One with a minigun, and if something happens, he can support by fire, over."

"Roger, roger," Tippy answered.

"OK, and Oscar Four, you stay where you are, and be prepared to support him as well. And be advised, it'll be at least an hour or so before One and Two can get into position to help you."

During the time it took OPs One and Two to get into position to support their comrades on the ridge beyond them, nothing had happened to indicate that the Russians were doing anything more than sitting there protecting the flanks of the advancing armored column. That theory was confirmed when two more Mi-8 loads of infantrymen were deposited on top of the mountains flanking the column several kilometers farther south. Then, in the late afternoon, the Mi-8s returned to pick up the men guarding the ridge near Tippy, and they deposited the troops even farther to the south.

By then most of the combat elements of the motorized rifle regiment had passed to the south. Now the logistical support elements were entering UWOA Sword.

Denton had sent his radio operator on the mission to support Tippy's Oscar Three element and had held SFC O'Neill at the base camp. He needed his senior NCO's opinion about how to respond to the message from 1st SOCOM. He also called Chief Warrant Officers Stephens and Goodwin, the helicopter pilots, to ask their advice. When they arrived he noted that Goodwin's arm was in a sling, his wrist red and badly swollen.

"Can you fly with that thing?" Denton asked the wounded pilot.

"Not very well, I'm afraid, sir."

"We've got a solution, though, Major D.," Stephens said. "We were just coming up here to tell you about it."

"What's that, Red?"

"Cat."

"What?"

"Cat. Sergeant Whitaker. She's got about thirty hours flying Hughes 500s."

"Wait a minute," Denton said. "Are you proposing to let her fly one of the helicopters? A female? She isn't a qualified pilot, is she?"

"Depends on what you mean by 'qualified,' sir," Stephens said. "She isn't rated, but I can tell you this—she's a better pilot than a lot of these kids we're getting right out of flight school."

"Red ought to know, Major," Goodwin said. "He's the one who taught her to fly."

"You guys must be out of your minds," Denton said, shaking his head in disbelief. "Have you forgotten about the stink raised in Panama for letting women fly *support* missions, much less *combat* missions?"

"Now, hang on, sir," Stephens said. "With all due respect, I think I know a little better than you do what makes a good pilot. Cat's a natural. I want to use her as my copilot and let Miles here fly with Bart Evans."

Denton just looked at them, and Goodwin said, "Major Denton, we've got two flyable helicopters, and the mission to kill as many Soviet vehicles as we can before they get down to Khash. Without Whitaker we can't fly but one bird at a time. Not only does that mean we have only half as much firepower, but it makes the crew out there by itself a hell of a lot more vulnerable. Now, if you don't want to take resp—"

"If that's what you think is best for the mission," Denton interrupted, "then do it. Now, let's figure out how to reply to this message from SOCOM." And that was it. With no further discussion Mark Denton had agreed to allow Catherine Whitaker to copilot one of the H-500s.

The four men then discussed how they might best

improve their chances of further impeding the Russian regiments' advance. They concluded that the concept had worked extremely well so far, but the Soviets were already beginning to take effective steps to counter them. By putting heliborne troops on the hills flanking their columns, O'Neill pointed out, the Soviets had already found a way to deny his team the freedom to operate from there.

"Not necessarily, Harry," Denton said. "So far, they're only using that trick to cover the combat elements. That leaves their support vehicles wide open, and if we can deny them fuel, we can deny them mobility."

"Yeah, that's a damn good point, sir," O'Neill admitted.

"The thing that bothers me most," Stephens said, "is the damned Su-27, or whatever it was that painted me with his radar. With a look-down/shoot-down capability like they have . . . well, we were lucky last night, that's all I've got to say."

"How do we counter that?" Denton asked.

"With great bloody difficulty," Stephens replied. "I mean, our fuzzbusters let us know when his radar hits us, and when that happens, we might be able to land and shut down in a hurry, like we did last night. But sooner or later we'll be too late, and 'blooey'!"

"Too bad we don't have an AWACS to watch out for 'em, like the one that vectored us to the ships," Goodwin said.

"Yeah. . . . Wait a minute, Miles. What range do the radars on those things have?"

"Don't know. It's classified. Part of it depends on the altitude of the aircraft they're tracking, though. The higher, the better."

"Maybe," Stephens said, "just maybe. . . . The Su-27 does operate at a pretty high altitude. It wouldn't hurt to ask, Major D."

"You're right there, Red. We won't know if they can help us if we don't ask."

"If the AWACS *can* work for us, then I recommend we

get a few more little birds in here to help us hit the Russians," Stephens said. "There aren't any more H-500s set up like ours, but there's plenty of OH-58Ds. They're not as easy to fly or maintain, but they have through-the-mast target acquisition and carry the same weapons. It means we'd have to get a lot more fuel and ammo in here, though. And somebody to hump it."

"We'll see what they say," Denton said, hastily scribbling notes. "What do you want to ask for, Sergeant O'Neill?"

Before O'Neill could answer, Oscar Three called on the radio. "We've moved off the hill and linked up with everybody else, Base. Should be at your location within an hour."

"Roger, Oscar Three. Standing by, out."

"What I'd like to have, sir," O'Neill said, "is at least twice as many men as I have now. For one thing, it's sort of like the choppers—the more you have shooting at 'em, the more damage you can do, and the more the bad guys have to divide their reaction. At the rate they're moving now, we'll have to try to hop way ahead of them in time to set up before they get there."

"What about training the new men, though?"

"Shit, I guess we'll just have to give them on-the-job-training on the equipment when—if—they get here. Or, better yet, I can take one guy from each OP here and marry him up with one of the new guys."

"OK," Denton said, "that being the case, I'll request one A team. Eight of them can man OPs, and the others can act as a reserve, or replacements, if we need 'em."

"Yeah," O'Neill said, "especially if somebody gets scarfed up, like Tippy almost did today."

"With Cat flying, we could use them at the rearm/refuel point, too," Stephens said.

"What about weapons, Harry?" Denton asked O'Neill.

"TOWs. If we had TOW 2s, we wouldn't have to worry about that damned reactive armor. Right now we're having to choose our targets carefully with the Dragons. Their new warheads still don't seem to be doing the job.

We're getting less than fifty percent effective rounds on the T-80s. And with more than twice as many guys to hump ammo, we could give those Russian bastards hell."

"Done, then," Denton said. "I'll ask for—what?—four launchers and thirty-two rounds?"

"Yes, sir. I don't think we could handle more than that," O'Neill said.

"Anything else?" the B-30 commander asked the group. "What about a couple of Weasels?"

O'Neill laughed. "Boss, most of what you come up with is brilliant. We proved that yesterday, I think. But that goddam mechanical monstrosity of a remote recon vehicle is the exception to the rule, I'm afraid."

Denton's brow furrowed, then he smiled. "Yeah, well, we have to save *something* for the next war, anyway."

"You know, we could use some kind of vehicle, though," O'Neill said. "How about some of those little all-terrain vehicles like we used to haul the Weasel around at NTC?"

Denton considered the request, then said, "I don't think so, Harry. They'd need fuel, they'd be channelized into the valleys, like the Russians, and they'd leave tracks."

O'Neill nodded in agreement. "Sure would be nice to have some mobility, though."

"Shit!" Red Stephens said. "I really have my head up my ass, Major D.!" The others gave him a quizzical look, and he said, "When we were packing up to leave, they were getting a couple of MH-60Ps ready to send to Masirah. I'm sure they're there by now. If we could get one of those in here . . ."

The others beamed. The MH-60P Stealth Hawk helicopter had only recently been delivered to the army, and there were only four of them. Two had been sent to Europe to support Special Operations Command, Europe. The other two were in Stephens's unit, 1st Special Operations Aviation Detachment (Provisional). Like its predecessor, the MH-60K, it was a long-range, all-weather version of the helicopter that had first proved its combat fitness on Operation Urgent Fury in Grenada in 1983. Like the "K" model of the Blackhawk, the recently fielded "P" model could be refueled in midair, had sophisticated map-of-the-earth instrumentation, and was capable of lifting more men than could possibly be stuffed in its cargo compartment. But the "P" model had one characteristic the MH-60K lacked—it employed "stealth" technology, which made it almost impossible to detect on radar. The Stealth Hawk was an ideal machine for operations behind enemy lines, with three exceptions: compared to the MC-130 Combat Talon aircraft, it had room for only one A team, and little of its equipment; it had a much shorter range, if it couldn't be refueled; and it had only about half the speed of the Combat Talon. But it was, if employed properly, a superb aircraft for such operations.

"Red Stephens," Denton said, "you brilliant son of a bitch. We're going to see just how serious these guys are about sending us what we want."

He dismissed the others and had his radio operator punch in a long message to 1st SOCOM headquarters.

While he waited for a response, Denton walked down to one of the camouflaged H-500s, where Sergeant Cat Whitaker was sitting in the copilot's seat, refamiliarizing herself with every aspect of the helicopter's cockpit. When she saw Denton approach she smiled and said, "Hi, Major D. I was glad to hear you're gonna let me fly with Mr. Stephens."

"Was it a good decision?" he asked.

"Sir, I'm the second-best H-500 copilot in Iran. The other one's wounded in the arm. It was a good decision, sir. A damned good decision."

To reinforce her commander's confidence she began to explain to him how everything in the cockpit of the little helicopter worked. She was still doing so half an hour later when Darryl Tippy and the other Special Forces men arrived at the base camp.

Denton gathered the Green Beret NCOs around him, congratulated them for the outstanding job they had done so far, then outlined for them what he had requested from 1st SOCOM headquarters.

"Boss," Tippy said, "you get us a Stealth Hawk or two in here, we'll *really* kick ass. But meanwhile, what are we gonna do about hitting these bastards tonight?"

1215 hours GMT (1545 hours local time), 27 September
Unconventional Warfare Operations Area Shark
Makran Mountains north of Chah Bahar, Iran

Captain Bill Davidson and his team sergeant, Master Sergeant Jimmy Slater, sat on either side of their Baluchi guerrilla chieftain, listening in astonishment to one of his messengers. The man had arrived by horseback a few minutes earlier, and the chieftain had summoned the Americans to his tent to hear what the messenger had to say.

According to reports he had gotten from other messengers arriving in Zaboli, the guerrilla force to their north had shot down four Soviet helicopters with Stingers two nights earlier.

"All right, Rocco!" Davidson said. "That's why the bastards never showed up in our UWOA. Rocco and his team took out all four of them out before they got down here."

The messenger continued. The previous afternoon, he said, there was a major battle on the road southwest of Zahedan. The Soviets had lost many vehicles and had been able to make little progress.

"How many vehicles did the enemy lose?" Slater asked.

"Twenty—maybe more," the messenger reported. "And last night there was more fighting, this time on the road east of Kuh-e Taftan, although the results of the battle have not yet been reported. And an enemy aircraft—a jet fighter—was shot down last night as well, thanks be to God. Our brethren from Pashku and Zaboli captured the pilots."

The messenger had no other information, and the chieftain invited him to stay and join him in a prayer of thanks. He dismissed Davidson and Slater.

As the two Americans walked back to their position Davidson said, "Get that info off to SFOB right away, Jimmy. And tell them that after today's training we'll be ready to take on a confidence target."

"Wilco, boss," Slater said.

By the time Slater had drafted the message, though, and the radio operator had set up the satellite radio to burst the message to the Special Forces Operations Base in England, Davidson and the Baluchi chieftain showed up.

"Hold off on that message," the American A team leader said. "Don't tell them that we want to hit a confidence target. That would cost us the element of surprise. Tell them instead that we're ready to deliver a major strike on the whole fucking airborne regiment."

Slater raised his eyebrows, then looked from his commander to the guerrilla leader.

"It is God's will," the Baluchi chieftain said.

CHAPTER 14

1540 hours GMT (1910 hours local time), 27 September
Unconventional Warfare Operations Area Sword

The leaders of Special Forces Operational Detachment
B-30 were discussing their options for continuing their
fight against the Soviets when Major Denton's radio
operator said, "Sir, there's a message from headquarters."

Denton went to the digital message device group of the
satellite radio and pushed the Read button. The following message scrolled across the face of the device:

SECRET: OOOO SWORD DE BASE: SFOD XX SFOD ALPHA DASH
THREE TWO THREE WILL REINFORCE YOU TOMORROW
NIGHT PD TWO MIKE HOTEL DASH SIX ZERO PAPA HELOS
WILL DELIVER TEAM PD ONE HELO WILL RETURN TO FOR-
WARD OPERATIONS BASE PD ONE HELO WITH CREW OF FOUR
WILL REMAIN IN UWOA SWORD TO SUPPORT BRAVO DASH
THREE ZERO OPERATIONS PD REFUEL REQUIREMENTS FOR
YOUR AIRCRAFT WILL BE EXPLAINED BY PILOTS ON ARRIVAL
PD SFOD XX SFOD WILL INFIL WITH FOUR EACH TANGO
OSCAR WHISKEY LAUNCHERS AND THREE TWO MISSILES AS
REQUESTED PD

The lengthy message went on to say that SFOD A-323,
which was being sent to reinforce Denton's team, would
receive an automatic resupply forty-eight hours after
their infiltration into UWOA Sword. The MH-60P that
would remain in the area to support Denton, the message
advised, would carry air-to-air missiles to defend itself

143

and the team. Also, beginning immediately, the AWACS aircraft over the Strait of Hormuz would start broadcasting, on the team's satellite radio voice net, the presence of enemy aircraft in the vicinity of UWOA Sword. There was a warning, however, that the AWACS could only detect aircraft that far north that were at altitudes in excess of nine thousand feet.

It directed Denton to select and transmit the coordinates of primary and alternate landing zones for the MH-60Ps and drop zones for A-323's resupply drop. The body of the dead helicopter pilot was to be sent back to Masirah, if possible, on the Stealth Hawk that would return there. The long message ended with a request for a summary of B-30's plans for the next twenty-four hours.

SFOD B-30 was being given everything they had asked for except more small helicopter gunships, and given it quickly.

Denton made no attempt to conceal his elation at the contents of the message. In the fading light of early evening he ran to each camouflaged position where his subordinates were hidden to tell them the good news. SFOD B-30 was to be reinforced by a full Special Forces A team—the twelve men of SFOD A-323. In addition, one of the Stealth Hawks that delivered A-323—and four TOW launchers with thirty-two rounds of ammunition—would remain in the UWOA to support the team. It was much more than he had expected to be granted.

"When you're the only game in town, boss," Harry O'Neill remarked, "you get what you ask for. And A-323's one of the best teams in Group—with the exception of that asshole in command of it."

"Who's that?" Denton asked with obvious concern.

"I don't know his name, but Pete Puchinelli, his team sergeant, says he's one inflexible, thickheaded son of a bitch."

"Puchinelli, huh?" Denton replied. He had heard of Master Sergeant Pete Puchinelli, who had the reputation of being one of the best team sergeants—if not *the* best on Smoke Bomb Hill, the area of Fort Bragg where the Special Forces units were located. "Well, if he gets off on the wrong foot, Harry, I'll just put his ass back on the Stealth Hawk that's returning to Masirah. I'd rather go down this river with one good man, as ol' Charlie Beckwith used to say, than a whole boatload of shitheads."

After Denton had delivered the good news to everyone in his team he told Red Stephens and Harry O'Neill to join him at his command post.

"We've got to give them our plans for the next twenty-four hours and select LZs and DZs for the infil and automatic resupply," he said. "Harry, I'll let you select the LZs and DZs, but first, I want to decide what we should do tonight."

The three men discussed the matter. The H-500MDs had only three Hellfire and three TOW missiles left in the pods and at the rearm point. But they had two miniguns and ten thousand rounds of ammunition for the rapid-firing, six-barreled rotating gun systems. And O'Neill's men had eight Dragon missiles in the nearby ammo cache as well.

"The miniguns ain't worth a damn against armor," Red said, "but they'll tear the hell out of fuel trucks."

"Same for the Dragons," O'Neill said.

"OK, Red," Denton said, "get ahold of the AWACS on the satcom and find out if he can warn you about the Russian fighters. If so, we'll see what damage we can do to their logistical tail before we move south. Would you be able to lift a few Dragon teams up north a few klicks, so we can hit them with the rest of our missiles?"

"Sure," Stephens said, "as long as we don't mount the minis until after we deliver them."

"Good," Denton said. "Then as soon as it gets dark we'll drop teams in the valley between here and the west road, every five hundred meters. While we're making our way to the top of the ridge with our Dragons you can come back here and mount your miniguns. Then, when everybody's ready, we'll salvo the column with half of what we've got, change firing positions, and give it to them again. Harry, we'll then haul ass to the west a ridge line or two and start moving south."

"Sounds good to me," O'Neill said. "Let me give the guys a warning order and select those LZs and DZs for A-323, and we'll be ready to go."

"I'll dismount the TOW and Hellfire pods and get the crews ready," Stephens said. "We can take the few missiles we have left south with us."

"OK, let's do it," Denton said. It was obvious from his "we this, we that" that he intended to take the place of the NCO with the twisted ankle for the coming night's action. "I'll let SOCOM know what the plan is."

*1555 hours GMT (1925 hours local time), 27 September
Unconventional Warfare Operations Area Tiger*

Not long after Major Mark Denton received the encouraging message from his headquarters, Captain Rocco Birelli—now linked up with the rest of his team, all of the Baluchi guerrillas under Lakha Nawaz, and the two captured Soviet fighter pilots—received a message from SFOB. The Special Forces Operations Base in England directed Birelli to be prepared to evacuate the Soviet pilots aboard an MH-60 helicopter the following night. It requested the coordinates of the pickup zone and indicated that the time of pickup would be given in a later message.

The pilot whose leg had been broken during his emergency parachute jump was beginning to respond to the kindness of the Green Beret medic who was caring for him. The medic had not only set and splinted the compound fracture and dressed the puncture wound, but he had shared his food with the Soviet pilot, made him as comfortable as possible, and checked on him frequently to ensure that the prisoner was not in too much pain.

The Russian had excellent command of the English language, and when he asked the medic if the injury to his leg would be permanent, the medic replied, "No. If we can get you evacuated out to an American hospital before long, it should be completely healed in a few months. If not, and gangrene sets in, well . . ."

"I'll be sent to an American hospital?" the Soviet airman asked.

"Sure," the medic replied. "It may not be for a while, but we'll get you out. You know, if you could give us some good information, Yuri—something of really good intelligence value—I'm certain our headquarters would find a way to get you out of here right away. Think about it."

He left the Russian airman alone for quite a while then and let the injured man consider his situation.

The Soviet expedition into Southwest Asia was a very unpopular move to most Russians. Gorbachev, before he lost his open access to the press, had expressed his reservations about the wisdom of such a move, and the Soviet people had gotten the message. There was considerable unrest not only among the civilian populace of the USSR, but in the armed forces as well. The pilot was one who thought it was reckless and stupid to reinvade Afghanistan and move into Iran but, out of fear of reprisal, had not voiced his opinion. He knew of some army units in which resistance to the invasion had led to open rebellion—and the subsequent quick slaughter of the rebelling soldiers. And now he was being offered an opportunity to go to an American hospital. If the Politburo was going to get rid of Mikhail Gorbachev and return to the oppressive policies of the past, it would be terrible. But here was a chance, Senior Lieutenant Yuri Kalenkov realized, to hedge his bet. If he told the Americans what he knew, not only would he be out of the war and away from the Baluchi tribesmen he constantly feared would take him from the Americans and torture him to death, but he would be evacuated to an American hospital. There he could see what was going to happen with respect to the conflict in Iran. If the Americans got the upper hand and Gorbachev was able to prevail and have the Soviet forces withdrawn to their homeland, he would be repatriated to the Soviet Union. If not, and the

Soviet Union—and thus the hard-liners in the Politburo —prevailed, he would simply defect to America.

He called for the medic, and when he felt assured that his disclosure of Soviet secrets would, indeed, lead to his early evacuation, he offered to tell all he knew.

"Make sure you milk him dry for everything that could be of help out here," Jake Brady said to his intelligence sergeant, who would question the man. "If we wait to get feedback from that bunch who'll interrogate him back in the rear, it'll be too late to do us any good out here—if it ever even gets back to us."

1730 hours GMT (2100 hours local time), 27 September
Unconventional Warfare Operations Area Sword

An hour after dark the H-500MD helicopters of SFOD B-30 began ferrying the Special Forces men and their Dragon weapons to the area from which they would attack the Soviet motorized rifle regiment's logistical tail.

There was only one pilot in each of the little helicopters, to enable each to carry two passengers and their bulky Dragons. To further demonstrate to Denton his confidence in Cat Whitaker's ability to fly, Red Stephens had her fly one of the aircraft while he flew the other. They darted up the valley in the darkness after verifying with the distant AWACS aircraft that there were no "bogeys" at high altitude over the area. If any appeared, the AWACS crew would notify the B-30 base radio operator, who would immediately relay the information to the choppers over the frequency-hopping PRC-117.

Mark Denton, sitting in the seat beside the young female sergeant, watched with real interest as she expertly zipped along behind Stephens's aircraft just a few feet off the valley floor. As they approached the coordinates of the first landing zone they had selected from a map reconnaissance she nosed the helicopter up to slow it, then settled smoothly to the ground twenty meters behind Stephens.

The man in the back of each helicopter jumped out, and as soon as the men and their weapons were clear they lifted off, darted to their next LZ, and once more touched down smoothly. Before he hopped out of the seat beside her, Denton patted Cat Whitaker on the leg and said, "Good job, Cat. I think I made the right decision."

As he stepped to the ground she gave him a thumbs-up and, when he was clear, lifted smoothly off, pivoted, and headed back to pick up the next team.

While the men were climbing aboard, the radio operator's voice came over the pilots' earphones. "Aphid Flight, Roulette reports two bogeys at eighteen thousand, eighty miles north."

"Kill the engine, Cat!" Stephens ordered.

They shut down, got out, and monitored the satcom as the AWACS reported the enemy aircrafts' movements. The Soviet jets flew south over their regiments' columns, then back and forth above them for nearly an hour. Stephens went to his helicopter and turned on the radar detector. When the Russian jets were over B-30's area, the detector buzzed an alarm. They were searching the skies below them with their down-looking radars for moving aerial targets. But they found none, and Roulette finally said, "They've moved out of our range to the north, Aphid. There's nothing on the screen to indicate anyone's taking their place."

Stephens and Whitaker delivered the other four men to their LZs, then returned to the rearm point and, with the other pilots' help, mounted their minigun systems, each loading a long belt of two thousand rounds of ammunition aboard.

"Wish we could test fire these damn things," Stephens muttered as the crews inspected the rapid-firing miniguns. "OK, Sparky, check with Roulette and see if there's any bad guys up there."

The AWACS reported detecting no aircraft near, or moving toward, UWOA Sword.

"All right, Cat," he said. "Let's go qualify you as the first female gunship pilot to see combat."

She climbed in the lead aircraft beside him while Bart

Evans got into the pilot's seat of Aphid Two and the injured Miles Goodwin took the copilot's seat.

By the time they lifted off, all four of the two-man Oscar elements reported that they were in position and ready to attack the column of trucks creeping south on the narrow dirt road in the valley below them.

CHAPTER 15

In UWOA Tiger Rocco Birelli's intelligence sergeant was summarizing all of the information he had gotten from the Soviet Su-24 Fencer pilot.

"Now listen to this," the intel sergeant said after he had covered the Russian airman's personal history and military background. "When he was shot down they were trying to hit some people who were up on the ridges, shooting up a tank regiment on one of the roads just south of Zahedan—people being supported by a bunch of helicopter gunships."

"Helicopters? Whose helicopters?" Birelli asked.

"He has no idea. He assumes they're American, but he says they might be Iranian Cobras. They still have a few from the Shah's regime, although our intel brief said they were all down for parts."

"Yeah," Birelli said. "But that's the same thing they told the Delta Force about the Iranians' F-14s before they went on the rescue raid back in '80. The damned things bombed Baghdad a week or two later."

"Well, anyway, whoever they are, the people and their gunships that hit the Russian tanks and a motorized rifle regiment on the other road earlier in the day apparently did a hell of a job. According to our boy Yuri, there were dozens of vehicles burning on each road. And they destroyed a couple of Hinds and a Halo yesterday, too, not to mention the Su-24 our prisoners were flying."

"Damn!" Master Sergeant Brady said. "That's *great!* Did the Russians get any of the gunships?"

"Negative. He says he talked to an Su-27 pilot on the way there who said he had just locked onto one when it disappeared from his radar screen. The '27 fired a missile, but it didn't hit anything. So Yuri started hitting the ridges where the missiles were being fired at the tanks from, and the next thing he knew, something kicked his airplane in the ass, and he had to eject."

"Did he know what kind of missiles were being used against the tanks?" Birelli asked.

"He says he heard that there were several types being used—some wire-guided, some laser-guided, and some type that—"

"Lasers?" Birelli said, interrupting him. "Denton! Major Denton from G-3, and those guys who went out to NTC to test some concept about fighting armor with Hughes 500s and electronic OPs with lasers and all sorts of other gadgets."

"You mean Harry O'Neill and his team?" Jake Brady asked.

"Yeah," Birelli said. "I'll bet you a dollar to a bucket of shit that's who's up there. I'll be a son of a bitch!"

"If it is, I hope Group will move them down here when the Sovs get here," Brady said. "If they don't get their asses shot off, that is."

"Look, Jake," Birelli said, "we'd better burst that info to SFOB right away. And anything else the pilot knows that could be of value to Denton and them, and help keep them going."

"Will do," Brady said, then, to the intel sergeant, "Get back with the pilot and pick his brain for anything else he knows about the situation up there."

1835 hours GMT (2205 hours local time), 27 September
Unconventional Warfare Operations Area Sword

Red Stephens eased the helicopter up above the ridge overlooking the blacked-out Soviet truck convoy.

"There we are, Cat," he said to the woman beside him as they scanned the enemy vehicles with their forward-looking infrared sensor. The image on the little screen looked like a black-and-white television picture being taken in broad daylight.

"All right. You see those four tank trucks in a row there?" the pilot asked.

"Yes, sir. Got 'em."

"OK, they'll be our first target. I'll do the flying and trigger pulling this first run. You watch the instruments and the area around us. If you see anything, sound off, take the controls, and try to evade, OK?"

"Will do, sir."

Stephens keyed his transmitter to call the Dragon teams and his wingman. He and Cat were north of the ridge line along which the ground teams lay tracking the convoy with their sights. Aphid Two was just to the Dragon teams' south.

"This is Aphid One," Stephens said. "Everybody ready?"

"Oscar One, roger."

"Oscar Two, roger that!"

"Oscar Three's up."

"Oscar Four. Ditto."

"And Aphid Two's ready when you are."

Stephens flipped his ANVIS goggles down, lifted the little gunship over the ridgetop, and nosed over, diving at the trucks in the valley below. As he did so he said, "Fire at will!"

Off to their right Cat Whitaker saw several flashes from the top of the ridge as the Dragon gunners fired their first rounds. Before they struck their targets she saw the line of trucks as Stephens closed rapidly on them, swung right when he was almost to them, and triggered his minigun, pouring fifty rounds a second into the line of fuel trucks.

Cat watched in amazement as a steady stream of

tracers from the H-500 moved along the line of trucks, then ceased as Stephens, almost on top of the front truck, released the trigger and banked hard to the left. As he sped toward a gap in the ridge on the opposite side of the valley, she saw several vehicles to their south explode as the Dragons found their marks.

Stephens shot through the gap and dived behind the protecting ridge.

"We set any of them afire?" he asked.

"Not that I could tell," Cat replied.

"Shit!" Stephens exclaimed. "Must be diesel. OK, let's hit them again before they have time to get their shit together. There ought to be fuel all over the road now. The tracers will get it going. All right, Cat, soon as you get your goggles down, it's your airplane."

She flipped her goggles down, grasped the control stick and collective handle, and applied pressure to the pedals.

"Got it," she said.

"OK, now ease up till the mast's above the ridge . . . back off a little . . . that's a girl." With his goggles up, Stephens was glancing back and forth between the instruments and the FLIR screen. As the sensors at the top of the rotor mast peeked over the hill he said, "All right, the rear tanker's on fire after all. The others are stopped . . . probably got the drivers, so the fire should get them, too. Back down, and let's go north a ways."

She backed the helicopter away from the ridge, then dived off to the right and headed north along the ridge line.

"Where you at, Aphid One?" they heard Bart Evans ask from Aphid Two.

"Couple of miles north," Cat replied. "How'd you do?"

"Shot up a tanker that must've been carrying Mogas. Damn thing blew up right in our faces. You hit anything, Cat?"

"Chief hit four tankers," she replied. "One's burning."

"OK," Stephens said, "pull up between those peaks, and let's have a look."

She eased the helicopter up, and they saw a line of trucks bunched up and halted in the road.

"Choose your poison," Stephens said.

She flipped up her goggles long enough to scan the FLIR screen, working the pedals to allow her to see some distance along the line of trucks.

"All right," she said. "See those three pulling trailers?"

"Yep. Go for it."

"Here goes," she said, lightly feeling the stick-mounted trigger with her right hand as she flipped her goggles down with her left. She crossed the ridge and flew toward the trucks she had chosen to hit, boring in on them from their left rear.

"Get in close!" Stephens said. "Closer . . . closer . . . now!"

She squeezed the trigger, and the stream of tracers tore into the ground beneath the rear truck. She kept the trigger depressed and raised the nose slightly, and the stream of fire from the minigun bored into the rear trailer. She nosed the chopper slightly to her left, and the tracers raked along the side of the truck, then into the next trailer. It exploded brightly when she was fifty meters from it, blinding her momentarily. Stephens grabbed the controls and pulled the chopper sharply up, making a left turn as he did so. Shrapnel from the explosion showered against the helicopter's Plexiglas bubble but did no apparent harm.

When he was fully in control of the helicopter and speeding back up toward the ridge top Stephens said, "All *right*, cat lady! You got an ammo trailer! You blew up a fuckin' ammo trailer."

"It blinded me," she said. "It blinded me, and I almost lost control of the chopper."

"That's why the copilot shouldn't ever look directly at the target," Stephens said. "If I'd been looking right at it, it would have blinded me, too. You all right?"

"Wheh!" the female sergeant said. "Yeah, I'm fine, chief. Let's hit 'em again!"

"Aphid One, this is Oscar One," Harry O'Neill called over the radio. "Those explosions way up north your doings?"

"That's most affirm!" Red Stephens said. "The cat lady just became the first American female gunship pilot in combat, over."

"Break, break! Aphid, this is Base. Roulette has two bogeys headed south at two zero thousand!"

"One, roger! Sit down and shut down, Bart."

Stephens found a niche in the side of the ridge near the bottom, big enough for the helicopter, and set it down. He and Sergeant Whitaker hopped out and began folding the rotor blades. They were finished and had taken off their shirts to drape over the reflective shine of the windshield before the "fuzzbuster" sounded. The warning from the AWACS had come in plenty of time.

Stephens turned on the radio and heard Major Denton, temporarily using Oscar Two's call sign, say, "OK, as soon as we fire, let's all move downhill to the west. Harry, you roll us up from north to south. As soon as the AWACS says the sky's clear, we'll get the killer eggs to pick up the first load on their way home, over."

"Oscar Two, this is Base."

"Go ahead, Base."

"Roger. Roulette now sees four bogeys, two at twenty thousand overhead, and two more at ten thousand, sixty miles north, over."

"This is Oscar Two, roger that," Denton said. "OK, let's fire up a few more vehicles and get the hell out of here before the fighters show up, out."

Five minutes later a pair of Su-24 ground-attack fighters bombed the ridge line from which Denton and his men had launched their missiles. Fearing the enemy's Stinger missiles, the Soviets dropped their bombs from high altitude. Although the Americans didn't know it, one load of bombs was off target and destroyed two more of the vehicles on the choked road below.

It was more than an hour later when Base relayed the

AWACS report that the skies over UWOA Sword were clear of Soviet aircraft.

When B-30's members were back in their base camp, preparing to leave it for their next cache sites to the south, Mark Denton tallied up the score of their latest attack. He estimated enemy losses from the attack at fifteen trucks from the Soviet regiment's support units.

In 1st SOCOM's intelligence section the next morning the image interpreters who examined satellite photographs of the road south of Zahedan counted twenty-two burned-out Soviet vehicles that hadn't been there the day before.

The count of enemy tanks, vehicles, and aircraft destroyed by Denton and his little detachment and their two small helicopters now stood at sixty.

1210 hours GMT (0810 hours EDT), 28 September
Headquarters, 1st Special Operations Command
Fort Bragg, North Carolina

By the time the 1st SOCOM staff briefed the number to the commanding general, most of the men—and the lone woman—of SFOD B-30 were asleep in their new hide site, some fifty kilometers south of the burned-out hulks for which they were responsible.

"Incredible," the general said. Turning to his deputy commander, Brigadier General Porter, he added, "I would never have believed it was possible, Bill."

"Take the right men, give them the opportunity to try out their bold ideas—especially when they're supported by the best of American technology—and this is what it can lead to, sir. The important thing, if I may say so, is to remember their limits as human beings."

"Yes. Well, I hope that with more men, weapons, and a Stealth Hawk to support them they can keep it up for at least a few more days. We've *got* to keep the Soviets from reaching Chah Bahar until after Corps gets a couple of brigades ashore. They still need two or three more days to prepare fully. If our boys can't hold them off until then, well, I'm afraid there's little hope for getting a cease-fire from the Soviets."

"What about the request from Captain Davidson down in UWOA Shark, sir? Are we going to get permission for them to hit the airborne regiment?"

"The big brass is in a meeting in the NMCC (National Military Command Center) right now," the 1st SOCOM commanding general replied. "I expect they'll give us the go-ahead. The more punishment we can give the sons of bitches now, the better the chances of getting a cease-fire . . . Christ, Bill. I wish I were a captain again."

Porter chuckled. "I've been thinking the same thing, sir. But remember—I was a lieutenant when you were a captain. We were so fucked up, it's a wonder we ever got promoted."

The other general laughed aloud, then, in a serious tone, said, "I wonder if we'd have had the balls to try what we're asking those kids to do, Bill."

"Don't know, boss," Porter replied. "But I wish I had the opportunity to find out."

"Yeah. Well, if these guys can't get it done, I doubt if we could."

Porter checked his watch and said, "It's about time for the Hawks to leave Masirah now. I'm going to go over to the radio room and see how it goes."

CHAPTER 16

The MH-60P Stealth Hawks carrying the twelve members of Special Forces Operational Detachment A-323, en route to UWOA Sword to reinforce Mark Denton and his team, lifted off Masirah Island shortly after dark. Both helicopters were crammed full of men and equipment, and there was no way the men were going to be comfortable during the two-and-a-half-hour flight.

Eleven of them accepted their discomfort as inevitable, but their detachment commander, Captain Dick Warner, did not. After all, he was the only commissioned officer on the team, and that, he felt, should be reason enough for the others to make certain he was comfortable. But not this Special Forces crowd. They seemed to think that everybody was the same—that the so-called "experience" of being in the army longer than he had been somehow equaled the superior training he had acquired during four years at the Military Academy.

Warner pushed his feet against the legs of one of his men, forcing the NCO to draw his knees up into an even higher, more uncomfortable position.

The team sergeant of A-323, Master Sergeant Pete Puchinelli, saw Warner push against the man's legs, tried to make a bit more room for him by drawing up his own knees, then glared at Warner, wondering what the officer was thinking.

What Captain Warner was thinking was that for the first time since he had come to Special Forces nearly a

159

year earlier, he was glad he had done so. Since the formation of the United States Special Operations Command in 1987 and the lessening of tensions in Europe as a result of the disintegration of Communism and the withdrawal of most of the Soviet troops from Eastern Europe, he had decided that a tour in Special Operations would be good for his career. Once he earned a Special Forces tab and spent long enough in an assignment to get that particular ticket punched, he would bail out and go back to the "real" army. It would be a pain in the ass, but since most of his competition in the mainstream of the army weren't smart enough to see that a special ops tour might one day be a good thing to have on one's record, it would be worth it.

Warner had been anxiously waiting for his year to end so he could leave Special Forces and go find a good staff job in the Pentagon when Panama had been invaded. He hadn't made it there until after the fighting was over, but he had managed to make it long enough to pick up a couple of minor medals. Then this thing with the Russians had come up. At first he had hoped he would get only as far as the forward operations base, because that would be all he needed to get an Armed Forces Expeditionary Medal. But now that A-323 was being deployed to assist B-30 in harassing the Soviets, he should really be able to get a leg up on his peers.

Warner looked around at the half of A-323 that was on the lead Stealth Hawk. They would be the key. If he could send them out to heap enough glory on the team, it would do wonders for his career. And if some of them became casualties, well . . . he wanted them to come away with as many medals as possible as proof of his leadership and the team's overall bravery. Besides, the more medals he put them in for, the more likely they were to reciprocate. If they just didn't do something stupid, such as get captured and compromise the hide site—or something else that would risk *his* well-being— then he'd be miles ahead of his competition. Panama would be long forgotten after they got involved against a *real* army, like the Soviets.

Best of all, though, would be if Denton became a casualty before they finished the short mission. That would make *him* the B-30 commander, and that would *really* be a feather in his career cap.

He pushed his feet harder against the legs of the NCO, making himself as comfortable as possible, then closed his eyes and dreamed of the day he would become a general.

The AWACS vectored the two MH-60P Stealth Hawks and the aging MC-130 aerial tanker to the rendezvous point at the beginning of the aerial refuel track. Through their night-vision goggles the Stealth Hawk pilots could see the refuel hoses deploy from the wingtips of the tanker. They pulled their helicopters up on either side of the converted Combat Talon and extended the probes from the front of their aircraft, then eased forward until the probes nosed into the baskets at the trailing end of the hoses.

When the probes were locked in, fuel from the tanker gushed into the Stealth Hawks' tanks. As each helicopter reached full fuel capacity its pilot backed off from the refueler until the connection was broken, then retracted the probe. The refueler retracted its hoses, turned left, and headed back toward Masirah. The Stealth Hawks, with enough fuel to allow them to fly well over a thousand miles, turned right and entered Unconventional Warfare Operations Area Sword. Fifteen minutes later they touched down on the landing zone where Mark Denton and his men were waiting.

Quickly, as Captain Warner watched, his men and the members of Denton's B-30 began unloading the equipment from the helicopter. Seeing Warner standing there idly, one of the men who was hurrying past with a TOW missile stopped beside him in the darkness and said, "You! Your goddamn back broken or something? Get your ass over there and help unload these choppers!"

"I'm the detachment commander!" Warner replied indignantly. "Where's *your* detachment commander? And what's your name, troop?"

The figure faced him, shoved the missile into Warner's arms, and said, "My commander's at Fort Bragg, and my name is Denton, Captain—*Major* Denton. Now get over there and help unload the Hawks, or I'll kick your ass so high up on your shoulders that your nose'll be sticking out of your asshole!"

"Yes, sir," Walker mumbled, then under his breath he added, "Oh, that's just great. Another undisciplined Green Beret knuckle-dragger. . . ."

When the helicopters were unloaded Denton and Harry O'Neill placed the decaying body of Hardin Boone, the crewman who had been killed on the infiltration jump, into a body bag the Stealth Hawks had brought along. Then they gently set it in the cargo compartment of the chopper that was going back to Masirah Island, saluted, and turned away. While O'Neill found the A-323 team sergeant, Pete Puchinelli, Denton went to the pilot's window of the chopper and said, "I'm Major Denton. Thanks for your help. We'll take care of your wingman. You guys have a good flight home."

"Will do, sir. If you need any more help, just holler."

"You bet," Denton said. "I owe you guys a keg of beer when the war ends."

The pilot laughed. "*You* kill the Commies, sir. *We'll* buy the beer. In fact, we'll have a keg iced and waiting for you when you get home."

Denton stepped back, the pilot yelled, "Clear!" and the Stealth Hawk's engines began to whine. Two minutes later it was gone, and Denton walked over to the crew of the other Hawk to introduce himself and brief them on their mission. He was pleased to find that the MH-60 pilot was an old and close friend of Red Stephens, the lead pilot of the little Hughes 500 "killer eggs."

As Denton discussed the mission with the Stealth Hawk crew and showed them the place he had chosen for their hide site, Harry O'Neill took the members of A-323 and showed them the two-man positions he had selected for them in the rocks on the side of the ridge. Captain Warner complained that he had intended to put his team into three-man positions, and O'Neill said, "Well, the ones I've selected are probably a little small for three men, sir. Why don't you take a look in the morning, and you can change them then if you'd—"

"Sergeant Puchinelli," Warner interrupted, "I want you to find suitable positions—three-man positions—for the team while I send an initial entry report back to SFOB. You, the XO, and I will share one position. And make sure ours is big enough for us to spread out, so I can have plenty of room for planning and preparing situation reports."

"Sir," Puchinelli said, "I think it would be best if you let Major Denton handle the reporting. He *is* in charge, I believe."

"Sergeant," Warner said, "just follow my orders and stop wasting my time and yours, will you? Of course Major Denton is in charge of B-30. But the last time I checked, my team was subordinate to B-32. Until I receive orders to the contrary, I'll do what I think is best for this team. Now carry on as I directed."

"Captain," Harry O'Neill said, "I think you'd be well advised to report to Major Denton *now,* so he can give you a little guidance. He has some pretty specif—"

"Let me know when you've found a suitable site for my headquarters element, Sergeant Puchinelli," Warner interrupted again. "I'll be waiting right here."

Another figure appeared beside them in the faint moonlight just then. It was Denton's radio operator. "Captain Warner?" the man said.

"Yes. Right here."

"Major Denton wants you, your team sergeant, and Sergeant O'Neill at the CP right away, sir."

The men made their way to the B-30 command post, which was a small open space beneath a rock overhang. Denton, Red Stephens, and the Stealth Hawk pilot were already there when they arrived.

"Have a seat, gents," Denton said. The six men sat in a tight circle in the darkness, and Denton confirmed that everyone had been introduced to one another. "Now," he said, "let's discuss how we're going to use all these new assets to kick a little Russian ass."

"It's my belief," Warner said, "that I can best perform my mission, Major, if you give me an area of operations, the Hawk and the TOWs I brought in with me, and let me decide how to employ them. That way, your span of control doesn't become too great."

"I see," Denton said. "Well, it's *my* belief that handling a platoon-sized element is within my abilities, Captain Warner, and that the effort needs to be commanded and coordinated from one point. We've got the ability to start hitting both columns simultaneously. That'll cause the Sovs to have to divide their response and enable us to make the best use of our most critical asset, which is time. The way I see it, we've got maybe forty-eight hours or so to do what damage we can before the majority of them get south of UWOA Sword. Now, here's what I was thinking. The men from Harry's team are tr—"

"Harry?" Warner asked.

"SFC O'Neill," Denton replied. "Since his guys are the only ones trained on the remote OPs, I was going to put one of them and one of your men on each OP, so they could get on-the-job-training. But I think it would be best, in the interest of time, if we leave them as they are and put remote OP teams and TOW teams together to hit both columns. We'll send the killer eggs to wherever the best targets appear and use the Stealth Hawk to ferry the teams, to handle casualties—if that, God forbid, becomes necessary—and to move supplies. What do you think?"

"Well, frankly, Major," Warner said, "I don't like the idea of splitting my team, *nor* of a single command post. I mean, what happens when you become a casualty?"

"Well, in that case, Captain Warner," Denton replied, "you take command from the alternate CP, of course."

"But my orders from B-32 didn't say anything about working for anyone else. I think it would be best if I remained in command of my own te—"

"What *did* your orders say, Warner?" Denton inquired.

"That my team, with one MH-60P attached, was to

enter UWOA Sword and conduct offensive operations to impede, harass, and destroy Soviet forces moving south on the Zahedan-Khash-Chah Bahar axis. They said nothing about attaching my team to your ad hoc B team, that I can recall."

"Captain Warner," Master Sergeant Puchinelli said, "I thought it was made pretty plain that we were coming in here to work for Major Denton. True, the operations order didn't specifically say that, but as quickly as they threw it together to get us out here, that's no surprise. And every verbal briefing we got made it plain that our job is to reinforce the major, here, in whatever way he deems—"

"Sergeant Puchinelli," Warner said angrily, "this is a matter between Major Denton and me. If—"

"You're right, Captain," Denton interrupted. "It *is* a matter for us to settle, if you have any doubts." To the NCOs he said, "Will you excuse us, please?"

The noncommissioned officers disappeared, and Chief Warrant Officer Stephens said, "You want us to take off, too, boss?"

Denton didn't answer him. Instead, he leaned over until his face was close to Warner's and said, "Now, let's get one thing straight here, Captain. You're in UWOA Sword now, and I don't give a damn what you think your orders said or didn't say. The last time I checked, I was still in charge of this area of operations, and until someone who outranks me shows up, that means you'll damn well do *what* I say, *when* I say it—and if you don't get your ass off your shoulders, I'll start telling you *how* to do it. Now, I don't know what your problem is, but we don't have time for all this bullshit. So you can make a choice—either continue being a problem, or start being a solution to the problem we have out here, which is killing as many Russians as we can, as quickly as we can. So which will it be, Captain?"

Denton could feel the SFOD A-323 commander's hateful glare in the darkness. "Major," Warner said, "I think we would be well advised to have this conversation away from the presence of junior officers. I—"

"Oh, really?" Denton said. "Well, I disagree, Captain. If I send these warrant officers away, who's going to pull me off when I start beating the living *shit* out of you? Now, I'll tell you one more time, Warner—either I start hearing a whole bunch of 'yes, sirs' from you, or I'll relieve you of command of A-323."

"Are you threatening me, Major?" Warner said.

"No, Captain. I'm *promising* you. As of this moment, you're no longer in command of A-323. You're now the executive officer of B-30. From now on your job is to handle the logistics of this operation. You will ensure that the aircraft are fueled and armed and ready to fly. You will ensure that every man here is fed and rested, and that casualties are properly cared for. You'll keep me informed of the status of supplies and equipment, and you'll make damned certain that this hide site—and any others we occupy—are well camouflaged and appropriately defended. And you'll do these things properly, or I will relieve your ass of those duties and put you on drop-zone surveillance of Dasht-e Lut, that wonderfully hospitable desert somewhere out to the west of us. Do I make myself clear, Captain Warner?"

"But—"

"But nothing, Warner! Now, I suggest you go start performing your duties as XO of this detachment—and while you're at it, send O'Neill and Puchinelli back over here. We've got a war to plan and fight."

Warner stood. He decided he'd better leave it alone for now. At the first opportunity he'd radio back to the rear and tell them that Denton was obviously too fatigued or otherwise unfit to command the little force in UWOA Sword. Meanwhile, he'd perform those duties Denton had outlined to him. At least he'd be safe, managing the logistics of the operation. And if Denton were to become a casualty, well, then things would be done *his* way. If not, he would see what happened and try to get in the major's good graces. He saluted, said, "Yes, sir," and headed off to find the senior NCOs as Denton had directed.

"Where do they come up with assholes like that?" Stephens said when Warner was gone.

"I don't know, Red," Denton said. "Maybe he's just nervous about being in combat. He seemed to be relieved when I told him he'd stay here and run the refuel/rearm point. Anyway, we've got more important things to think about right now. All right, here's the plan. . . ."

0245 hours GMT (0615 hours local time), 29 September
Vicinity of Kuh-e Taftan mountain, Iran

By sunrise, Denton's plan for his detachment's next engagement of the advancing Soviets was being put into place.

Centered some fifty kilometers north of Khash is a large hill mass called Kuh-e Taftan. Rising to a height of almost 13,000 feet, it is more than twice the altitude of the high desert surrounding it. The two roads between Zahedan and Khash wind along the lower slopes of the mountain on both sides of it. The western road splits at the village of Eskalabad on the southwest side of the mountain, but both of these western roads end up in Khash. Anyway, Denton's plan was to hit the Soviets well before they reached the intersection where the west road split. At the same time he would hit the armored column on the eastern road along the other side of the big mountain.

With the AWACS to warn them of any Soviet aircraft approaching UWOA Sword, Denton decided to use the Stealth Hawk to drop off his observation posts and missile-launching teams during daylight, so that they would be in position to hit the Soviets that night. Although the sophisticated helicopter would no doubt be seen by some of the Iranian and Baluchi herdsmen in the area, he doubted that the information would reach the Soviets, and even if it did, there would be little they could do except halt their columns and mount a massive attempt to find it—a venture that stood little hope of success in the big, rugged hill mass in which it would hide.

By midafternoon, with the Hawk's invaluable help, the teams were resupplied from his center cache site, and Denton had his force in place and ready.

On the western road he had two observation posts manned, each with two remote electronic OPs consisting of TV cameras and laser target designators, and each with four 84-mm AT-4 antitank rockets. The AT-4s, rigged for remote firing, were sighted in on the road at choke points. If they were able to destroy vehicles at those points, it would halt the column until recovery vehicles could be brought forward to remove the destroyed targets. In addition, each OP team had a Stinger antiaircraft missile and two Dragons.

Also on the western road was positioned one of the four TOW teams of A-323. From high on the mountain above the road they would be prepared to pick off key targets within the motorized rifle regiment's column, change positions to where they had other rounds cached, and hit the enemy again.

On the road that wound through the eastern slopes of the mountain the other three TOW teams and the other two remote OP teams were ready to take on the column of vehicles of the Soviet tank regiment that was moving in that direction. Each TOW team had four deadly tandem-warhead missiles to expend in the coming night's battle.

The little Hughes 500 helicopters, armed with two Hellfire missiles and two TOWs each, would strike the column that reached B-30's killing ground first. The Stealth Hawk, with its electronic countermeasures and air-to-air Stingers, had the mission of providing defense against low-flying Soviet aircraft and was prepared to ferry the OP and TOW teams south to their next positions. Shortly before daylight it would leave UWOA Sword just long enough to rendezvous with an aerial tanker over the desert and take on a fresh load of fuel.

Captain Warner did an outstanding job of coordinating the move, resupplying the teams from the cache that had been dropped days earlier to Denton's men, and ensuring that the killer eggs were armed and fueled. Denton was about to approach him with some conciliatory remarks, but Warner found him first and lodged a protest about the fact that a woman—and one not officially qualified, at that—was flying one of the Hughes 500MDs in a combat role.

"Captain Warner, it was not my decision to have Sergeant Whitaker sent out here as a combatant. Our mission is to destroy as many Soviet vehicles as we can, and in order to do that we need both killer eggs flying. So unless *you* or someone else on your *former* team is qualified to fly one of them, Sergeant Whitaker will continue to do so. That's my decision, and so far it's proved to be a good one. Now, you've done a fine job—an *outstanding* job—of keeping things flowing smoothly today. You let me worry about who's assigned what tasks and just make sure that when the shit hits the fan you keep the ammo and gas flowing—including aboard the chopper that Sergeant Whitaker's flying. Any questions?"

"No, sir. But I intend to report the fact that you've got an unqualified pilot—a *woman*—flying combat missions, at the first opportunity."

Denton glared at him. He wanted very much to beat hell out of the malcontented officer, but instead he said, very calmly, "Captain Warner, you're a very capable officer, and if you could just get the chip off your shoulder and work *with* me instead of *against* me, we could . . . ah, never mind. Why don't you get some rest before the Russians show up? There's going to be a lot of work to do when that happens, and I want everybody as rested as possible."

Denton took a short nap, then went down to the helicopter hide site to ensure that all was ready. He found Warner sitting in a makeshift bathtub consisting of a poncho lining a depression in the ground, having a bath. He stood over the captain and said, "Captain Warner, what the hell do you think you're doing?"

Without looking at him, Warner replied, "Taking a

bath, sir. It may not be the policy of B-30 to be washed and clean-shaven, but it's mine . . . just like in the *real* army."

"I see," Denton said, controlling his temper. "And how much of our precious water is your fastidiousness costing us?"

"One five-gallon can."

"And how much is left in the cache, Captain Warner?"

Warner looked up at him. "Exactly sixty gallons."

"So if everyone decided to indulge himself in a poncho bath, we'd be out of water before half of them got to do so, am I correct?"

"Yes, sir."

"Then what you're doing doesn't make a hell of a lot of sense, does it?"

Warner said nothing. He knew Denton was unquestionably right this time.

"Get rinsed off and get out of there, Warner," Denton said. "It's bad enough to waste water like that, but if a Soviet aircraft happened to show up and see the glare off your bathtub, you could cause somebody to be killed as a result, and that would make me even angrier than it would to die of thirst out here." With that he walked away.

His radio operator caught up with him. "Sir, OP One reports a column of dust about five miles to his north. Looks like they'll be here before dark."

"OK, Sparky," Denton said. "Let's get the chopper crews standing by."

CHAPTER 17

1400 hours GMT (1730 hours local time), 29 September
Khash, Iran
Northern boundary of Unconventional Warfare Operations Area Tiger

In Unconventional Warfare Operations Area Tiger preparations were also being made to take on the Soviet motorized rifle and tank regiments when they arrived. Captain Rocco Birelli and his A team, along with their guerrilla force of one hundred forty Baluchi tribesmen, were anxious and ready for action. From the intelligence reports they were receiving from the Special Forces Operations Base in England and the news broadcasts from the BBC they knew the Soviets would probably arrive in Khash sometime the following day.

It had been a busy day for Birelli, his teammates, and their Baluchi guerrillas. Shortly after the MH-60P Stealth Hawk had arrived the night before to exfiltrate the Soviet pilots they had captured, Birelli had received a message from SFOB:

SECRET: 0000 TIGER DE BASE: ENEMY FORCES BEING SUCCESSFULLY DELAYED BY ELEMENTS TO YOUR NORTH. NATIONAL COMMAND AUTHORITY WANTS MAXIMUM EFFORT BY UNCONVENTIONAL WARFARE FORCES TO STOP ENEMY NORTH OF TWO EIGHT DEGREES NORTH LATITUDE. PROCEED NORTH AS SOON AS POSSIBLE AND ENGAGE ENEMY IN AND AROUND KHASH XX KHASH WITH ALL AVAILABLE RESOURCES. ESQUIRE XX ESQUIRE WILL RECEIVE DROP OF ADDITIONAL MUNITIONS VICINITY KHASH TONIGHT. YOU ARE TO LINK UP WITH HIM VICINITY COORDINATES LIMA MIKE THREE THREE SIX ONE FIVE NINE ON ARRIVAL. IF

NEGATIVE CONTACT WITH ESQUIRE RADIO BASE FOR IN-
STRUCTIONS. ACKNOWLEDGE. SECRET: KKKK

When he received the message Birelli had called for his
Baluchi counterpart, the guerrilla force commander,
Lakha Nawaz. At the time they were some fifty kilometers southeast of Khash, while the other half of the force
was moving into position along a road many miles to
their west. Birelli explained the message to Nawaz and
showed him on a map that twenty-eight degrees north
latitude was twenty-five kilometers south of Khash.

"You remember I told you about the news conference
the president had a couple of days ago?" Birelli asked.
"Well, apparently he wants us to help show that he was
dead serious. Do you think we can get there in time?"

"God willing, we can," Nawaz replied.

As they were making preparations to load their weapons and equipment on horseback for a hurried move
north, one of their security outposts had sent a message
saying that a truck was coming south along the road near
them. It stopped a mile from the base camp, and a
Baluchi man got out and walked straight toward the
outpost. It was a messenger from their chieftain, Chakur
Nothani.

"He sends God's blessings and offers this truck to
carry as many weapons as possible to kill Russians," the
messenger said.

"How did he know where we would be?" Birelli asked
Nawaz.

"Chakur Nothani knows such things," Nawaz answered.

"What about the rest of our men, Nawaz?" the American asked, and the messenger said, "There is a truck en
route to them now as well."

"And Nothani knows where they are, too?"

"Of course."

The Special Forces soldiers of A-326 and their guerrilla force spent the rest of the day moving men and
equipment by truck, horseback, and foot to Khash.
Rocco Birelli met Dick Medlin—"Esquire"—at the

appointed place south of the town. From the CIA operative Birelli learned what had been delivered by the previous night's parachute drop, which had been received by Medlin, Nothani, and some of the men from the underground organization they had established in Khash. There were more TOW and Dragon missiles, 60-mm mortar rounds, and antitank and antipersonnel mines. And there was a large amount of explosives, as well as additional medical supplies.

"Christ," the A team leader said to Medlin as he read the list showing the equipment that had been dropped. "There's enough stuff here to turn Khash into another Stalingrad!"

"You've got the picture, Rocco," Medlin said. "We can't let them get past us—not in any strength, anyway. Now let's get into town so you can plan how to put all of this stuff to use."

Khash was full of feverish activity. Men, women, and children were at work digging shelters and fighting positions in the floors of the stone and mud buildings of the town and chiseling holes in the walls of many of them.

"What's the purpose of the holes?" Birelli asked. "Firing ports?"

"Yes," Medlin answered. "Firing ports and bunkers to hide in."

When they reached the northern edge of the town they got out of the battered old Datsun pickup that Medlin was driving. Rocco Birelli surveyed the approaches to Khash, trying to envision what two regiments of Russians would look like approaching the town in tanks and armored personnel carriers. He shuddered at the vision of more than two hundred armored vehicles—most of them tanks—bearing down on the town.

He carefully studied the ground around him.

The town of Khash sits on a flat desert floor at an elevation of about 4,500 feet between two ridgelines oriented northwest to southeast. One ridge, four kilometers to the west of the town, rises to a height of 7,451 feet. On the east, some three kilometers from town, is a ridge that averages 5,500 feet in height. One deep wadi, or riverbed, runs from the northwest just past the west side of the town.

The wadi and the town itself are the only real obstacles to tracked vehicles for the entire seven-kilometer width of the desert valley in which the town sits. It would be an awesome task for Birelli and his force to try to stop them. He suddenly felt ill at the thought. Perhaps, with a reinforced American tank battalion supported by artillery and engineers, it would be possible to stop two Soviet regiments. But he had no tanks, no artillery support, and about one company of men—albeit a company armed with a large number of antitank missiles and a thirst for Russian blood.

"What I wouldn't give for an engineer battalion," the Special Forces captain mumbled, "and a week for them to put in a minefield." Then a thought struck him, and he turned to Medlin.

"Wait a minute!" he said. "Why not?"

"Why not what?" Medlin asked.

"Why not a mine field? I mean, if stopping the Soviets is so damned important, why shouldn't we be able to get an air-delivered mine field laid out here, north of town? Let's get back into town, Dick, so I can get on the radio."

He sent an urgent message back to the Special Forces Operations Base requesting the delivery of such a mine field, ending with the assessment that "Unless such support is given prior to arrival of enemy forces, the likelihood of stopping or even slowing them for long north of the two eight degree latitude is remote."

He received an initial reply from SFOB just a few minutes later. "The employment of aerial mines was previously considered and rejected by Joint Chiefs of Staff. However, in view of current situation, Commander, 3rd Special Forces Group, will press for approval on urgent basis. Will advise."

"Shit!" Birelli exclaimed when he read the reply. "By the time the request gets run through the damned bureaucracy the Russkies will be in Chah Bahar." He sighed deeply, then gathered his teammates and the

Baluchi leaders around him and outlined his plan for trying to halt—however temporarily—the Soviet juggernaut that would soon be reaching the eastern Iranian village of Khash.

In the southernmost Unconventional Warfare Operations Area—UWOA Shark—Captain Bill Davidson and his A team were planning to do their part to show the Soviets the folly of their invasion, too. A short time earlier they had received an order to move toward Chah Bahar and the nearby airfield and conduct an initial attack against the airborne regiment anxiously waiting there for reinforcements from the north.

But before the Soviets could reach Chah Bahar, or even Khash, they would be required to run the deadly gauntlet on either side of Kuh-e Taftan, the high mountain mass centered fifty kilometers to the northwest where Major Mark Denton and his determined force were going into action.

1545 hours GMT (1915 hours local), 29 September
Unconventional Warfare Operations Area Sword
Kuh-e Taftan Mountain, Iran

It was nearly sunset when the lead element of the Soviet motorized rifle regiment reached the killing ground chosen by Denton and his men. Four Mi-8 helicopters made a high pass over the roads on both sides of the mountain, dropping an occasional flare in an attempt to confuse any Stinger missiles that might be locked in on the heat of their engines. When no missiles were fired, the helicopters descended, dropping security troops off at four points high up on the mountainside. The nearest was more than three kilometers away from any of Denton's men and therefore presented little threat.

Again the four vehicles of the regiment's combat reconnaissance patrol—three BTR-80 armored personnel carriers and a ZSU-23-4 antiaircraft gun system—were allowed to pass unharmed. But the lead vehicle of the forward security element—a BTR-80—was destroyed by a remotely fired AT-4 rocket as it reached a narrow stretch of road between two high, rocky banks. The vehicle behind it tried to push the eight-wheeled carrier out of the way so the column could pass, but it was killed by the first TOW round fired by the three-man team manning the single TOW launcher above the west road. Special Forces Operational Detachment A-323, sent to reinforce Mark Denton's team, had fired its first round in anger. The result was three Soviet soldiers killed, six wounded, and the vehicle's other two passengers scrambling for cover. The vehicle itself burst into flames, further plugging the narrow defile and preventing the vehicles behind from passing.

The remaining BTRs in the forward security element and the platoon of T-80 tanks attached to them began firing wildly at the area from which the AT-4 and the TOW had been launched. Unfortunately for them, the Soviet squad atop the ridge also began firing at the position from which the antitank team had fired their first round. As the Americans scrambled through a narrow, protecting draw to their next firing position, the weapons of the Soviets on the road were shifted to the source of fire of their comrades on the ridge top, killing or wounding four Russian infantrymen and scattering the rest.

The next effective round fired was a Hellfire missile launched by one of the H-500MD helicopters. Guided by the laser beam from one of the remote observation posts, it slammed into the ammunition of the lead T-80 tank, the turret of which flew out of the big fireball of the explosion and landed atop the BTR-80 in front of it. Several seconds later a TOW missile from the other killer egg knocked out an antenna-laden BTR-80, ending the life of the commander of the lead Soviet motorized rifle battalion.

Two Mi-24 Hind helicopter gunships approached from the north, one flying low, the other several thousand feet above it, looking for the telltale flash and smoke trail of any Stinger missiles that might be launched at his wingman. In the fading light, neither the crew of the higher Hind nor its radar saw the Stealth Hawk approach to a range of three thousand meters to their right rear. By the time they saw the Hawk's first Stinger it was nearly to the Hind's engine. The Soviet gunship twirled crazily around in the sky for several seconds, then its rotor blades flew off, and it plunged to earth and exploded.

The second Hind made one gun run on the ridgeline above the road before it fell victim to the Stealth Hawk's second Stinger. It managed to crash-land on a small plateau just west of the road, but as the crew attempted to scramble to safety a Hellfire missile from Red Stephens's little H-500 slammed into its rocket pods, and it erupted in a series of secondary explosions.

By dark the Americans on the west road had accounted for the destruction of five BTR-80s, three T-80 tanks, and two Mi-24 helicopter gunships. In addition, the Soviet infantrymen sweeping the ridges for remotely fired rockets had discovered three AT-4s and a remote OP. But they had paid a heavy price, as two of the rockets and the remote OP were blown up in their faces, killing several of the Russians and wounding several more.

The AWACS over the Strait of Hormuz warned the helicopters of approaching aircraft just as darkness fell. Within two minutes both Hughes 500s and the MH-60 were shut down in their hide sites, their weapons pods being replenished for the next engagement.

There was a lull of nearly half an hour until a Soviet bulldozer-blade-equipped tank arrived from well back in the column to push the destroyed vehicles off the narrow road so the rest of the column could pass. A-323's TOW team destroyed it as it arrived to clear the narrow defile, further blocking the gap.

Well to the northeast of the killing zone along the eastern road, across the hill mass from the latest Soviet victims of Denton's men and their high-technology weapons, the Russian tank regiment continued its slow but steady advance. Master Sergeant Pete Puchinelli, in charge of the two OP teams and three TOW teams waiting to engage the enemy tank column on the east road, knew they were coming. He reported to Major Denton that his northernmost observation post could see the faint images of the lead tanks with the low-light-level television camera of one of their electronic OPs.

"They're still about seven or eight klicks from our initial point of engagement," Puchinelli said. "And they're either halted or moving real slowly, over."

"Roger, Pooch," Denton answered. "Keep me advised of their progress. We're going to sit tight here until Roulette—the AWACS—advises there's no bogeys near. If the tanks haven't reached you by then, I'll use the killer eggs for one more hit on the west road, then send them to support you, over."

"This is Pooch," the steady old NCO answered, "roger your last. How much damage you done over there?"

"Five BTRs, three tanks, and a couple of gunships so far. Best thing is we've got a tight spot in the road blocked with three burning vehicles. I plan to have O'Neill and his guys lay low until they try to clear the wrecks again. No sense wasting ammo or giving away our firing positions as long as we've got 'em stopped, right?"

"That's affirm," Puchinelli said. "I've got a couple of spots near the end of the killing zone where I think I can plug up this road, too. But I believe we can kill a few tanks before they get there, over."

"Roger, Pooch. Keep me informed," Denton said.

It was nearly half an hour before Puchinelli called Denton again.

"Base, this is Pooch," he said. "Be advised, the tanks are definitely halted about six kilometers northeast of us. I guess you guys have got 'em scared to move this way, over."

"We'll see, Pooch," Denton answered. "Roulette just advised us we've got clear skies, so the killer eggs are about to do their thing again."

"And Base," Red Stephens broke in, "this is Aphid lead. We're topped off, reloaded, and on the way to lay some eggs on the red brick road, over."

"Roger, Aphid," Mark Denton said. "Good hunting."

Over the intercom Stephens said to his female copilot, "OK, Cat, bag us some trophies."

Sergeant Catherine Whitaker led the pair of Hughes 500MD helicopters in a long arc through a valley that curved northeast then northwest behind the crest of the mountain. When she was several kilometers east of the enemy motorized rifle regiment she headed due west up another valley, which led to a gap in the mountain range overlooking the road. There she slowly raised the helicopter until she could observe the road through the mast-mounted sight. She held the little aircraft there for nearly a minute while Red Stephens observed the Soviets on the TV-like screen of the forward-looking infrared sensor.

"OK, Cat," he said. "In the flat area on the other side of the road they've set up an artillery battery. The trucks behind the guns are probably the ones with the ammo in them. Let's hit them."

"All right, sir," she said. "Hellfire or TOW?"

"Uh, let's use a TOW while we still have surprise working for us back here."

"Roger," she said, then she keyed the radio mike to advise Bart Evans and his wounded copilot, Miles Goodwin, of the target. "Aphid Two, this is Aphid One. Where are you now?"

"We're a couple of hundred meters behind you, One."

"Roger, Two. We're going to hit a howitzer battery just across the road to the west. Find a firing position and let me know when you're ready to fire, over."

"Wilco, Cat," Evans said, and he turned, flew south several hundred meters, then lifted his chopper up near the top of the ridge line. There he spotted the target but also saw, south of it, a ZSU-23 antiaircraft gun system.

"I've got a ZSU in sight over here, One. I'd better take him on first, then shift to the arty battery."

"Roger, sir," she replied. "I'll let you fire first, then."

"OK, Cat. Stand by. . . . Hellfire armed . . . and fired!"

She saw the flash of Evans's Hellfire, popped up, and

launched a TOW at the truck nearest to the enemy howitzers. The flash of Evans's missile striking its target was visible to her left front well before her TOW round hit home, but she held the crosshairs steady on the side of her target until it exploded. The TOW's warhead caused the immediate sympathetic detonation of scores of 122-mm high-explosive artillery rounds, lighting the hillsides for kilometers in every direction.

"Nice shot!" Stephens exclaimed as Cat pivoted the helicopter and dived back down the valley to go to another firing position.

By the time Aphid Flight returned to the rearm/refuel site half an hour later, their eight missiles had accounted for a ZSU-23-4 antiaircraft system, two ammunition trucks, three BTR-80s, and a BRDM-2 antitank guided missile carrier.

Meanwhile, another vehicle farther south on the road had been destroyed by the ground-mounted TOW fired from the ridge top by A-323's three-man crew.

Soviet artillery started falling while the H-500s were being prepared for another sortie. In an attempt to stop their hidden tormentors, the Soviets began a steady volume of artillery and mortar fire on the crests of every hill and ridge within three kilometers of the road. In addition, they began to launch a salvo of 122-mm Katusha rockets at every site within the hill mass that looked as if it might be a good hide site for the helicopters. In the case of one salvo, their guess was correct. Two of the big rockets landed within the perimeter of Denton's hide site. The first Katusha landed near the rearm/refuel point, where Bart Evans was helping Cat Whitaker's fellow ground crewman, Specialist Wally Christian, reload a Hellfire missile into Aphid Two. Fragments of the exploding warhead tore into the men and their aircraft. Evans's left leg came off at the knee, and his left hand was smashed. Christian was even less lucky—a large chunk of steel tore off the back of his skull, taking much of his brain with it. He was dead before the second rocket hit with another ferocious but harmless explosion seconds later.

Cat Whitaker, sitting alone in Aphid One, was already in the process of cranking up her helicopter by the time the second rocket hit. Shielded by Aphid Two, her helicopter was untouched by the explosion of the first round. The second was even farther from her, but, not knowing if the hide site had been discovered and was being targeted by enemy artillery, she was determined to get the helicopter out of the area before it was destroyed or damaged. As soon as she had enough RPMs to lift off she did so, buzzing away down the narrow valley to the northeast.

She tried to raise Base on the radio but got no reply. SFC O'Neill, some distance northwest, heard her unsuccessful attempts to raise Denton or his radio operator and called her. "Aphid One, this is Oscar One, over."

"This is Aphid One. I can't get Base to answer. They were under artillery fire when I left. What should I do, over?"

"Is Aphid Two with you?"

"Negative. I took off just after the first couple of rounds hit. One explosion was pretty near the other 500. I don't know if it and the crew were hit, over."

"OK, Cat," O'Neill said. "See if you can find a safe place to set down. The major and them are probably just away from the radio right now, sorting things out. Just sit down and take it easy for the time being."

The crew of the Stealth Hawk, sitting in a small valley near the northern edge of the hill mass, where they were waiting to engage any intruding enemy helicopters that dared to appear over the battle area, heard the conversation.

"Aphid One, this is Hawk," the aircraft commander called over the radio. "What's your position?"

Cat Whitaker read her coordinates off the aircraft's global positioning system indicator.

"Roger, Aphid," the MH-60P pilot said. "Sit right there. We're on the way there now to give you a hand."

At the rearm/refuel site Red Stephens, Mark Denton, and Denton's radio operator were working feverishly to tend to the amputated leg and smashed hand of Bart

Evans. Miles Goodwin, wounded in the arm days earlier, was watching them.

"Somebody had better get on the radio," Denton said as he tied a tourniquet on Evans's leg. "Where the hell's Captain Warner, anyway?"

"Don't know," Goodwin said. "But I'll man the radio."

"OK," Denton said. "Let the OPs and the other helicopters know what the situation is. And if you see that damned Warner, tell him to get down here."

As he approached Denton's command post under a ledge of rock Goodwin heard someone say, "Halt! Who goes there?"

"Oh, for fuck's sake, Captain Warner," he replied. "It's me, Mr. Goodwin. Major Denton wants you down by the rearm site."

Warner appeared from behind a rock, his rifle leveled at Goodwin. Without a word he turned and walked stealthily toward the light of the flashlights Stephens and the radio operator were holding for Denton as he worked to save Bart Evans's life.

Goodwin got on the radio and called O'Neill, Puchinelli, and the helicopter pilots.

"We took a couple of rockets in here," he said when the others had answered his call. "Christian's dead, Mr. Evans is pretty badly wounded, and Aphid Two's probably damaged, though we haven't had a chance to check it out yet. What's everybody else's situation, over?"

"This is Oscar One," Harry O'Neill answered from his position behind the ridge above the west road. "We've been taking sporadic artillery fire up here, and we have one man from A-323's TOW team slightly wounded. And the TOW launcher took a frag. It's out of action."

"Roger, Oscar One," Goodwin acknowledged. "What about you, Oscar Three?"

"This is Pooch at Oscar Three," Puchinelli reported. He was in position above the east road. "The bad guys are still stopped several miles from us. There's been a few stray artillery rounds well to the west of us, but that's all we've seen, over."

"Roger, Pooch. What's *your* situation, Hawk?" Goodwin asked.

"We're on the way to link up with Aphid One," the Stealth Hawk pilot reported.

"Break, break!" O'Neill's voice interrupted. "This is Oscar One, over!"

"Go ahead, One," Goodwin said.

"We're in a fire fight with troops just north of us on the ridge line! Probably the ones the Mi-8 dropped off this afternoon! I've got two wounded—one real bad. They've got us pinned down with a couple of machine guns."

The other Americans listening to their radios could hear the sound of small-arms fire in the background as O'Neill spoke.

"I'm afraid they're gonna keep us pinned and bring mortar fire in on us," he continued.

"I'm on the way, Oscar One," a feminine voice said over the radio. "What's your position?"

"This is Hawk. Give us a couple of minutes, and we'll set down and give you a copilot."

"No time," Sergeant Whitaker replied as she lifted off and headed for the top of the ridgeline to her west. "Say your posi . . . disregard. I've got the tracers in sight!"

She maneuvered behind a hilltop about a kilometer from where she could see two streams of green tracers— the color of Soviet tracer ammunition—intersecting at a point she assumed to be the position of O'Neill and his men.

"You where the green tracers are hitting, One?" she asked as she fixed her sight on one of the enemy machine-gun positions.

There was no need for her to use a callsign. Hers was the only feminine voice on the net.

"That's affirm, Cat," SFC O'Neill replied.

She armed a Hellfire, activated the laser in the mast of her killer egg, made sure it was on the source of one stream of tracers, and fired. The missile darted to the target and exploded in the midst of the enemy machine-gun crew. Whitaker did a slight pedal turn, waited for the second Soviet machine gun to fire again, then launched her second Hellfire. The results were the same.

She quickly moved to a position behind a point of rock about five hundred meters east of O'Neill as he said, "All right, ma'am! Good shooting! No fire from either machine gun now! We're pulling out."

"Don't 'ma'am' me, I *work* for a living!" Cat said, elated at her destruction of the enemy that was threatening her comrades-in-arms. "Move out. I'll keep you covered."

"OK," O'Neill said. He had one walking wounded, one litter patient, one dead, and four healthy men, including himself. "It's going to take us a few minutes to get improvised litters rigged up."

"Roger," Cat said. She scanned the ridge above them with her FLIR—forward-looking infrared—sensor and saw one Soviet soldier raise himself above a boulder to fire at O'Neill's position. Quickly she aimed and fired a TOW, which struck near the man. When the smoke and dust cleared she could see two more men standing some distance from where the TOW had hit. They had their hands raised high above their heads.

"Hey!" she reported over the radio. "I've got a couple of bad guys up there who want to surrender!"

"Say again?" O'Neill said.

"There are two Russians up there with their hands up! They're trying to surrender."

"Well, just keep 'em there," O'Neill said. "We don't have the time—or the people—to fuck with 'em."

"Uh, roger that," Whitaker replied. She put the sight on them and activated the laser. The men dived for cover.

"I just gave them a burst from the laser," she said, edging her little helicopter closer to the Russians' position. "They're scared shitless of it!"

"Aphid, this is Hawk," the MH-60 pilot called. "We've got you in sight. If you can hang in there a while, we'll hop up there and pick up Oscar One's people."

"Can do easy, Hawk," Whitaker said. "You copy that, Oscar One?"

"That's affirmative," O'Neill said. "We'll mark our position with an IR strobe, Hawk."

Within two minutes the MH-60 had picked up O'Neill and his men and was headed back to the rearm/refuel point.

As he lifted off the pilot said, "Good job, Aphid One. Follow me on back to base."

"I'll be there shortly," Cat Whitaker said. "I need to unload this last TOW first, though."

She turned her helicopter southwest, found a gap in the high ridge line, and buzzed through it, hugging the ground as she sped down to the road, crossed it south of the Soviet column, then turned north. A short distance later she came to a hover behind a hill, raised her H-500MD until she could see over it, and scanned the road. About fifteen hundred meters north she found what she was looking for—the four vehicles of the enemy regiment's point element, which had been allowed to pass untouched that afternoon. She fixed the crosshairs of her sight on the ZSU-23-4, whose four 23-mm guns were oriented toward the east, away from her. She popped up and fired her last missile. The TOW sped to the point on the vehicle on which her sight was steadily fixed, and it detonated.

"That's for Mr. Evans and Christian, you Communist bastards," she said. Then Sergeant Cat Whitaker, the first American female gunship pilot ever to know combat, turned her helicopter toward the south and, alone in the cockpit, headed for the hide site.

Captain Dick Warner watched Major Mark Denton feverishly working to save the life of Chief Warrant Officer Bart Evans. The flashlights held by Stephens and the radio operator were concentrated on the bloody stump of Evans's leg, and Warner fought back the urge to puke.

It wasn't the way he had imagined it would be. It was all so distant, so alien to him. These were not helpless pawns of soldiers waiting dully for some superior officer to direct their every action. These were battle-tested

American soldiers—thinking, independent men and women risking their lives by aggressively attacking and pursuing their enemies, trying, at the same time, to take care of one another. He looked at his hands, still shaking from the fear of the Soviet rocket attack. *Oh, God,* he thought. *Oh, God, it's so different from what I thought it would be.*

He had never known such humiliation as he now felt. He was the one—the only, single one of them—who had let fear control his actions. The only one who had not reacted as a member of a team. He wanted to hate them, to despise them for making him feel small, but he could not. He could only hold them in awe and envy. He was a failure.

Warner, rubbing his hands together in an effort to still their shaking, felt Denton's gaze and looked up at him in the dim glow from the flashlights.

"Think you can take over here, Warner? I need to get on the radio."

Warner felt his eyes cloud up, threatening to spill over. Failure or not, he was needed—*needed!* He took a deep breath. *Show them what you can do,* he thought. *Show them what you can do . . . show* yourself *what you can do, you son of a bitch.*

He jumped to his feet and said, "Yes, sir. I'll get Mr. Evans all fixed up, then check on what material damage the rockets did and get back to you with a report, Major Denton."

Denton watched for a few moments as Warner quickly and smoothly took over the dressing of Evans's wounds, then moved off to man his radio.

CHAPTER 18

In the town of Khash, fifty kilometers southeast of the
tiny helicopter in which Sergeant Catherine Whitaker
was making military history, Captain Rocco Birelli,
using night-vision goggles, was watching an event that
did much to relieve the sense of dread he was feeling
about trying to stop the Soviets with his A team and their
Baluchi guerrilla comrades.

The National Command Authority of the United
States had decided to honor Birelli's request for an
aerial-delivered minefield on the approaches to Khash.
Since it did not involve a direct attack by American
aircraft on Soviet forces, which would have constituted a
major escalation of the conflict in Southwest Asia, and
since the president was determined to back up his
warning to the Soviets that they had better not cross the
twenty-eighth parallel, the Chief of Staff of the United
States Air Force was ordered to comply with the Special
Forces captain's request.

The Air Force Chief of Staff complied with the order
by dispatching a full squadron of FB-111 swing-wing
fighter-bombers from England to deliver the aerial
mines.

Now, as Rocco Birelli, Dick Medlin, and their Baluchi
counterparts—Lakha Nawaz and Chakur Nothani—
watched, the FB-111s were appearing just to their north
at one-minute intervals. Each aircraft made one pass
over its assigned portion of the minefield, its long wings

swept forward to enable it to sow its deadly seeds
accurately at low speed. As one aircraft after the other
swept past, discharging a string of deadly AT2B mines
over a three-kilometer-long strip of the desert floor north
of Khash, Birelli leaned over to Medlin and whispered,
"If they'd been able to come in low and slow like this
over Tripoli a few years ago, Khadafy would have
become a martyr long before Khomeini did."

A quarter of an hour later the FB-111s, their wings
swept sharply back and their afterburners kicking their
speed to well over twice the speed of sound, were out of
Iran and over the Indian Ocean.

"Please ensure, Chakur," Birelli warned the Baluchi
chieftain, "that everyone in the region understands how
these aerial mines work. There are four things that will
trigger them: pressure, the magnetic attraction of a mass
of metal, movement, and time. In other words, something pressing down on them—whether it is a Baluchi
child or a Soviet tank; a mass of metal—even a man with
a heavy weapon—passing within a few meters of the
mine; any disturbance of the mine, such as a kick or an
attempt to pick it up; and time—something between
forty-eight and ninety-six hours, depending on the time
delay in the mine's self-destruct device—and it will
explode with deadly force. Most of the blast will go up,
but much of it will spray outward. They are terrible,
terrible weapons, and I beg you, for God's sake, to ensure
that everyone in and around this village understands
that. My president would not have sent these seeds of
death if he thought they would do harm to any of your
people."

Medlin gave Birelli a look of respectful approval, then
added, "Captain Birelli is correct, of course, Nothani. It
is your duty to make certain that your people understand
that these weapons lack souls. If your people fail to heed
the warnings that accompany them, they will be as if they
were unbelievers, dying for an unrighteous cause. Instead
of righteous martyrs, they will be only dead, for no good
cause."

The Baluchi chieftain looked at the dim figure of each

man. "They will understand by the time the sun shines on the field of mines your president has just caused to be sown," he said. "And we will give thanks to God that the deadly harvest will allow many of our people to save their martyrdom for a later time in their lives."

"If it is God's will," Dick Medlin said, and Birelli added, "God willing."

When the Baluchi leaders had left to spread the word about the deadliness of the aerial-delivered minefield Medlin sat down on the warm, rocky floor of the high desert of Baluchistan. Young Captain Rocco Birelli sat down beside him.

"You realize, Rocco, what the delivery of this minefield means, don't you?"

Birelli considered the question for a moment before answering. "Yes, I think I do. If the president was willing to risk sending that squadron of FB-111s in here, he's counting on us to give all we've got to stop the Russians here. Is that what you mean?"

"Yes," Medlin replied. "That's exactly what I mean. We've got to do the very best we can to hold them right here. Based on what we've been hearing on the BBC, it seems to me that it could well mean the difference between a diplomatic solution to all of this and a major fight between American and Soviet forces—ground, air, and sea. And God only knows where that might lead."

Both were silent, thinking their own thoughts for a long time, then Birelli said, "Those guys up north of us—Major Denton and whoever he's got with him—sure seem to be doing their share of slowing the Russians down. I'll bet the Soviets expected to be in Chah Bahar before now."

"Yeah," Medlin agreed. "You know, there was a goat herder who showed up here from up near Zahedan this afternoon. He says there're burnt-out tanks and trucks all over the roads up that way. Says he counted more than thirty on one road, and a couple of crashed helicopters, too."

"Well, I hope Nawaz's guys have reached the mountain by now. It sure will be helpful to know when the Russians

189

get past Denton and his people—and whether the tanks or the rifle regiment is leading."

"It's a pretty tough climb," Medlin said, referring to the steep southern slopes of the almost-13,000-foot mountain of Kuh-e Taftan. Although it was out of UWOA Tiger, Birelli had agreed to allow the guerrilla leader to send two men on horseback up to the mountains in which Major Denton's team was battling the Soviets. They were to observe the roads the Soviets were using and to report on their small AM radio when the enemy vehicles appeared on the roads to Khash. The radios were unsecure, but the Baluchi men would use simple code words to render their reports to Nawaz.

"Any word from SFOB on your request to establish radio contact with Denton?" Dick Medlin asked.

"Not yet," Birelli said. He had asked for Denton's frequencies and cipher in order to contact him and coordinate the attacks on the Soviets as they left UWOA Sword and entered Tiger. Also, he wanted to advise Denton of his readiness to assist him, if need be.

"Well, I bet they'll give you permission to do so next time they contact you," Medlin said.

"Yeah, it makes sense. As desperate as the government is to try to stop them here, they're bound to realize we can use all the help we can get."

1916 hours GMT (2246 hours local time), 29 September
Kuh-e Taftan Mountain, UWOA Sword

As Cat Whitaker swung south around the slopes of Kuh-e Taftan, the warning lights on the instrument panel of her helicopter all flashed, then went out. At the same time the engine of the Hughes 500 quit. She was only some fifty feet above the ground, but well up on the side of the slope.

"I'm going to crash," she thought, but even as she did so she turned right and let the helicopter descend parallel to the slope.

For a trained helicopter pilot the loss of engine power is not a great problem as long as he has adequate altitude to enable him to build up speed so he can flare his aircraft by changing the angle of the rotor blades shortly before he sets down. Much like the twirling seed pod of a maple tree, the helicopter's rotor blades enable it to "glide" to a relatively soft landing. Fortunately for Sergeant Whitaker, this maneuver, known as "autorotation," was one of the things Red Stephens had taught her when he was giving her unauthorized flying lessons.

Now her instincts as a natural aviator took over, and as she glided down the slope of the hill she allowed the aircraft to pick up speed, its rotor blades increasing RPMs as it did so. Through her ANVIS-7 night-vision goggles she saw a small, level area several hundred meters ahead and made the decision to try to land there. As she neared it she flared, the helicopter slowing both its rate of descent and forward speed as she did so. She almost got it right, but she was a little too high, and about ten feet above the ground the helicopter stalled, then dropped straight down, hard, onto the rocky surface. The strut on the right side of the helicopter broke, causing it to list sharply to that side, and the rotor blades chewed into the earth.

Whitaker was unhurt in the crash landing, but displeased with herself for flaring too high.

"Shit!" she said aloud. "I didn't even make a damned Mayday call." She keyed the radio, but the aircraft was totally without power. Obviously the helicopter's batteries were disconnected.

Quickly she scrambled out of the tilted helicopter, took the flashlight from her survival vest, and assured herself that there were no fuel leaks. Then she opened the hatch to the battery compartment—her first priority being to restore power to the radios so she could call Base or the Stealth Hawk for assistance.

Suddenly Cat felt a presence and turned around to find a man standing nearby, his AK-47 assault rifle leveled at her.

"Aphid One, Aphid One, this is Base, Base, over." Mark Denton had been trying for more than five minutes to raise Cat Whitaker on the radio. He was beginning to fear the worst.

Red Stephens, beside him, turned to the Stealth Hawk pilot and said, "Crank it up, buddy. We'd better go look for her."

"Right," his fellow aviator said. "But we're going to have to break off and meet the tanker over the desert in about an hour and a half."

"Are you sure you have enough fuel to go look for her?" Denton asked.

"Yes, sir. We're good for another three hours and twenty minutes."

"All right. Take O'Neill and a couple of his people with you for security, in case you have to set down somewhere. And one of the medics," Denton directed.

"Will do, sir. Christ, I hope we can find her. I can't believe she'd go off by herself like that with no copilot and no wingman."

The MH-60P Stealth Hawk had just departed in search of Sergeant Whitaker and her Hughes 500MD when the senior medic from Puchinelli's A team came to the command post and said, "Sir, we've got to get Mr. Evans evacuated or we're going to lose him."

"I'm going to contact headquarters right now," Denton said. "Once the Hawk gets a full load of fuel, I'll send him out on it, along with your man with the gut wound and Christian's body. I'm going to try to get them to send the other MH-60, with a surgical team on it, to meet them somewhere between here and the coast. Do you think he can hold out for a few more hours?"

"Yes, sir. I believe so. I've got a direct transfusion going into him now from one of the guys with his blood type. And I've got another man standing by to give him more if he needs it."

"Good," Denton said. "I'd better get on the radio."

While he was composing his request for the evacuation of his wounded, Denton received a burst of data on his digital message device group.

SECRET: 0000: SWORD DE BASE: CONTACT COMMANDER, SFOD XX SFOD ALPHA THREE TWO SIX, IN UWOA TIGER XX TIGER VICINITY KHASH XX KHASH FOR COORDINATION OF OPERATIONS AGAINST ENEMY FORCES . . .

The message went on to give Birelli's frequencies and cipher key and to explain that Birelli was also being advised of the fact that Denton would contact him and would assume command of A-326 and UWOA Tiger, as well as his own B team and A-323. Once that occurred, B-30 was to fall under the direct command of the 3rd Special Forces Group commander, who was now at the Special Forces Operations base in England.

Before he acknowledged the message and contacted Birelli, though, Denton had the matter of his wounded men and the missing Cat Whitaker to deal with. He punched a message into the DMDG explaining the urgent need to evacuate Bart Evans and the badly wounded TOW crewman from A-323.

He would have to wait for a reply before he could reset his radio frequencies and cipher to enable him to communicate with Birelli in UWOA Tiger.

While he waited, Master Sergeant Puchinelli called on the frequency-hopping PRC-117 to advise that the Soviet tank column was beginning to move toward him on the east road.

"Roger, Pooch," Denton replied. "I'm afraid there isn't a hell of a lot we can do from here to assist right now. Just do the best you can with what you've got. And be advised that once you start to engage them, they'll probably do like they did over here and try to take you out with mortars and artillery, over."

"Understood, Base," Puchinelli said. "I've decided to wait until we get the lead tank in this narrow defile down here, like Harry did over on the west road. We may not kill as many tanks that way, but at least we can keep them bottled up for a while."

"This is Base," Denton said. "That sounds like the best plan, in view of the current situation. Just be careful."

Mark Denton was near exhaustion and becoming increasingly worried. He had to find Cat Whitaker, if she was still alive. And he had to get the wounded men—and any casualties Puchinelli and his element might receive in their coming fight—out of Iran. But at the same time he had to start planning how he was going to continue using his dwindling resources to battle the two Soviet regiments trying to get to Chah Bahar. He suddenly found himself wishing that he could just pack everyone up and leave—go back to Fort Bragg and let XVIII Airborne Corps put their two waiting brigades ashore to fight the Soviets.

His greatest regret at the moment, though, was that he had allowed Sergeant Whitaker to fly one of the helicopters. He wondered if she was alive—if she would ever be seen again.

1924 hours GMT (2254 hours local time), 29 September Kuh-e Taftan Mountain

Cat Whitaker was alive, but she was beginning to wonder how long that would be true. The man with the AK-47 had thrown her to the ground while a second man took her flashlight and examined the wrecked H-500MD helicopter. As the first man held the muzzle of his rifle under her chin the two men held a conversation in a language she could not understand. It was only then that she realized they were not Soviet soldiers. In the darkness she had not initially noticed their native dress, and until they held their conversation in a language she knew was not Russian, she had simply assumed that her worst fears were true—that she had been captured by Soviet soldiers.

Now she began to try to explain to the men that she was an American.

"I'm American. American soldier. *No* Russian—*American!"*

Again, the men held a conversation, and this time she realized that their dialogue included words that were apparently the words—in the strange tongue the men were using—for "America" and "Russia."

"Yes," she said. "American. Me United States of America soldier. Michael Jackson . . . Muhammad Ali . . . uh, Bruce Springsteen . . . Ronald Reagan . . . George Washington . . . Abraham Lincoln!"

The man with the weapon backed off slightly, and she reached up and removed her aviator's helmet while the men had another brief conversation, the tones of which made their confusion apparent. Then one of them took a radio from his load-bearing equipment and made a call on it.

She wondered whom he was calling—whether it was the Soviets or other Iranians. After several exchanges over the radio the man who had been using it handed it to her and said something she interpreted as an order to speak to the station on the other end. She held the radio for a moment, until the man with the AK-47 waved it under her nose and made it apparent that he wanted her to speak.

"Uh, hello. . . . Is anybody there?"

An American voice on the other end said, "Unknown station, this is, ah, Yankee Doodle. Say your call sign, over."

She looked at the radio in amazement, then said, "Yankee Doodle, I'm a Yank, too. Where are you, over?"

"This is Yankee Doodle. The men with you claim you were flying a helicopter. Is that correct, over?"

She didn't know whether the voice on the radio was truly that of an American, and as relieved as she was to hear English spoken, she decided she'd better be cautious before giving any information.

"Uh, Yankee Doodle, I'm sorry, but I don't know

who you are. Are there any other Americans there with you?"

"That's none of your business," the voice said, then, "You sound as if you're a woman. Is that correct, over?"

"And you sound as if you're a redneck. Is *that* correct, over?"

"Oh," the voice on the other end said, "so we're going to have one of those World War II authentications, is that right?"

"That's affirmative," Cat replied, becoming increasingly confident that the voice on the other end was, indeed, an American. "Just like World War II. Uh, let's see. . . . Who won a Grammy for 'Eight by Ten' a couple of years ago, Redneck?"

"Why, Randy Travis, of course," the voice on the other end said. "Would you happen to know where he's from, ma'am?"

"I think he's a Tarheel, isn't he, Redneck?"

"Roger," the man on the radio replied. "You know much about the Old North State?"

"Well, let's see," she said. "Who's the coach of the team in blue?"

"Well, there's the Blue Devils and the *real* team in blue. I presume you don't mean Coach K., but the other guy. What's *his* handle, unknown lady?"

"A guy named Smith whose team plays in . . . what's the name of that facility?"

"The Dean Dome," the man replied, now completely satisfied that the voice on the other end was an American familiar with North Carolina basketball. "I believe you're a fellow Carolinian, unknown lady. You got somebody else there who can verify it?"

"That's a negative, Redneck. Just these two guys who gave me the radio to call you on."

"OK, ma'am. You gotta understand, this is mighty strange. . . . Put one of the men with you back on the horn."

She held the radio out to the man who had given it to her, and he took it and made a call. The voice of the man to whom she had been talking was audible over the radio's speaker, but this time he was speaking the same foreign tongue her captors used. After a brief conversation the man with the radio helped her to her feet, and the one with the weapon leveled at her put it on safe and slung it over his shoulder. Then the man with the radio gave it back to her.

A different voice came over the radio and said, "Unknown station, this is Yankee Doodle."

"Go ahead, Doodle," she said.

"I'm going to need one more bit of authentication here," the voice on the radio said. "Give me the first initial of the guy who's in charge of you up there. Then I'll give the second, you give the third, and so forth. You copy?"

"That's affirm," she replied. "First initial, last name, is 'delta'."

"Roger. Second initial 'echo', over."

"November," she said, giving the third letter of Denton's name.

"Tango."

"Oscar."

"November," the man's voice said. "What's the next one?"

"That's all she wrote," Sergeant Whitaker replied.

"OK, ma'am. I'm convinced. I understand from the men with you that you had a chopper crash. Are you hurt?"

"That's correct," she said, "but I'm fine. Who are these guys here with me, anyway?"

"Allies," Birelli said. "You can trust them. They'll take care of you, over."

"Roger. Do you have any contact with my boss?" Cat asked.

"Negative. I've requested permission to contact him, but so far I haven't been given his frequencies."

"OK," she said. "How 'bout telling these men to let me work on the chopper, so I can see if I can get the radio working, over?"

"Wilco," Birelli said. "Hand the radio back to one of them."

After Birelli explained to the guerrillas what she wanted to do, she was able to quickly locate the severed electrical line and temporarily repair it. That done, she turned on the radios and was rewarded by the sound of Red Stephens calling, "Hello, Aphid One, Aphid One, Aphid One. This is Hawk, over."

"Hawk, this is Aphid One, over!" she responded.

"Cat!" Stephens answered with surprise. "Shit, I thought we'd lost you! Are you all right?"

"I'm OK, sir. But I'm afraid I've wrecked your aircraft, over."

"What's your location, Cat?"

"Uh, wait one, and I'll get a reading off the GPS," she said.

When she had passed him the location of the crashed helicopter he said, "Good copy. We're on the way there now! Break . . . Base, this is Hawk, you copy that?"

"Roger, roger!" Denton said with obvious relief in his voice.

"This is Aphid One," Cat said. "Hawk, be advised, there's two guys—two locals—here with me. They're friendlies who have radio contact with some other Americans."

"Understood," Stephens replied. "Probably the A team to our south. Let them know we're friendlies, will you?"

"Wilco." She gestured to the man with the radio to indicate that she wished to use it again, then called Birelli. "Please advise these guys that there's another chopper on the way in here to pick me up, Yankee Doodle."

"Will do, Unknown Lady. And tell your boss that I've been advised he'll contact me on the other radio net, over."

"This is Unknown Lady. Wilco, out."

While Birelli told the Baluchi tribesmen that another American helicopter was en route to the crash site to pick up Whitaker, she called Denton and passed him the message from Birelli.

Within five minutes, while Major Mark Denton established electronic contact between his digital message device group and that of Captain Rocco Birelli, the Stealth Hawk arrived at the site of Sergeant Cat Whitaker's wrecked helicopter.

While Whitaker and Red Stephens examined the damage to the little Hughes 500, Mark Denton began to exchange messages with Rocco Birelli. At the same time, on the ridges above the road to the east of the mountain called Kuh-e Taftan, Master Sergeant Pete Puchinelli was preparing to launch his initial missile attacks against the Soviet tank column approaching his positions.

CHAPTER 19

2003 hours GMT (2333 hours local time), 29 September
Above the east road between Zahedan and Khash
Unconventional Warfare Operations Area Sword

Puchinelli had three three-man TOW antitank missile teams and two electronic observation posts to use in trying to halt the advancing column of T-80 tanks. In addition to two antitank missiles, each TOW team had a Stinger antiaircraft missile launcher at its position. The two OP teams, with their remotely manipulated TV cameras, each had several AT-4 rockets armed and targeted on the road, and they were prepared to remotely fire them when the Soviets passed their fixed points of aim.

Puchinelli was with the center TOW team, and as the Soviet tanks neared the kill zone he called the others to reiterate his plan to hit the Russians with two TOWs from each position in rapid succession. During the thirty seconds or so that the attack was taking place, the OP teams would fire their AT-4s at any vehicles passing their points of aim. Once the second TOW from each target was fired, the OPs would detonate any remaining AT-4s and the destructive devices attached to the electronic observation posts. Then Puchinelli and the twelve men with him would scramble behind the ridge to preselected positions in the rocky mountainside. There they would wait out the barrage of Soviet artillery and mortar fire that was expected to be fired in response to their half-minute missile attack.

The attack had the expected result. The first three TOWs struck home with deadly accuracy, and during the time the TOW teams were reloading, two vehicles passed points at which the remotely fired AT-4s were aimed. One of them damaged a T-80, and the other destroyed a BMP tracked vehicle.

The Russians tried to mask their column with smoke from the tanks' on-board smoke generators, but the only result was that their tank gunners were unable to see the firing positions of the enemy TOW teams. The thermal sights of the TOWs, unaffected by the smoke from the Soviet tanks, destroyed two more T-80s and most of their crewmen and disabled another.

Puchinelli and his men quickly scrambled to their protecting positions behind the hill, and by the time the Russian artillery and mortar fire began to pound the hill, they were well hidden, deep within the rocky terrain of the mountain range. Except for one near miss that caused one American's nose to begin bleeding from the concussion, the forty-five-minute barrage did Puchinelli and his men no harm.

The Soviet tank column, however, suffered the destruction of five T-80 main battle tanks and one BMP. Two other T-80s were damaged. Soviet personnel casualties were seventeen men killed and nine wounded. And the missile ambush had the added effect of littering the narrow road with burning vehicles, two of which made it impossible for others to pass until they could be removed.

Over the radio to Mark Denton, Pete Puchinelli passed the initial report of damage his men's attack had done to the enemy. Then he crawled deep beneath a rock ledge to wait out the ineffective rage of the enemy artillery barrage.

Meanwhile, Red Stephens and Cat Whitaker examined the cause of the loss of power she had experienced with the killer egg. A fragment from the Soviet 122-mm rocket that had landed in the hide site had hit the helicopter, nearly severing the main power cables of the electrical system. The remaining strands of wire had eventually burned in two from the overload of electricity, causing her to lose all power and crash. But it appeared that they could get the chopper flying again by repairing the power cable and replacing two rotor blades and the broken strut with ones from the badly damaged H-500MD at the hide site. They had Birelli explain, over his radio link to the Baluchi tribesmen, that they were going to leave for a while, then come back and repair the damaged helicopter.

The Stealth Hawk took them back to the hide site, where Stephens and Whitaker removed the necessary parts. The Hawk then returned them to the crash site before heading out over the desert to meet the aerial tanker that would refill the sophisticated helicopter's long-range fuel tanks.

There were still several hours of darkness remaining by the time the little helicopter, now repaired, returned to Denton's command post location. The refueled Stealth Hawk, meanwhile, had flown to a position near Puchinelli and his men, who, after waiting out the Soviet artillery barrage, had moved with their TOW launchers to the pickup zone.

Major Mark Denton gathered the others around him to brief them on the current situation and plans for the immediate future.

"All right, I know everybody's immediate concern is the wounded men. The other Stealth Hawk is on the way here from Masirah right now—ETA is about forty minutes from now. We'll get Mr. Evans and the sergeant from A-323 out on it—and Christian's body. And I'm sending Mr. Goodwin out, too. The medic says the wound he got a couple of days ago is getting infected, and since we only have one killer egg left flying, there's no need for him out here.

"Now," Denton continued, "we've used up the electronic OPs we have up here, although we still have some in the southernmost cache we put in at drop zone One, west of Khash. When we get finished doing what damage we can here, that's where we'll be heading. We'll service that cache, then link up with another A team—A-

326—who are getting ready to engage the Soviets in and around Khash, when they get by us."

"A-326?" Puchinelli said. "That's Captain Birelli and Jake Brady's team. It's a good one."

"I hope so," Denton said. "Anyway, we'll be reinforcing them down there once we leave Sword. Meanwhile, though, I intend to have one last, hard go at the Russians before we leave here."

Turning to SFC O'Neill, he said, "Harry, I've asked the chopper that's coming to pick up the wounded to bring me three more TOW launchers and as many more missiles as they can carry. That'll give us six serviceable launchers—three with Pooch, and three with you.

"OK, Pooch, I'm going to send your three TOW teams up north toward Zahedan in the Hawk we have here right away. By now the bad guys should be all jammed up back there, and there should be plenty of targets. And I don't think they'll be expecting any attacks up there."

"What about Cat and me, Major D.?" Red Stephens asked.

"Well, if you think Aphid One's fully flyable, Red," Denton replied, "I'd like for you to go up there and scout out the targets for Pooch to hit—you know, find some targets, let the Hawk set his teams down, then support his attack. Think you can do it?"

"Yes, sir . . . if Cat's not too tired to fly copilot."

"I'll be fine," the female sergeant said.

"Look, I know everybody's tired as hell," Denton remarked. "So if you don't think you can handle these additional missions tonight, then say so. I'd rather wait until we get with Birelli's team down at Khash than have anybody go out here and get hurt because he was too tired to think straight."

"We can rest when the war's over," Master Sergeant Puchinelli said. "Right now the whole damned U.S. Army—the whole Department of Defense—is counting on us to give the Russians everything we've got. So let's get on with it."

"All right," Denton said. "Red, I want you, Pooch, and

the Hawk crew to get together, do a map recon, figure flight routes, times, and all of that, and go after the Soviet support elements southeast of Zahedan."

"As soon as he drops them off," Denton said to SFC O'Neill, "the Hawk will come back here and get you and your guys, Harry. By then the other Hawk will have dropped off your TOW systems and headed home with the wounded. You'll hit the motorized rifle regiment's rear from the hills on the west side of their route about thirty kilometers below Zahedan. Now, there shouldn't be any artillery left that far north to bother you, and if they react to you, it'll probably be with gunships or fighters, so have your Stingers ready. If the Hawk's there at the time, he can use his air-to-air Stingers again. Everybody got it so far?"

The Stealth Hawk pilot, both senior noncommissioned officers from the TOW elements, and Red Stephens all indicated that they understood, so Denton continued to outline the plan for delivering B-30's next blows to the staggering Soviet regiments. "Sergeant O'Neill, by the time the Hawk drops your team off, Sergeant Puchinelli should be ready to hit his targets, so when you get the word that the chopper's inbound to your pickup zone, Pooch, you go ahead and fire your six missiles. And Red, you and Cat can support the attack with your TOWs and Hellfires. As soon as you've launched your second volley, Pooch, hustle down to your pickup zone, load up, and get back here. Then the Hawk will go back up to O'Neill's pickup zone. You'll do the same thing Puchinelli did, Harry—fire your six missiles, hop on the Hawk, and get back here. From here we'll head south to drop zone One, then link up with Captain Birelli and his team and get ready to help him fight it out at Khash when the Russians get there."

He paused to allow everybody to absorb the plan. Then, to ensure that everyone understood, he had each of the pilots and team leaders brief back their actions. There were minor adjustments made to the plan; then, satisfied that everyone understood it, Denton said, "OK,

Pooch, you and the Hawk crew get going. You, too, Red. And good hunting. Harry, let's get down there and get set up to receive the chopper from Masirah. He should be here in about ten minutes."

Red Stephens and Cat Whitaker led the way north in their hastily repaired killer egg, with the Stealth Hawk—its cargo compartment crammed with the nine men and their TOWs and Stingers—flying some distance behind.

While they picked their way north through the valleys toward the hills above Zahedan, the other Stealth Hawk arrived after its long flight from Masirah Island in the Indian Ocean.

An army doctor and a physician's assistant hopped out as soon as it touched down, and they were directed to where the wounded men lay waiting on improvised stretchers to be evacuated. The two medical men immediately went to work to prepare the injured soldiers for the flight back to Masirah.

After offloading the additional TOW launchers and missiles for Harry O'Neill's men, Denton and his reluctant executive officer, Captain Dick Warner, helped load the wounded men and the body of the dead ground crewman, Specialist Christian, onto the helicopter. When Denton leaned into the cockpit window to thank the crew for coming to B-30's assistance again, the pilot said, "Sir, I was told to let you know that if you want us, we'll head back up here to help you first thing tomorrow night. We hear you're probably going to get in a pretty good punch-up around Khash in a day or so."

"Oh, that would really make a difference. That's great!" Denton said. "Your wingman could use a little help hauling us around. And it wouldn't hurt if you brought the docs back with you, too. And some more TOW rounds."

"We can do that, boss," the pilot said. "Just send a request to SFOB. We've already got the skids greased back on Masirah."

"I sure will!" Denton said. "And thanks. Now, you'd better get these wounded guys back to Masirah."

Even before the sound of the departing helicopter disappeared, Denton was punching the request for its subsequent return into the keyboard of the DMDG.

"Major," Dick Warner said to Denton after he had transmitted the request, "you got a minute?"

"Sure, Captain Warner. Excuse us, will you, Sparky?" he said to his radio operator.

When the other man was gone Warner said, "Sir, I guess I got off on the wrong foot with you, didn't I?"

"Yeah, Captain Warner, I guess you could say that."

"Well, I . . . I apologize for that, sir. I mean, I guess I had this weird idea about what combat would be like. You know what I mean, Major?"

"Yeah," Denton said. "I know what you mean."

"It's, well, I mean, after seeing what's gone on out here the last couple of days—the rocket attack, and Mr. Evans with his leg blown off, and the NCOs going out again and again to hit the Russians—after seeing all of that, and especially after seeing Sergeant Whitaker go off killing Russians by herself, then crashing, and still going out after them again . . . it leaves me feeling like a self-serving, chickenshit, son of a bitch."

So, Denton thought, *maybe the guy's going to be all right after all.* "Well, Captain Warner, there's a lot of us who sort of get off track with our ideas about the army. You know, we seem to act like the army—and the troops—are here to serve us, instead of the other way around. You think maybe you had that sort of attitude?"

"Yes, sir. It's *exactly* the way I thought. I hate to admit it, but when we came out here I saw this operation as a way to get a little glory for myself. I mean, I was all set to sacrifice some of my own men just so *I* could make a name for myself. I guess I've succeeded in making a name, all right—Joe Shit, the ragman."

Denton chuckled. "Let me tell you a little war story, Captain Warner. A few years ago I was a platoon leader in 1st Ranger Battalion. I never had been in combat, but when we got orders to jump into Grenada I said to myself, 'OK, Denton. All you gotta do is get these hard-dicked Ranger privates to fight like hell, and you can claim all the credit for being a wonderful leader.' I was gonna be a real hero at their expense. I got hit by a sniper in the first half hour, though, and missed most of the action. Then, after those young Rangers *did* fight like hell, in comes the 82nd and claims all the medals. On paper they look like the heroes, even though the Rangers did almost all the fighting. But *they* know—and, I daresay, those ambitious, medal-hunting officers from the division know—who the real heroes were. And in the end, you know the only thing that'll matter? It's like Colonel Mike Malone used to say—'That last moment, when we're laid out on a cold, gray slab, and we're looking up in the mirror just before the lights go out— when that time comes, the guy in the reflection will decide whether we were good officers or not. And that's all that'll really matter.' Am I making any sense?"

"Yes, you are, Major Denton. A whole lot of sense."

"Well, I'll tell you what we'd better do then, Captain Warner. We'd better get down to the LZ and get you linked up with Sergeant O'Neill. He's only got two men on one of his TOWs. The chopper will be back soon from dropping Pooch off, and I'd hate for you to miss the chance to go with 'em. But let me give you one final bit of guidance before you take off."

"What's that, sir?"

"Don't fuck up. . . . That's all, Warner—just don't fuck up."

When Denton told O'Neill that Captain Warner was going with him as a member of the understrength TOW team, the crusty NCO started to protest. But he had developed a great deal of trust in the officer who had been his boss for the past few weeks, since they had begun preparing to demonstrate Denton's concept, which had since proved so devastating to the Soviets in Iran. So he said simply, "Very well, sir."

Captain Warner further improved the situation when he said, "It's your show, Sergeant O'Neill. You're the guy with the experience. Just tell me what you want me to do."

"Will do, sir," O'Neill replied. "Stick with me, and I'll

see that you get caught up on experience real quick like. You know how to operate a TOW system, Captain?"

"I was a TOW platoon leader in the 82nd," Warner replied. "And being an arrogant bastard, I hogged more than my share of the practice rounds we got."

"Well, sir," O'Neill said, his teeth showing in a grin in the moonlight, "grab that there launcher. We're fixin' to see what kind of TOW gunner you are in combat."

CHAPTER 20

2300 hours GMT (1900 hours EDT), 29 September
(0230 hours Iran time, 30 September)
The Pentagon, Washington, D.C.

In the United States, the National Security Adviser was in the National Military Command Center, meeting with the Joint Chiefs of Staff and the commanders-in-chief, U.S. Special Operations Command and U.S. Central Command. The National Security Adviser listened intently as the JCS briefing officer outlined the current tactical situation in southeastern Iran.

"North of Chah Bahar, in Unconventional Warfare Operations Area Shark, Detachment A-325, with more than 200 Baluchi fighters, continues to move toward the Soviet airborne regiment's positions around the port and the airfield northwest of it. They should be in position to launch their attack by dark tomorrow evening—that's shortly after noon tomorrow, Washington time."

The head of the National Security Council nodded in acknowledgment.

"As of two hours ago, the forces in Unconventional Warfare Operations Area Sword," the briefer continued, pointing to Denton's UWOA on the large map beside him, "have continued to keep the Soviets from passing the Kuh-e Taftan hill mass. They have been resupplied with three more TOW weapons systems and eighteen additional rounds by the MH-60P that was dispatched from Masirah to recover their battle casualties—one KIA and three WIA. The casualties are now aboard the USS *America.*

"They currently have one AH-500MD and one MH-60P working for them, and they plan to attack the Soviets once more on both their axes of advance before retiring to Unconventional Warfare Operations Area Tiger, where they will link up with Special Forces Operational Detachment A-323 in and around the town of Khash."

"When can we expect the Soviets' lead elements to reach Khash?" the National Security Council chief asked.

The commander-in-chief, USSOCOM, answered him. "That's difficult to say, sir. Actually, we expected them to reach Khash yesterday, but Major Denton and his people seem to keep finding ways to prevent them from passing. Still, if they ever manage to get past the guys in Sword, they could reach Khash in a few hours."

"I see. And how long do you estimate they'll be able to hold the Soviets at Khash?"

This time the commander of CENTCOM responded. "Again, it's really difficult to say. Once the fight starts, it'll depend on how long it takes the Sovs' attack formations to arrive and build up for their assault. And a lot depends on how willing they are to throw everything they have at the defenses there. From the reports we're getting from CIA, they're having a lot of trouble with desertions, vehicle maintenance—even getting enough fuel to their forward battalions. If all goes well, from their point of view, they could break through in a few hours. But my best guess is that it'll take them at least twenty-four hours."

The commander of USSOCOM voiced his agreement with the latter estimate. "With the Baluchi guerrillas and the A detachment that's already in Khash, Major Denton will have about ten times as many men as he started out with, and he's already held them off days longer than we thought he could. If we could give him some Apache attack helicopters, there's—"

"But we're not going to do that, General," the National Security Adviser said. "Not until they cross the twenty-eighth parallel. And then it'll be CENTCOM's fight, with all the air support two carrier groups can muster, followed by everything we can push in there, until the bastards either quit, or the whole thing escalates into World War III."

Turning to CINCCENT, he asked, "Are you ready to do that, General?"

"The 3d Brigade of the 82d Airborne will be in six hours after we say 'go,' sir, followed by an armor-heavy brigade from the 24th Division. The two Marine MAUs will be in reserve until we get another brigade from each division in. That will put a reinforced division ashore about ninety-six hours after H-hour."

For a moment the leaders of one of the world's two most potent armed forces silently considered what the results might be if they were forced to meet the other superpower on the battlefield. Then the Chairman of the Joint Chiefs broke the silence by asking, "What do the possibilities of a negotiated settlement look like, sir?"

"They're getting better all the time. Gorbachev's popular support, even among the ethnic minorities in the Soviet Union, seems to be the key. They're finally coming to the realization that if he goes, their freedoms go with him, to be replaced by Russian tanks again. And none of them want that. We're hoping that the new concessions the satellite states and the internal dissident groups are beginning to make— just to keep him in power—will cause the rest of the Politburo to agree to back off. The other thing that's key, of course, is what's going on in Iran. They know we've only got a handful of troops in there, and they're beginning to see that if two regiments can't defeat a handful of Americans, how the hell are they going to stand any chance of beating *divisions* of them? But let's get back to the current tactical situation, and then I need you to brief me on exactly what's going to happen if they get through before there's a settlement."

Southeast of Zahedan, Red Stephens was easing his
Hughes 500 up behind a hill overlooking the village of
Kacharud, on the east road out of Zahedan. As the
mast-mounted sight cleared the top of the hill, Cat
Whitaker, observing the forward-looking infrared screen
on the instrument panel between them, said, "Holy . . .
look at that, Red!"

He flipped up his night-vision goggles and looked at
the FLIR screen. Beside the road several kilometers to
his front was almost every helicopter supporting the
two Soviet regiments. As he manipulated the pedals to
swing the sight north and south Cat counted the aircraft.

"It looks like about six Hind gunships, five Hooks or
Halos—I can't tell which—and five or six Mi-8s," she
said with astonishment.

Realizing that such a concentration of enemy forces
was bound to be well defended, and probably surrounded by outposts, he eased the chopper back behind
the hill and radioed the Stealth Hawk, hovering in a
valley several kilometers behind him.

"Hawk, this is Aphid. Looks like we've found their
main rotary-wing airfield. We've got about sixteen or
eighteen helicopters laagered off the road near this little
village up here."

"Roger that!" the Stealth Hawk pilot said. "But, hey,
the guys in back only have six missiles. Why don't we
drop them off, go back and get the other TOW teams, and
try to do them *all* in?"

"Sounds good to me, Hawk. Can you pop up back
there and try to get Base on the radio?"

Because the helicopters were down low behind the hill
mass between Denton's base area and them, they
couldn't talk to Denton on their PRC-117 FM frequency
hoppers, so the MH-60P began climbing and calling him.
The helicopter was several hundred feet above the
ground before Denton heard the call and replied, "Hawk,
this is Base. Go ahead."

"This is Hawk. We've found their helicopter airfield up here. There's at least sixteen aircraft, and God knows how many other targets. Recommend we drop these guys off to get into position, then come back there for the other TOW teams and try to take them all out at once. What say, over?"

Denton thought he must have heard the number of aircraft wrong and replied, "Say again number of aircraft, Hawk."

"I say again, sixteen. One six, over."

"This is Base. Drop those guys off and get back here ASAP for the rest of us. And tell Aphid to sit down and shut down somewhere. He needs to save his fuel until the attack starts, over."

"Hawk. Wilco, out."

Forty minutes later the Stealth Hawk had dropped Puchinelli's TOW teams off, picked up Denton and the three teams under Warner and O'Neill, and—its cargo compartment crammed with every additional missile they could fit into it—returned to the area where Stephens and Whitaker sat waiting for them. Puchinelli's teams had already moved forward to find firing positions from which to hit the airfield.

"All right," Denton told the additional teams. "Let's move up with everything we can carry. We'll leave the rest of the missiles in the Hawk, and as soon as the shooting starts he can hop forward to a position behind us and drop them off so we can fire up the rest. Let's move."

The components of each TOW launcher weigh nearly two hundred pounds, and each of the missiles, with its heavier tandem warheads, weighs about sixty-two, so that the ten men, with three launchers and six rounds, were carrying an average of almost a hundred pounds apiece of antitank missile gear strapped to their rucksack frames. Add to that the weight of their individual weapons and equipment, and the total weight each man struggled toward the firing positions with exceeded 130 pounds.

But the adrenaline flowing from the knowledge that they were going into combat with the Soviet forces several kilometers to their front enabled the well-conditioned Special Forces men to cover the distance to the firing positions in less than an hour.

When they arrived behind the row of low hills about two kilometers west of the Russian helicopters, three of Puchinelli's men were there to guide each team to the firing positions Puchinelli had reconnoitered for them.

There, each team extended the missile launcher's tripod, placed the traversing unit atop it, and affixed the AN/TAS-4 optical/thermal sight and the launch tube. Then they placed the missile guidance set beneath the tripod legs, hooked it up, and tested the system. That done, each team loaded a missile, then reported to Denton that they were ready.

Denton had moved to a position beside Master Sergeant Puchinelli and was observing with fascination the field of targets before him. There were six Mi-24 Hind gunships visible, laagered on the south side of the improvised airfield. On the north side were four big Mi-26 Halo and two older Mi-6 Hook cargo aircraft. Between those two groups sat four Mi-8 Hip helicopters and a little Mi-2 Hoplite. Just across the road were a half-dozen fuel trucks and, parked behind them, four other large trucks. A hundred fifty meters south of the Hind gunships, on the edge of the Iranian village, several tents were set up. A BMP tracked personnel carrier and two light utility vehicles were parked beside the largest tent.

Denton and Puchinelli discussed the numerous targets before deciding how to attack them. They agreed that the first priority should be the Hind gunships, followed by the four big, powerful Halos—each capable of carrying more than a hundred combat troops or twenty tons of fuel.

Denton said he thought the fuel trucks should have the next priority for attack, but Puchinelli said, "Suppose they're empty, though, boss? Anyway, what good will the fuel do them if there's no helicopters to put it in?"

"Yeah, you're right there," Denton said. "OK, we'll go with the choppers first—the six gunships with the first volley of TOWs, and the six cargo helicopters with the second. Meanwhile, the killer egg can work on the Mi-8s. Once the Hawk gets here with the other eight TOW rounds we'll just go for targets of opportunity."

He got on the radio and assigned a specific pair of targets to each TOW team. He told Stephens to crank up his helicopter and move toward the area, then attack the Mi-8 troop-carrying helicopters as soon as the shooting started.

When all TOW teams advised that they were prepared to attack their first targets, Denton said, "Roger. Stand by . . . at my command . . . fire!"

The whole area west of the enemy airfield was lighted by the blasts of six TOW missile systems being fired, and Denton watched in awe as he saw the burning rocket motors of the six missiles streaking toward the helicopters. Before they reached their targets he saw a laser's straight, thin beam appear above him, the narrow shaft of light ending on the side of one of the Hip helicopters. As the TOWs began to strike their targets, another missile—Stephens's Hellfire—cracked past.

The entire improvised Soviet airfield seemed to erupt with explosions, the Hellfire and the six TOWs' tandem warheads creating giant fireballs as fuel cells erupted, throwing burning debris all over the area. It seemed that the whole field was a giant ball of orange flame. Almost immediately rockets and missiles from the burning gunships began cooking off—some careening in crazy spirals through the air, others blasting straight out of their launch tubes. Several of the rockets slammed into other aircraft, the tents and the village behind them, and into the trucks across the road. One fuel truck exploded just as the killer egg's second Hellfire flashed overhead, riding the pencil-thin laser beam into another enemy Hip.

Then the six TOW launchers began firing again. One after the other, six more American missiles began their fast flight toward new targets, and a stream of green tracers arched toward the firing positions from the top of a small hill beyond the road.

Cat Whitaker saw the source of enemy fire just as Red Stephens was about to launch the first of his two TOW rounds, and she said, "ZSU! There, on the hill across the road!"

Stephens relaxed his trigger finger, then said, "I don't see it! Take the aircraft."

With her eyes fixed on the location from which she had seen the four rapid-firing 23-mm guns fire, Cat took the controls and said, "I have it," just as the ZSU 23-4 fired another long burst at the TOW teams. She fixed the crosshairs on the position and launched a missile. The ZSU kept up a steady stream of fire on the TOW firing positions as Cat's missile flew toward it, seeming to her to take forever. There was another series of explosions in the foreground of her sight as most of the TOWs from the ground teams found their marks. But she held the sight steadily on target, and her missile finally arrived, striking amid the muzzle flashes of the four enemy guns. The deadly stream of 23-mm rounds ceased immediately.

But they had done some damage before they were silenced by the American woman's return fire. Two of the TOW gunners had been distracted by near misses; they lost the targets in their sights as a result and missed them with their missiles. And one of the ricocheting rounds glanced off Dick Warner's thigh just after he launched his second missile. He fell back, pulling the launcher's muzzle up as he did so, and the weapon's electronic guidance system, following the sight, caused the TOW missile to arch upward into the sky. But, fighting the pain in his leg, the young captain quickly got back into position on the launcher and moved the sight back on his target. The missile, following the movement of the sight, turned toward the target once more and struck home. Another Soviet helicopter exploded in flames.

The Stealth Hawk flared to a landing behind the hill Denton's men were using for their firing positions, and one man from each team raced downhill toward it to secure another missile for his team's launcher. While they did so, Cat Whitaker loosed her last round toward the BMP beside the tents two kilometers to her east when she observed the vehicle's 73-mm smooth-bore gun go into action against the TOWs. Her missile not only silenced the enemy gun, but its shaped charge tore into the vehicle's ammunition stores, turning it into a giant fragmentation weapon whose shards of steel ripped through the Soviet tents.

"Aphid is out of ammo," Stephens advised over the radio net, and the Stealth Hawk pilot replied, "We've still got two TOW rounds in the Hawk."

"Roger that," Stephens said. "We'll be right there to pick 'em up!"

While the men with the last rounds of ammunition for the ground-mounted launchers struggled uphill to the firing positions, Mark Denton ran from launcher to launcher. He wanted to see what damage the ZSU 23-4 and the three rounds of 73-mm from the BMP had done. He learned that Captain Warner's leg had been broken, and that the two men on the southernmost team had been severely wounded while their teammate was getting a missile from the Stealth Hawk. In addition, their launcher had been badly damaged.

He yelled to the men of the neighboring team to give him a hand with the wounded. One of them ran to his assistance immediately, but the gunner and the ammo bearer, just loading another round, ignored him. They were caught up in the blood lust of action and fired their last round into a fuel truck before moving to Denton's position to assist him.

"We've got to get these guys to the Hawk," he said.

"Let us take their last round and expend it first, sir," one of the NCOs said, anxious to get in another blow against the enemy.

"All right," Denton agreed. "But hurry it up, dammit!"

They were back within a minute, their last round

having been expended against a damaged but not burning Hook helicopter.

As Denton and the other men from the two southern positions moved downhill toward the Hawk with their badly wounded comrades, they saw the Hughes 500MD lift off. The last two missiles the team had with them were in the helicopter's TOW launcher, and Stephens and Whitaker were off in search of more targets.

"Let's go north a ways and see what we can find, Cat," Stephens said as he maneuvered the little aircraft behind the hills.

A few minutes later they were hovering in a deep wadi several kilometers north of the burning enemy helicopters, observing the area before them with their FLIR. There, on the straight stretch of road in front of them, sat a giant six-engine AN-225 Dream cargo plane. In a desperate attempt to resupply their expeditionary force with badly needed repair parts, replacement troops, and munitions, the Soviets had landed the huge airplane on the road to discharge its much-needed cargo. The nose section, through which cargo was loaded and unloaded, was in the process of being raised.

Red Stephens and Cat Whitaker couldn't believe their luck. Without hesitating, he said, "Arm TOW!"

"Armed!" Cat replied as she flipped the arming switch.

Red raised the helicopter, fixed his sight on the gaping hole in the nose of the giant transport, and fired. Several seconds later the missile disappeared into the cavernous cargo compartment of the AN-225 and exploded.

Nothing the two Americans had ever seen was comparable to the eruption of the big plane and its cargo. Both fliers were momentarily blinded as a brilliant flash came from within the AN-225. The fuselage of the monstrous craft seemed to expand and burst like a huge balloon as the munitions within it erupted, and then it disappeared in a fireball as the tons of fuel in its tanks ignited.

Miles to the south, the other Americans, loading their wounded men and TOW launchers aboard the Stealth Hawk, saw the flash of the explosion and froze momentarily, wondering what it was.

Red Stephens's voice over the radio gave the answer. "We blew up a giant fuckin' airplane!" his excited voice reported. "I've never seen anything like it in my goddam life! We blew up the biggest airplane in the world! You wouldn't bel—" Then "Fuzzbuster, fuzzbuster!" he warned as his radar detection device sounded an alarm.

Above the H-500 a Soviet Su-27 Flanker counterair fighter saw the blip of the helicopter on the screen of his down-looking radar and attempted to lock in on it with the radar. Stephens, however, dashed into a narrow valley to his west, and the Fencer, flying at only four thousand feet above the ground, lost the blip of the helicopter's radar reflection as it disappeared behind one of the valley walls.

The Russian pilot, realizing what had probably happened, radioed his wingman to climb to three thousand meters, and the two Su-27s turned their noses to the sky and climbed. The Stealth Hawk saw them on his own radar as they climbed, but before he could do anything about it they were above the range of his Stingers.

As the Soviet fighters gained altitude they leveled off, then swung back toward the area where Red Stephens was working his way through another narrow valley, back toward B-30's hide site. Stephens heard the alarm of his radar detector again and realized the enemy aircraft had locked in on him once more. Just as he crested the ridge at the top of a valley he heard the Stealth Hawk pilot call, "Bogey missile launched!" Immediately Stephens flew straight at the bottom of a cliff in front of him, flaring just before he reached it—barely able to keep his little helicopter from hitting the cliff wall. But his desperate maneuver worked, because the missile was approaching from an angle that was masked by the cliff, and although the fighter's radar was still locked on the helicopter, that of the missile lost its target and exploded harmlessly into the ground.

The Stealth Hawk, en route to the hide site with the first load of men and equipment from the attack site near the Soviet airfield, went into action. In an attempt to confuse the fighters, the pilot nosed the helicopter up, pointing it in the direction his radar showed the Soviet fighters to be, then launched two air-to-air Stingers in that direction.

Although the infrared sensors in the missiles were not locked on the enemy aircraft—which were beyond the range of the Stingers anyway—they sped through the dark sky in the general direction of the Fencers. Seeing the missiles on their down-looking radars, the fighters broke off their attack against Stephens's helicopter and took evasive action to avoid the Stingers arching up toward them.

"Red, sit down and shut down *now!*" the Hawk pilot called. Stephens did so, and the Soviets saw two flashes as the Stingers self-destructed upon reaching their maximum range. The fighter pilots immediately searched for Stephens with their radars again and found the blip of his still-turning rotors on their screens. But before they could fire again the Stealth Hawk launched another pair of Stingers, and again the Russians took evasive action when they detected the missiles coming in their direction. By the time the second pair of missiles exploded harmlessly below them and they began their radar search for the American helicopter again, Stephens and Whitaker's aircraft was shut down on the floor of a valley, and the Soviets' radars could not distinguish it from the ground clutter below.

Because of the magic of its stealth technology, the Russians never did see the MH-60P on their sophisticated, look-down/shoot-down radars.

It had been a near disaster for Red Stephens and his female copilot, Cat Whitaker, but Red's quick thinking and flying skill—and that of the Stealth Hawk pilot—had saved them from destruction.

Compared to the damage the attack had done to the Soviets, the wounding of three of the TOW crewmen barely mattered. The last attack of SFOD B-30 in UWOA Sword had left at least thirteen Soviet helicopters destroyed, including all six of their Hind gunships and most—if not all—of their cargo helicopters. A ZSU-

23-4 antiaircraft system and a BMP, with its 73-mm gun, had been destroyed as well.

But the biggest blow to the Soviets resulted from the TOW missile that had entered the giant AN-225 Dream transport. Not only were the huge, new aircraft and tons of ammunition and badly needed repair parts lost, but scores of Red Army replacements and air crewmen were killed, and scores more were maimed and burned in the fiery blast.

CHAPTER 21

0114 hours GMT (0444 hours local), 30 September
Unconventional Warfare Operations Area Sword

While the Stealth Hawk returned to the pickup zone near the blazing rubble of the Soviet airfield, Mark Denton saw that the wounded men were being cared for, then directed his radio operator to send a spot report to the SFOB in England. When that was accomplished he sent a message to Captain Rocco Birelli near the town of Khash, some sixty kilometers to the south.

> SECRET: 0000: TIGER DE SWORD: WILL ARRIVE YOUR POSI-
> TION IN APPROX ONE HOUR WITH THREE WOUNDED. BE
> PREPARED TO ASSIST. HELICOPTER WILL TAKE THREE SOR-
> TIES TO RECOVER MEN AND EQUIPMENT FROM THIS LOCA-
> TION. ALSO, ONE H-500MD XX H-500MD WILL BE ARRIVING
> YOUR AREA . . .

Denton also included the frequency on which the aircraft would be operating so that Birelli could guide them in to the positions at which he wanted them to land.

The Stealth Hawk returned to the hide site with the second load of men and TOW launchers, then left to recover the last of the men from the pickup zone—Master Sergeant Puchinelli and five others. Because of the need to lay the wounded men in the floor of the cargo compartment during the first sortie, they had been unable to take all of the remaining men and equipment on the second lift.

Red Stephens and Cat Whitaker, having heard their

radar detection alarm remain silent for several minutes, cranked up the H-500MD and headed for the hide site as well.

At the hide site Denton and the others were feverishly preparing to abandon the area for the move to Khash. The camouflage nets were folded and ready for loading, and most of the remaining fuel, rations, and water were hidden and camouflaged as an emergency cache. The 5.56-mm miniguns that had been dropped in for use by the killer eggs, and the ammunition for them, along with several cans of fuel, were put aside for movement to Khash, along with the four remaining Stingers the team had.

The Stealth Hawk called to report that he was on short final, and as he eased down toward the landing zone, the area around the hide site erupted with small-arms fire and exploding RPG-16 rounds.

The commander of the Soviet motorized rifle regiment, fed up with the battering he was receiving at the hands of his elusive enemy in the hill mass above the road, had made a fateful decision. When night had fallen he had dispatched two battalions of infantrymen into the hills to patrol the area and try to locate the Americans. They had found nothing until one patrol saw the Stealth Hawk, carrying Denton and the wounded back from their latest battle, land at the hide site. The Soviet patrol had radioed their find, and while the Hawk continued to ferry men from the site of their latest missile attack, they had reinforced the patrol with others in the area. Now, as the Stealth Hawk eased in with the last six men, the Russian infantrymen opened fire with everything they had.

Rounds of 7.62-mm ammo slammed into the sophisticated helicopter, and a rocket-propelled grenade exploded almost underneath it. One door gunner was badly wounded by both rifle fire and fragments from the grenade. The copilot took a round through the thigh, and one of Puchinelli's men was killed by a bullet through the brain. Puchinelli himself received a grazing wound to the forearm.

With the first burst of enemy fire the pilot reacted quickly to get his aircraft out of the landing zone. The modified UH-60 Blackhawk helicopter, with the majority of its fuel expended and with a fairly light load in the cargo compartment, leapt from the ground as most of the Soviet riflemen continued blasting wildly away at it. Puchinelli's men, recovered from the shock of the sudden onslaught, were returning fire with their rifles, and the unhurt door gunner was firing at the enemy muzzle flashes with his machine gun.

The Stealth Hawk disappeared into the night sky.

At the hide site, the Soviets turned their attention toward the men remaining on the ground there, raking the area with 7.62-mm fire and rocket-propelled grenades from their RPG-16 launchers.

Captain Dick Warner dragged himself quickly behind a boulder as the Russian infantrymen ended the lives of the two wounded men lying beside the landing zone. One of the men with SFC O'Neill took the full brunt of an exploding RPG and was blown nearly in half. Another of O'Neill's men took a 7.62-mm round through the lungs and crumpled to the earth. The remainder of the men scrambled to cover and began returning fire with their M-16s. Denton and his radio operator, slightly higher up the hill, opened fire at the enemy muzzle flashes and were soon receiving most of the fire from the three Soviet squads.

Denton changed magazines, then rose to unleash another burst of rifle fire at the enemy. Two rounds slammed into his chest, flinging him backwards. It took him a moment to realize what had happened, and he tried to move his hands to his chest. His arms refused to respond to the commands from his brain, however, and he realized he was paralyzed.

"God damn it, Sparky," he muttered. "I should have known better. No security. Never have a position without security around it."

His radio operator didn't hear him. He was already dead from a bullet through the head.

Major Mark Denton was surprised to find that he felt no pain. And, although he could see red and green tracer rounds ricocheting around and saw the flashes of explosions, he heard nothing. He suddenly felt peaceful. No pain. No noise. Just a euphoric feeling as his brain demanded all the resources it controlled to soothe itself, desperately trying to hang on to life.

Then Mark Denton's heart surrendered to the damage it had suffered, his dying thoughts of his wife and children, playing in the backyard of their tidy little bungalow at Fort Bragg.

Aboard the Stealth Hawk, Pete Puchinelli yelled to the pilot, "Set down and let us out above them!" as he pointed to the top of a ridge above the hide site.

The pilot nodded, and, as he descended, Puchinelli yelled, "Can this thing keep flying?"

"Hell, yes! These things are hard to hurt!" It was an understatement. During the invasion of Grenada in 1983 several Blackhawks had taken dozens of rounds—some as large as 23-mm—and had been able to keep on flying. Since then the helicopter's survivability had even been improved.

"How 'bout fuel?" Puchinelli asked.

"Plenty!" the pilot replied.

"All right, as soon as you drop us off, take the wounded men to Khash, get the A team there—and as many guerrillas as you can carry—and get back here! We'll try to keep them off Denton and them till you get back!"

The Stealth Hawk came to a hover two feet above the ridge, and the pilot yelled, "Take the door guns and ammo with you!"

"I'll stay with 'em!" the uninjured door gunner yelled as he dismounted his machine gun from its window mount.

That gave Puchinelli six men, including himself, and they scrambled from the helicopter and along the ridge toward the firefight a kilometer away.

Red Stephens and Cat Whitaker were nearing the base

area and saw the red and green tracers richocheting into the sky.

"Base, this is Aphid. What the hell's happening?" he called. No one answered, and he repeated his call.

This time the MH-60 pilot responded. "Aphid, this is Hawk. We got hit at the LZ. I've dropped six guys off on the ridge to their north, and I'm going to Khash for more. Do what you can to help, out."

"Aphid, roger. Break, break. Any ground station, this is Aphid, over."

Puchinelli heard the call on his PRC-117 and answered.

"Aphid, this is Pooch. I'm moving into position above the bad guys to their north. You got any ammo left?"

"Affirm. I've got one TOW. I'll buzz up there and see what I can do with it."

"Roger. See if you can get a machine gun or RPG. I'll have two machine guns and a few rifles in action in a minute."

As Stephens buzzed to a position behind the ridge from which Puchinelli had been dropped off he could see the former hide site and the green enemy tracers being fired at it from the Soviet squads to the west and northwest.

"OK, Cat," he said on the intercom. "Let's see if we can scare 'em with the laser like you did before."

He activated the helicopter's laser target designator, his sight on the area from which the enemy fire was emanating. The Russians' fire slackened immediately, but one enemy machine gun continued firing bursts into the battered American position. Red placed his crosshairs on the enemy gun and said, "Arm TOW."

"Armed."

He triggered the missile, and it flew to the Soviet machine gun and exploded, destroying gun and crew. But the H-500 was now out of ammunition.

"Aphid, this is Pooch."

"Go, Pooch."

226

"We've got no night sights on these guns. Can you see the bad guys when they aren't firing?"

Cat Whitaker answered his question. "I can see them on the FLIR—some of them, anyway."

"Roger," Puchinelli said. "How 'bout marking them with the laser so we can shoot?"

"Wilco," Stephens replied, then over the intercom he said, "You take the controls, Cat. I'll keep my goggles on and make sure you don't bump the ridge."

She spotted a grenadier with an RPG-16 rising to launch a rocket-propelled grenade, fixed the sight on him, and triggered the laser. Almost immediately Puchinelli's gunners fired several bursts at the beam's point of termination, and Cat saw the man pitch forward.

"Got him, Pooch!" she said. "Stand by!"

She found another machine-gun crew, apparently reluctant to fire as a result of the destruction of their comrades by the TOW missile and the machine guns above them. But their attempt to avoid revealing their location by not firing proved fruitless. Whitaker illuminated their position with the laser beam, and again Puchinelli's machine guns made short work of them.

In the area of the hide site, O'Neill was rallying his remaining men and assessing the situation. At first he thought there was no hope and was about to order the survivors to attempt to evade from the area to their rally point. But then the H-500's TOW and Puchinelli's laser-assisted machine guns had improved things markedly. Now, under the protective watch of the killer egg's FLIR and Puchinelli's machine guns and rifles, he scrambled around the hide site in search of people and a functioning radio.

It took the Stealth Hawk, flying at 150 knots, less than fifteen minutes to reach Khash. En route the pilot received a call from Birelli, who had been advised by the two Baluchi tribesmen on the south slope of Kuh-e Taftan that a helicopter had passed near them, headed south.

"Sword aircraft, Sword aircraft, this is Tiger, Tiger, over," Birelli called.

"Uh, Tiger, this is Sword aircraft—call sign 'Hawk,' over," the Stealth Hawk pilot replied.

"Roger, Hawk. This is Tiger. Understand you have three wounded aboard, over?"

"This is Hawk. Be advised, we just got hit in our hide site. I have several casualties aboard and more back there—at least three, probably more." He went on to explain that they needed Birelli's Special Forces men and some of their guerrillas to fly back with him immediately, to enable Denton and his men to extricate themselves from the mess they were in.

"Tiger, wilco!" Birelli responded. Turning to his executive officer, he told him to alert the Americans and the guerrilla commander, Lakhar Nawaz. Then he asked the pilot, "What's the enemy strength, disposition, and weapons, Hawk?"

"I'm not sure. I'd say there's a platoon or so. They've got machine guns and RPGs, at least. They're on the hillside to the west, above our people. I dropped off six of our guys up there with my door guns. They'll try to hold the Russians off till we get back. Also, we've got one little H-500 gunship working, but I think he's out of ammo, over."

"This is Tiger, roger," Birelli said. "What's your ACL?" he inquired, wanting to know the aircraft load of which the Stealth Hawk was capable.

"All you can cram in here!" the pilot said. "Around twenty, if you really pack 'em in. Also, if you have anybody with flying experience, I need him up front with me. My copilot's one of the wounded."

"Roger, I'll check. What kind of ammo does the H-500 need, Hawk?"

"TOWs and Hellfires, if you have 'em."

"We've got negative Hellfires, but I can bring TOWs. How many?"

"Uh, see if you can fit four. Also, you got any Stinger rounds, so I can rearm in case any enemy air shows up?" the pilot asked.

"Affirm. Are they the same as the ground-launched ones?"

"Roger, roger. . . . I've got your town in sight now, Tiger."

"OK, Hawk. Be advised, we have an LZ marked southwest of town. Do not—I say again, do *not*—come in below a hundred feet until you reach town," Birelli warned. "We have a minefield all across our front to the north, and they'll blow if you cross them too low, how copy?"

"Hawk copies—maintain at least one hundred feet AGL until I reach the town. I'm about two minutes out."

The Stealth Hawk touched down in the triangle of lights Birelli's men had set up to mark the landing zone. His American medics immediately tended to the wounded copilot and door gunner, and they had the body of the dead member of Puchinelli's team removed while Birelli conferred with the pilot.

Dick Medlin climbed into the copilot's seat and donned the wounded airman's helmet.

"You a pilot?" the aviator asked him over the intercom.

"Single-engine fixed wing," Medlin said. "But that's more than anybody else here. Also, I've got a few hours in Hueys a long time ago."

"No sweat," the pilot said. "We'll make it work. Hold what you've got. I'm gonna hop out and load these Stingers."

While he did so, six members of Birelli's team, under the command of Chief Warrant Officer Fred Kaminski, along with Nawaz and fourteen of his guerrillas, crowded into the cargo compartment and the empty door gunners' seats. They also had four TOW missiles for the H-500MD.

When they lifted off and headed north the pilot looked at Medlin and said, "I'm Rosie Rosengrant. Thanks for helping out."

"Dick Medlin. Hope I *can* help."

"Medlin?" Rosengrant said. *"The* Medlin, from Son Tay, and the Iran raid?"

"Yep," Medlin replied, and Rosie said, "Christ! Is there anything you *can't* do, sir?"

"Yep. I can't fly *this* thing, so tell me what you want me to watch for on the instrument panel while you do the flying."

Rosengrant told Medlin what to watch on several of the gauges, then called Stephens on the radio.

"This is Aphid," Stephens replied. "They're starting to throw artillery in here now. O'Neill is moving northeast down the wadi with three wounded—two walking wounded and one on a litter. There're four dead, including Denton, he's having to leave behind. Pooch is up near where you dropped him, covering O'Neill's withdrawal, over."

"Hawk, roger. I've got about twenty men, plus four TOW rounds for you. Where do you want me?"

"Set down five hundred meters or so northeast of base in the wadi bed," Stephens advised. "O'Neill should be there by then, and I'll drop in and pick up the TOW rounds from you."

The Stealth Hawk landed ten minutes later, and Kaminski, his Special Forces men, and their guerrillas quickly unloaded. While Nawaz and his men secured the area the Special Forces men loaded their wounded comrades on the Stealth Hawk. The H-500 landed behind the Hawk, and Red Stephens hopped out. With the help of Kaminski's men he loaded two TOWs into the helicopter's launcher and stowed the other two behind the seats, then took off again.

Kaminski got with O'Neill, whom he had known for years, to see what else needed to be done.

"We've gotta hurry, Harry," Kaminski said. "It's gonna be light in less than an hour."

"Let's send the wounded out with one of the medics," Harry said. "Then, when the artillery quits, we can go back and get the major and the other bodies while Pooch covers us."

"OK," Kaminski said. "But if they don't quit firing by the time the Hawk gets back, we'll have to leave them for later, I'm afraid. We're going to run out of darkness, ol' buddy."

They dispatched the Stealth Hawk with the three wounded men and the two unhurt men O'Neill had left, as they were too exhausted to be anything but a liability. Kaminski sent his medic out with them to care for the wounded en route to Khash. Then they settled in to wait for the Soviet artillery fire on the devastated hide site to slacken so they could recover the bodies of the four dead Americans.

Stephens and Whitaker flew north along the hill mass of Kuh-e Taftan until they found a gap in the ridge line leading west, then turned toward the Soviet rifle regiment. To their left front they could see flashes from the muzzles of the Soviet 122-mm artillery that was firing on the American position. Working his helicopter along the ridge line until he could see the artillery pieces along the road below him, Stephens said to Cat Whitaker, "All right, cat lady, let's see if we can shut those assholes down."

He maneuvered until he was on the flank of the six enemy howitzers, then launched a TOW missile that struck between the middle two, silencing both. With his second round he disabled the nearest gun and crew, then flew east until he could find a flat place to set the helicopter down and rearm the launcher with his two remaining missiles.

While he did so, the three remaining artillery pieces turned their fury on the ridge line from which he had fired, thinking they were engaging ground-mounted weapons.

With artillery rounds no longer landing on the hide site, O'Neill, Kaminski, and most of the others moved quickly up the wadi and recovered the four dead Americans, their radios, weapons, and the two miniguns and several jerrycans of fuel for the H-500MD.

Only two bursts of fire came from the Soviet troops above them. Puchinelli's machine gunners, and the combined fire of Kaminski's Special Forces men and their guerrillas, quickly silenced them.

By the time Kaminski's men arrived at the pickup zone in the wadi, the Stealth Hawk was on the way in to land. Red Stephens, meanwhile, was covering the withdrawal toward the pickup site of Pete Puchinelli and the five men with him.

Quickly, most of the guerrillas and the bodies of the dead Americans were loaded aboard the Hawk for the flight to Khash.

"We'll move farther to the east for the next pickup, Hawk," Kaminski advised over the radio. "No sense using this PZ for a third time."

After landing briefly to take on the fuel the guerrillas brought to the pickup zone, Stephens radioed O'Neill to say that he and Sergeant Whitaker were going to fly to the site of the killer egg that she had crash-landed earlier, to remove some parts from it. "We've got two TOW rounds left," he said, "so if you need us, just holler."

O'Neill didn't hear him. Exhausted from the ordeal of the last few days, and especially the stressful battle at the hide site, he had sat down and fallen asleep as Kaminski and his men were preparing to move out to the east.

CHAPTER 22

There was one more battle between the Soviets and the Americans in Unconventional Warfare Operations Area Sword.

As Rosie Rosengrant flew the MH-60P Stealth Hawk north out of Khash to pick up the last load of Special Forces men and the handful of guerrillas with them, he turned to Dick Medlin, in the copilot's seat, and said, "Oh, hell. The satcom's not turned on. Flip that number three switch on the radio panel, will you, Dick?"

Medlin did so and heard the sound of a voice saying, ". . . is Roulette, Roulette, over."

Medlin keyed the radio and said, "Roulette, say again station being called, over."

"This is Roulette," the controller in the distant AWACS aircraft said. "I'm trying to get ahold of Sword, over."

"This is Hawk, Roulette. Send your traffic, over."

"Roger, Hawk. I have two bogeys at eighteen thousand, in orbit fifty miles south of Zahedan, over."

"This is Hawk. Roger, roger," Rosie said, then over the intercom, "That's above the hide site." He switched the satcom channel to receive only, and the PRC-117 channel to receive/transmit, and he tried to raise Aphid One. There was no reply. At the site of Cat's crash-landing she and Stephens had shut their helicopter down and were stripping the damaged Aphid Two of its key components.

Rosengrant began climbing rapidly in the nearly emp-

ty Stealth Hawk. He didn't want to activate his radar, as
that would enable the enemy to locate the source of his
radar emissions, negating the invisibility to radar that
the aircraft's stealth technology allowed.

He called the AWACS on his satellite radio again.
"Roulette, this is Hawk. I'm going to try to find the
bogeys using passive systems only. Keep me advised of
their direction of flight and altitude, please."

"Hawk, this is Roulette. Wilco, over."

The radar detector began to sound the alarm periodi-
cally, and Dick Medlin glanced at Rosengrant with a look
of concern.

"Don't worry about that," Rosie said. "As long as it
keeps going on and off, it means they're only searching
around with their radar."

"And if it *stays* on?" Medlin asked.

"Then we take this damn thing back to the stealth
technology contractors and ask for our money back."

"Hawk, Roulette. They're at sixteen thousand, north
end of their orbit, turning south now."

Rosengrant checked his altimeter. The Stealth Hawk
was at just over eleven thousand feet. He kept the nose of
the Hawk up slightly and slewed the tail back and forth
somewhat as he watched the screen of his forward-
looking infrared sensor. He flipped the arming switches
of his number one and number two Stingers to On.

"There!" he said a moment later, pointing to a small
blur on the screen of his FLIR. The beep from the Stinger
system, indicating it had acquired an infrared heat
source, began, and when it became steady, indicating it
was locked onto the heat of one of the enemy aircraft's
engines, he said, "Still too far."

As the image of the two aircraft became larger on the
FLIR screen, he launched a Stinger. The Soviet Fencers,
about a mile to the Hawk's front and several thousand
feet higher, were coming head-on toward the helicopter
when the missile intercepted them. With its sensor
guiding it to the source of heat from one of the engines, it
took the shortest route toward the rear of the nearest

aircraft—through the air intake. Even if it hadn't exploded, the missile would have caused the engine to fly apart violently. With the added effect of the warhead's detonation, the Russian aircraft exploded immediately. The second Fencer, flying just to its right rear, was struck by debris from his wingman's ruined plane. The pilot made a hard right turn as Rosengrant launched the second Stinger, but the missile was still locked onto the heat of the first aircraft. It flew into the flaming debris of the first plane and exploded, enabling the other aircraft to limp away without further damage.

As Rosengrant nosed his chopper over in a rapid descent Medlin watched with fascination as the flaming wreckage fell toward the wasteland below.

The AWACS controller said, "Uh, Hawk, this is Roulette. The bogeys . . . they collided or something. One of them came apart, and the other has turned to the north, over."

"Roger, Roulette," Rosie said. "You have anything else on your radar screen?"

"Uh, negative, Hawk. Just the one that's headed north."

Over the intercom Rosengrant said, "Well, I guess this stealth stuff works after all."

Below them, Red Stephens and Cat Whitaker saw the explosion of the Russian fighter high in the lightening sky. Red ran to the helicopter and turned on the radios.

"Hawk, this is Aphid, over."

"Go ahead, Aphid."

"Say your location, Hawk."

"I'm descending through seven thousand, just east of the mountain peak."

"Roger, Hawk," Stephens said. "Did you see an explosion up there?"

"I didn't just *see* it, old buddy—I *caused* it."

"Wow! With a Stinger?"

"That's most affirm," Rosie said.

"A fighter kill with an air-to-air Stinger? That's a first, Rosie. You owe a case of beer!"

Rosengrant laughed and said, "Can do." Then, his voice returning to a tone of seriousness, he called Puchinelli.

"Pooch, this is Hawk, inbound. What's the situation, over?"

"This is Pooch. All's quiet down here now. We're ready for pickup, over."

They loaded the dead and the equipment they had recovered from the hide site, then the remaining men, American and Baluchi. In the growing light of dawn the Stealth Hawk lifted off and headed for Khash.

Stephens and Whitaker, after stripping the damaged Aphid Two of its key components, loaded the parts into the back of Aphid One. Then they, too, took off and flew to the town that was to be the site of the next battle with the advancing Soviet regiments.

It took the Russians most of the day of 30 September to recover their patrols from the hill mass of Kuh-e Taftan. Meanwhile, the pace of their point elements was literally slowed to that of a walking man. For they were unaware that the enemy who had done them such devastating damage had withdrawn from the area, and, to prevent further attacks, the commanders of the regiments on both roads had ordered foot patrols to clear the flanks as they moved.

As the Soviet columns crept forward, their tormentors, near exhaustion from the stress and exertion of battle, fear, and the carrying of heavy loads to and from their attack positions, were asleep.

Birelli made certain the survivors of SFOD B-30 were made as comfortable as possible. The wounded were placed in the building on the south side of town that his medics had set up as a field hospital, and the others were given a hot meal, then put to bed in several of the adobe buildings nearby.

It was midafternoon before they began to awaken, one at a time. The bearded, filthy men found pans of water, soap, and towels waiting for them. Quietly, each rose, undressed, and bathed himself. Then each took his razor from his rucksack, shaved, and changed into his spare uniform.

In the building in which she slept alone, Sergeant Cat Whitaker awoke, unable at first to remember where she was. Then she remembered, and for nearly half an hour she lay on the woven bed beneath the wool blanket, recalling the shocking changes that had occurred in her life since she had been alerted for immediate movement from Fort Bragg just a few days earlier. A hurried trip from airplane to airplane ending in a perilous, frightening parachute jump into the rocky wasteland of southeastern Iran. Maintaining and rearming a small helicopter, whose pilots, with a handful of other Americans, were battling two Soviet regiments. Men wounded and dying in the battle. Mr. Stephens taking her into battle as a pilot, although she was barely—and informally—trained to do so. Hiding in desolate little valleys while, above, high-technology Soviet fighters searched for her aircraft with their weapons systems— once nearly blowing Stephens and her from the sky. Boring in on enemy tanks and antiaircraft systems and unleashing missiles and minigun fire at them, then watching them explode, the men inside being horribly burned, maimed, killed. The frightening explosion of the Katusha rockets in the hide site when she flew off alone, then attacked the Soviets by herself. The crash landing, and finding herself unhurt—alone, until the two tribesmen arrived, one throwing her to the ground and shoving his weapon beneath her chin. The relief of hearing an American voice on the radio, and finally being picked up and returned to her comrades. The sight of the huge AN-225 aircraft exploding in a giant fireball. The artillery attack on the hide site, and the deaths of more Americans, including the man who had consented to allow her to fly into combat—Major Mark Denton.

She wept silently for a while, then rose, bathed, and went off to find her helicopter. There was much repair and maintenance work to be done to it before she and Chief Warrant Officer Stephens could take it back into battle. And nobody was more capable of doing work on the little Hughes 500MD "killer egg" than Sergeant Catherine Whitaker.

She and Stephens were meticulously going over the helicopter's small but powerful turbine engine when Sergeant First Class Harry O'Neill approached and said, "Chief, Captain Birelli is having a meeting of the key people. He'd like you to come to his CP."

"Go ahead, sir," Cat said. "I can finish up here."

"OK," he said. "Rosie says he's ready to take us over to the cache at Drop Zone One to pick up more fuel and ammo whenever we're ready. We can go when this meeting's over."

At the command post Rocco Birelli surveyed the men gathered before him.

Nine members of his own team—A-326—were there, one medic remaining in the improvised hospital to tend to the wounded men. Only the man who had been evacuated by surface-to-air recovery the night of his team's parachute infiltration into UWOA Tiger made Birelli's own A team less than fully manned.

Of the ten Special Forces soldiers Denton's Special Forces Operational Detachment B-30 (Provisional) had sent into battle, only SFC O'Neill and two others remained alive and unhurt. Of the pilots and ground crewmen of B-30's battered Aphid Flight, only Stephens and Whitaker remained effective.

The Stealth Hawk crew was down to the pilot and one door gunner, although Birelli had received a message from SFOB indicating that the second MH-60P Stealth Hawk would arrive at Khash that night. In addition to a medical doctor, anesthesiologist, and physician's assistant, it would bring in another pilot to fly with Chief Warrant Officer Rosengrant.

SFOD A-323, which had been sent in to reinforce B-30 in UWOA Sword, was relatively intact. The detachment commander, Captain Dick Warner, was present, although wearing a pneumatic cast on the leg the medics suspected was fractured. Two of the NCOs in his team were wounded, but not so badly that they couldn't function in the coming battle. As the recently commissioned warrant officer who had been A-323's executive officer had been killed the night before, Master Sergeant Puchinelli was in charge of the team's other nine NCOs.

Altogether, that left Birelli with a total of twenty-four American Special Forces men for the coming battle. He would also have a medical team, one H-500MD, and two MH-60P Stealth Hawks to assist him. And the remarkably capable CIA operative, Dick Medlin.

In addition, the Baluchi chieftain, Chakur Nothani, and his guerrilla commander, Lakha Nawaz, had 140 fierce, if hastily trained, guerrillas available to fight the Soviets.

When everyone he wanted in the meeting had arrived at the one-room adobe school he was using as a command post, Rocco Birelli said, "First I want to say that what you men and the female sergeant did up in UWOA Sword is almost unbelievable. We expected the Soviets to get to our UWOA days ago, but not only did you hold them up for days, you've destroyed so damned many of their vehicles and helicopters that maybe—just maybe —if my team and our Baluchi comrades can fight nearly as well as you have, we can stop them here—at least long enough to get so many of CENTCOM's units time to get ashore that they'll never stand a chance of holding Chah Bahar."

He waited while Dick Medlin translated his remarks for the Baluchi leaders, then said, "Now, there's all sorts of speculation on BBC news about the possibility of a cease-fire, and big problems in the Soviet Union, even threats from their former comrades in the Warsaw Pact countries, and all of that. But I got another message from SFOB a while ago saying that we're to do our best to hit the bastards here, as hard as we can and as long as we can. So that's what we're going to do.

"OK, let's go over what assets we've got to do that with, and let me tell you my plan for getting it done. And if anybody has any suggestions about how to do it better, interrupt me. It's like George Patton said—'The only tactical principle which is not subject to change is to bring the maximum amount of death, wounds, and destruction on the enemy in the minimum time.'"

He listed the number of men available for the fight, then the weapons at their disposal. In addition to their individual weapons there was a large number of machine guns, light and heavy, and there were numerous Dragon missiles and Soviet-made rocket-propelled grenade launchers.

"But our big guns," Birelli said, "are the TOW 2s. Including the launchers you brought from up north, we have a total of eleven serviceable launchers and thirty-six missiles."

"Is that including the ones in our cache west of here?" O'Neill inquired.

"What cache?" Birelli asked.

"You mean you don't know about our cache at the first drop zone we used?" O'Neill said.

During the hectic activity of the previous night, no one had made Captain Birelli aware of the big cache of supplies B-30 had hidden near their first drop zone forty kilometers to the west of Khash the night of their infiltration into Iran.

"Oh, you'll love *this*," O'Neill said with a smile. "We've got a whole *bunch* of Dragons, AT-4s, and a few Stingers cached west of here a ways."

"And there's fuel, Hellfires, TOWs, and minigun ammo for the killer egg, too, sir," Stephens added.

"How many?" Birelli asked.

"I don't remember exactly," O'Neill said. "But I think it's something like twenty-four Dragon rounds, sixteen AT-4s, and a few Stingers."

"There's also eight each TOWs and Hellfires, and about 10,000 rounds of 5.56 for the minis," Stephens said. "And about two hundred gallons of JP-5 fuel."

"Aren't there a couple of electronic OPs, too?" asked one of the survivors from B-30, Staff Sergeant Tippy.

"Yeah, that's right," O'Neill said.

Red Stephens said, "Rosie's going to take us over there

in the Hawk as soon as you're finished with us, Captain B."

"OK, great," Birelli said. "But let me go over how we're going to deal with the Soviets first."

He turned to a drawing he had made of the area around Khash on the blackboard of the one-room school. It showed the town sitting between two ridge lines oriented northwest-southeast. Four kilometers west of the town the ridge was almost 3,000 feet higher than the town. The ridge three kilometers to the east was, on average, about 1,000 feet higher than Khash. He had also drawn in the deep wadi that ran from the northwest past the western edge of town.

There was a red swath drawn from ridge to ridge just to the north of Khash, and Birelli pointed to it and said, "This is the minefield the FB-111s delivered the other night. The only real problem with it is that even though they're painted to match the terrain here, they're still sitting on top of the ground. But if a tank—any vehicle, for that matter, or even a man carrying a lot of metal—passes near one of the mines, it'll detonate. And even if they see the mines, they'll have to slow down to pick their way through them, and they'll be easier targets for our missiles that way."

"Rocco," Captain Dick Warner, leaning on his crutches at the back of the room, said. "Suppose you hit them with a couple of rounds—your 60 mortars, for example—as they approach the mine field? Wouldn't that make them button up inside their vehicles and make it harder for them to see the mines?"

"Yeah, Dick. Good idea," Birelli replied. Then, turning to his executive officer, he said, "Make sure that happens, Fred."

"OK," he continued, "since the Dragons can't reach the whole way between the ridges and town, I want the TOW gunners to engage only targets that are more than a thousand meters away. Leave the closer shots for the Dragon gunners."

He pointed to the symbols for his various weapons

spread across the front of the town and along the ridges to either side and said, "As you can see, I've got about half the Dragon teams here in town, and the rest divided between the two ridges. Also, there's going to be three TOW launchers here, three on the east ridge, and five out here to the west. I put more on our west because, number one, the space between here and there is greater than it is between here and the other ridge, so they're more likely to try to bypass us to that side. And, number two, from the greater height of the west ridge they can see more targets and get a better angle of attack."

"Uh, Rocco, have you considered using airmobile TOW teams to hit them from the rear?" It was Dick Warner.

"You mean the 'killer egg,' as Mr. Stephens calls it?" Birelli asked.

"No, I'm talking about putting a TOW team or two aboard the Stealth Hawk," Warner said. "They could fly around to the flanks of the second echelon and hit them from there, then hop back on the chopper, fly somewhere else, then hit them again."

"I agree, sir," Puchinelli said. "Or we could leave the TOWs for the long shots here and take some Dragons for that."

O'Neill agreed with Puchinelli's idea, adding, "Anyway, the Dragons will be a hell of a lot more effective on the rear and sides of the tanks. We found out up north that the reactive armor on the front of 'em pretty well negates the Dragon warheads."

"All right. Pooch, you decide how many men and Dragons you want to do that mission. Also, you'll have the mobility to act as a reserve, if I need you to reinforce somebody."

"I'll take O'Neill and his two men, and the rest of my team, then," Puchinelli said. "That'll give me six men for each chopper—three Dragon teams per bird."

"What about the AT-4s?" O'Neill asked.

While Birelli considered how best to employ the short-range 84-mm antitank rockets, Captain Warner said, "You're going to move your CP up on the ridge to the west, aren't you, Rocco?"

"No, I'm going to put Fred up there with the alternate CP. I'll stay here in town, in the middle of the fight, where I can control it best."

"I don't think that'll work, Rocco," Warner said. "You won't be able to see shit from here, especially when they start hammering this place with artillery, like they're bound to do. Why don't you let me stay here in town and run things, and you fight the battle from up where you can see better?" He didn't add, "and where you have a chance of surviving." He didn't have to, because every man in the room knew that Khash would become the immediate, most heavily pounded target of the enemy tanks and artillery when the battle was joined. The chances of anyone in the town escaping unharmed—especially anyone on the forward edge, where they would have to be in order to observe and engage the enemy—were much lower than in the relative safety of the ridges above town.

"Come on, Rocco," Warner said. "I've got to be somewhere, and it's for damned sure I can get around town on these crutches a hell of a lot better than I could up on those ridges. Tell him," he said, looking around the room at the other Special Forces men. "We all know the best place for the CP is up on the hill."

The men looked at Warner, many of them thinking how much he had changed since tasting battle on the slopes of Kuh-e Taftan. He had entered UWOA Sword a self-serving coward. Now, instead of using his broken leg as an excuse to avoid the battle, he was volunteering to command the most dangerous sector of the battlefield.

"Captain Warner's right, sir," Pete Puchinelli said. "You need to be up on the ridge. He can handle things here in town." He looked over at Warner and gave him a nod of professional respect.

"I agree with Captain Warner, too," the CIA man, Dick Medlin, said. "I'll be here in town myself. We need you up on the hill, where you can manage the whole fight better."

Birelli knew the others were right. The only reason he had intended to put his command post in the town anyway was that he didn't want to leave someone of lesser rank to be in charge of the area that was bound to be the most dangerous. Since Warner, a fellow captain, had volunteered to do so, he would move the CP to the hill, where it really belonged.

"Very well, then," Birelli said. "You'll have the alternate command post here, Dick."

"Good," Warner said. "So let me have the AT-4s. They'll be best put to use here in town if the bad guys manage to get here."

They went on to discuss the movement of the wounded to the mine at the foot of the western ridge and the evacuation of the women and children to the south at nightfall. Then, arrangements complete, the meeting ended, and the men went to their battle positions to improve them.

Rosie Rosengrant took Stephens, O'Neill, and two other men to the cache site forty kilometers to the west to retrieve the ammunition and equipment from there. It took them two sorties to get it all back to Khash and the hills above it.

It was almost dark when the two guerrillas, high up on the southern slopes of Kuh-e Taftan, radioed that they could see Soviet vehicles on the roads that converged south of the mountain. The tanks were going to be first, the guerrillas said. And, having remounted the men who had swept their flanks until the lead elements cleared the hill mass, the Soviet vehicles were moving fast, now. The guerrillas expected that the lead elements of the enemy would arrive at the minefield north of Khash in two or three hours.

CHAPTER 23

1620 hours GMT (1950 hours local time), 30 September
Unconventional Warfare Operations Area Shark
Just north of the port of Chah Bahar, Iran

As darkness fell on southeastern Iran that night the men
in Khash were not the only group of Americans and
Baluchi guerrillas about to go into battle against the
Soviet forces in Iran.

Far to the south, in Special Forces Operational Detachment A-325's area of operations—UWOA Shark—
the twelve-man team of Captain Bill Davidson, with a
newly trained and equipped force of 324 Baluchi tribesmen, was on the move.

They were en route to hit the Soviet paratroopers
securing the town of Chah Bahar and, twenty-five kilometers to the west, across a broad, half-moon-shaped bay
on the Arabian Sea, an airfield, also being secured by the
Soviet airborne force.

The Special Forces men and their Baluchi comrades
had been on the move for two days, leaving their base
camp in the Makran mountains north of the coast in two
groups—one headed for the little port town, the other
for the airfield.

Both elements, each 168 men strong, were burdened
with heavy loads of weapons and ammunition. Even
more ammunition was waiting for them in cache sites
near their targets, placed there, along with cans of
much-needed water, by Baluchi carrying parties during
the previous several days.

As they neared the cache sites, robed Baluchi guides
appeared out of the darkness, exchanging greetings with

their fellow tribesmen, then leading them silently to where the additional munitions were hidden. Each site was in a wadi less than two kilometers from the Soviet positions, and as the column of men moved through it each man was handed two 60-mm mortar rounds to carry forward.

When they reached the positions from which the attacks would be supported by the mortar section attached to each element, the mortar rounds were neatly stacked while the mortarmen and their American advisers quickly laid in the mortars and aiming stakes.

It was an uncomfortable moment for Captain Bill Davidson when the Baluchi guerrilla leader with his element approached him to say that he was ready to depart.

"Go with God, then," Davidson said to his counterpart. "And please know that if the decision were mine, my men and I would go with you." Both men knew it was true that if it were Davidson's choice, he and his Special Forces soldiers would accompany the tribesmen in their assault on the Russian positions. But he had been ordered to stay behind—to keep himself and his men from becoming directly involved in the assault. When the attacks were ordered, SFOB had sent him a message saying that under no circumstances were the members of his A team to enter the Soviet positions at Chah Bahar or the airfield twenty-five kilometers to the northwest. The risk of capture was too great.

"Yes, I know that is true," the guerrilla leader said. "And you must not feel bad, my brother. If it were not for you and your men, and the weapons and training you have brought us, there is no way we could do this—no way we could prove to the Shiites that while they remain impotent to strike a blow against the Russian infidels, we, the Sunni nation of Baluchistan, can demonstrate our determination and independence by doing so. For that we give you our thanks and ask God's blessings upon you."

"Then be careful, my brother," Davidson said, embracing the Baluchi man. "And remember that, although a man killed for his faith may be a holy martyr, he is still dead. And if he is dead, he can no longer fight for the independence of his brethren here on earth. May you and your men live to fight many battles."

The Baluchi guerrilla leader laughed. "Davidson, my friend, we are not pawns of the Shiite mullahs, who bled their nation to death by sending children against the guns of Iraq. We are Sunni warriors. Our holy men fight beside us, so we know that if we live or if we die, it is God's will, not man's. And now we go to do our duty."

At precisely the same time, from the deep, dry bed of each wadi, two camels emerged, each pair being led by a Baluchi tribesman and his family.

The camels appeared almost immediately on the screens of the PSNR-1 battlefield surveillance radars the Soviets were employing to guard their positions. At each location the radar operator notified his superiors of the presence of something several hundred meters outside the perimeter of their positions.

From the perimeter of the airfield two vehicles emerged a short time later, and one approached the family with its camels while the other vehicle guarded the encounter from a distance. Seeing that it was only a family passing by the airfield, the Soviet patrol leader gestured to the Baluchi man that he must move north, away from the airfield. The man and his family began moving away as ordered.

From the Soviet positions around Chah Bahar, however, the commander of the airborne battalion manning the perimeter there made a different decision. After going to the PSNR-1 radar position to see for himself that there was something slowly approaching from the north, he watched the screen for several minutes, then ordered that warning shots be fired over the heads of the potential intruders. The crew of a 12.7-mm NSV machine gun fired a long burst over the heads of the Baluchi family and their camels.

The burst of fire had the desired effect, but also an unexpected one. For it was the time of the locusts along the coast of the Arabian Sea, when billions of the creatures swarm there as they do twice each year, and this year they were present earlier than usual, and in unusually large numbers. The startling crack of the machine-gun rounds caused them to lift off the fields in huge numbers, and their presence blurred the screens of the Soviet battlefield surveillance radar.

The result was that, as the Baluchi guerrillas rose to move against the Soviet positions when the machine gun began firing, they were not detected. On they moved toward the Russians as the locusts swarmed around them. The Soviets ignored everything except the insects, swatting them away from their faces as the Baluchi tribesmen moved closer.

Near the airfield the radar operator saw his unit's patrol vehicles arrive at the site of the unidentified blips, then pause for several minutes before moving back toward the perimeter. Then, as the Americans had expected he would when they recommended the ruse to the guerrillas, the radar operator kept his sensor concentrated on the camels while they moved slowly away to the north. He failed to detect the force of over a hundred men as they emerged from the wadi and trotted toward the perimeter of the airfield.

The first rounds at the airfield were fired by a sleepy soldier in a listening post a hundred meters from the shallow, sandy foxholes surrounding the airfield. The Baluchi tribesmen were nearly upon him when he fired, and he got off only one short burst from his AKM before he died. But that was enough to cause the locusts there to rise in fright, and soon the airfield, too, was swarming with hordes of the insects.

The 60-mm lightweight mortars went into action then, three tubes from each firing position dropping high-explosive rounds onto the Soviet positions. Half of the fuzes on the mortar ammunition were set to explode in a low airburst, to wound those Soviets who had no overhead cover. The rest were set to detonate on impact, to defeat the light overhead cover some of the Russians had, and to do greater damage to materiel.

Right after they began firing, the guerrilla machine

gunners dropped to earth and started pouring streams of bullets at the flashes of the Soviet weapons that began to fire as the guerrillas breached their defenses.

The confusion of the sudden attack and the hordes of locusts swarming this way and that as the firing kept them stirring, caused many of the Russian paratroopers to fire wildly, the muzzle flashes of their weapons identifying their positions for the assaulting guerrillas.

The Baluchi tribesmen at both objectives saw the locust swarms as help from God, and their ferocity was increased by this divine assistance as they swept across their targets, shooting or bayonetting the Russians in each position. They quickly overwhelmed the forces at their points of attack and roamed deep within their targets, grenading and stabbing and shooting Russian paratroopers, and destroying their aircraft and vehicles with shoulder-fired incendiary rockets, until the Soviets finally began organized counterattacks.

By then the swarms of locusts, seeking more placid skies, began to move well away from the firing, and they disappeared into the night. The Baluchi guerrillas took this to be a sign from God that it was time for them, too, to withdraw, and they made an orderly withdrawal back to their rally points, one squad from each platoon laying down a base of fire at the Soviet positions as the rest of each platoon leapfrogged past them until another squad took up the covering-fire role.

From the mortar positions the American Special Forces men could see numerous fires on the objectives as the guerrillas returned, some carrying the dead and wounded. But there was a surprisingly small number of guerrilla casualties in the fierce, brief surprise attack. At the airfield only eight men were dead or missing, and only four were wounded seriously enough to require litters.

The force that had hit the enemy at Chah Bahar suffered eleven killed or missing and nine nonambulatory wounded, plus another two killed by a Soviet mortar round that hit the column as it moved north up the wadi toward the distant mountains.

It was a highly successful attack with scores of Soviets left dead and wounded, much of their aircraft, vehicles, and fuel stores aflame, and their ammunition dumps continuing to explode into the night sky far behind the withdrawing tribesmen and their American advisers.

To a man, the Baluchi guerrillas felt that the locust swarms had been sent by God to assist them in the attack. Many of the Special Forces men, too, were wondering if it was more than simple luck.

Whether the presence of the locusts was a matter of divine intervention or not, the fact that most of the Soviets had their backs to the guerrillas when the attack began was not. It was the result of a deception plan developed at the Special Forces Operations Base in England and executed by the ships and aircraft of the U.S. Navy in the Arabian Sea. Several hours before the guerrillas' attack began, some of the ships enforcing the exclusion zone began steaming toward Chah Bahar. As the time for the Baluchi attack drew nearer, aircraft from the U.S.S. *America* began making feints nearer and nearer to the Soviet airborne regiment's positions. The Soviet commander, believing the expected American landings were about to occur, reinforced his coastal positions, thus weakening his defenses in the north, where the Baluchi attack was then delivered.

The infrared photographs from the SR-71 ultra-high-altitude reconnaissance aircraft the U.S. Air Force sent over the airborne regiment's positions shortly after the guerrilla attack showed much greater damage than had been hoped for. The hard-liners in the Politburo were handed another setback. And General Secretary Gorbachev would use the attack to further his argument that the invasion of Iran was, like the occupation of Afghanistan more than a decade earlier, a reckless military adventure that could only be supported by a continuing loss of young Soviet lives—a price the increasingly rebellious population of the U.S.S.R. was no longer willing to accept.

1708 hours GMT (2038 hours local time), 30 September
North of Khash, Iran

A few kilometers north of Khash, the two Soviet regiments that had, for a week, been trying to reinforce the paratroopers at Chah Bahar were bunched up and moving fast. Once they had managed to escape the hill mass where Denton's force had done them so much damage, they had picked up a considerable amount of speed. But the road converged south of Kuh-e Taftan, and until they cleared Khash, where the road split again on parallel routes to the south, both regiments would be confined to a single road. In order to clear that road as quickly as possible so his sister regiment could continue its move, the Soviet tank regiment commander had his lead elements all bunched up. Instead of a small combat reconnaissance patrol leading the forward security element by five kilometers, with the regiment's main body another five kilometers behind them, the tank regiment was in a single unbroken line as it approached the minefield north of Khash.

Valentin Popovich Valnikov fought to breathe as he sat in the commander's hatch of his T-80 tank. The choking dust and diesel fumes of the tightly packed column of rumbling war machines burned his lungs and his tired, bloodshot eyes:

"Look out!" he yelled to his driver as the tank nearly ran into the one in front of it.

The driver locked the tracks, slamming Valnikov's rib cage against the hatch opening and skidding to a halt just two meters behind the tank in front of him.

"Son of a whore!" the driver exclaimed over the intercom. "Comrade Lieutenant, I can't drive under these conditions. At these speeds we're bound to run into this bastard in front of us. I can't see a damn thing, can't breathe, and—"

The big tank jolted, and Valnikov's leather helmet banged back against the open hatch cover. "Shit!" he yelled, looking back at the commander of the tank behind him. "Watch it, you cabbage-headed son of pig!"

He called the remainder of his company to warn them to maintain adequate interval, then switched to the battalion net and gave his battalion commander a call.

"We've got to slow down and increase our interval or we're going to be running all over one another," Valnikov explained.

"Just a little farther, comrade," his new battalion commander answered. "The rear of the regiment is nearly clear of the road junction, and the reconnaissance element will be in Khash soon."

"All right," Valnikov replied as the vehicle in front of him started moving again. "But please advise me when we can slow down and pick up the proper interval. Also, we're going to need fuel within a couple of hours."

"Understood," his commander said. "Regiment plans to refuel as soon as the forward security element clears Khash."

"Understood," Valnikov said, then he switched to intercom and told his driver, "All right, Sergei Ivanovich. Move out, but keep enough interval to avoid running into the tank in front, like that stupid pig's prick behind us."

Shortly after, the reconnaissance element's lead tank struck one of the aerial-delivered mines lying in the road, and because the regiment remained bunched up, many more tanks than those of the combat reconnaissance patrol were within range of the three TOW launchers in Khash.

With the explosion of the mine the TOW gunners launched their missiles. Before the Soviet tank gunners could react, the missiles struck, destroying two more tanks and finishing off the one that had struck a mine. In the first few seconds of the battle of Khash, three Soviet tanks and their crews were eliminated.

The vehicles behind them—the combined arms team consisting of three tank platoons and a platoon of infantry in BMP armored personnel carriers, which was supposed to be the forward security element—immediately deployed on either side of the road behind the burning tanks. As the TOW crews scurried to their alternate firing positions the T-80s and BMPs began firing their 125-mm and 73-mm guns at the positions from which the TOWs had been launched.

As they did so the 60-mm mortars behind the town rained a short barrage of high and low airburst rounds on the Soviet column, and those crews who had not already done so quickly buttoned up, closing the vehicles' protective hatches, but severely restricting their vision by doing so.

The remainder of the lead tank battalion—two companies of T-80s, well below full strength as a result of B-30's earlier attrition—began deploying to the flanks of the forward security element. When the entire battalion was thus on line, they were ordered forward, firing as they went.

Because of the dust and smoke and noise of battle, they were well into the mine field before they realized that many of the explosions were not from antitank weapons, mortars, and the report of their own tanks' main guns, but of mines exploding beneath and beside them. And by then many of the vehicles were within range of the TOW launchers to their flanks. While the confused Russian gunners continued to pour fire into Khash, the first volley of TOWs from the ridges struck the tanks. Seven more T-80s joined the blazing hulks of those destroyed by the initial volley from Khash and the deadly field of high-technology, multipurpose mines.

Some tanks continued to press forward toward Khash, but most were disabled by the mines or destroyed by the second volley of TOW missiles from the ridges.

As the second battalion of Russian tanks began deploying into a line formation behind their battered comrades, the artillery and mortar batteries of the forward security element were attempting to go into action. But the indirect fire of the 60-mm mortars, raining a mixture of airburst and point-detonating fuzed projectiles on the enemy gunners and mortarmen, dealt them a number of casualties and prevented them from getting into action in good order. Their job was further complicated when, from their flank, a laser beam suddenly illuminated one of their ammunition carriers. A few seconds later a Hellfire missile from Red Stephens's killer egg tore into the ammo carrier, killing or wounding a number of the gunners, damaging much of the nearby equipment, and adding significantly to their fear and confusion.

A ZSU-23-4 crew, having spotted the source of the laser beam, attempted to bring the four barrels of their 23-mm guns to bear on it. Before they could do so, however, Stephens turned off the laser, flew several hundred meters north up the wadi from which he had popped up just long enough to fire, and was again peering at the mass confusion before him. Cat Whitaker saw the ZSU unleash a long burst of tracers at the area from which the Hellfire had been launched a short time before. She took control of the helicopter, sighted in on the antiaircraft system, activated the laser, and destroyed the enemy weapon with the second Hellfire.

Ten kilometers to the northeast Master Sergeant Puchinelli and five other men with Dragons were atop a low ridge, peering through the night sights of their launchers at the line of enemy vehicles several hundred meters away. They were waiting for SFC O'Neill, half a kilometer to his south in a wadi, to report that his men, too, were sighted in on their targets and ready to fire.

"Dragon One, Dragon Seven," O'Neill called. "Seven through Twelve are up and ready to fire."

"This is Dragon One," Puchinelli replied. "Fire at will!"

Almost immediately twelve Dragon antitank missiles were snaking their way just above the ground toward their targets. Eleven of them struck home, destroying another six vehicles and damaging five more. Before effective fire could be brought on the Americans, they were scurrying toward the Stealth Hawk pickup site a kilometer behind their firing positions. The Stealth Hawk, well to their east with more missiles aboard, would swoop in and pick the men up when they reached the pickup site. Then it would take them to their next firing positions.

While Puchinelli, O'Neill, and their Dragon gunners were moving to rendezvous with the Stealth Hawk, the Soviet force at the gates of Khash was continuing to fall victim to the TOW gunners in and near the town and the minefield before it. An effort to clear a path through the minefield with two tanks equipped with mine rollers, which were pushed in front of the tanks, had failed. Captain Dick Warner, firing a TOW from a rooftop in Khash, destroyed one of the tanks with a missile that struck it where the turret joined the hull, decapitating the enemy vehicle. Red Stephens killed the second mine-rolling tank with a TOW missile from the flank.

Stephens then took out another ammunition carrier with the last missile of his initial load, effectively ending the Soviet 120-mm mortar battery's participation in the battle when the mortar ammunition exploded, taking the fire direction center vehicle with it.

While Stephens and Whitaker swooped into the rearm/refuel point behind the west ridge to load more missiles into the H-500's launchers, the Stealth Hawk picked up the Dragon gunners and moved them to other positions overlooking the road on which much of the two enemy regiments were stalled. As Stephens was preparing to take off he heard someone call Captain Birelli to report that enemy infantrymen or engineers were dismounted in the minefield, trying to clear it of mines.

"Let's drop the TOWs and mount a minigun," the H-500 pilot said to his female copilot, and they jumped from the little gunship to do so. By the time they took off again, however, the men in the mine field were under fire from the Baluchi-manned 60-mm mortars. Those who were not wounded by exploding mines were cut to shreds by airbursts from the mortars or were sent fleeing back to their armored personnel carriers.

The Soviet tankers and their supporting artillery were not totally without success.

Valentin Valnikov, peering through the boiling dust

and smoke of the raging battle, spotted a flash of flame as a TOW was launched from a rooftop of the town two kilometers to his front. Keeping his eyes fixed on the spot, he brought the ranging battle sight of the tank's main gun on it as he commanded, "Load HEAT!"

"HEAT selected!" the gunner replied as the automatic loader rammed a high-explosive antitank round into the breech. "Up!"

"Fire!" Valnikov said, and the T-80 rocked violently as the gun blasted the round at the target.

The round was true and exploded on target. The TOW crew, including one of the NCOs from Birelli's team, was killed.

As the tanks before him continued to erupt from enemy mines and missiles Valnikov attempted to call his battalion commander on the radio. He couldn't raise him, but the regimental commander's voice came across the air.

"Valnikov, the battalion is yours now. Take your tanks to the right. Swing right around the hill mass west of the town, then attack the town from the rear. Acknowledge, comrade Valnikov."

"Understood," Valnikov replied, thankful that he and his men would be spared—at least for the moment— from the deadly stream of missiles pouring from the town.

In addition to the TOW crew killed by Valnikov, one of the TOWs atop the east ridge suffered a near miss from an artillery round. The missile guidance system was damaged, and two crewmen—one American, the other Baluchi—were wounded. Also, two Baluchi mortarmen were killed and two wounded as they were displacing their weapons to alternate firing positions beneath a hail of Soviet artillery.

The artillery had become the greatest immediate threat to Birelli and his group of U.S. Special Forces men and their Baluchi guerrilla comrades-in-arms. The detachment commander hoped the second Stealth Hawk would arrive soon from Masirah. Not only did he need the medical team there to deal with the mounting number of casualties, but he wanted to use the helicopter to deliver a raid force to the enemy artillery positions. Rosie Rosengrant had already warned him that, after delivering Puchinelli and the Dragon gunners to their next firing position, he would have to head northwest and rendezvous with the incoming Stealth Hawk Two and the Talon tanker from which both Hawks would draw fuel before reappearing in the battle area.

"Tiger Boss, this is Aphid," Stephens said, calling Birelli. "Be advised, I have two Hellfires and a minigun with two thousand rounds ready to work next targets, over."

"Roger, Aphid," Birelli said. "See if you can find their damned artillery. They're starting to hit us pretty bad."

"Wilco," Stephens said over the radio, then, to his copilot on the intercom, "We'll head due north until we see gun flashes to our east, Cat. That should be their artillery positions."

As they headed north just fifty feet above the ground Cat saw several flashes to their east and said, "There, sir. I think that's their guns."

Stephens slowed the chopper, turned right toward the area from which Cat had seen the flashes, and came to a hover. There were several more flashes from the area, but they were not from Soviet artillery pieces firing on the American and Baluchi positions—they were from Soviet vehicles igniting as they were struck by Dragons launched by Puchinelli, O'Neill, and their men.

Stephens turned left and headed north once more. A short time later he saw the almost incessant flashes of the tank regiment's two remaining howitzer batteries, which were pounding Khash and the ridge lines east and west of the town.

As Stephens dashed behind a hill near the flashes and peered over the top of it with his mast-mounted FLIR he could see twelve type 2S1 122-mm self-propelled howitzers lined up almost hub to hub, in typical Soviet fashion.

"Well, shit, Cat," he said. "This minigun ain't going to

257

be much use against those armored gun carriers. Let's see if we can get ahold of the Hawk and have him bring Pooch and the Dragons up here to hit them. We can help out with our Hellfires, then go find somebody to shoot with the minigun."

"Sounds good to me, sir," the young sergeant said.

Stephens called the Stealth Hawk but got no answer from the helicopter. Puchinelli answered, though.

"Aphid, this is Pooch. The Hawk's gone west to link up with the tanker and the other Hawk. We don't expect him back for another ten minutes or so."

"Roger, Pooch. I was going to get the Hawk to bring you up here to hit this artillery with your Dragons. Guess we'll have to do what we can with what we've got, though."

"Breaker, breaker! Aphid, this is Hawk Two. Say your position, over."

"Hawk Two, this is Aphid," Stephens answered over the frequency-hopping radio. "We're about ten klicks due north of Khash, getting ready to take on two batteries of SP artillery, over."

"Roger, Aphid," the pilot of the second Stealth Hawk said. "I'm fresh off the tanker, headed for Tiger's position to drop off the Band-Aid team. What can I do to help, over?"

"Contact call sign 'Pooch' and get him up here ASAP. We've got to do something about these big guns—they're doing too much damage!"

"Uh, Aphid and Hawk Two, this is Pooch. I'm afraid we won't be much help until Hawk One gets back. He's got our last missiles aboard, over."

"Aphid, Roger. We'll do what we can now with our Hellfires, out."

"OK, Cat," Stephens said as he observed the line of self-propelled howitzers, "here we go!"

He lifted the H-500 above the hill, fixed his sight on the turret ring of the nearest 2S1 howitzer, and activated the helicopter's laser. After adjusting his aim slightly he launched a Hellfire missile and watched it slam into the enemy vehicle. The eruption of the ammunition in it caused an explosion that not only destroyed the 2S1 and crew but damaged the vehicle beside it. Two Soviet 122-mm howitzers were out of action as a result of Stephens's first missile. Without ducking behind the hill he illuminated the third vehicle in line and knocked it out with his other Hellfire. As soon as the second missile struck he nosed the little gunship over and sped toward the line of howitzers. When he was nearly on them he triggered his minigun, and the little rotating cannon began to spew a steady stream of tracer ammunition at the vehicles. Stephens's targets were the auxiliary fuel barrels sitting atop the vehicles, and as the stream of bullets struck, the diesel fuel in the barrels began pouring out onto the vehicles and the ground around them. But the tracers failed to ignite the slow-burning fuel during his first pass, so Stephens made a quick turn and sped back at them, again spraying the self-propelled howitzers with minigun fire.

As Red made his second run the radar warning indicator began a steady tone. Radar—probably from a ZSU-23-4 antiaircraft system—was locked in on him. He dived toward the front of the line of enemy howitzers, temporarily silenced as a result of his Hellfires and the minigun attacks. The skids of his helicopter nearly hit the ground as he zoomed along just in front of the guns, and the first burst of fire from the ZSU-23-4, atop a low hill a kilometer to the north, sped at his radar signature. The enemy howitzers protected him from the initial burst, however, and he did a sharp left turn, keeping the row of vehicles between his helicopter and the source of antiaircraft fire. The second burst also missed the ground-hugging helicopter, most of the rounds again slamming into the lightly armored self-propelled howitzers. The 23-mm shells exploded, in some instances doing slight damage to the howitzers, but—more important, from the Americans' point of view—igniting the diesel fuel around several of the now-silent vehicles. As the flames grew, spreading to the ruptured fuel cells of other vehicles, several of the crews abandoned their howitzers. Only two drivers had the presence of mind to pull their

L. H. BURRUSS

vehicles out of the growing flames, but the crew of one, whose auxiliary fuel tanks were still leaking onto the hull, had to abandon theirs anyway.

With most of the Soviet mortars and artillery silenced, the Americans and Baluchis in and around Khash who had been forced to seek cover from the hail of exploding Russian fire were able to get out of their protective bunkers, man their antitank weapons, and bring the enemy armor under effective fire again.

CHAPTER 24

Captain Dick Warner crawled from the rubble of the building on the leading edge of Khash toward the partially collapsed building behind it. He was coughing from the dust and smoke that hung over the battered town like a heavy, dry fog. His ears were so badly damaged from the near miss of the Soviet tank round that had exploded above him that he could hear nothing except a loud, incessant ringing. He knew he was fortunate that the shell's fragments had missed him, but the throbbing pain of his broken leg was so bad that he barely cared about anything else.

He had destroyed two Soviet T-80 tanks with the TOW he and two Baluchi gunners were manning before another tank had zeroed in on their position. Since the concussion of the near miss had knocked him temporarily unconscious—he had no idea how long ago that had been—he had seen nothing of the Baluchi men. He had no idea whether they had escaped or lay in the rubble of the building with the damaged TOW system. All he knew was that he could see from the flashes of light through the heavy dust cloud that the battle was still raging around him. He dragged himself into the building behind the one from which he had just escaped. His confused mind was aware that there was something in there he wanted to get, but he couldn't remember what. "It must be water," he thought. "I've got to have some water."

He groped around in the dark, dusty room for a while

but found nothing, then let himself yield to the pain in his leg and in his head and drifted into unconsciousness.

Several buildings away the CIA man, Dick Medlin, and the Baluchi chieftain named Chakur Nothani were lying on the floor of another building. The crash of exploding artillery around them had all but ended, although they could still hear occasional explosions a short distance to their north.

"It sounds like their artillery has stopped," Medlin said in Baluchi. "That's tank fire north of us, I think. And machine-gun fire—probably also from the tanks."

They listened for a short while longer, then Medlin said, "I must go see if I can find Captain Warner. Or a radio, so I can talk to Birelli."

"I will try to find some of my men," Nothani responded, "then meet you back here."

Medlin ran north toward the building where Warner had gone with the TOW system and two guerrilla crewmen some time earlier. The building was nearly leveled.

"Damn!" Medlin said. *There's no way they could have gotten out of that mess,* he thought.

He dashed across the street into the building south of the rubble just ahead of a burst of machine-gun fire that tore up the street behind him, tripping on something as he entered and falling forward onto the dirt floor. He reached back to feel what he had tripped over and found a body. Pulling a penlight from his shirt pocket, he twisted it on. By the dim light he discovered that he had tripped over the legs of Captain Warner. The young officer was lying unconscious on the floor, the pneumatic splint on his broken leg nothing but a sleeve of shredded plastic.

Medlin felt the man's neck, discovered that he was still alive, and rolled him over. He could find no serious wounds on Warner, although he noticed that a small amount of blood had leaked from his ears.

Medlin searched around the room for something with which to splint Warner's broken leg and spotted a PRC-117 radio and two AT-4 antitank rockets. He grabbed the radio, turned it on, and heard a conversation between Rocco Birelli on the ridge west of Khash and Birelli's team sergeant, Jake Brady.

"Kaminski and Washington are both down," Brady was saying. "We have two or three missiles left. After that we've got nothing left but RPG-16s and the machine guns, over."

"OK, Jake," Medlin heard Birelli say in reply, "Just do the best you can with what you've got, out. Break, break, Warner, Warner, this is Birelli, Birelli, over."

Medlin keyed the radio and spoke. "Birelli, this is Medlin, how copy?"

"Roger, Dick, I've got you loud and clear. Is Warner with you?"

"Affirmative, but he's unconscious. What's the situation, over?"

"It looks like they've stopped trying to punch through the mine field," Birelli explained, "but they're trying to bypass us to my west. I'm moving almost everything I have left to the west side of the ridge here, but we're damned near out of antitank ammunition. What's the situation in town, over?"

"The artillery and tank fire pretty well leveled the place," Medlin replied. "Nothani's trying to round up everybody we have left here. All I know for sure we have left is a couple of AT-4s that are here with me, but there ought to be a couple of RPGs around here somewhere. I'll let you know as soon as I link back up with Nothani."

"Roger. Can you get Warner and your other wounded to the south side of town? I've got the medical team over with Brady on the east ridge. I'll get Hawk Two to pick them up behind Khash and fly them over there for treatment," Birelli said.

"Hawk *Two?*" Medlin asked. "We got both Stealth Hawks in here now?"

"Negative," Birelli answered. "The fuel probe on Rosie's bird went tits up on us, and he couldn't take on any fuel from the tanker. He's sitting out in the desert southwest of here, out of gas."

"What about the killer egg?" Medlin inquired.

"He took a hit in the rotors and had to set down. Hawk

Two's picking him and the girl up now to bring them back here to the rearm point to get spare parts. Then he'll take them back, pick up Pooch and his people, and bring them back here. By then, unless the artillery starts up again, the chopper should be able to pick up your wounded from south of town and get them to a safer area."

Medlin could barely grasp the rapidly moving situation. He was glad to see that Rocco Birelli seemed to be on top of it, though—and glad that the capable young captain had taken Warner's advice and moved his command post to a position on the high ridge west of Khash.

"OK, I'll splint Warner up and get him moved south of town for pickup," Medlin said. "Any word from SFOB, by the way?"

"Negative," Birelli replied. "My satcom took a hit from the artillery, and I haven't had a chance to find the spare and get it up on the air yet. Call Hawk Two when you have your wounded south of town, out."

Medlin tore two legs off a table that was in the room and used his shirt to tie them onto Warner's broken leg as a splint. He was about to go to the building where he and Nothani had been when he heard the creaking of tank tracks just to his north. He peered around the doorway of the house and saw a Soviet T-80 tank turning into the street.

"Shit!" the American intelligence agent muttered, then he grabbed one of the 84-mm AT-4 rockets from the corner and climbed through the back window of the house into the narrow alley behind it. There he prepared the antitank rocket for firing, thinking, as he heard the enemy tank creaking through the rubbled streets, that if the tank was allowed to go unmolested, the Soviets would realize that the town was nearly abandoned. They might then press their attack through Khash instead of—or in addition to—attempting to bypass it to the west, where Birelli was now concentrating his forces to attempt to stop them.

The front of the tank appeared down the alley in front of him, and he raised the rocket launcher to his shoulder.

When the center of the turret appeared he fired the rocket into the side of the tank. He didn't destroy it, but the tank commander and his gunner were wounded, and the tank filled with smoke and fumes. The three-man crew abandoned the tank almost immediately, fleeing toward an open doorway on the far side of the street.

Chakur Nothani and a number of his men, several buildings to the south, had been preparing to engage the T-80 with rocket-propelled grenades when Medlin's rocket disabled it. They saw the crew stumble into the building and immediately maneuvered against it. The stunned crew surrendered to them without a fight.

Medlin called to Nothani to ensure the chieftain knew who he was, then ran to the building. There he found the Baluchi men searching the Soviet tankers. The gunner was badly wounded in the back, the driver was unhurt, and the tank commander, wearing the rank of senior lieutenant, was only slightly injured.

Taking Nothani aside, Medlin said, "The one with the injured leg is a senior lieutenant. He must be the commander of one of the tank companies. We need to find out what he knows."

"Shall I kill the others?" the Baluchi chieftain asked.

"No," Medlin replied. "They are brave warriors. They are the only ones who have made it to Khash. We will hold them captive. How many of your men were you able to find?"

"Of twenty-eight I found only seventeen. Of them, only ten are not dead or badly wounded. And I found one of your Americans. He is dead. Did you find the other?"

"Yes," Medlin answered. "He is in a building just across the street there, unconscious. I also found a radio. Most of the Russians are trying to bypass Khash to the west of the ridge. We must get the wounded to the south of town. A helicopter will pick them up there and take them to the aid station on the east ridge."

"And the rest of us?" Nothani asked.

"We will stay here and ensure that no Russians get past us," Medlin said. "And we will find out what the officer knows of their plans."

"Very well," Nothani said. "We are nearly out of ammunition, but we will fight with what we have left. They will not pass as long as one of my men can fight."

Medlin looked out in the street. The Soviet tank was still running, although smoke was rising from the tank commander's and driver's hatches.

"Get some of your men to take Captain Warner to the helicopter, please," Medlin said. "And have someone get the radio and the rocket from beside him and bring them here."

As Nothani began giving orders to his men, Medlin ran to the tank, crawled into the driver's hatch, and lowered the seat. Although his eyes burned from the acrid smoke, he located the steering laterals and transmission. He threw the tank into gear, pulled back hard on the left lateral, and gunned the throttle. The tank pivoted in the street until it was headed north, from which it had come. Releasing the lateral, he guided the big war machine back to the northern edge of town, then locked both laterals to halt it.

He climbed out of the driver's hatch and up onto the turret, then lowered himself into the tank commander's hatch. Crawling down to the gunner's position, he found the controls for the turret and the main gun. Placing his burning, watery eyes on the infrared sight, he traversed the turret, surveying the smoke-filled battlefield before him. There seemed to be burning vehicles everywhere. Finally he found a tank that was still moving—heading north out of the battlefield, away from Khash. He was unsure how to operate the ranging sight, so he placed the crosshairs high on the other tank's turret.

"Now let's see if this damn thing's loaded," he muttered to himself, and he depressed the triggers on the control yoke.

The big tank bucked as the main gun fired and recoiled beside him. Pressing his eyes to the sight again, he saw a bright flash on his target.

"Got him!" Medlin exclaimed aloud. He began looking around the smoky, cramped gunner's compartment, trying to figure out how to reload the big 125-mm smooth-bore main gun for another shot at the enemy.

He was still looking around the smoky interior of the tank when a rocket-propelled grenade struck it.

One of the Baluchi guerrillas whom Nothani had not found had pulled himself from a rubbled building on the northwest corner of the artillery-blasted town when the firing had stopped. Seeing the Soviet tank pull back out to the northern edge of town, he assumed it was going to join the others that were moving back to the north. He fired his last RPG at it, striking it in the side of the turret. It detonated with a bright flash, and the guerrilla, having used the last bit of strength in his badly wounded body, gave thanks to his God as he saw the explosion and collapsed onto the rubble.

Normally, replacing a couple of rotor blades on a Hughes 500 helicopter is not a difficult task. But in the black of night, with enemy forces nearby, it becomes difficult. Nevertheless, Chief Warrant Officer Red Stephens and his helicopter mechanic and copilot, Sergeant Cat Whitaker, had nearly completed the task.

Stephens, perched atop the helicopter, holding the rotor blade in place as Whitaker bolted it on, heard her say, "OK, sir, now rotate it toward the rear a little so I can insert the locking pin."

He leaned forward to do so but lost his footing and fell from the side of the helicopter. His face struck the front of the multibarreled minigun, lacerating his right eye and eyebrow, and his left hand, trying to break his fall to the wadi bed, was bent far back, badly spraining his wrist.

"Damn, Mr. Stephens," she said. "Are you all right?"

He was sitting on the ground, his injured wrist hanging loosely at his side, his right hand pressed against his lacerated eye. "Christ!" he said. "I nearly tore my eye out."

She leaned near him and examined his eye with her penlight. She moved his hand and tried to raise the blood-covered eyelid with her finger.

"Ow!" he cried, but she had seen enough. The eyeball had a short but deep cut in it. As she removed a battle dressing from his survival vest to tie over the eye he said, "I think I broke my damned wrist, too, Cat."

"Can you move it?" she asked. He moved his hand back and forth at the wrist and said, "Yeah, but it hurts like hell."

"Well, at least it probably isn't broken," she said as she tied the battle dressing around his head, the gauze pad firmly over his injured eye.

That done, she stood and said, "I still didn't get the damned locking pin in."

Stephens climbed to his feet and, with his good hand, picked up one of the damaged rotor blades they had replaced. "If you can climb back up there with the pin, I'll try to hold the blade up with this broken one."

She did so, and after several tries at aligning the hole in the coupling so she could insert and lock the pin, they got the last rotor blade locked into place.

"That's it, sir," she said as she lowered herself to the ground. "Let's get in, and I'll see if this thing will fly."

Their radios had been off while they repaired the helicopter, and after she started the engine Stephens reached over and turned them on, then called Birelli.

"Tiger Base, Tiger Base, this is Aphid, over."

"This is Birelli," came the reply. He had long since given up using proper call signs for the ground elements of his force. With the confusion of battle, men being killed and wounded, and others moving from one location to another, it was much simpler just to use names.

"This is Aphid. We've got the little bird fixed, I think. What's the situation, over?"

"Hawk One's still down in the desert. Hawk Two has moved the wounded from Khash to the east ridge and is now en route to pick up Pooch and his people and bring them back here. I still haven't been able to call SFOB to tell them our situation, but when Pooch gets back with his LST-4 I'll call them. . . . How's your fuel situation, Aphid?"

Stephens looked at his aircraft's fuel gauge. "Pretty

low. I'm only good for about half an hour or so. We'll be back there to pick up some more in a few minutes."

"I'm afraid not, Red," Birelli replied. "The refuel point took a hit from the artillery a while ago. It's burning."

"Oh, hell," Stephens said. "What about the ammo?"

"We saved a couple of the Hellfires, but I've already fired the TOWs you had left. And we've got a couple of cans of minigun ammo, over."

"OK, comin' out," Whitaker said over the intercom. She lifted the little helicopter off the ground, did a quick hover check and a check of the gauges, then nosed the aircraft over and started south down the wadi.

"Come right to two-seven-zero," Stephens said over the intercom.

Cat lifted the helicopter out of the wadi and turned west, asking, "Where we going?" as she did so.

Stephens answered her question by calling Birelli and saying, "Give me Hawk One's coordinates. We'll go find him, siphon off any gas he's got left, and pick up the Dragons he's carrying for Pooch and them."

"Break, break!" a voice on the radio said. "This is Hawk Two, Aphid. We're headed for Hawk One's pos now. We'll give him enough of our gas to get back here, then return here with the last twelve Dragons ASAP. How copy?"

"Aphid has a solid copy. We're heading for base to load whatever ammo's left, then, over."

Cat turned the H-500 back toward the south. To their left they could see countless fires just north of Khash.

"Jesus," she said to Stephens, "look at that. How much longer can this go on?"

"Not much, cat lady," he said. "One more load of Hellfires and whatever's left of the minigun ammo and we're finished. And from the sound of things, Birelli and whoever he has left will be dry, too, when they fire that last bunch of Dragons."

CHAPTER 25

1945 hours GMT (1545 hours EDT; 2315 hours Iran time),
30 September
National Military Command Center
The Pentagon, Washington, D.C.

The Secretary of Defense looked down the table at the
civilian men who were the service secretaries of
the armed forces of the United States, and at the four-
star officers comprising the Joint Chiefs of Staff. He
had just been told that contact had been lost hours
earlier with the American Special Forces men in
and around the southeastern Iranian town of Khash.
It had to be assumed, he was told, that they had
been overwhelmed, and that the Soviet forces moving south toward Chah Bahar, if they had not already done so, would soon reach the twenty-eighth parallel.

"Well," the secretary said, "that's it, then, gentlemen.
The Soviet foreign minister was advised earlier today, in
the most straightforward of terms, that the passing of
that line would be viewed by this government as a
declaration of their intentions to go to war with the
United States and her allies—that's the bad news. The
good news is that most of the NATO nations have finally
come on line to declare that they, too, will view it as a
direct act of war on the alliance and will respond
accordingly. And the other part of the good news is that
the Soviets—behind all the bullshit rhetoric—are making it plain to anyone who will listen that they *do not*
want this thing to escalate beyond the current area of
conflict, and they do not want it to go nuclear—under

any circumstances. And, of course, we believe that . . . about as far as we can *throw* the Soviet Union."

"Are they speaking with *one* official voice now, Mr. Secretary?" the chairman asked.

"Yes—although Mr. Gorbachev still doesn't seem to be fully in control of the hard-liners—especially those in the Soviet High Command."

"Are we going to mobilize, Mr. Secretary?" the chief of staff of the army asked.

"Yes. As soon as we have CENTCOM's lead brigades ashore we're going to begin mobilization of every damned man, woman, and child on the troop lists, as we discussed earlier."

The generals and admirals looked at one another. The United States of America was about to go to a full wartime footing for the first time since World War II. Much of the rest of the world, they knew, would follow suit.

The big difference this time was that, for the first time in the history of the planet, the warring nations would possess the ability to totally annihilate each other. Every man in the room was fully aware of that fact, and for several moments they were all silent.

Then the Chief of Staff of the Air Force asked, "What will be the state of alert of our nuclear forces, sir?"

"I regret to say that the president has been forced to order that our nuclear forces alert status will be—"

"Excuse me, Mr. Secretary," an army major general apologized as he burst, breathless, into the room. "They've reestablished contact with the Special Forces commander at Khash." He looked around the room at the other men, uncertain to whom he was supposed to pass the rest of the information.

"And what does he report, General?" the Secretary of the Army asked.

"Uh, well, we don't have much information from him yet, sir. Actually, we're only speaking to the Special Forces Operations Base in England. But *they've* got contact. All they've reported is that he says he's still fighting the Russians, and they haven't gotten past him yet. I, ah, thought you'd want to know that much, though."

"Yes," the Secretary of Defense responded. "Yes, thank you, General. Will you let us know as soon as there's any more information?"

"Uh, yes. Of course, Mr. Secretary. Shall I bring it straight in here, sir?"

"Yes, General. Please do—as long as it's something of significance."

"Of course, sir," the major general said as he backed out of the room.

The Secretary of Defense looked at the Chief of Staff of the Air Force. "What was your question again, General?"

"Nukes, Mr. Secretary," the air force general replied. "What's to be the alert status of our nuclear forces?"

"Yes, of course," the secretary said somberly. "As I was saying, the president, after a great deal of thought, has decided the following. . . ."

*1950 hours GMT (2320 hours local time), 30 September
Ridge line west of Khash, Iran*

Almost halfway around the world Captain Rocco Birelli was on the secure voice satellite communications system he had been able to patch together with components from the various elements under his command. He was speaking to the commander of the 3d Special Forces Group at his SFOB in England.

"We're getting ready to hit them with just about everything we have left here, Eagle," Birelli was saying. "Then we'll have to break it off, unless you can get some more weapons and ammunition—and people—up here, over."

"This is Eagle," the group commander said. "I'll see what I can do, Rocco. But even if we get approval, it'll probably be tomorrow night before we can get any help in to you. What are your plans meanwhile, over?"

"After this next go at 'em, I'm going to find out what I have left. I'll send the wounded out on the Hawks, if they have enough gas, and take the rest of the people east somewhere, and hide out until we get resupplied. . . . We've done just about all the damage we can for the time being, over."

"You've done well, Rocco," his group commander replied. "CINCCENT has had much more time than he planned on to get his forces ready to go. Looks like it's up to them now. Do what you can with what you have left, and then lay up for a while. I'll do what I can to . . . wait, out."

Birelli handed the radio handset to his slightly wounded radio operator, Sergeant Percy Hanson. "It's the group CO," he said. "I've got to get down the hill with Pooch. Let him know what's going on till I get back."

"Will do, sir."

Birelli scampered down the hill toward Puchinelli and his men, who were waiting until enough vehicles were within range of their Dragon missiles so they could launch their last remaining antitank rounds in a final, deadly salvo.

The Soviet tanks were echeloned to the left as they turned and headed south past the western side of the ridge, their turrets turned so that the long 125-mm guns were trained on the ridge where Puchinelli's men waited for his order to fire. All twelve men were aware that, unless they fired within about a second of each other, the tanks would have time to adjust their guns and fire on any of the Dragon gunners still tracking their targets as the missiles flew toward them. The men whose targets were farthest away were most in jeopardy, as their missiles would be in flight the longest, and they would have to hold their sights on the targets until the wire-guided missiles hit, or they would miss their assigned tank. Worse, there was little place for the men to hide after they fired. Any tanks not knocked out by the salvo were almost certain to begin firing immediately at the fleeing Americans with both their main guns and coaxially mounted machine guns, as well as the tank commanders' guns.

Puchinelli was just about to give the order to fire when Birelli reached his position. Turning to the captain, he said, "Sir, it's going to be hell here once we launch our missiles. I recommend you get back over the hill, and quickly." It was a long two hundred meters from the firing positions to the first low ridge, where there was adequate cover from the tank fire.

"Pooch," Birelli said, "I'm not going to let you fire from here. It's too damned far to reach cover before they hit you, and you're bound to get a lot of guys hit. Move 'em back up the ridge and fire a salvo at the few tanks nearest to you. Half these damn Dragons won't kill the tanks they hit anyway."

"But Captain, they're going to get past us if we don't hit 'em now."

"They're going to get past us anyway, Pooch. Even if we knock out this lead company, the ones behind them will just bypass farther to the west. Anyway, we're out of antitank ammo after this, except for a few RPGs. Now get the men moving uphill."

"Yes, sir." The detachment commander was right. They *would* get by, even in the unlikely event that the last salvo he was about to fire took out all the tanks in the lead company. And it was unlikely that many—if any— of his men would make it to cover before they were gunned down.

"All right!" he called to the men nearest him. "Pass the word! Weapons safe, and move up the ridge to the rally point! Do it now!"

By the time the men had reassembled at the rally point behind a foothill of the ridge, Cat Whitaker was calling on the radio. She and the injured Red Stevens had made it to the rearm point and had reloaded the Hellfire launcher and the minigun with the last of the H-500's ammunition. Stephens had hopped into the copilot's seat, but she told him that with his injuries, he was only adding unnecessary weight to the almost fuelless helicopter. After some argument he agreed to climb out, and she took off toward the west.

"Pooch, this is Aphid, over," she called.

"Go ahead, Aphid."

"Pooch, I'm prepared to support you with my last two Hellfires. I don't want to shoot the same targets you're after, so tell me what you want me to hit."

"OK, Aphid," Puchinelli said. "Wait till I get my guys set to fire, and we'll hit them together. We'll take the six closest to us. You can hit anything west of them, over."

"OK, but hurry it up," she said. "This thing's almost out of gas."

Puchinelli assigned one tank to each pair of Dragons, then called Cat.

"Aphid, this is Pooch. We're ready. We'll let you take the first shot. That should divert their attention long enough to let us fire and track. Be careful."

"Roger," she replied, then she lifted her mast-mounted sight above the southern tip of the ridge. She scanned the desert floor with the forward-looking infrared, doing an easy pedal turn to the left as she did so. She mentally counted off the six tanks nearest the ridge, then set the crosshairs of her sight on the seventh. Then she eased the helicopter up, illuminated the side of it with her laser target designator, and triggered a Hellfire missile.

At the blast of the missile's launch most of the tank commanders began to shift their guns in her direction, even though the Hellfire struck its target before they had a chance to engage her. As she backed the helicopter up and lowered it behind the ridge she saw flashes from the north as Puchinelli and his men salvoed their last Dragons. Above her, streams of tracers aimed at her firing position cracked harmlessly overhead.

"All right, Cat," she said to herself as she turned and headed south, "let's get around to their other flank and give 'em one last Hellfire."

The Dragons destroyed two of their targets and disabled three more. The sixth tank's reactive armor saved it from major damage, however, and even as the last missile closed on its target the gunner, seeing that his sight was aligned on the row of flashes from the firing site, loosed a 125-mm high-explosive round, following it up with a steady stream of fire from the coaxially mounted machine gun. The main gun round exploded almost in Staff Sergeant Tippy's face, killing him instantly and severely wounding the man nearest him. Rocco Birelli ran to their assistance but was knocked down immediately by a round from the enemy machine gun. Master Sergeant Puchinelli ran to him and dragged him behind the ridge just before another burst of fire almost hit him, too.

Birelli was shot through the face, his jaw a mass of broken bone and torn flesh. He was trying to breathe in short gasps, but his throat was clogged with his nearly severed tongue. Puchinelli reached his finger deep into the officer's throat, trying to clear it so he could breathe, but was unable to do so. Quickly he drew his trench knife from the scabbard on his load-bearing equipment, pulled Birelli's head back, and felt for the groove in his Adam's apple. Marking it with the tip of his finger, he plunged the knife into the officer's throat with his other hand. Then he took a ball point pen from his shirt pocket, unscrewed it, and threw all but the barrel away. He bit the bottom end of the plastic tube off, then pushed the remainder into the hole he had punctured in Birelli's throat. Immediately he heard air begin to whooze in and out of the plastic tube.

"OK, *paisano,*" he said to the wounded captain, "you'll be OK now. Just hang on for a while, and we'll get you to the docs."

Birelli nodded his head slightly in acknowledgment, unable to speak, but amazed at the lack of pain he felt, and at the way he was able to breathe deeply, even though no air was passing through his nostrils or his battered mouth.

The fuel warning light of the H-500MD had been illuminated for several minutes when Cat Whitaker launched her last missile from the right flank of the enemy tanks. It took the turret off another T-80, and she followed that up with a long burst of minigun fire, although it did no harm. She was just trying to lighten the aircraft as much as possible in the hope that she would be able to make it back to Khash, or at least behind the ridge.

As she headed east toward the ridge line—easily detected by the burning vehicles at the foot of it and the furious barrage of 125-mm and 7.62-mm fire now being directed against it—she was only about two kilometers south of the leading tanks. She was afraid to hug the flat desert floor, as she would not have sufficient altitude to auto-rotate to a safe landing if the fuel ran out before she got to the ridge. It was a wise decision. Suddenly, its fuel cells emptied, the helicopter's instrument panel flashed a loss-of-power warning, and the engine began to wind down.

Thank God I have enough altitude, she thought as she allowed the helicopter to descend rapidly, then used that speed to flare the helicopter to a textbook landing as, on the radio, she called, "Mayday, Mayday, Mayday!"

Puchinelli heard the call as he was about to radio Hawk Two, the only helicopter with sufficient fuel remaining to continue flying, to crank up and come to the back side of the ridge to evacuate the wounded.

The Stealth Hawk pilot answered Cat's call immediately.

"Roger Mayday, Aphid! Say your position, over!"

There was no answer, so he tried again. "Aphid, this is Hawk Two. Roger your Mayday! Say your position, over!"

Again there was no answer, so the MH-60 pilot said, "All stations, this is Hawk Two. Anybody know where Aphid went down?"

Puchinelli had seen a tank erupt well to the west and assumed it was from Sergeant Whitaker's last Hellfire. He scanned the horizon from there to the south with a pair of night-vision goggles he took from one of his men.

"There she is!" he said aloud as he spotted the helicopter to the southwest of the ridge. He grabbed the radio to let the Stealth Hawk know her position, but even as he did so, the man to whom he handed back the night-vision goggles said, "Oh, shit! They got her!"

Looking where he had seen her, Puchinelli saw the flash of a Soviet tank gun and, seconds later, some distance south of the tank, the explosion of the second round of tank fire as it slammed into the already-destroyed Hughes 500.

"Hawk Two, this is Pooch. They just put two rounds of 125 into her chopper, over."

"Roger. What's the location? We'll go see if she got out."

"Negative, Hawk," the master sergeant said sadly. "It's right out in the flatlands. If you go out there, the bastards'll just get you, too. Anyway, the tanks will be there by the time you could get there. But I have a couple of critically wounded I need you to pick up from the east side of the ridge. I'll have them at the mine entrance in about ten minutes, over."

"Uh, roger, Pooch. We're going to shut down till you get the wounded there, to save gas. Call us when they're ready."

The tank fire ceased as the Soviets realized they were receiving no more fire from the ridge line and continued their slow advance to the south. Puchinelli went to the position atop the ridge that Birelli had been using as a command post earlier, while his uninjured men took the wounded captain and NCO and the body of Staff Sergeant Tippy to the mine on the east side of the ridge. With Major Denton dead, and captains Birelli and Warner and their warrant officer XOs out of action, he was in command of the Special Forces men now—what remained of them. He needed to get on the satellite radio, and let SFOB know their situation, and ask for further orders.

As he reached the position, Puchinelli saw the radio operator, Sergeant Hanson, lying sprawled on his back. One of the young NCO's legs was lying several meters away. The man was dead, and his radio, a victim of the same tank round, lay shattered beside him.

Dick Medlin, barely aware of which way was up, saw a circle of dim light. Although his eyes and lungs were seared by the acrid smoke within the Soviet tank, and his muscles were barely able to expand and contract from the lack of oxygen reaching them, he reached toward the open hatch, managed to grab onto something, and pulled his weakened body upward. When his head was finally outside in the fresh air he gulped deeply, the cool night air of Khash soothing his burning lungs. Oxygen, absorbed by his bloodstream, reached his brain before it reinvigorated his muscles. "Rest now," his brain seemed to say. But his warrior soul said, "Move!" He obeyed the latter impulse, pulling himself out of the hatch, jumping from the hull of the damaged T-80, and crawling, on his hands and knees, to the doorway of a half-collapsed building behind the tank. There, aware that he was free of the suffocating environment of the interior of the burning T-80, he pulled himself to his feet by clawing his way up the rough wall. Reeling as he stood there, he said aloud, to himself, "You're not done yet, Medlin. Move!"

He stumbled back out into the street, looked to his left, and recognized the dim doorway from which he had run to board the tank sometime earlier. He had no idea whether it had been minutes or hours since he had done so. All he knew was that there was something he was supposed to be doing. He stumbled into the doorway and saw several figures. They spoke to him in a language he failed to understand at first, until he heard the name "Medlin." Then he remembered. It was the Baluchi chieftain, Chakur Nothani, and he was asking if Medlin was hurt.

"Thanks be to God," the CIA operative responded, "I am all right."

"You drove the Russian tank," Nothani said.

"Yes," Medlin said. "Yes, I did. And I destroyed another tank with it. It was God's will."

"God blesses you with skill and courage," Nothani said.

"He does," Medlin said. It was the first time in his life that he had acknowledged that anything except his own determination might be responsible for his actions—and his success as a warrior. Some inner strength moved him then, and he said, "Our brothers—Baluchi and American—have fought well, Nothani. Now it is time to bring them together, and to decide what to do next. Do you have the radio that was with the captain?"

"We do, Medlin, my brother. Sit and have some tea, and use it as you wish."

Medlin sat beside the Baluchi chieftain. One of the men set the AN/PRC-117 radio before him, and he took the handset and said, "Tiger, this is Medlin, over."

Pete Puchinelli answered his call. "Medlin, this is Pooch. Where are you, and what's the situation there, over?"

"I'm here in town," Dick Medlin replied. "Nothani is here, and so are some of his men—about a dozen of them, I think. Ah, what's the situation with the enemy, over?"

"This is Pooch," Puchinelli said, thinking, *If Medlin's still at it, we're OK.* The legendary soldier and Agency man had always managed to take the worst of situations and turn them around. The sound of his voice brushed away the feeling of defeat that had been settling into Puchinelli's mind, and he said, "We ain't in very good shape, ol' buddy. But we can get together, figure out what's left to hit these bastards with, and at least give them one more go. Where do you want me to meet you?"

"Is the mine still safe?" Medlin asked.

"That's affirm, Richard," Puchinelli replied. "Meet you there?"

"Roger," Medlin said. "We'll see you there in about, oh, ten minutes."

Another voice came up on the radio net. "Pooch and Medlin, this is Warner. Is there any reason we can't meet on the east ridge instead of at the mine, over?"

"Uh, Warner, this is Medlin. Last time I saw you, you were *non compos mentis.* Where you at?"

All three men, subconsciously elated at the fact that they had survived the carnage around them, began the sort of lighthearted banter soldiers in that situation often engage in.

"Speak English, Medlin," Captain Warner said. "I'm over behind the east ridge. How 'bout if I send the Hawk over to pick you guys up and bring you back here? And if you have contact with higher, bring your radio. I need to get ahold of them and tell 'em what heroes you are—and ask them how the hell they're going to get us out of here, so we can go down south and kick these fuckers' asses some more . . . over."

Medlin and Puchinelli both chuckled before answering. Medlin keyed his handset first and said, "Hey, Cap'n, you're talking good. But if you think you're in charge of this bunch of hard-dicked mothers, you're gonna have to show us, when we get there, that you've got all three 'iles,' over."

"Iles?" Warner inquired.

"Roger that," Master Sergeant Puchinelli interjected. "Mob-ile, ag-ile, and host-ile."

Warner laughed, then pressed the push-to-talk button on the radio handset and said, "If that's all it took, I'd be the Secretary of Defense—except that I used to be a pretty good scotch drinker, I did more womanizing than the guy from Texas—and I'd rather be here killing Commies than working in Washington."

"Bullshit, Cap'n," Puchinelli responded. "Last time I talked to you, all you could say was how wonderful you were gonna be when you finally got to D.C. You had a change of heart or somethin'?"

"Hey," the captain said from his command post below the ridge east of Khash, "I've been through a lot of changes since you bastards dragged me out here to this place. Now get your asses over here, and let's decide what to do next, over."

There was a sudden seriousness in Warner's voice that made the others drop the levity they had been using to take their minds off the death and fear and destruction that surrounded them.

"This is Pooch. I've got one dead American here, and the satcom radio's shot. You'll have to use the chopper's satcom to contact higher, over."

"This is Warner. All this damn dust out here has put the chopper's satcom out of commission. They haven't been able to contact SFOB or the AWACS all night."

"Roger, sir. I recommend you pull the radio and try to repair it, then. This one's literally shot to hell. There's no way it can be fixed, over."

O'Neill entered the net to advise Hawk Two that he had the wounded at the mine and was ready to be picked up and flown to the east ridge, where the medical team was tending to the other wounded American and Baluchi soldiers. Then he called Puchinelli to ask him if he was on the way down to the mine as well.

"Roger," the weary team sergeant replied. "I'll carry Hanson's body down. Be there shortly."

With that he hefted Hanson's body onto his shoulders and started downhill, then stopped, went back, and picked up the dead soldier's severed leg by the ankle. Then, stifling a wave of nausea, he moved down toward the mine.

Behind him he could hear the creaking treads of the Soviet tanks as they continued to crawl to the south.

CHAPTER 26

2033 hours GMT (1633 hours EDT), 30 September
(0003 hours, Iran time, 1 October)
National Military Command Center
The Pentagon, Washington, D.C.

The Secretary of Defense had finished his discussions with the service secretaries and the Joint Chiefs and was ready to leave for the White House to advise the president that all was being made ready for the United States to go to war. He turned to the director of the Joint Staff and said, "Before I go, General, how about checking to see what the latest word is from the Special Forces commander in Iran?"

The lieutenant general—the lowest-ranking man in the room—reached for the secure telephone beside him, but before he could pick it up, it began to buzz. He answered it, then turned back to the Secretary of Defense.

"It's for you, sir. It's the National Security Adviser."

The secretary went to the telephone and listened to the message the president had asked his National Security Adviser to deliver.

"Yes," he said. "I understand completely. I'll pass the word here, then be right over there."

Turning to the men in the room, he said, "It looks like there's been a change of plans, gentlemen. The Soviets have agreed to an immediate cease-fire. They say they'll remain north of the twenty-eighth parallel and will commence withdrawal of their forces—including those at Chah Bahar—as soon as we can guarantee their safety."

The sense of relief shared by the men in the room was

almost tangible. Most broke into smiles, then the army chief of staff said, "We have to let our Special Forces people know that right away, sir."

"Yes," the Secretary of Defense agreed. "And when you do, tell them that . . . well, just tell them that the president will want to see them when they get home."

0145 hours GMT (0515 hours local time), 1 October
Ridge line just east of Khash, Iran

In the small, rock-strewn valley in the hills just east of Khash, Captain Dick Warner, his fractured leg encased in a new pneumatic splint, was listening to status reports from the men under his command.

Harry O'Neill's report on the status of the remaining personnel from Special Forces Operational Detachment B-30 (Provisional) was staggering. Of the sixteen men, including H-500 crews, who had parachuted into Iran a week earlier—and the one woman who had been sent in to replace the ground crewman killed during infiltration—only O'Neill remained effective. Stephens was injured and incapable of flying but was, as he put it, "still on my own two feet, anyway."

From his own team—A-323—Warner had six effective subordinates.

Master Sergeant Jake Brady and five other Special Forces soldiers from his team—A-326—were still capable of action, he reported. He turned to Chakur Nothani and said, "I'm afraid I don't have accountability of your brave soldiers, Nothani."

"Talwar Allah is blunted but not broken," the Baluchi chieftain said, "although the tip of its point, Lakha Nawaz, has been martyred. I have seventy-two men still capable of fighting, including those with minor wounds—one hundred and seventy-two if you allow me to count Medlin, who is worth a hundred men."

"You do me too much honor, Nothani," the CIA man said. "I am but one man, but one who is ready to fight to his death beside you."

"Mr. Rosengrant?" Warner asked the pilot of Stealth Hawk One.

"Seven rotor-headed soldiers still good to go, boss—four pilots and three in back. But my bird's almost bone dry again, and Hawk Two's down to a little over two hours."

Warner tallied up the numbers and said, "Counting the three-man medical team, we've got twenty-five Americans and seventy-two Baluchi still on their feet. What's the story on the wounded, Jake?"

The A-326 team sergeant, Jake Brady, said, "Doc says he's got about forty wounded, including six Americans, who will live if we get them evacuated soon. If not, he says he'll lose two—maybe three—Americans and about ten Baluchi. Also, he's got a lot of bodies stacked up outside. . . ."

"In other words, he's got thirteen men who have to be evacuated, right?"

"That's about right, sir," Brady replied.

"Can you get thirteen wounded onto Hawk Two, Rosie?" Warner inquired.

"Depends on how we stack them, sir. I mean, if we rig up the cargo compartment right, we probably can. No room to work on them or anything, though."

"It's a moot point anyway, unless we can get one of the satcoms up and get a tanker up here, sir," Hawk Two's pilot said. "We probably don't have enough fuel to get to the fleet with them—assuming that's where you want to take them."

"No time to set that up, even if the radio *was* working," Warner said. "It'll be daylight soon. We can't send your bird out in daylight anyway. But there's time to get most of the way to Nok Kundi."

"Where?" Rosengrant asked.

"Nok Kundi, Pakistan," Warner answered, pulling out his large-scale map and pointing to a Pakistani airfield northwest of Khash. "It's only about eighty-five or ninety nautical miles from here—less than an hour's flight."

"Pakistan?" Stephens said. "They'll have your ass if you do that, sir. Plus they'll probably lock the crew up, even if they don't shoot the bird down on the way in."

"How're they gonna shoot us down if they don't see us until we land?" Hawk Two's pilot asked. "You forgotten why they call us 'Stealth Hawks,' Red?"

"Well, what about when they lock you up, then take all those magic boxes?" Stephens said.

"You have destruct mechanisms built into all the secret shit, don't you, Chief?" Warner asked the MH-60P pilot.

"Of course, sir. But, uh, they'll really be unhappy if—"

"Fuck 'they,'" Warner said. "We've got men dying here. Let's get them loaded up and headed for Nok Kundi—now, on my orders." The pilots shrugged, and Warner added, "What are they gonna do? Cut off my hair and send me to Iran? Get going."

Dick Medlin had been translating the Americans' comments into Baluchi for Chakur Nothani.

"There will be no problems at Nok Kundi," the Baluchi chieftain said. "That is still Baluchistan. Give them this," he said, drawing his ceremonial dagger and handing it to the pilot as Medlin translated his words into English. "Just tell them who it is from."

It was becoming light in the east when the Stealth Hawk took off about half an hour later, its nose and sides taped with white in the shape of a crescent and star—the Muslim equivalent of the Christian world's red cross.

Meanwhile, the men who had been trying to repair the satellite radio from the helicopter were having no luck.

Jake Brady said, "Well, we're supposed to receive an emergency resupply drop at twenty-three-fifteen hours Zulu the second night after we fail to make a scheduled contact. It has radios and survival gear in it. If we're still not in contact by tonight, I'll take a couple of guys and head that way to receive it."

"Where's the emergency drop zone?" Puchinelli inquired.

"Down near Pashku," Brady said. "Just about where the Russians will be by tonight."

"Don't count on it, Jake," Warner said. "It's my guess that as soon as they hit the twenty-eighth parallel CINCCENT is going to have a big surprise for them. Like ass-kicking airstrikes, for example."

"Look, boss," Puchinelli said. He paused a moment before continuing. "Boss" had become a key word in the relationships between Special Forces NCOs and their officers. It was more formal than the use of the officer's first name, which crossed the line of excessive familiarity. But it was less formal than addressing the officer by his rank or "sir." It was used sparingly by senior NCOs —only after, in the eyes of the NCO, the officer had proved his worth and acceptability. Both Warner and Puchinelli realized that it was the first time the NCO had called Captain Warner "boss."

Warner grinned. "Yeah, Pooch?" he said.

Puchinelli returned the smile and said, "I think I ought to take O'Neill and a radio back over to the west ridge and see what's passing us. That way, if we reestablish commo with the outside—or any friendly air that shows up to take on the Soviet columns—we can designate targets for them."

"Good idea," Warner said. "Have you still got a serviceable LTD, Harry?" A laser target designator, such as O'Neill and his men had used to mark targets for the H-500D's Hellfire missiles early in the war, would be invaluable if any U.S. aircraft with laser-guided munitions showed up.

"I sure do, boss," O'Neill said. "I'll take it along."

"OK," the young captain said, wincing with pain as he tried to move his fractured leg to make it more comfortable.

In the growing light Puchinelli was able to see how pale and drawn the officer's face was. "Boss," he said, "you all right? You look like shit."

Warner didn't answer him. Pain, stress, and exhaustion had caught up with him again, and he was unconscious.

"You'd better take somebody else and get on up the ridge, Harry," Puchinelli said to O'Neill. "Looks like I'm in charge of this bunch of ragtag Green Beanies, at least until the boss here revives."

As O'Neill and his sole uninjured teammate made their way across the valley toward the west ridge an aircraft passed high overhead, flying from the south. The three Baluchi gunners who still had serviceable Stinger missile launchers heard it and attempted to acquire the aircraft, but it was far too high.

"Probably just a reconnaissance flight trying to see what the hell's going on down here," O'Neill remarked to his teammate as they again turned their attention to the ridge, dreading the tough climb that lay ahead of them.

The aircraft was not a reconnaissance flight. It was a United States Air Force B-1 bomber that had entered Iran only about ten minutes earlier, coasting in at Mach 2 just two hundred feet above the Indian Ocean. At that speed it would have reached Khash in under eight minutes. But when the navigator told the pilot, Major Huey Harlow, that they were abreast of the towns of Iranshar and Zaboli, some sixty miles south of Khash, Harlow said to the aircraft's occupants, "Hang onto your shit, guys. This puppy's going cock skyward."

Behind him, Sergeant Major Carey Funston and his Delta Force teammate, Sergeant First Class John Lassinger, lay on their backs and watched the three instruments in the pod above them. As Harlow took manual control of the aircraft and pulled back on the yoke the Delta Force NCOs were pressed against the reclined seats in their little compartment in the aircraft's ordnance bay. As a force nearly five times that of gravity pushed down on them Lassinger noticed the sudden movement of the altimeter needle as the powerful engines pushed the aircraft skyward. When the airplane reached the vertical, darting up, the men in back looked at their wrist-mounted altimeters and compared them to the winding instruments on the panel above their faces. Their compartment was intentionally unpressurized, and the men had to open and close their mouths in rapid motions beneath their oxygen masks to keep their inner ears open during the rapid depressurization. In what seemed like no time they were at twenty-eight thousand feet, and Huey Harlow called, "Coming level. One minute," as he nosed the supersonic bomber over until it was parallel to the earth's surface and throttled back, his airspeed decreasing quickly.

In their little compartment Funston and Lassinger watched the altimeter needles slow down, then cease climbing at thirty-two thousand feet, their bodies straining against the restraining straps as the B-1, going "over the top," tried to press them toward the ceiling with almost as much force as that with which they were pressed downward a minute earlier. The airspeed had decreased to four hundred knots and was continuing to decrease, according to the digital readout. The men felt weightless for a moment as the bomber leveled out— their cue to release the restraining straps. In level flight the pull of gravity was normal. Quickly they checked each other's equipment. They were about a half minute from their exit point.

Lassinger flashed Funston a thumbs-up, and Funston returned the signal and said, over the intercom, "A-OK in back."

"Roger," Harlow replied. "Twenty seconds."

"Twenty seconds," Funston said. "Off O-two and intercom." As the ordnance bay doors of the aircraft opened behind them, replacing the cool air inside with the sixty-below-zero temperature of the air outside, he looked Lassinger in the eye, disconnecting his oxygen mask and intercom cable from the panel above them, and drew deeply on his mask to ensure that the bottles of compressed oxygen on his parachute harness were now feeding him. Lassinger did the same, and each man gave the other a thumbs-up simultaneously to indicate that all was well.

There were twelve seconds on the digital counter and two hundred sixty knots indicated airspeed on the speedometer as they got on their hands and knees and faced the big hole in the floor of the ordnance bay. Funston looked down. From thirty-two thousand feet the wasteland below looked like nothing but a National Geographic photograph of a desert. Funston had no idea whether they were exactly above their release point or a thousand miles away. No matter. If the pilot let the digital counter reach zero, they were getting out. He grasped the bundle release handle on the bulkhead beside him and turned to look back at the digital counter, which showed four seconds. John Lassinger had him tightly by the ankle, ready to hold on even when they were out of the aircraft and in free fall, to keep their separation to a minimum.

The counter read one, then zero, and Funston yanked the bundle release handle and pitched forward at the same moment, leaving the ordnance bay a split second behind the bundle. Lassinger left with him, hanging onto his team leader's ankle for dear life. The 260-knot blast of air from the slipstream hit them as they left, and Lassinger released his hold, tumbling twice before he could get aerodynamic control of his body and stable out, falling face to earth. He had difficulty seeing because of the restricted vision caused by the oxygen mask, but he looked around the cloudless sky beneath him, trying to find Funston. He saw the small drogue chute of the Parapoint bundle several hundred feet below him first, then saw Funston, body elongated, tracking toward it. Lassinger brought his arms and legs in closer to his body, causing his rate of descent to increase, then began to tumble out of control. In the cold, super-thin air at thirty thousand feet, he quickly learned, stable free-fall is considerably more difficult to maintain than in the heavier air at lower altitudes, especially with a rucksack and weapon attached to his harness. Lassinger extended his arms and legs and quickly regained stability. His unstable fall had brought him almost level with Funston and the bundle, and all he had to do to close with them was extend his legs and glide toward them.

Funston saw him closing and gave a thumbs-up, and Lassinger returned the signal, then checked his altimeter. They were just above twenty thousand feet.

The B-1, meanwhile, had dived off to the west and was nearly level a short distance above the ground, the crew grunting at the four-plus Gs caused by the aircraft pulling out of its steep dive. As they leveled off at two thousand feet, then dropped quickly to two hundred in their supersonic run toward the Indian Ocean, Harlow said, "How'd we do, Wizzo?" to his weapons systems officer.

"No problem. They painted us when we were almost at the top, then lost us when we started that bodacious dive. The Russkie radar operators probably think we were one of their SAMs, that's all."

Now the two Delta Force men, still in free-fall with one hand grasping the side of their accompanying bundle, were concentrating on the ground below them. The peak of Kuh-e Taftan, rising high above the surrounding terrain, was easily recognizable to their north. Almost directly beneath them they could see dozens of gray streaks stretching away to the northeast. It was only when they reached about fifteen thousand feet of altitude, however, that the men realized what the gray streaks were. They were columns of smoke—the smoke of burning armored vehicles destroyed by the men they had been ordered to try to find.

Quickly scanning the area around Khash, Funston saw, to the west, the dots of a large number of vehicles casting long shadows in the early-morning sunlight.

With a minute of free-fall left he concentrated on the ridge line to the east of Khash. Their plan was to open low, just on the other side of the ridge, and land there. But they were too far west. They needed to open higher than planned and glide, with their MT-3 high-glide airfoil canopies, over the ridge before landing.

As they passed nine thousand feet on their altimeters —4,500 above Khash—Funston confirmed that Lassinger was watching him, then grasped the manual release ripcord on one side of the bundle. He made a series of exaggerated nods with his head. On the third nod he pulled the bundle's manual rip cord—a thousand feet before it was set to open automatically—then pulled his own main parachute rip cord as Lassinger did the same. At 3,500 feet above the ridge east of Khash the men checked their parachutes, released the brake loops on the control lines, and turned to the east. Funston turned on the small control box used to control the Parapoint bundle guidance system, setting it on "automatic," which caused the bundle to home in on the transmitter. He looked back over his shoulder and saw that the Parapoint, high and behind him, was turning in his direction. Lassinger was fifty feet below him, so Funston did a quick 360-degree turn, losing altitude and bringing him level with his teammate. He checked the bundle and saw that it was still following them. Lassinger guided his parachute over beside Funston's until he was only twenty-five feet away.

Both men reached up and unhooked their oxygen masks, then cleared their ears by pinching their noses and blowing.

"Christ," Lassiter yelled. "What a ride! Did you see all those damned vehicles burning north of the town?"

"Yeah! Looks like these guys kicked ass, doesn't it? There's a lot more vehicles out to the west, though. OK, see that light-colored area at our one o'clock, about five hundred meters?"

"Got it," Lassinger said. "That our landing point?"

"That's it."

The Delta Force men concentrated on landing, checking the smoke from the burning Russian vehicles to determine the direction of the ground winds.

Everyone on the ground heard the sonic boom of the B-1 as it went supersonic again during its dive back to earth. But no one around Khash saw it, although many of them scanned the sky above them for a time. The only people who heard the ripping sound of the parachutes opening above them some two minutes later were Harry O'Neill and his teammate, climbing the west ridge above Khash to establish an observation post. It was a familiar sound to O'Neill, once an avid sky diver. He searched the sky to his northeast where he had heard the sound as he said to his teammate, "Parachutes!"

He had trouble spotting the canopies at first because of

their mottled, light-gray color, which blended in well with the sky. Then he saw them. "There! Two . . . no, three canopies! Mottled gray—that's the new pattern they use on MT-3s." He grabbed the handset of his PRC-117 and called Puchinelli.

"Pooch, this is O'Neill. I've got three ram air canopies over Khash, headed your way, over!"

"O'Neill, Pooch. Say again?"

"I say again, there's three ram air parachutes above Khash at about, oh, three thousand feet, headed your direction. They look like our guys—gray MT-3s, over."

There was a pause of about fifteen seconds, then Puchinelli said, "Got 'em in sight!"

At a thousand feet above the ground the men passed almost directly over Puchinelli, who was quickly spreading the word to everyone not to fire on the men, but to keep them covered with their weapons when they landed.

The two parachutists turned crosswind over what they thought was a pile of brush, although it was actually Rosie Rosengrant's camouflaged Stealth Hawk. The parapoint was dutifully following the men, responding to the electronic commands of the Parapoint guidance system.

Carey Funston landed first, flaring to a five-foot-per-second descent as he did so. John Lassinger was ten meters behind him. He flared, touched down, and ripped his cutaway pillow off to release the parachute canopy. Funston immediately switched the Parapoint control device from automatic to manual. The bundle passed just above him, and when it was ten feet above the ground he slid the brake control button to seventy-five percent. The servos in the guidance system above the bundle responded instantly, drawing the control lines in, and the bundle flared to a soft landing. Funston looked over at Lassinger and saw him standing there with his hands in the air. Two Baluchi tribesmen were standing nearby, each with a weapon leveled at one of the men. Funston, too, raised his hands. A third man appeared from the rocks behind the tribesmen—a filthy, bearded man with an M-16 leveled at them.

Funston studied him a moment, then said, "Pete Puchinelli, you look like hell."

Puchinelli didn't recognize the Delta Force man until he removed his helmet and goggles.

"Funston! I'll be a son of a bitch! What the hell . . . ?"

"Heard you needed a radio," Funston said. "Thought I'd drop in and lend you mine."

CHAPTER 27

"Yeah," Funston said as he sat with Puchinelli in the camouflaged hide site, watching Lassinger assemble the satellite radio components, "we were still out at Yuma, getting ready to party to celebrate our jump tests from the B-1. Then this flash message comes in from SOCOM, and the next thing we know, we're aboard the damn B-1, headed for Seymour Johnson airbase at Mach 2. They gave us the bundle, two hours to study the map and devise an escape and evasion plan, and zip—we're headed for Iran at Mach 2 again. The only time we slowed down was to hit the refuel tankers. I was scared shitless, claustrophobic, wishing I'd been going to church, and regretting ever having joined the army. And I've never been so goddam glad to finally be in free-fall—even though I wasn't sure we were over the right country, much less your UWOA. It wasn't until I saw all those damned tanks burning that I realized we were in the right place. How many of those damn things did you guys knock out anyway, Pooch?"

"Don't know," Puchinelli replied. "About fifty last night, I guess. Could've got more, but we ran out of antitank ammo—and killer eggs. You wouldn't believe how much damage those H-500s did to the bastards. There was a fem—"

"Base, this is Tiger Tail," SFC Lassinger was saying into the handset of the secure voice satellite radio, causing Puchinelli to cease his discussion with Funston.

"Tiger Tail, this is Base. You on the ground, over?"

"This is Tiger Tail. Affirmative. On the ground and in contact with Tiger and Sword, over."

"Roger, Tiger Tail. Stand by for the group Charlie Oscar." The 3d Special Forces Group commander came on the radio then and said, "Tiger Tail, this is Eagle. Well done. Be advised, you're now attached to the senior American there until exfil. Let me talk to him, over."

"Who's the senior man, Pooch?" Lassinger asked. "The group commander wants to talk to him."

Puchinelli took the handset. "Eagle, this is Tiger— Sergeant Puchinelli, here, over."

"Uh, roger, Tiger. Be advised, we are in a cease-fire situation with the Soviets—I say again, we have a cease-fire with the Soviets, how copy?"

"This is Tiger," Puchinelli replied. "Understand cease-fire. That's good news, sir. Thank God."

"This is Eagle. The terms are as follows: The Soviets will remain in place, north of the twenty-eighth parallel, until we can guarantee their safe withdrawal north. They will avoid approaching within five kilometers of Khash until that is done. How copy so far?"

"This is Poo . . . uh, Tiger. Solid copy, Eagle."

The group commander went on to explain the terms of the cease-fire as they affected the men in UWOA Tiger. As soon as both sides could confirm a "weapons tight" situation for air defense weapons systems, they were to report it, and then medical evacuation aircraft would be brought in by both sides to evacuate their wounded. He asked Puchinelli the status of the wounded on his side, and Puchinelli explained about Hawk Two having left for Pakistan with the most seriously wounded shortly before daylight. He expected the colonel to question the decision—even be hostile about it. But the Special Forces officer replied, "Roger, Tiger. Good decision. We'll contact the embassy there ASAP and see that they're taken care of, and that the Stealth Hawk and crew are taken care of, too."

He asked for the status of the remaining American and Baluchi troops and was told about the rest of the wounded, and the small number of effectives remaining. He was also informed about the missing Sergeant Cat Whitaker and the two Baluchi tribesmen who were to the north, on the slopes of Kuh-e Taftan. They were the only people under American Special Forces control who were still outside a five-kilometer radius of Khash, Puchinelli reported, then he added, "But you'd better let me check with Nothani to be sure, over."

"Roger," the colonel said. "Do that, then get back to me. Eagle, standing by, out."

Puchinelli went to the head of the draw, where most of the remaining Americans and several of the Baluchi men, including Nothani, were asleep after the long night of action. He woke them all to tell them about the cease-fire, and to confirm that Nothani had no one outside the five-kilometer area around Khash other than the two men on the mountain to the north. The Americans were jubilant about the cease-fire. Nothani, more reserved, said, "I'll believe it when they are off Muslim land and back in the Soviet Union." He reported that all of his guerrillas, except the two on the mountain, were camped nearby.

After making certain that Nothani would send someone to explain the cease-fire to the guerrillas and to collect the remaining Stinger launchers, Puchinelli returned to the Delta Force men and their satcom.

O'Neill, now atop the west ridge, was on the frequency-hopping PRC-117 FM radio with Sergeant Major Funston. Funston handed Puchinelli the handset and said, "He says the Soviets have halted and laagered up at a number of locations west and north of him. I told him about the cease-fire, too."

Before calling O'Neill, Puchinelli asked Funston, "How come you guys didn't tell me about the cease-fire, anyway?"

"Didn't know about it," the Delta Force man replied. "It must have happened while we were on the way here."

Puchinelli told O'Neill to maintain surveillance on the Soviets and report any activity he saw. The other Americans were gathering around him to eavesdrop on the transmissions from SFOB when Captain Warner hobbled up on his crutches. One of the Americans had run across the hill to the makeshift aid station to report that the Delta Force men had jumped in with a satellite radio, and that a cease-fire had been agreed to. Warner, now conscious and able to move about, had come to see what the full story was.

"How you feeling, boss?" Puchinelli asked the officer.

"I'm OK, Pooch. The doc fixed me up with some pretty good painkillers. How 'bout briefing me up?"

Puchinelli introduced his detachment commander to Funston and Lassinger, then brought him up to date on all he knew about the situation.

Warner said, "OK, let me talk to SFOB and clarify a couple of things, then we'll have a team meeting and sort out what we do next."

He called SFOB and advised the group commander that he was able to function as detachment commander, adding, "at least as long as the painkillers hold out. If I can't hack it, I'll give it back to Pooch, sir. Meanwhile, can you give me an idea on when we can expect our wounded to be evacuated, over?"

"Negative," the group commander replied. "It'll be at least twenty-four hours, I imagine, before JCS can get with the Soviet High Command and work out the details. Is there anywhere within your five-K radius that we could bring a fixed-wing in when we get permission, over?"

"Yes, sir," Warner responded. "There's a straight stretch of hardtop road just south of Khash that's several kilometers long. We could put a medevac bird in there with no problem—unless the Soviet artillery cratered it too badly. I'll send somebody down there to check it out and advise whether or not it's usable. Also, we'll continue to monitor the Soviets north and west of here and advise you of their activity. Anything further for me, over?"

"This is Eagle. Not at this time. Keep me informed, out."

Warner gave the handset back to Lassinger. "All right, top," he said to Puchinelli. "Let's have a team meeting. There's still some unfinished business to take care of."

When the Americans and the Baluchi leaders were assembled, Warner sat on a boulder and briefed them on the situation. He paused after each sentence or two to allow Dick Medlin to translate his comments into Baluchi for Nothani and his men.

"Now," he said, "this is what I propose to do. First, we have to send somebody down to the road to make sure it's usable as a landing strip."

"We can do that for you, sir," Sergeant Major Funston volunteered. "Then we can relieve your outpost up on the hill, if you'd like. Those guys must be dead tired."

"Thanks, Ser'n Major," Warner said. "That would be a big help."

"Next, we've got to try to get to Sergeant Whitaker. She might even still be alive, and—"

"She?" Funston interrupted. "You've got a *woman* out here?"

"The hardest fighting son of a bitch on the team," Puchinelli said.

"She jumped in to replace a killer egg mechanic who wrapped his static line around his neck during infil," Red Stephens explained. "When my wingman and copilot got nailed, Major Denton let me put her in the cockpit. I taught her to fly myself, back at Bragg. She was a natural."

"What happened to her?" Lassinger asked.

"She was out killing tanks—flying by herself, since I fucked up and sliced my eye and sprained my wrist," Stephens said. "We heard a Mayday from her, but the Sovs nailed her with two main-gun tank rounds when she landed."

"Jesus," Funston said. "A female sergeant flying a gunship against the Russians—*by herself.* You sure they got her?"

The men were momentarily silent. Sergeant Major Funston's remark had suddenly made them realize what a remarkable thing Cat Whitaker had been doing. Then Warner spoke.

"Damned near unbelievable, isn't it?" he said. "I guess we were so involved in trying to hammer the bad guys—and in the case of some of us, like me, worried about our own asses—that Whitaker's gutsiness didn't really sink in until now. Anyway, there's a superb American soldier out there somewhere, and dead or alive, we're going to take her with us when we go."

"How we going to do that, boss?" Puchinelli asked. "I mean, we're supposed to stay in this goddam five-kilometer circle around Khash. If she was alive, she'd have been here by now."

"Maybe she was hurt," Stephens said, "and couldn't make it. Or more likely, if they *didn't* kill her, they probably captured her."

Medlin was still translating the American's remarks into Baluchi for Chakur Nothani, who now offered a comment.

"She is a woman with a warrior's soul," he said. Those who knew Baluchi realized that in that language, "warrior" was a masculine noun only. There was no noun in Baluchi for a female warrior. "I will see that she is returned to you whether she is a martyr or only a hero." There was no feminine equivalent of "hero" in Baluchi, either.

Medlin translated Nothani's remarks into English.

"How can you do that?" Warner inquired.

"We have three Russians," he replied through Medlin, adding, "and there are probably some out there with the tanks who are still alive. We will take them and trade them for your warrior woman."

Warner considered Nothani's proposal. As the senior Special Forces man in the UWOA, it was his responsibility to ensure that not only the Americans but also the Baluchi guerrillas they were advising adhered to the terms of the cease-fire. And those terms required that they stay within a five-kilometer radius of Khash. Still, Sergeant Whitaker deserved—dead or alive—to go home with her comrades-in-arms. And Nothani's comment about Soviet tankers reminded him that indeed there probably were wounded men out there amid the ruined vehicles. They were the enemy, but they were soldiers. And now that he had known combat, he had a new respect for what that meant. They had fought, and bravely. Those who had lived through the battle deserved to be saved. He would not let them die, neglected, while the generals on both sides negotiated their recovery.

"All right," the young captain said. "All right. This is what we will do. . . ."

An hour later Senior Lieutenant Valnikov, now commanding the remnants of the lead battalion of the Soviet tank regiment, was awakened by an excited call from the lieutenant he had placed in charge of the reconnaissance element southwest of Khash. There was a battered red pickup truck traveling toward him on the winding dirt road that skirted the southern edge of the ridge west of the town. He requested permission to engage it. Valnikov wiped his burning eyes, then said, "What is in the truck? Can you see?"

"Not yet," the reconnaissance element leader replied, "but it is leaving the five-kilometer zone of Khash. I think we should engage it."

Valnikov said, "No, not yet. Halt him some distance away, but do not engage him." He could envision another enemy missile flying toward one of his tanks, another trio of his men being consumed by shrapnel and exploding ammunition and flaming fuel, so he added, "Unless you suspect that he is going to fire on you first—then destroy him."

"He has a white flag," the recon man reported.

Valnikov wondered if it was a trick. What would the enemy expect to gain by that, though? The advance was stopped, the battle ended. He would have to see. He radioed his subordinate. "When he approaches, stop him some distance away. Hold him there. I will be there in a few minutes."

He woke his driver and told him to take him to the reconnaissance element's position on the west flank.

When he got there ten minutes later he saw the truck—a battered red pickup, a square of white cloth on a stick above it. From two hundred meters away he saw a man get out and begin hobbling on crutches toward the newly arrived tank. The gunner brought the main gun to bear on the man, but he continued walking toward the tank. Valnikov dismounted, saying, "Wait here," as he walked to meet the man.

When he was ten meters away Valnikov stopped. The other man saluted and said. "I am Captain Richard Warner, United States Army. Do you speak English?"

Valnikov stared at him. The man was clean, freshly washed, and wearing a plastic cast on his leg. His uniform, though wrinkled, was clean and in good order. He returned the American's salute and approached him, saying, "I speak some English. I am Senior Lieutenant Valnikov of the Army of the Union of Soviet Socialist Republics. What do you want, Captain?"

"I want to arrange for us—your soldiers and mine—to recover our dead and wounded and get them treated and prepared for evacuation."

"Speak more slowly. I do not understand English so well."

Warner gestured back to the pickup truck and said, "I have a man who speaks Russian very well. May I ask him to come here?"

"Yes," Valnikov replied, and without looking back Warner circled his hand above his head, then tapped himself on top of his camouflage cap. The man in the truck got out and walked to them. When he arrived, the man saluted Valnikov, and Warner said, "This is Sergeant Major Funston."

In Russian, Funston said, "Hello, sir. I will serve as Captain Warner's translator."

The three men stood there for a while, talking. Then Valnikov returned to his tank to tell his regimental commander who the men were and what they wanted.

Twenty minutes later the regimental commander, newly appointed to that position after his predecessor was killed by an American TOW missile, arrived in a BMP personnel carrier. He spoke to Valnikov for a long time, then returned to his BMP and left without meeting Warner and Funston.

The Soviet senior lieutenant returned to the American soldiers and said, "He has agreed, but he is worried that the mine field will kill more men."

"No," Warner said. "All the mines will have self-destructed by now. At least, I think that's true. But your recovery party must be careful."

"He wants to know where your wounded are, that you must leave the five-kilometer radius of Khash to recover them," the Russian officer said.

"There is only one," Warner said, pointing a crutch to the north. "The pilot of the helicopter up there. Do you have her?"

"No," Valnikov said. "We have no one."

"Have you looked in the helicopter?" Funston asked.

Valnikov said nothing, so Funston repeated himself, and then the Russian said, "Yes. We stripped it for our intelligence service to examine. It is a deadly machine. But the pilots are gone."

"There was only one," Warner said. "A woman."

Valnikov stared at him. He didn't believe Warner—neither that there was only one pilot, nor that a woman was flying it. Americans didn't send women into combat, especially after their experience in Panama.

"You don't believe me, do you?" Warner asked.

"No."

"Nevertheless, it is true. And you didn't find her?"

"No. There was no one. We could find no footprints, although that is not surprising, because of the battle and the tanks maneuvering, and the wind."

"Will you take us to look for her?" Warner asked.

"Yes. But your vehicle can't make it. You must ride with me."

Valnikov and Funston helped Warner up onto the hull of the tank. The broken leg was hurting him badly, so he took a couple of pills and washed them down with water from his canteen. As he did so he saw Valnikov lick his cracked lips with a dry tongue. He passed the canteen to

the Russian and said, "Have some, Lieutenant Valnikov."

The Russian hesitated, then took it and sipped gently.
He handed it back to Warner, saying, "Thank you. Most
of us are out of water."

"Then give your driver and your gunner the rest. I have
another canteen."

The Soviet officer passed the canteen as Warner said,
"There are wells south of Khash. Send a vehicle there to
get water for your men when you wish to."

Funston had a PRC-117 radio on his back, and O'Neill
called. Funston answered, and O'Neill said, "I see you on
the tank, headed north. Everything all right?"

"Affirmative," Funston said. "We're going to the killer
egg to look for Whitaker. Be advised, they've agreed to
ignore the five-K radius to recover their wounded.
They'll use wheeled vehicles only, as we asked, and no
more than ten of them, over."

"Roger," O'Neill said. "You say they claim they
haven't seen Whitaker?"

"That's correct," Funston answered.

O'Neill, with no means of backing up his threat, said,
"Well, tell the bastards she'd better turn up—or else." It
was a useless thing to say, they both knew, but it was
indicative of the way the men felt about Sergeant Whitaker now that the battle was over and they had had time
to realize what she had done—what they *all* had
done.

"We'll find her," Funston replied.

The sun was getting high now, and the soldier lay in the
wadi with the enemy all around, trying to decide whether
or not to surrender, and thinking, *If I don't, I'm going to
die of thirst. Why aren't they moving?*

There *was* movement—the sound of tank treads
creaking not far away. Climbing slowly up the crumbly
edge of the two-meter-high wadi wall, Sergeant Catherine Whitaker peered over the top and saw a tank moving
toward the scattered remains of the little helicopter.
There were men sitting on top of the tank, which stopped

between her and the wrecked chopper 150 meters away. One man hopped off, then helped another down—a man on crutches. A third man climbed out of the commander's cupola and joined them. They disappeared behind the tank, and she slid back down into the wadi, thinking, *Some more of them come to look at my helicopter, I guess.* There was no shade in the wadi now. The sun was directly overhead. She wondered if she would be strong enough to wait for dark to come, so that she could try to sneak past the Russians and make it to Khash. Just the exertion of climbing to look over the wadi wall had been difficult, and she could only breathe in short gasps, her ribs were hurting her so. She was certain they had been broken when she fell into the dark wadi as she ran from the helicopter. She had barely gotten away from it when the first round hit it, and she didn't know what else to do but run. It had been a violent fall, and she was glad that she still had her helmet on when she fell, or she would have smashed her skull.

"Got to hang on until tonight," she whispered to herself, then, exhausted, she curled up on the floor of the rocky wadi.

She was asleep when Carey Funston found her. He figured she had to be in the wadi; there was no place else to hide. He called, "Whitaker?" when he saw her lying there, twenty meters away. She didn't answer, so he ran to her and said, "Sergeant Whitaker!"

She heard him then and woke up, rolled over, and looked up at him with wide eyes, startled.

"Who . . . who are you?" She didn't recognize the man, but he was in an American uniform, and he smiled and bent over her and said, "You all right?"

She wanted to believe it—that she had been found by an American, that she had been saved. Then she remembered the tanks all around, the war, the exploding vehicles and dying men. A trick. Well, at least her decision about whether or not to surrender had been made. She looked up at the man again and said, "Whitaker, Catherine S., sergeant, four one nine, two tw—"

"There's been a truce. I'm an American. You're not a prisoner, Sergeant Whitaker."

She looked at him again, wanting to believe it. But he was a stranger, so she said again, "Whitaker, Catherine S., sergeant, four one ni—"

"You sure trashed old Aphid One, Cat," another American voice said, and she looked up and saw Captain Warner and another man—a Russian.

"Come on, Cat," Warner said. "We've got to get back to Khash. Red Stephens will have my ass if we don't get you back there so you can tell him how you managed to wreck his killer egg."

CHAPTER 28

1110 hours GMT (1440 hours local time), 2 October
South of Khash, Iran

The fat new C-17 jet transport used less than half the length of the strip of road that Puchinelli had marked for it to land on. When the plane stopped, he drove forward in the little pickup—the only transportation the Special Forces men had available other than the Baluchi horses. He waved for it to follow him, then turned around and drove up the road toward Khash. When he was abreast of the clump of trees beside the well where the dead and wounded lay waiting he stopped, got out, and signaled the crew to turn the big plane around. When it had done so, the engines shut down and the cargo doors and ramp at the rear opened.

Several people walked off the ramp toward him. From the trees around the well Captain Warner appeared, hobbling on his makeshift crutches.

The man leading the others from the airplane was the 3d Special Forces Group commander, Colonel Bob Thomas.

He saluted the two Special Forces men, then shook their hands, saying, "It's good to see you, men. God damn, it's good to see you. Uh, show the docs here where the wounded are, will you?"

Puchinelli nodded and waved for the medics to follow him, then headed for the well, leaving Warner and Thomas standing there behind the airplane.

"Captain Warner . . . Dick, isn't it?"

"Yes, sir."

"Dick, I hope you realize what happened here, what
. . . well, what it means."

Warner chuckled, and the colonel looked at him.
Warner said, "I tried to say something like that to
O'Neill—SFC Harry O'Neill, sir, one of the best soldiers
in your group. He said, 'It don't mean nothin', Captain.'
I didn't know what he meant at first."

"It's from Vietnam. 'Don't mean nothin''—that's
what the troops used to say over there when they didn't
know what else to say."

They were watching the first of the wounded being led
toward the airplane, the walking wounded. Another
group of men was walking toward the well from the
airplane, carrying body bags for the remains of the dead.
The captain said, "It takes a long time for history to
decide what means something and what 'don't mean
nothin',' doesn't it, Colonel?"

The colonel thought about it, then said, "Sometimes,
Dick. But sometimes you know when it happens that it
means something." He looked at his captain and added,
"Like this time."

Now the guerrillas and the uninjured Special Forces
men came, carrying nonambulatory wounded from beneath the trees by the well, and the captain said, "Here
come some more of your men, sir. Sir, this is Special
Forces, and I think you ought to help carry them."

"Of course," the colonel said, and he moved off to
help. All the wounded were being carried already,
though. So he went to where the men were putting the
bloated remains of other soldiers into the thick, green
plastic body bags, and he stifled an attack of nausea.
When the first bag was zipped up he reached down and
grasped the carrying handles at one end of it, and
someone reached for the handles on the other end. It was
a woman, and he looked at her with his mouth open and
his back bent and he said, "You're Sergeant, uh, Whitaker."

"Yes, sir," she said, lifting her end of the bag.

They carried it toward the airplane, and he said,

"Sergeant Whitaker, what you did out here . . . it was—"

She interrupted him with, "Don't mean nothin', Colonel."

They passed Captain Warner, who was standing in the road. He was supporting himself with one crutch under his left arm. He was standing as straight up as he could, and his arm snapped up into a crisp salute when the body of his dead comrade-in-arms passed. The colonel fought back tears and said to the woman carrying the other end of the dead soldier, "Yes, it does, Sergeant Whitaker. It means a lot. It means everything."

Senior Lieutenant Valnikov of the Soviet Army arrived in a BTR-80 as the last dead American was being carried toward the aircraft. He hopped down and stood beside Captain Dick Warner, saying nothing as the body bag was carried past, but joining the American Special Forces officer in a salute to the dead soldier.

"Thank God there will be no more," Valnikov said.

Warner looked at him. "Yes. Thank God."

"Good-bye, Captain. Perhaps someday we shall meet again."

"Yes," Warner said. "Perhaps we shall. Good-bye, Lieutenant Valnikov."

The men shook hands, and Valnikov stepped back and saluted. Warner returned the salute, and then they turned away from each other and started home.